THE LEGACIES OF TRAITORS

FORSAKEN LEGACIES SERIES
BOOK ONE

THE LEGACIES OF TRAITORS

C.M. LEYVA

KRISTON PRESS

Hardcover: 979-8-9905241-2-5

Paperback: 979-8-9905241-1-8

Ebook: 979-8-9905241-0-1

First edition August 2024

Printed in the United States of America

Published by Kriston Press, Tampa, FL

To those once broken,
who forged themselves into someone unbreakable.

While *The Legacies of Traitors'* primary theme is creating hope, it's also a story about morally gray rebels, and there are several thematic elements that, while handled with care, may not be suitable for all readers. The story contains, but is not limited to, depictions of medical errors, alcohol abuse, grief, death, depression, anxiety, oppression, sexual activity, violence, blood, murder, plague, torture, poisoning, and PTSD. Readers, if any of these elements are sensitive to you, please take note.

◄——————►

Welcome to the rebellion.

PART I

AGE OF APATHY

Excerpt from the journal of Katherine Wells –
Summer 2259

Nature is resilient. It took nearly a century for us to heal as we hid in our underground bunkers made of cold hard steel, while outside these walls, nature thrived in our absence. All that once was, now hidden under the lush, vibrant green that surrounds us.

So we rise from the dark, shielding our eyes to the brightness of the new world. Nothing more than ghosts of what we once were. Skin gray, eyes sunken, bodies frail.

What a beautiful day to be born again.

1

MISCALCULATIONS

E ach slow, deafening tick of her father's watch brought Maia one second closer to the end of the life she knew. The life she'd been naïve enough to think she had earned. A single moment—much like this one, where seconds felt like lifetimes—was all it took for her mistake to change everything.

She swallowed, lifting her gaze from her white-knuckled hands knotted in her lap, to the man sitting excruciatingly silent across from her. In the year since becoming one of Mr. Thomas' healing apprentices, she'd never seen him lost for words. He always had an answer, but challenged her to find it. This, however, was not something either of them could fix. And as a man dedicated to finding solutions, being forced into this situation only added to the tension of his already suffocating office.

"What happened yesterday?" he asked, voice steady in a forced way as his jaw clenched under his trim, white beard.

She had spent all night replaying the moment over and over again...

The sterile exam room that reeked of infection.

The grayish tint of her patient's face.

Her frantic pulse thundering in her ears.

The glass bottle clutched in her trembling hand.

But worst of all... the units stamped into the brown glass, forcing her to accept the terrifying truth. "I grabbed the wrong tonic bottle from the shelf, sir."

"How?"

Because the world has been trapped in a permanent fog since my mother passed.

If Mr. Thomas had anyone he cared about, it was something he kept secret. There were no pictures on the dark wood walls that now seemed to close in around her. Only an oil lamp and inkwell to bear witness to her downfall. And that fact alone made her certain he wouldn't understand the hole that now existed in her heart.

"I wasn't paying attention, sir."

"You weren't paying attention..." he repeated, each word short and clipped in time to the tick of the watch. "You realize you nearly killed him?"

The relief that washed over her eased the nauseating dread churning in the pit of her stomach. Her patient was still alive.

"I know," she whispered. "It was an unforgivable mistake. You have no idea how sorry I am."

That's not what he wanted to hear though. What he wanted wasn't possible. No words could change what happened. A thousand apologies would never be enough.

"Maia." The way he said her name was too soft, and his lips pressed together in pity. She recognized it for what it was—the moment before everything changed. "I know you're hurting right now. Red lung is an awful disease that takes from everyone touched by it. It claimed your mother, but it's infected your soul."

Infected. Tainted. Dangerous.

There was a reason he chose that word, and she felt it slither into the dark corner of her mind, taking root.

"As healers, we give our lives to serve others," he continued. "We do this to bring hope and comfort in the darkest of times. It's a thankless job that requires discipline and devotion. Your mother understood that. But I don't see that in you. Not anymore."

His words sucked the air out of her. No, not just the air, but something deeper. It was as if he'd carved out her core, leaving her hollow. A shell.

What would she be if she couldn't follow in her mother's footsteps?

"Mr. Thomas, please don't do this." Maia's words heaved from her as she leaned forward onto his desk. The oil lamp rocked precariously, drawing his attention. "It was an accident."

He slid the lamp closer to him, but despite its warmth, his gaze grew cold and distant. "Williamsburg is a small town, Ms. Avalos. People talk. They see you stumbling out of the tavern each night. Something easy enough to correlate with your... miscalculation."

None of it was true. It was never more than one drink. Something to numb the pain of loss. But lies spread quicker than truths ever could.

"Please," she choked out.

His lip curled in disgust. She'd never been this vulnerable with him—this desperate. And it seemed to confirm his decision as he smoothed his navy-blue suit vest. "I won't let you destroy my name while you search for your purpose."

"This *is* my purpose!" She'd completely lost control of herself, allowing tears to spill down her cheeks. She needed him to see her. To understand how important this was. That without healing, she had nothing. She *was* nothing. "Sir, please. This is all I have left of her."

He opened a drawer, removing his leather-bound inventory log and fountain pen. "Healing was your mother's purpose... but not yours. I'm sorry, Ms. Avalos, but this is where we part ways."

Maia stared—numb, yet shattered—as she dropped back into the suddenly uncomfortable and stiff leather chair. Her eyes traveled around the office again, realizing it was meant to be as inhospitable as the man who occupied it. The version of him the rest of his apprentices whispered about. The version he had spared her from until now.

She nodded vacantly. "I understand."

Mr. Thomas flipped open the log, starting his evening paperwork. "You can go now."

Grabbing her jacket, she quietly stood, pushing open the door leading to the apothecary storefront.

The sun lazily seeped in through the dusty windows draped in hanging herbs. It glinted off the tonic bottles stacked on rows upon rows of shelves as it did each evening before close.

This used to be her favorite part of the day—filling bottles while Mr. Thomas tested her with patient cases.

The mortar and pestle she'd used just yesterday still sat on the wooden counter. Even the brass weights Mr. Thomas had knocked over as he rushed to save her patient remained scattered next to the bronze scale.

Everything looked the same, but already felt like a fading dream. She closed her eyes, the tick of the watch filling the silence as fear gripped her chest.

Her apprenticeship was over. She could no longer follow her mother's path.

Gathering what little composure she had left, she forced her feet to the door.

Stepping out onto the dirt road, the soft spring breeze soothed her burning cheeks while dusk set fire to the cloudless sky. Townspeople passed with worn work clothes and weary faces on their way home for the evening. They avoided her empty gaze, something she'd grown used to. A consequence of her criminal father's actions.

Or maybe it was a consequence of her own now.

Without healing, she was exactly what she'd always feared...

A disappointment.

Maia's scuffed, brown boots weaved through the dwindling crowd with purpose, even if the purpose was delaying the walk back home. She could hear their whispers. Feel the looks of disappointment searing into the back of her head.

"Just like her father," a woman muttered as she passed, followed by a collective tsking from the group flocking behind her.

Balling her hands, Maia painfully grit her teeth, fighting the urge to confront them. Nothing good would come of it. It was just further evidence to validate her snide remark.

So, instead, she tucked into a narrow alley, her steps faltering as two Portico guards entered from the other end.

How was it possible for her day to get any fucking worse?

The gold buttons on their red jackets were too polished for a town like Williamsburg, and their heavy boots approached with the authority their uniforms granted. It wasn't often Portico made an appearance in their small town, but every now and then, they liked to send a reminder of who was in control.

A traveler sat against the wall between them, tucking away the threadbare cap he'd been holding out for coin.

"Whatcha got there?" the taller guard asked, reaching for the traveler's cap. "You know beggin' ain't allowed."

Dropping her gaze, Maia took advantage of the distraction and continued past them.

"Hand it fuckin' over. Do you know who we are?"

It wasn't a question, but a warning. According to the history texts, Portico Trading Company was the first successful government of the New World. Founded a year after the survivors of the Old World could finally leave their bunkers. A group of men and women specializing in different trades formed a council tasked with establishing new law and order.

What the texts didn't say is that power only goes so far without control. In the three decades since, Portico established its own standard currency and took over all trade posts in the Forest Region, as well as the major port of Jamestown in the Coastal Region. It was this unchecked power that created men like the ones behind her.

"I know exactly who you are," the traveler mumbled.

With a quick glance over her shoulder, Maia watched as the traveler hocked up a wad of spit, sending it onto the guard's boot.

This petty act of defiance would become the man's death sentence, but it stirred something dangerous inside Maia.

"Looks like we found ourselves a fuckin' rebel," the guard growled, grabbing the man by the shirt and lifting him to his dirty feet. "You're going to regret that."

Even tucked away in the alley, Portico's propaganda surrounded them, showing the death and destruction caused by the rebels quietly growing in numbers.

Buildings burned to the ground. Homes robbed of anything worth a few coin. Maia's father had been one of the many corrupted by the rebellion.

It had become his death sentence too.

The traveler's wet cough turned the air glacial, freezing Maia's footsteps at the end of the alley.

The same cough her mother had. It was when she realized fear had tones.

It was her mother's screams, piercing the calmness of the night as she fought to survive.

"He's got red lung."

But it was also the whisper that escaped the guard as he realized his own fragile mortality.

"Just cover his head, Heath," the other guard suggested, a slight tremble in his voice. "We'll get rid of him in the woods."

Maia looked down at her father's watch and closed her eyes. Had she not been there for her mother, would the guards have taken her to the woods too?

Wrapping her fingers around the scuffed watch face, she slowly turned to them. "He's not a fucking animal."

They lifted their collars to their mouths as the traveler coughed again, freckling the dirt with blood. The guard named Heath turned to her. "You don't need him contaminating your town."

"He's sick. What's your excuse?"

The traveler didn't need to be her burden, but Maia's footsteps moved protectively toward him nonetheless. It was the reason her mother warned her about being too much like her father.

Heath's strong brow lifted with amusement, reminding her of her insignificance. "What's your name?"

Maia stood in silent defiance, knowing her words wouldn't hold the same strength.

He nodded, thin lips curling into a cruel smirk. "Suit yourself, darlin'. I'll figure it out on my own. It's only fair the people of Williamsburg know who they can blame for their red lung outbreak."

The guards took turns spitting back at the traveler as they walked away.

With her adrenaline now dissipating, Maia's shoulders slumped, and she dared a look down at the stranger. His face burned red, lines etched deep between his brows, and guilt suddenly washed over her.

There was no cure for red lung. Whatever days he had left would be torture. Maybe she was wrong for denying him a quick death by Portico's hands. Especially knowing he couldn't stay here without condemning them all to the same excruciating end.

"I'm sorry, but you have to go." The cruel words tasted bitter on her tongue.

He pushed himself up, tucking the coins from his hat into his pocket. "You shouldn't have done that."

He was right. Despite the rebel propaganda surrounding them, their world wasn't any better under Portico's control. He lifted his hat to his head and trudged out of the alley, her steps quietly following behind him.

The sign for Folly's Tavern creaked above her in the gentle breeze as voices carried through the weather-beaten door. But she waited, watching as the traveler's silhouette disappeared into the shadows of the surrounding woods, before pushing open the door and stepping into the drunken chaos.

Niall stood in front of the oxidized mirror lining the back wall of the bar. He tugged at his red beard speckled with silver, eyes pinned on what appeared to be the start of an argument in the corner.

His flannel button-down hugged tight across his waist as he leaned over the counter to shout at them. She was certain that, like everyone else in Williamsburg, he couldn't afford to buy new clothes that fit.

"You lookin' to become a regular?" he asked as Maia approached, removing a glass from under the counter.

Rows of greasy liquor bottles reflected the dim light from the two oil lamps hanging above him. He'd put minimal effort into his establishment, with its unsteady chairs and splintered tables, but none of these things deterred his usual crowd.

She ignored his question as he poured her the same two fingers of whiskey she asked for each night. Her gaze drifted to the other end of the bar, where a man with sad, distant eyes hovered over an untouched lager.

He had arrived only a couple weeks ago, but his quiet demeanor had made him a source of gossip. Maia, however, only wondered what would bring this man to a town everyone else hoped to escape.

Niall slid her glass over, and she carried it to a table in the corner, dropping into a chair. With a slow sip, she closed her eyes, savoring the burn of the whiskey as it eased the tension in her shoulders.

Absentmindedly, she traced the jagged *x* scratched deep into the wood, while her thoughts forced her to relive her mistake. The quiet of the exam room, the bottle in her hand, the subtle change in her patient's breathing—

"I'm sorry about your mother."

She jumped, surprised to find a shadow hovering beside her.

"Thank you," she mumbled.

Stealing a glance, she expected familiar sympathetic eyes.

Instead, she found a stranger.

"May I?" He removed his hat and motioned towards the chair across from her.

Maia's mother used to tell her she had a talent for overthinking things. *If your eyes are open, the moment will always reveal itself,* she'd often said.

At that moment, Maia couldn't deny the nervous energy radiating from the man, like static from an approaching storm.

"No offense, but I've had a shit day and would rather be alone right now."

The man's brows shot up in surprise. "Oh, yes, of course. I understand." He turned to leave, but his step wavered. "Your mother was a strong woman. Kept your father in his place."

How did this stranger know that? It had been years since anyone talked about her father. Even her mother only mentioned his name when the hallucinations took hold on her final night.

Maia let her curiosity get the best of her. "What do you want?"

The man took her words as his invitation, pulling out the seat.

His worn face was covered in stubble, and the silver streaks in his dirty-blond hair hinted he was around Niall's age. He placed his hat on the table with dirt-covered hands, and his vibrant, blue eyes met Maia's.

Her stomach dropped. Why did she recognize those eyes?

"Christian was quite the conversationalist. I suppose your father didn't pass that gift down to you."

All she'd wanted since her mother passed was to be left alone. She wished people would look at her the way she looked at the sad man at the bar.

Distant pity—she'd even take apathy—but what Maia learned was that a broken man was left alone, while a broken woman became a target.

"No. He didn't."

The stranger remained undeterred. "He was a good man—"

"Most people would beg to differ."

Her words struck something within him this time, and the man's face hardened. "Most people like to see the world in black and white."

What he meant was good and evil. Persuasive words, now nearly as diluted as the watered-down whiskey in her glass. A drink her mother never allowed in their house. Her father's favorite.

She leaned back, the chair clunking hard onto the slightly shorter back leg. "I'll ask again—what do you want?"

He drummed his fingers on his hat. "I wish the timing was better, but I'm here to offer you a job."

"I already have a job." Her stomach dropped as she realized that was no longer true.

"This is bigger than healing, Maia."

Goosebumps traveled up her arms as her name rolled off his tongue with an unnerving familiarity. He leaned forward, and their corner of the room suddenly shrunk.

"You feel it, don't you? The feeling that something isn't right."

She gripped her glass, glancing around the room. Everyone remained in their place, adrift in the world outside of their corner.

"I see you scanning the room, preparing a distraction. Your mother taught you all those things. But she learned them from your father."

"Who are you?"

"Your parents called me Rowan."

Her mother had mentioned his name, but it was years ago.

"Well, Rowan, I appreciate the offer, but I'm not interested."

"Maia—"

"Stop saying my name," she snapped.

He lifted his hands in a truce. "You need to calm down."

"Don't tell me to calm down. Tell me the job you're here to offer or leave."

"I'm looking for someone with your talents. Someone who can look at a situation, assess it, and find a solution. That's what healers do, right?"

His words allowed Maia a second to breathe. If he was looking for her help, it meant she still maintained some control.

"I'm not a healer. I'm..."

He didn't need to know about her mistake. She didn't owe him any explanations.

"But you know enough to be useful to the cause."

Or dangerous. "Whose cause?"

"The rebellion's."

There it was. The reason he'd found her.

Rowan was recruiting her to pick up where her father left off.

"I'm not interested in becoming a criminal."

"Criminal?" His penetrating gaze forced her to look away. "Is that what you think your father was?"

She didn't know her father. At least, not the way everyone else seemed to. She knew him as a man who was gone most of her childhood, even before he died.

Rowan leaned back and folded his hands on the table, allowing the room to expand around them.

"I've been on your side of the table, Maia. You need something to believe in right now. You're angry and lost. You need purpose. That's what your father gave me. And that's what I'm here to offer you."

It bothered her that he was right. She *was* angry and lost and hated that she suddenly saw herself reflected in his worn face.

"So, then tell me. Who was my father?"

Rowan's brow creased in thought, and for a moment, they sat in silence.

"Did you know it took nearly a century before the survivors of the Final War could leave the bunkers? Can you imagine how infinite the sky felt when they finally emerged?" He paused, as if expecting her to answer. "That's why our leaders chose to go by the names of the stars. A reminder their duty is to watch over us in this hostile world." His gaze dropped to a string bracelet holding a round piece of metal. Punched into it were seven holes forming Orion's constellation. "The rebellion knew your father as Sagittarius—Taris for short. Now we follow Orion."

"So, you're saying my father led the rebellion?"

He reached into his pocket, removing a torn piece of paper.

"The truth is reality, not the propaganda that surrounds you. I'll give you some time to figure that out."

Standing from the table, he hesitated, eyes suddenly distant. "Your mother once told me not to let fear guide my decisions. I've lived by those words and wish I could have told her that." He tapped the table with the brim of his hat, bringing himself back. "Goodnight, Maia."

2

PURPOSE

Maia waited until the tavern door closed behind Rowan before reaching for the scrap of paper left on the table.

Your mother's tree. One week.

There were only three possible outcomes. One, Rowan would walk away alone in a week. Two, Maia would be waiting by her mother's tree to join the rebellion her father died for. Or, three—

The doors opened and the chaos surrounding her hushed to whispers as the two Porticc guards entered.

Shit.

Maia crumpled the paper in her hand, stuffing it into her pocket.

The guards continued towards the bar with Mayor Alper behind them, clearly unsettled by his impromptu visit to Folly's.

"To what do I owe the pleasure of this unexpected visit, Mayor?" Niall asked, sarcasm dripping from his words.

Mayor Alper adjusted his jacket as if remembering the weight of his title. "These guards believe a rebel is hiding in your tavern."

Maia's stomach plummeted, stealing her breath. *They don't know.* Still, she couldn't slow the furious beat of her heart. The last thing she needed was to be trapped in the corner again.

Throwing back her drink, she quietly stood, hoping the shadows would keep her hidden as she inched towards the exit.

Niall lifted a red brow. "Is that so?"

Scanning the room, Heath's gaze stopped on Maia, his lips twisting dangerously. The look of a hunter who had just found his prey. "There she is."

It was humiliating the way the sudden attention of the room now heated her cheeks. Hadn't she lost enough for one night?

"Maia?" Mayor Alper couldn't hide his surprise. "You must be mistaken. Her father was the rebel, not her."

Heath ignored him, taking slow, commanding steps toward Maia. There was certainty in his gaze, like he already knew how this would play out. The other guard dropped onto a barstool, requesting a lager from Niall.

"Tell him what you did," Heath demanded, his voice no more than a whisper as he hovered over her.

Despite his controlled steps and menacing posture, she could see the tremble of his lip from his barely contained rage. This wasn't about the traveler or red lung. This was about power. He was here to remind her what happened when you made an enemy of Portico.

But there were two truths to be told. Theirs and hers.

Maia's nails bit into her damp palms. She pulled back her shoulders, face hardening under his gaze. "I stopped you from killing an innocent man."

"What was that, Maia?" Mayor Alper asked, taking a hesitant step toward them. "I didn't catch what you said."

She pulled her gaze from Heath and glanced around the room. There was a charge in the air she hadn't noticed until now. Anticipation building as eyes spoke words no one was brave enough to say out loud.

Portico had made enemies in this room. The guard sitting at the bar felt it too, one hand still on his lager while the other hovered over the pistol on his belt.

"Careful with your next words," Heath warned, pulling her attention back to him.

She swallowed before clearing her throat to address the mayor. "I stopped them from killing an innocent man, sir."

Mayor Alper's lips pressed together as if realizing his night was about to get much more complicated than he hoped.

"He had red lung!" Heath shouted, spit flying from his lips while his cheeks quivered with rage. "And now he's wandering your town—"

"No, he's not!" Maia shouted back.

Heath's eyes grew wide at her interruption, but she refused to flinch.

Niall was now beside her, his freckled arms crossed. "Maia ain't that reckless. She's Mr. Thomas' best healing apprentice." Maia appreciated his confidence as he unknowingly lied. "She wouldn't put us in danger like that, and you know it, Mayor."

"Yes," Mayor Alper said, nodding in agreement. "Clearly a misunderstanding. Isn't that correct, Maia?"

All eyes were now on her—the mayor desperate for her to agree, and Heath daring her not to. It took everything in her to keep her hands at her sides. Heath's eyes fell to her fists, his eagerness suddenly palpable.

"Maia…" The mayor's tone was nothing short of a plea.

She could push back all she wanted, but it wouldn't change who won. "It was a misunderstanding, sir."

The mayor seemed to collapse in relief, clapping his hands together. "Wonderful, so we have nothing to worry about, correct?"

"Correct," she said, eyes now dropping to her scuffed boots.

He patted Heath's shoulder. "As always, we appreciate you keeping our beautiful town safe. Isn't that right, Ms. Avalos?"

Heath's eyes lit up, and his terrifying smile sent a chill through her. "Something tells me we'll be seeing each other again soon, Ms. Avalos."

Niall tensed beside Maia, but Heath was already moving towards the exit with the mayor. Throwing back his lager, the other guard rushed after them.

The tension around the room lifted the second the door closed behind them. Conversations slowly started up again, and Maia was relieved to no longer be the center of attention.

Niall remained beside her, arms still crossed. "Your mother said Rowan would come looking for you one day."

"You know him?"

"I know he only shows up when something bad has happened."

The quiet man at the bar slid off his stool and started for the door. His eyes met hers with what looked like respect, and she wondered what she'd done to earn it.

"Are you one of them?" Maia asked, glancing back up at Niall.

He barked out a laugh, as if even the thought was ridiculous. "You don't need to be a rebel to do the right thing." He removed the towel from his back pocket and grabbed an empty glass from a nearby table, returning to the bar. "Go home, Maia."

The orange glow of oil lamps and soft, comforting scent of vanilla greeted Maia as she stepped into the parlor of her home. Hannah sat at the formal table, now pushed into a corner. At one point, it had been the dining room where their family would sit together for meals, but now it hid under piles of brightly colored fabrics. Hannah leaned closer to the lamp, threading a needle.

Her skin looked waxen and sickly under the light, but her golden-blonde hair still glowed as it cascaded past her thick shoulders. A new light-blue dress hugged her curves that had grown more pronounced since their mother passed.

Where Maia used whiskey to numb her broken heart, Hannah had turned to food. Neither worked.

"Were you out drinking again?" Hannah asked, without looking up.

A month ago, Hannah would have been serving tea in their front room while they studied with the other healing apprentices, laughing at absurd patient stories. Death had a way of making even the living disappear.

Maia didn't think there was anything more that could break her tonight, but Hannah's disappointment burned like salt on a wound. "I'm going to bed."

She walked through the kitchen, retreating into her room for the night.

The bed remained unmade, as it had since Hannah moved into their mother's old room. Maia kicked a pile of clothes out of her path and forced open a sticking dresser drawer. Hidden under a stack of shirts was an unlabeled bottle of whiskey. She snatched it, nudging the drawer closed with her shoulder. The sight of fresh peonies in a vase on her desk made her pause.

Hannah's way of saying she missed her. Or rather, the version of Maia that existed before their mother fell sick.

Maia's mother adopted Hannah at five after her parents died in the same accident that claimed Maia's father. Fawns on their own were easy prey, and children were no different. Maia remembered the look of embarrassment on Hannah's face when the kids would make fun of her for her loss.

She didn't remember dropping her bag or pushing through the crowd, but Maia did remember her fist making contact with the boy's nose. Hannah screamed as he turned to Maia and charged. The fight was insignificant, no more than a minute, but it changed everything. The girls walked home in silence—Maia with a black eye, and Hannah just a little taller.

Maia reached for the flowers but stopped. They weren't children anymore. Even at nineteen, Hannah was already like their mother, with her comforting words and gentle touch. Confessing her mistake to Hannah, only to disappoint her more, would be too much. Instead, Maia picked up her sketchbook and popped the cork off the bottle, hoping to numb at least some of the guilt and worry for now.

⋘⟶⟶⟶⟶⟶⟶⟶⟶⟶⟶⟶⟶⟶⟶⟶⟶⟶⟶

Time felt different.

Excruciatingly slow as she struggled to fill her days and busy her mind.

Yet surprisingly fast as Rowan's deadline arrived.

Vendors shouted from their wooden stalls in the crowded market square, but it was the taunting smell of freshly baked bread and pastries that called to Maia. She rubbed the slip of paper in her pocket, balancing a bag of rice she bought for the week on her hip. It felt especially heavy today, knowing their coin was quickly dwindling.

Hannah would soon finish her apprenticeship, but even that wouldn't be enough. Not without Maia bringing coin home too. How was it possible for her to destroy all their hopes and dreams so easily?

Frantic shouts carried over the crowd, and Maia was surprised to find Hannah forcing her way to her. "Maia! Two men are throwing everything out of the house!"

"What?" There was no way she heard Hannah right. She reached for her sister, allowing her a second to catch her breath.

"Two Portico guards. They barged into the house and started throwing everything into the street." Hannah's tear-stained cheeks were flushed as she sobbed between gasps of air. "They were looking for you."

The bag of rice fell from Maia's grip, splitting as it hit the dirt road. She straightened her back, every muscle tensed, every nerve on edge, every ounce of her seething. They had gone too far.

She sprinted across the market, cutting through the same alley where she created this problem. The guards stood outside her home, dumping drawers of clothes into a pile in the road.

"What the fuck are you doing?" Maia shouted, grabbing her sheets from Heath's arms. "You can't force yourself into our home like this."

He snatched the sheets back and threw them into the dirt. "This ain't your home anymore, darlin'. You owe a month's worth of taxes, which means it belongs to Fortico Trading now."

"Our mother just passed," Hannah pleaded, winded from chasing after Maia. "We'll pay whatever we owe."

"I would have been willing to negotiate, but *she* ruined that for you," he said, pointing at Maia.

Hannah's face twisted with confusion, her gaze trailing back to Maia. "What did you do?"

Ignoring her, Maia took a step towards Heath, face burning and resolute despite him towering over her. "If you take one more thing out of this house…"

His brow lifted, daring her to finish her sentence.

"Enough, Maia!" Hannah snapped.

A smirk crossed his thin lips as he leaned forward, his pungent aftershave assaulting Maia. "You picked the wrong fight, darlin'. Next time, make sure you ain't the only one who's got something to lose."

"I wasn't going to let you kill him." There was no fear left within her, only fury.

"With red lung, he was already dead."

The other guard tossed Hannah's fabrics to the ground. Seeing them strewn across the dirt dropped Hannah to her knees as she desperately pulled her fabrics into the safety of her arms.

"We expect this trash to be gone when we get back tomorrow," Heath sneered. "Let's go."

They walked away, leaving the sisters in the wake of their chaos. Eyes peered from the surrounding windows, but no one would risk helping. Not after what they just witnessed.

Maia offered Hannah her hand, but she pushed it away, standing on her own.

"I'm sorry. I'll fix this," she said, following Hannah as she stormed down the road. "They can't just take our house like that."

Hannah's pace quickened. "They just did."

"It was out of spite. I'll figure out how to get it back."

"You don't get it," she spun to Maia, red traveling up her neck. "You know what they're capable of, but you still can't keep your mouth shut."

"Because we shouldn't!"

Hannah's face hardened at Maia's outburst. Two men stood quietly, watching them through the gray clouds of their smokes as they leaned against the wall outside of Folly's.

Hannah took Maia's arm, pulling her into the shadows of a building.

"Did the rebel put these thoughts in your head?" she whispered, eyes flickering back to the men watching.

"How do you—"

"Niall told me." Maia couldn't tell if she was angry at the fact that it was true, or that she had to find out from Niall.

She thumbed the piece of paper in her pocket again. Rowan would be waiting by their mother's tree tonight. Maybe this was how she could fix things.

"The rebellion can offer us a roof and keep us safe until we get this sorted out."

"Safe?" Hannah's voice grew shrill. "Joining the rebellion is a death sentence. My parents fought with them, just like your father. I won't die like them. Not for a lost cause."

It was only a lost cause if they allowed it to die with their parents.

"I'm tired of having to stay silent, Hannah. This is how I make things right. Not just for us."

Hannah shook her head in frustration. "The rabbit can only run so long from the wolf."

It was something Maia's mother used to say to her father, and he always had the same response. "A wolf against a wolf stands a better chance."

"But what do you sacrifice to become the wolf?"

It wasn't a question Maia could answer through words, only actions. If she stayed, it would only be because of the fear of change gripping her stomach. The same fear she saw in Hannah's eyes.

"I don't want to leave without you."

"Then don't," Hannah begged. "We can find another—"

"Mr. Thomas ended my apprenticeship because of my mistake." Hannah's big, blue eyes stared as she stood lost for words. For a moment, Maia stopped and thought about the life she could still have in Williamsburg. Even after her mistake, she knew Niall would offer her a job at Folly's cleaning tables or pouring lagers. A safe life, or at least the appearance of one.

That's what Portico had done—created the illusion of safety with their rebel propaganda. When, in reality, they kept everyone in line through fear. If she stayed, nothing would change. All of it could be taken away again.

She reached for Hannah's hand. "Please don't make me choose."

Her sister's lips curled in disgust, and she yanked her hand to her chest. "I'd rather get a room with the lowlifes at Folly's than willingly put a target on my back. If you walk away, it's *your* choice. Not mine."

Her words pierced Maia like a knife. Their mother had taught them to be strong and stand by their convictions. But she also made them promise to never let these things get in the way of standing by each other. Tonight, they would break that promise.

"Okay." Maia tucked her trembling hands into her pockets, wishing she was strong enough to walk away without feeling another tear in her heart.

"Maia," Hannah choked. "Promise me this isn't goodbye. I'll be here when you decide to come back."

She smiled gently, the same shattered smile she gave Hannah when they had walked away from their mother's freshly planted cherry blossom. "I promise."

Empty words.

There was a stillness to the evening that Maia was only beginning to understand. In the weeks since her mother passed, all she wanted was to scream, to cry, to tear down the walls of her home. But now, she felt a chilling nothingness as she approached the cherry blossom tree overlooking the lake on the edge of town.

The New World didn't believe in mausoleums and gravestones. Those temporary monuments had been reclaimed by the lush green now blanketing their earth. To live on was to return to nature.

Lo que el monte nos dio, el monte lo recogió—what nature gives, nature takes. It was a saying her father created in his native tongue. A reminder that whatever kindness their world gave, it always took back.

The full moon silhouetted the harsh twists of the cherry blossom's branches, like mangled fingers stretching protectively across the calm surface of the water. Maia dropped to her knees, sinking into the soft dirt where she had buried her mother's ashes three weeks earlier. Her fingers grazed the long petals of the freshly planted lilies.

"Mom," she whispered, reaching her hand out to the rough bark.

The sharp pain in her chest took her breath away—a new crack in her already splintered heart.

"I miss you so much."

It was pathetic how desperate she sounded. The same desperation she had the night she begged her mother not to go to the shantytown.

There had been rumors of a red lung outbreak just outside of Williamsburg. Stories of how it wasted its victims away to nothing, before drowning them in their own blood. Even knowing this, Lena Avalos still walked out the door.

Maybe Mr. Thomas was right about Maia. If she could do it all over again, she would sacrifice the entire shantytown if it meant her mother survived. And *that* was the difference between her and her mother.

She wiped the tears from her cheeks, feeling the grittiness of the dirt still on her hands.

"All I ever wanted was to make you proud." Her words caught in her throat as she thought about the slip of paper crumpled in her pocket. "I just need to know I'm making the right decision."

Had her mother been there, she would have given Maia words of wisdom to ease the fear painfully twisting her stomach.

Instead, there was only silence as Maia waited for something she'd never have again.

"Christian would be proud of your decision," Rowan said from behind her.

With a sigh, she pushed herself to her feet, noticing fresh dirt on his knees.

"And my mother?"

"Lena would want what's best for you."

His avoidance of an answer meant it probably wasn't this.

"Are you ready?" Rowan asked, eyeing the bag on her shoulder. "It's a long walk back to the safe house."

"Which is where?"

He looked towards the shadowy entrance of the woods. "Hidden. For obvious reasons."

She glanced back at her mother's cherry blossom one last time. All she wanted was a sign that she was right to walk away from everything she knew. The freshly planted lilies danced in the soft breeze. Her mother's favorite.

Maia's eyes drifted back to the dirt stains on Rowan's knees. *If your eyes are open, the moment will always reveal itself.*

She remembered now why his eyes were so familiar. Rowan was a man from a different life—a man her father once called a 'friend.' She could still see him sitting at their kitchen table, laughing with her father when she was just a child, their eyes filled with the same effervescence as Rowan's in this moment.

Two years later, he was bringing her mother lilies as they stood over her father's freshly buried ashes. Her mother had taken his hand and spoken the same words he told Maia that night at the tavern. *Never let fear guide your decisions.*

There was a reason Rowan found her when he did—why Maia had to lose everything tonight. Her mother's footsteps were no longer her path, but her father's now appeared laid out before her. If she didn't take these next steps, she'd always wonder if she walked away from her true purpose.

"You could have turned me in to those guards, Maia, but you didn't. I need you to trust me too." Rowan's voice was different, softer.

"I do," she said, lifting her hood and stepping past him into the darkness.

It was time to disappear.

3

HUNTERS & PREY

The beasts may stalk us, but it's the sweetest smelling flowers that cut the deepest.

K. Wells – Summer 2259

I t was impressive how inconspicuous the two-story plantation home appeared, hidden behind wild vegetation. Tendrils climbed the white columns and stretched along the walls, slowly consuming it. A relic of the past that only remained standing because nature allowed it.

A gentle creak carried from the small front porch where two white-washed rocking chairs swayed in the evening breeze. Even the twinkle from a wind chime seemed to welcome her home. The rebellion had done its job creating the illusion of conformity.

Maia followed Rowan up the cracked brick steps of the porch. "How long have you been here?"

Rowan pushed open the front door, stepping inside. "This house has been in my family since before the war."

Most houses were shells of pre-war structures. Which made her wonder how he knew—over a century after the Final War—that this specific house belonged to him.

She wiped her boots before entering, and her mouth fell open in shock as she stepped inside.

Cathedral ceilings and white marble floors all remained untouched by time. A stark contrast to the decay outside. Gathered around a coffee table in the parlor was a small group of rebels arguing over paperwork, while two others descended from the grand staircase.

"You need to work on your poker face," Rowan said, closing the door behind them.

Maia lowered her hood and shook out of her jacket. "I expected something… different."

Definitely nothing so bright and extravagant.

"Always anticipate but never expect."

Like that, she was suddenly back in an apprenticeship. And this was lesson one.

Rowan hung their jackets on a coat rack and took Maia's bag as the man and woman descending the stairs approached.

"Maia Avalos," the man said, voice rough like gravel as he put out his hand. "It's good to finally meet you. You look just like your father."

A thick scar traveled down the right side of his neck, making him look deadly. Maia took his hand, surprised by the rebellion tattoo on the inside of his wrist. Wearing the symbol so blatantly made him either very brave or very stupid.

"You knew my father?"

The man eyed Rowan, his thick brows knotting with confusion, and Maia wondered if she had said something wrong.

The younger woman beside him broke the tension by taking Maia's hand. "I'm Jackson. So sorry to hear about your mother. It's been years since I lost mine, but the hole in my heart never seems to heal."

Brightly colored strings and beads stood out against her sun-bleached, matted hair, while layers of hemp, leather, and shells covered her tanned wrists and neck. She looked like Mother Nature personified.

"I was just stopping by to pick up supplies for my team, but I'll be back to help with your training." Jackson gave Maia a wink that seemed surprisingly genuine. She turned back to the man beside her, elbowing him in the ribs. "Everything is set for the hit in three days. I'll report back on day four."

Despite her playfulness, his face remained stern as he dropped his burly hand onto her shoulder. "Be safe."

"Yeah, yeah," she said, waving him off.

Rowan guided Maia to the parlor, passing the group gathered around the coffee table, toward a set of chairs in front of a lit fireplace.

She took a seat next to the window, grateful for the comfort of the flames. A branch warily tapped against the pane, as if beckoning to share a secret only with her. The man from the foyer took the seat across from Maia, while Rowan grabbed a bottle from the liquor cabinet.

"I knew your father well," the man said. "If I'm not mistaken, he used to call you his little Sagitta."

Little arrow. It had been too long since she last heard those words, and a sad smile crept across her lips. "He did."

The man returned her smile with a soft one, contradicting his sharp jaw and hooded eyes. Rowan handed him a glass. "Your father truly was an amazing man, Maia."

"I wish I could have known him the way you did, sir," she said as Rowan handed her a drink too.

"You can call me Orion."

Her grip went limp around the glass. She barely caught it before it fell in her lap, ignoring the drops of whiskey on her hand. How did a name immediately change the perception of someone? Orion's brawny build and strong features transformed him from powerful to intimidating, and the scar along his neck suddenly made him seem invincible.

"What do you know about your father?" he asked, casually lifting his booted foot across his knee. It was effortless in a way that felt purposeful. An attempt to put her at ease in his overwhelming presence.

Her mind went blank. The stories she knew were from people who feared everyone in this room. Rowan dropped onto the loveseat in front of the fireplace and lifted his hand to his mouth, waiting for Maia's response. Her father's watch suddenly felt heavy in her pocket, digging into her thigh.

"Only that he was a rebel, sir."

Orion nodded, and she wondered if he knew her words were only half-truths.

"He wasn't just a rebel, Maia. Your father started the rebellion."

The argument from the parlor stopped.

Memories raced through Maia's mind, moments that felt so insignificant at the time, reborn with new meaning.

Her mother warning her that a name held power and to keep hers close.

Hannah finding a black hair comb in their mother's drawer, but it being gifted to Maia instead, only for her to discover the lockpick set hidden inside.

Her father and the rebellion had always felt synonymous, but she never realized they truly were.

A man with a strong five o'clock shadow stood from the group, pulling Maia from her thoughts. His brown skin and short, black hair reminded her of her father's.

"Mentiras," he whispered.

He even spoke Spanish like her father. Her mother once said it was a dying language. People had cut their roots once they escaped the Desert Region, and now it was rare for anyone to speak fluently. Her mother had stopped speaking it shortly after her father passed.

"You're the daughter of Taris?" The awe in the man's face made Maia realize he was younger than she thought. Closer to her own age than Rowan's.

Her face flushed as she realized how oblivious she must have looked. Was she?

Orion nodded, answering the man's question.

The sudden shift in power made Maia uncomfortable. "My name is Theodore Garcia, but *you* can call me Garcia."

A younger man with dark brown skin and soft features leaned back in his chair, grinning. "Don't let him flatter you. We *all* call him Garcia."

"Cállate, cabrón," Garcia snapped, waving the man off. "Let me introduce you to my team. The old bastard walking away is Edward."

Garcia pointed to an older man limping towards one of the front windows. The man didn't bother to look in their direction. Instead, taking a swig from a flask he pulled from his coat.

"He doesn't say much, but apparently is impossible to kill. Man's been shot, stabbed, and poisoned, but he keeps coming back for more. Jayce has the smart mouth, and his younger sister Kayla is a near-perfect shot."

Jayce's grin widened at his introduction, and his sister, no older than sixteen, sat with two pistols on her hips.

"Your father used to call us 'the voice of the people,'" Rowan said, pouring himself another glass. "I don't know if your mother ever told you, but Aquila—the leader of Portico—found Christian in a shantytown when he was about your age."

She had not.

"His parents died when he was a child, so your father spent most of his life on the streets. He was fortunate a man like Aquila took an interest in him. Weapons, espionage, manipulation... your father picked up all these skills quickly. Aquila called him a natural talent. But, when he was sent to poison the wells of the shantytown he grew up in, everything changed. He realized Portico doesn't create allegiance, they instill fear. The same people your father threatened just years earlier were the ones who helped him build the rebellion."

"Portico hasn't changed its tactics," Jayce said, walking over to join them. "Summer fever was rampant in our shantytown when Kayla caught it. They only offered the tonic to those who joined or paid a hundred coin. If any of us had a hundred coin, we wouldn't be living in that shithole. The rebellion stole the tonic from Portico's camp and offered us a chance at a new beginning. Kayla wouldn't be here if they hadn't arrived that night."

The siblings exchanged a glance, but Kayla looked away. Despite whatever he had already endured, Jayce still had a kindness to him. A warmth similar to the fire crackling in their silence. But life had hardened Kayla's eyes, and Maia wondered if her cold demeanor was because of the world, or the rebellion.

Garcia poured himself a glass from the bottle. "I was fortunate enough to meet Taris. My father worked the Portico coal mines and one day he just… didn't come home. My mother fought for his body so she could give him a proper burial—return him to the earth. Portico beat her to within an inch of her life, right in the town square, making an example out of her. When they threw us out into the street, your father brought her to *this* house, and your mother mended her wounds." A sadness washed over him that he tried to hide with a forced smile. "I wish I would have thanked them…"

"*That* is why we fight, Maia," Rowan added with a sigh. "To give a voice to those Portico has silenced with fear."

Orion lifted his glass. "To the rebellion."

The group followed, and Maia savored the burn as it anchored her in her new reality. There was a hope in their eyes that she hadn't seen in a long time, and she wondered if it reflected in hers.

"Training starts at 0700 for all of you," Rowan said, pushing himself up from the loveseat. "I'll show you upstairs to your room, Maia."

She stood, placing her empty glass on the fireplace mantel. As she followed Rowan, Orion's calloused hand found her wrist, causing her entire body to tense.

"Welcome home, Sagitta." The glow of the fireplace created harsh shadows across his face, and a loud screech of the branch against the window sent goosebumps up her arm. She shook away the unsettling feeling and smiled as Orion continued, "I look forward to seeing what we accomplish together."

Her stomach dropped as the weight of her father's legacy finally hit her. It was one thing to be a rebel, but to be the daughter of the man who sparked the revolution...

"Thank you, sir," she whispered, swallowing the bile working its way up the back of her throat.

Orion released her wrist, shifting his gaze back to the fireplace and allowing her to escape. Rowan was already making his way up the stairs, and she rushed to follow.

"Where are the rest of the rebels?"

"Moving," he said, handing her the pathetically-light bag with her belongings. "We don't gather in large groups anymore. Not since your father's death. There are small pockets throughout the Coastal and Forest Regions, but we tend to move in teams of no more than four or five. You're the first in your team. Garcia's team has most of the rooms on the left, but the rest are free for you to choose from."

She glanced down the dark hallway and turned back to Rowan, heart pounding. "What happens if I can't do this?"

He gave her a soft smile, as if seeing her again for the first time. "I know it's a lot, but your father's legacy was his. Your decision to join... that's where yours begins. Now, get some rest and don't be late."

Rowan disappeared into his room, leaving Maia alone in the hall. The wooden floor creaked under her boots, her steps stopping in front of the last door on the right. A shrill creak filled the silence as it rolled open, exposing a sterile room with a twin-sized bed, a wooden dresser, a desk, and a nightstand. Neatly folded on the bed lay a clean, white towel waiting for her.

She dropped her bag beside the door and took a seat on the stiff sheets, lifting the scratchy towel to her nose. Why did she think it would smell like home? Had her father once sat here? Had he always been this close on the nights she stayed up late waiting for him?

She still remembered one of their last nights together.

Her father had been picking at his bowl of stew most of dinner when he suddenly said, "They killed Simeon."

"Not at the table," her mother snapped, eyes narrowing in warning.

"We can't pretend anymore. Portico is becoming dangerous, and if we turn a blind eye, they'll be knocking on our door next."

She ignored his words, collecting the plates from the table. Desperate, he reached for her, but her mother turned away.

Maia remembered the sadness in his eyes, the worry scratched between his brows. She took his hand, hoping it would make him happy again.

With a sad smile, her father squeezed her small hand. "Don't worry. We're stronger than we look, my little Sagitta."

She pulled the rough towel to her chest as the wind picked up outside, unleashing a tortured howl. The knot in her stomach tightened as she realized Hannah would be alone at Folly's tonight.

Rowan's training was exactly what Maia had thought it would be—making them into the type of criminals he claimed they weren't.

They started by picking door locks in the house before moving on to Portico's supply caches. Advancing to the art of pickpocketing Portico's traders and, finally, self-defense for when either of those didn't go as planned.

Jackson slowly circled Maia, the straw stuffed mats of the training room crunching under her boots. A musty smell permeating from the concrete walls of Rowan's Old World bunker seeped into Maia's pores. After all the exhausting hours of training, she wondered if she would ever get the smell out of her hair.

"Rowan says you're pretty good with daggers." Jackson grinned, twirling her blade in her palm and catching it at the hilt.

Behind them, Garcia slammed Jayce onto the mat. The string of profanities that followed was impressive, but quickly overshadowed by Garcia's booming laugh, now echoing through the room.

Maia rubbed the sleep from her eyes, mentally berating herself for staying up late talking with Kayla. "I guess I'm alright."

"Long night?" Jackson asked.

Her answer came in the form of a yawn that Maia could no longer fight off. Before she knew what was happening, Jackson had Maia's arm twisted tight behind her back. She sucked in a breath as a smooth blade slid carefully against her throat.

"Don't let the enemy see your weakness," Jackson hissed, her breath sending a shiver through Maia as the skin prickled on the back of her neck.

She was awake now.

Her entire body tensed, and she threw back her head, finding Jackson's nose.

"Fuck!" She dropped her blade, covering her face. Maia took advantage of the distraction and scrambled to pick it up.

Jackson's eyes were already watering from the impact. Rubbing her finger under her nose, she checked to make sure it wasn't bleeding. "Go for the gut punch next time."

"That seemed to work just fine," Maia said, gripping the blade.

Garcia and Jayce took a break from sparring, dropping onto the wooden benches along the wall, now interested in the fight.

With a smirk, Jackson slid her second blade from the strap around her thigh. They were both circling now, daggers at the ready.

"The advantage of this weapon is you have complete control," Jackson said. With a quick spin, she gifted Maia a slice across her padded vest. "The disadvantage is you don't have the luxury of space between you and your enemy."

"You don't have any padding on," Maia said, taking a hesitant swing with the very real and very sharp knife.

Jackson dodged, grabbing Maia's arm and twisting it until the dagger fell from her grip.

"Good thing I don't have to worry about it." With a swift kick, Maia's only weapon went skidding across the mat.

She looked over and noticed Rowan leaning against the doorway, arms crossed and face stone. Maia's cheeks flushed. He hadn't said a word, but even that was enough to make her wonder if he was beginning to regret recruiting a failed healing apprentice.

"¡Oye!" Garcia shouted, grounding her back in the moment. "Brush it off. You got this."

The confidence in his face backed his words, fueling Maia. She straightened her shoulders and lifted her wrapped fists. Jackson nodded in approval. Bouncing on her toes, she took another swipe at Maia. This time she dodged it, sneaking a jab into Jackson's side. Without waiting for her to recover, she launched a kick.

A mistake.

Jackson's hand caught Maia's ankle, and she yanked hard enough to drop Maia onto her back.

For a terrifying moment, the world went dark. She gasped for air, trying to blink away the spots in her vision. Steps approached and Maia scrambled backward. Everything was a blur of panic, but she could still make out the towering figure now leaning over her.

"Use your legs," Rowan ordered. "It's the only advantage you'll have."

"No helping!" Jackson threw herself forward.

This was her chance. Maia dropped back and wrapped her legs around Jackson's neck, squeezing as hard as she could.

Panic washed over Jackson's reddening face as she clawed at Maia's legs, desperate to escape. Gritting her teeth, Maia struggled to maintain her hold. *We're stronger than we look, my little Sagitta.* She could do this.

Jackson's chokes were mirrored by a tapping sound on the mat.

"Maia," Rowan warned.

She opened her eyes to find Jackson's face turning purple as she slapped her hand on the mat, tapping out. Relaxing her legs, Jackson didn't hesitate to roll away, gasping for breath.

The thundering of Maia's heart was almost deafening as she dropped her head back on the mat. Her legs were trembling, and she greedily sucked in gulps of air, but she had won. Pressing her lips together, she fought back a smile.

"Have you ever killed someone before?" Jackson rasped, wincing as she touched the red marks already forming on her neck.

"No. And I wasn't planning on it, either, if that's what you're worried about."

Jackson was suddenly quiet, and when Maia glanced up, she found her exchanging a concerned look with Rowan. Were they hoping for a different answer?

"Maia's training with me tomorrow," he said, pushing off the doorframe.

The rebels may have been criminals, but their wrongdoings were nothing compared to the atrocities Maia watched Portico commit daily.

Acres of land seized from farmers and miners too poor to afford Portico's fluctuating taxes. That same land given to men and women who pledged allegiance—pawns content to play their role in Portico's corruption.

To be with Portico was to be untouchable.

Until now.

"Who's there?"

Rowan and Maia hid in the shadows of the tree line, quiet as the savage beasts that stalked the woods. They had been following their target for the last three miles, but it was a wild boar that triggered him.

Portico's fur traders were easy to recognize, because they wore it proudly in any season. Their target wasn't known for this, though. He was known for trading young girls. Something Portico conveniently turned a blind eye to.

The trader drew his blade, hunting the boar, while Maia and Rowan hunted him. Slowly inching forward, Rowan reached for his knife, but Maia quickly grabbed his arm.

His jaw clenched, and he threw a glare at her, clearly frustrated. But it was the flicker of doubt in his eyes that hardened her face to match his. She shook her head.

This target was hers.

Relaxing under her grip, Rowan nodded, and she stalked forward.

This was for Portico taking her home.

She picked up a thick branch, her footsteps soundless as she snuck up behind him.

For Hannah.

She swung, flinching at the crack the wood made against the back of the man's head.

For her father.

The trader would have an awful headache and a nasty bump, but death would have been a kindness. Maia pulled her blade and flipped him onto his back, taking her time as she carved a *tf* into his forehead, outing him as a trafficker.

Portico could no longer deny the truth, and Rowan stood watch, his thin lips tugging softly with pride.

It was then that Maia realized—if you weren't the hunter, you were the prey.

4

SCAVENGERS

My heart truly saw what my eyes never could.

K. Wells – Summer 2259

After three months, Maia's life had found a new routine with the rebels. When they weren't training, they spent afternoons hunting for food or loading supplies for teams coming and going.

Edward would usually disappear shortly after, heading to town for a drink while the rest wandered the grounds, looking for ways to entertain themselves.

"You're going to shoot your leg if you spin it like that," Kayla said, taking the pistol from Maia's hand. "It's about timing and pressure. One fluid motion to show your precision with both."

Maia grabbed her knife from its tip and flung it at the target drawn on the tree. It wasn't a bullseye, but it was getting close.

A wicked grin tugged at Kayla's lips.

"I know about precision," Maia said, starting toward the target.

A bullet whizzed past her, lodging straight into the bullseye. The sudden ringing in her ear dropped Maia to her knees in the soft grass. She lifted her trembling hand, wincing as it found the burning spot along the shell of her ear. The spot where the bullet had grazed her.

Muffled shouts approached, and Kayla yanked Maia violently out of her haze.

"What the fuck, Edward?" Kayla shouted, pulling Maia to her feet.

Did Edward just try to kill her? The moment of shock wore off, replaced by a blinding rage.

"I'm fine," Maia snapped, brushing off Kayla's hand.

Edward stood on the porch, holstering his gun while taking a drag from his smoke.

Walking to the tree, Kayla wrenched Maia's knife from it and handed it back to her. "Guess he's got somethin' to say."

She couldn't hide her still-shaking hands as she took the knife, shoving it into its sheath. With a steadying breath, she clenched her fists and started towards the porch. "What was that?"

Edward snuffed out his smoke, limping back to the rocking chairs. "You have no idea what you're getting yourself into, darlin'."

Darlin' seemed to be the name people used when they thought they knew more than her.

"Then why don't you tell me, asshole?"

He crossed his arms, but seemed to decide her insult wasn't worth the fight. "Your father used to say *follow the stars*. That's how you would know who to trust."

She climbed the steps of the porch and ran her thumb across Orion's constellation carved into the wood column.

"The stars are nothing more than a symbol though," he scoffed. "They won't protect you. If Portico finds out you joined the rebellion, none of us will."

"Is that a threat?"

He lifted his necklace to her. "These stars... they're a target. When Portico found out about my allegiance, they killed my fiancé and confiscated my land. They took everything from me."

"Isn't that why you fight?"

His eyes dropped, and for the first time since joining the rebels, she really looked at him. He wasn't lying. She recognized his sadness. It was one that came from sudden loss.

His bony shoulders fell, and he shook his head. "I don't fight anymore. There's only so much regret one person can live with. The lucky ones don't survive long enough to understand that."

The front door opened, and Garcia paused in the threshold.

"¿Estás bien?" he asked, eyeing Edward suspiciously.

Lifting his boot to his knee, Edward hocked up a wad of spit and sent it over the railing. He said what he needed to, and she wondered if he had given the same warning to the others.

"Yeah," she said, brushing the thought away. "We're good."

Garcia wasn't convinced by her response but nodded. "Vamos, cabrón," he said, walking over and shoving Edward's foot to the floor with a thud. "Our team just got called to fuck shit up in Jamestown. That should wipe the scowl off your face."

Edward's frown only deepened as he stood, disappearing back into the house.

"Not even death wants the bastard," Garcia said, shaking his head and leaning back against the railing. "Rowan asked for you. Sounds like you have your first solo mission."

Maia glanced around Rowan's concrete office with cold, gray walls and corroding-metal piping. Another one of the many rooms inside his Old World bunker tucked in the woods next to the house. She pulled the wooden chair across the floor, cringing at the deafening echo. Rowan looked up from his paperwork, watching her over the rim of his glasses, not hiding his annoyance.

"I believe I found our next recruit," he said, sliding her a folder. "However, he has some... vices. I need you to follow him to see if he's worth the effort."

Surprise slowly bloomed into a pride she quickly tamed. She must have done something right for him to trust her with this task. Reaching for the folder, she flipped it open to find a drawing of a man with a swollen left eye and busted lip. "Him? He looks like he's already lost one too many fights."

"His name is Briar Harper. I don't have a lot of information on him, but he's supposed to be one of the best fighters in the Forest Region. And, as you can see, he's not afraid to take a few hits either."

She flipped through pages filled with notes in different handwriting. Rowan had sent rebel scouts to follow Briar over the last few weeks, making her wonder what kind of notes he had on her. Was that why the quiet man with his untouched lager found his way to a place like Folly's?

She closed the folder, laying it on the edge of Rowan's desk. "Where do I find him?"

The air of the tavern was thick with greedy perspiration and stale smoke. Single lanterns on each poker table provided just enough light to make out the hooded eyes and carefully trained lips of the players. Maia turned back to the barkeep, dropping a coin and taking her drink to an empty corner table. She could sense eyes following her, confirming that she looked as out of place as she felt in the dodgy trading post town.

All she had to do was find her mark, and she would be out of here before anyone got a good look at her.

She took a sip of her drink and scanned the room when a man dropped into the seat across from her. The glass hesitated against her lips as her eyes met his hollow sockets, twisting her stomach into a knot.

His bulbous nose sniffed the air, and his lip curled as if he'd just smelled a secret. "You ain't supposed to be here."

The taunt in his voice sent goosebumps up her arms. She rubbed them away, grateful he couldn't see her reaction. "And how would you know?"

"I guess I could be wrong," he said with a rotten, tobacco-stained grin. He relaxed into his seat and took a sip from his lager. "So, who sent ya?"

"No one." she mumbled, wishing he was missing his tongue rather than his eyes.

He cackled. "And who is No One looking for?"

"For fuck's sake!" an older man at one of the poker tables yelled, throwing down his cards. "That's the third fucking hand in a row."

The younger man sitting across from him stood, reaching a tattoo-covered arm towards the center of the table to gather his winnings. The old man's hand pinned his arm, and the two locked glares.

"There's some shady business about you, boy."

The younger man should have been a menacing presence as he towered over the table, but the slight sway from one too many drinks betrayed him.

"Ya mind?" he growled.

Maia's eyes traveled around the tavern, watching swift hands swiping poker chips from those careless enough to divert their attention to the scene. Any one of these shady men could be her mark.

"I knew I recognized your face. You're Harper's boy, that sorry piece of shit."

Her eyes snapped back to the poker table. Of course, the drunk covered in tattoos was Briar Harper.

"You're just like your father, boy. Take only what you won and get the fuck out."

Briar pulled his arm from the old man's grip and dropped his coins into a worn leather pouch. With a grin, he chugged the rest of his lager and slammed it on the table, wiping his mouth with the back of his hand. He wanted every glare the men at the table were willing to provide.

"Enjoy your evenin', gentlemen." Briar's words were barely intelligible as they worked their way around his lager-heavy tongue. He stumbled from the poker table and tripped on his way out the door, allowing the world inside the tavern to continue without him.

"Poor boy's allowing the darkness to take hold." The blind man shook his head in disappointment. "Scavengers took my eyes, but since then, I've sensed more darkness than I ever saw. There's still light around him though. Faint, but it's there."

Maia's father used to frighten her with stories about the Scavengers. Men and women with beady eyes and long, sharp claws. Vultures of the human world, lurking along the edges of the Old World roads, waiting for travelers to pick bone-clean.

She could only imagine the horrors the man witnessed before his world went black. Dropping her gaze, she thumbed at a chip on the rim of her glass. "What do you know about him?"

"Portico's men show up every week or so to collect on a debt his father left him in his passin'."

"Did Portico kill him?"

The man shook his head. "A stab to the back. Portico would've made him look 'em in the eye as they did it."

Maia finished her drink and stood when the man gripped her arm.

"You see. Now saw."

Maia tore her arm from him. "What?"

"That's what the Scavengers chant as they take your eyes," he said, leaning back in his chair. "If Briar's who you're looking for, maybe there's still a chance for him."

"Why do you say that?" she asked, wondering what he sensed around her.

"It's a hard thing to find the light again once the darkness takes hold, which is why I hope not to see yours here again. You keep at whatever you're doin', and you'll end up like me," he said with a cackle.

The blind man's warning reminded her of Edward's. She shook away the unsettling feeling and continued out the door, hoping Briar hadn't made it too far.

He was still staggering down the empty dirt road to a sad gathering of neglected homes when Maia spotted him. Lifting the collar of her jacket, she kept to the shadows between the houses. His boot caught on the broken wooden porch steps, and he stumbled into the door. Jiggling the handle, he cursed when he found it locked. She expected him to force his way inside, but instead he pounded on the door, begging to be let in.

After a few minutes of no response, he slid to the floor, sniveling like a child before passing out across the cluttered porch. The sun peeked over the horizon, threatening to expose Maia's cover. It was time to head back to the safe house. She had seen enough. The man's vices far outweighed any good he had left in him.

She turned to leave when an aged woman stepped out of the house. There was a listlessness to her, like a woman who had no more tears to give to the world—face blank as she stepped over Briar with indifference. Even from where Maia stood, the resemblance between the two was uncanny. Not even his mother had patience for him anymore.

Waiting for the woman to be far enough away, she finally slipped out from hiding, hoping for a quick escape back to the safety of the woods. A violent tremble from Briar caused her footstep to falter. He looked so vulnerable in his fitful slumber—a softness he only allowed in his dreams...or nightmares. She took another hesitant step, but stopped again.

He's not your problem, she told herself, but it didn't seem to matter. Maia spun on her heels, yanking a sheet from the line and tossing it over him before disappearing.

"What do you know so far?"

The mustiness from the dripping pipes in Rowan's office was stronger, and Maia hoped their meeting would be short as she sat across from him.

"The man is a mess. An aimless drunk who doesn't know when to quit."

Rowan eyed her over his glasses, his icy-blue gaze suddenly as frigid as his office. "And why is that?"

He stared at her as though expecting something different from her assessment. She adjusted in the seat, reframing her next words.

"I guess because of his father. The man owed money to Portico, and his debt seems to have rolled over to Briar. Then there's his mother—callous and uncaring, but it looks like he still goes back to her every night."

"So, he's loyal."

She could still see him crying for his mother on the porch. "To a fault, it seems."

"Then, I believe we've found our next recruit," Rowan said, opening the folder in front of him and scribbling a note.

Maia chewed her lip, watching him tuck the folder into a drawer and debating whether to speak her next words.

With a sigh, she set them free. "What notes do you have on me?"

"You assume I have a folder for you." He stood before she could respond, removing the jacket from the back of his chair. "Come on, let's see if we can convince him to join us."

She eyed his desk before joining him at the door. He didn't want her to know what was in her folder, which meant she needed to.

Rowan shifted away from the old man with hollow eyes, taking a sip from his glass.

"You couldn't have picked a different seat?" he whispered to Maia.

The old man grinned. "I'm blind, not deaf, ya arrogant fuck."

Maia pressed her lips together to keep from laughing and gave Rowan a shrug. His face remained stone, making it clear he was not amused.

Briar had finished collecting his winnings for the night. He collapsed onto an empty stool, raising a finger for yet another lager.

"Don't you think you've had enough?" the barkeep asked hesitantly.

It didn't take more than a look, and the purposeful cracking of bruised knuckles before Briar had another drink in front of him.

"That's him," Maia said.

Rowan went to stand when a well-dressed man with a suit vest walked up behind Briar.

"Good evening, boy."

"Shit," Rowan hissed. "We need to leave."

There were two types of people who said *good evening*—people wanting to fight and people looking to collect.

"Fuck off," Briar slurred.

The man in the suit vest smiled and took his seat. One of Portico's collectors. Rowan grabbed Maia's arm, pulling her from the chair. He lifted the collar of his jacket to hide his face, and Maia followed suit, trailing him out the back door into the alley. She tucked her hands into her pockets, running her thumb over the raised, scrolled *P* of the Portico coins. As the door closed behind them, chaos erupted in the tavern. But she already knew who would win tonight.

Briar stumbled into the alley less than ten minutes later. He had a swollen left eye, busted nose, and broken lip, almost mirroring the sketch in his folder. The only thing not injured were his knuckles. Up close, Maia could now make out the intricate black tattoos covering his entire upper body. His shirt clung to his chest, coated in a mixture of booze and blood. He ran his hand through his hair, the stubborn longer pieces falling back in his eyes.

"I heard you were one of the best fighters in the Forest Region," Rowan said, stepping into the light of the moon as if it belonged only to him.

"Looks like Portico's collectors are better," Maia mumbled, joining him.

Briar spat blood onto the dirt. "It wasn't a fair fight."

"They rarely are." Rowan handed Briar a handkerchief. A genuine kindness that made Maia wonder who Rowan was outside of the rebellion. "What if I offered to pay off your debt?"

Briar laughed. "I'll tell you the same thing I told them... Fuck. Off."

Rowan frowned, tucking away his handkerchief. "You could get a clean slate. I'm offering you an opportunity to start over."

"I ain't gonna trade one man's pocket for another."

"The rebellion doesn't work like that," Rowan said with a chuckle. "By helping us, you keep others from being in Portico's pockets."

Briar wiped his nose, wincing in pain. "Rebels? Oh, I definitely ain't interested."

Whatever amusement Rowan forced a minute ago faded, replaced by a harshness he seemed to struggle to keep buried.

"I hope once the drink is out of your system, you realize what you're passing up. Maia will be back tomorrow to make you the same offer. If you turn it down again, there won't be a third chance."

Briar glanced between them with his good eye and laughed. "Whatever."

Maia and Rowan walked away without another word, but she couldn't help wondering how the rebellion could offer to pay off a debt without knowing the price. Rowan was clearly keeping more secrets than just the folders.

A woman's cry pierced the silence, and Rowan pulled his gun. Maia looked down to find her hands already resting on her daggers. Portico's collectors had found Briar's mother, dragging her by the arm up the front porch of her home.

"Are we going to—"

Rowan shook his head. "Maybe this will help Briar decide."

The collectors shoved the woman through the door. Shouts escalated into what sounded like a scuffle inside before a gunshot erupted. Maia gasped, slamming her hand over her mouth as the woman's frantic screams carried on the dense summer breeze.

Even if Rowan was right, everything about it felt wrong. Unphased, he continued towards the forest. How could he leave when this was their chance to actually help? Maia remained still, trapped under the heaviness of guilt, knowing he left her with only one option. To walk away.

5

TACTICS

We begin as we ended... in disagreement.

K. Wells – Summer 2259

T he house was silent as Maia watched a spider construct a web in the corner of her room. Sleep refused to come, leaving her too much time to replay the night's events. She had to believe Rowan knew the gunshot was just a warning. But the *what-ifs* kept tugging at her confidence, making her wonder if he was as honorable as he claimed.

Was it coincidence she lost everything when he arrived? Or had he played a role in her choice too?

She decisively threw off her covers and changed into clothes, careful to avoid the creaky floorboards as she slipped from the house towards the bunker.

A gentle tug on the handle confirmed Rowan's office door was locked. She reached into her hair, removing her mother's metal comb. Withdrawing the two center pins, she placed the picks into the lock.

It was more complex than the ones Rowan trained her on. Her frustration grew with each passing minute she spent exposed in the hallway. Wiping her hands on her pants, she let out a slow breath, sliding the pieces back into place.

Maia closed her eyes, slowly working the hook pick. She could hear Rowan's guidance as he paced behind her during lessons. *Lock picking is an art of patience. An understanding of subtleties.* Each pin fell into place with increasing gratification, and Maia smirked as she heard the final *click.*

The room was an impenetrable black, and she was grateful for the lack of furniture. Feeling her way around his desk, she eventually found the oil lamp.

The light from the flame danced to life, and she moved it to the floor to get a better view of the drawers. More locks, but at least these were insignificant compared to the door.

Inside the drawer were folders of varying thicknesses, neatly stacked. She reached in to remove them, flinching as her pinky nail caught on a small hole in the drawer's bottom. A curse escaped her, deafening in the quiet, concrete room. She shook away the pain and traced along the edges of the perfectly round hole.

Too perfect.

Placing the hook pick into the hole, she lifted the false bottom. Worn leather books peered up at her, *W. Wells, A. Wells, and K. Wells* embossed into the covers. Who were the Wells' and why were their journals hidden away? Maia winced at the deafening crack of the leather spine of *W. Wells'* journal, skimming the first sentence.

As with all quintessential moments in history, we must reflect. The fall of America was a slow progression of manipulation and apathy.

The book fell from her hands with a thud, but the softness of leather lingered on her fingertips. No one had a first-hand account of the end of the world, and yet, here it was in front of her. She reached for the paper, running her fingers across the delicate indentations written over a century ago. Her eyes darted from the door to the book, but she couldn't walk away. Not after reading those words. She collected the book and lamp, taking a seat in Rowan's chair.

No singular moment in history can mark the beginning of our descent, but rather a multitude of events that culminated into the one that changed everything.

W. Wells - 2132.09.21

The writer explained the gradual manipulation of those in power. Politicians corrupted by money, only pushing the agendas for those who could grow their standing. Pawns in a much bigger game than the one on the board. It all sounded too familiar.

Propaganda was a tool used to create hate, which allowed Wells to create violence. His journal was filled with detailed drawings and descriptions of the weapons, explosives, and war vehicles he created for the revolutionaries of the American Civil War of 2132. But two years later, he allied with the other side to avoid execution.

The Age of Apathy, as he named it.

It wasn't until 2155 when the revolutionaries finally succeeded in infiltrating the government. On December 14th, they assassinated the president, turning the war in their favor.

Wells went from a hero to an enemy in a single moment.

Desperation forced the government to change their tactics, shifting Wells' focus to biological warfare. Working with the best and brightest scientists, he created weapons from viruses. Documenting the process to cultivate diseases in painstaking detail.

Twenty million dead from a prototype, but I know there's potential for more.

W. Wells - 2158.03.19

His journal wasn't just the plans needed to guarantee absolute victory—they were a step-by-step guide to the apocalypse. Most Americans had already retreated into bunkers as foreign attacks took advantage of the chaos within.

August 25, 2163, the nukes were fired. The damage was worse than anyone anticipated. But isn't that what we wanted?

Russia and China retaliated, and before the radio went silent, the announcers informed us that most of the southeast was gone... gone.

So today, August 26th, our world has met its end. Outside is black and cold, much like this bunker we now hide within, and it will be decades before it's safe to return to the surface.

All of this over one man.

W. Wells 2163.08.26

Maia tucked the journal back into the drawer, clenching her hand to slow the tremble. Her footsteps echoed through the empty bunker, and she pushed open the heavy, metal door, shielding her eyes from the sun just beginning its ascent.

The fresh air felt liberating, and she wondered how anyone could survive a century within those concrete walls. Removing her boots, she cherished the softness of the grass between her toes as she wandered back to the house.

A rusted bike trapped within an oak tree. An abandoned tractor drowning in the lavender blooms of wisteria. Refuse of the Old World, now black stains on theirs. Relics touched and tainted, maybe by W. Wells himself.

"What's wrong?" She looked up to find Rowan reading on the porch.

Everything... "Nothing. Did Garcia and his team get back?"

"No, not yet," he said, returning his gaze to the book in his lap.

Maia reached for the door handle, but stopped. "Did you know Portico wouldn't kill Briar's mother?"

Rowan perched his head on his hand, lips pressed together in thought. Knowing him, he wasn't searching for his answer, rather the meaning between her words.

"The gunshot," she continued. "Did you know it was just a warning?"

"Yes—"

"How?"

Harshness returned to his face. "Because if Portico wanted to kill her, there would have been silence. Not a scream."

Sheer terror was the only difference between life and death for Briar's mother. Maia had to believe Rowan's words were true, which made her wonder if he would continue to speak truths.

"Who's W. Wells?"

Rowan's face flushed, and he slammed his book shut. "How do you know that name?"

"I found journals in your drawer—"

"Unbelievable. I don't have time for this," he said, shaking his head as if to brush it off.

She could allow him to dismiss her folder, but those journals in the wrong hands could end their world.

"What I read... no one should have that knowledge, Rowan. Those journals are a weapon."

He removed his glasses and pinched the bridge of his nose. "We are doomed to repeat a past we refuse to acknowledge."

"And what happens if Portico gets their hands on them?"

A silence fell between them, but Maia had said what she wanted. She pushed open the door and crossed the threshold before Rowan spoke again.

"Portico used to call my mother Libra—the scales of justice, but before that, she was known as Katherine Wells."

Maia turned back to him, slowly closing the door.

"She founded Portico on the belief that without order, there is no justice, and without justice, there is no hope."

"Those are your family journals..."

Rowan nodded, but didn't meet her gaze. "When Aquila *found* my mother dead in her room, I still believed in order. When he took control from me, I still believed in justice. And when your father arrived in Portico telling me we could make things right again, I still believed in hope."

Maia now understood what Rowan meant about knowing her pain and creating their own path. Their loss was the same, even if their legacies were on opposing sides.

"I should have been the rightful successor to Portico, but Aquila stole it from me. He offered me a place on his council as consolation many years ago, but I refused. Despite my work with the rebellion, he still asks me to consider his offer."

She dropped into the rocking chair next to him, processing his words. "Why?"

"I think somewhere deep within him there's a seed of remorse." Rowan scowled as he shook away the thought. "Regardless, my allegiance remains true to your father and the rebellion."

Maia removed her father's watch from her pocket, running her finger over the scuffed face. "And what would my father ask you to do with those journals if he knew?"

He leaned back in his chair with a sigh. "You may think it's selfish, but while the journals show my family's role in ending the world, they also explain what we've done over the last century to rebuild it. Destroying the truth doesn't prevent it from happening again."

"Look at the grand welcome home," Garcia shouted from the tree line, his team trudging behind him.

Sentimentality or penance kept Rowan in denial. If Portico got their hands on Wells' journals, they would have everything needed to guarantee complete control. Maia wanted to continue to argue, but she knew their conversation was over.

"Everything I told you needs to stay between us," Rowan whispered. "Do you understand?"

"Does Orion know?"

"About my lineage, yes. But not about the journals. Only you and I know those exist."

His response was deliberate. If the journals happened to disappear, she would be the only one to blame. "Fine."

He shook his head. "This is too important, Maia. I need your word."

"I'll give you my word, but I don't agree with your decision." Maia stood, hoping to escape before Garcia's team reached the porch.

"Fair enough." Rowan opened his book. "If I were you, I'd try to find Briar *before* he starts drinking."

It was early afternoon, but Briar already struggled to stay upright as he sat on his front porch. An empty glass jug lay beside him, and a shotgun rested on his lap.

"You best get out of here while you can," he slurred.

Maia leaned against the weather-beaten banister, crossing her arms. It creaked in protest, and she eased up, hoping the structure would remain standing.

"Good to know the shotgun isn't for me."

Briar's head dropped, swaying like a flag caught in the wind. "I would have got 'em their coin. I just needed more time. Fuck!" he shouted. "It didn't have to go this way."

"It still doesn't."

He picked up the jug, realized it was empty, and threw it into the street. "They had no right to lay a hand on her!"

The shatter of glass was too loud, and Maia waited to see if anyone from the surrounding hovels would care enough to investigate.

"You're right," she said, keeping her eyes on the road. "But if you kill them, they'll kill you."

"Like I fuckin' care anymore."

"The debt will still exist." Garcia's story forced its way into her thoughts. What Portico did to his mother for requesting to bury her husband's body. "They'll kill her too, Briar. If anything, just to make a statement."

His lip quivered, causing guilt to wash over her. Maybe she'd gone too far.

"What other choice do I got?" he choked out.

"Take the offer," she said, joining him on the steps.

The anguish that overtook his face tightened her chest, and her hand instinctively found his arm, barely wrapping halfway around it. He looked down in surprise, but his taut muscles eased at her touch.

"It's nearly two hundred coin now. I ain't worth that much."

"Rowan thinks you are."

They sat in silence, and she wondered what he did to deserve his mother's forsaking. Sure, he had his weaknesses, his love for his mother being one of them.

"I see why he sent you," Briar said, glancing at her out of the corner of his eye. He scrubbed his hands over his face and nodded, pushing back his hair. "Alright. If he's really good for the coin, then we'll try things your way."

Maia gave him a soft smile, removing the gun from his lap. "Alright."

"Glad you decided to join us," Rowan said as Briar and Maia entered the safe house parlor.

Garcia and his team stopped their discussion over another one of Rowan's mission folders.

"Why don't we have a big guy like that?" Kayla asked, looking Briar up and down.

Rowan ignored her comment and put his hand out to Briar. "I hope you take advantage of this new beginning. I know you have the potential to be so much more than the person alcohol makes you, and we're here to support you if that's what you choose."

"He just got here," Maia argued. "Give him a minute to settle in."

"This isn't your concern, Maia," Rowan warned.

Briar looked down at her. "I'd like to hear what you think."

Rowan lifted a brow as if to say *go on*. But he was right. It wasn't her concern, and she should have stayed out of it. He believed Briar could be better, even when everyone else had given up on him. Just as Rowan believed in Maia, even when the sting of disappointment from Mr. Thomas and Hannah were still so fresh.

She met Briar's gaze. "Detox is brutal. But if it's what you want—I'll help you through it."

"Then let's do it, boss."

Why would he call her that? She couldn't help but wonder if he was taking any of this seriously. His busted lip tugged at the corner, but his face remained uncertain.

He was scared. She saw it hidden in his forest green eyes, but for now, he seemed willing to trust her.

⇜———⇝

Briar spent the night heaving into a bucket while Maia rubbed his back. He gratefully took water between tremoring hands each time Kayla snuck into his room.

A few days later, the fevers took hold, trapping Briar in hallucinations. His words were rarely coherent, but Maia watched his guilty conscience bring him to his knees.

Jayce provided empathetic smiles as he brought in fresh towels, and Garcia told stories over delivered meals. Maia, however, remained firm at Briar's side day and night, as she promised.

Maybe Garcia's team felt pity for Briar—or maybe for Maia—but that in itself brought her closer to the man crying himself to sleep each night.

A little over a week later, Briar was finally well enough to leave his room.

"You clean up well," Jayce said with a grin as Briar and Maia entered the kitchen.

"I do," he said, pushing back his water-slicked hair.

He was wearing one of Rowan's crisp white shirts, easily a size too small, but looked polished nonetheless.

Kayla walked past, handing him a jam-filled pastry. "Glad to see you're feeling better," she said, continuing toward the large dining table.

Briar glanced around the kitchen, eyes wide as he took it in. It was a mixture of the Old World and new, with its hand-hewed ceiling beams and wood cabinets topped with white marble countertops. He followed Kayla, dropping into a chair and eating half the pastry in one bite.

"Fuckin' delicious. Thank you," he said, closing his eyes in satisfaction.

Kayla blushed and turned her gaze to the bay window overlooking the garden. "You're welcome."

He was surprisingly endearing with the alcohol now out of his system. Maia continued to the brick hearth, pouring herself a cup of tea. Jayce joined her, refilling his clay mug.

"You think he would have made it without you?" he whispered.

They watched Edward give Briar a commending pat on the back. He was the only one who never set foot in Briar's room during his suffering.

"You next, Edward?" Garcia asked, kneading dough for biscuits. "Might be the thing that finally does you in, ya bastard."

His booming laugh filled the room, pulling a smirk from Kayla.

"Fuck off," Edward mumbled, continuing out of the kitchen.

He nearly knocked Rowan over as they passed in the doorway.

"I was looking for the two of you," Rowan said, glancing between Maia and Briar. "Can we speak in the parlor?"

Quickly wiping his hand on his pants, Briar stood, holding the door open for Maia.

"After you, boss."

"Why do you keep calling me that?"

Her question came out harsher than intended, causing him to pause. "I'm only here because of you." The gratitude on his face told her he didn't mean just with the rebellion, but also for helping him through the last week. He looked away, continuing towards the parlor. "Plus, I sure as shit don't want to be in charge."

"Take a seat," Rowan said, handing them folders. "Inside is your first mission as a team."

Maia sat next to Briar on the loveseat and opened her folder. She skimmed the briefing while Briar flipped through the pages, too quickly to be looking at anything more than the drawings.

"The governor of Richmond has asked for the rebels' protection. In return, he's offered a secret he claims will finally give the rebels an advantage over Portico."

"Sounds like a done deal," Briar said, resting his arm along the back of the couch.

Rowan shook his head. "Governor Shaw is only where he is today because of Portico. He lives and breathes their corruption, and there are too many red flags for us to ignore. Which is why we're going to steal his secret."

Maia's stomach fluttered with excitement. "How?"

"Since our rebel pocket in Richmond has been compromised, we'll need help from someone unaffiliated. A woman named Senna Young owns the local brothel and is known for her ability to obtain useful information on powerful men." Rowan relaxed into the armchair. "She'll be a good place to start."

"It's almost *too* easy," Maia said, waiting for the catch.

A smile tugged at Rowan's lips, and he glanced at her out of the corner of his eye. "You haven't met Senna Young yet."

6

CARELESS

Shaded sconces and dark wood walls established an atmosphere of warmth and intimacy within the brothel. Women lazily sprawled themselves across lush chairs, fur throws, and the ornate rugs blanketing the floor. They were beautiful and carefree, holding some of Richmond's most dangerous secrets in their dainty hands.

Maia scanned the room, her eyes stopping on a woman's long, brown legs draped across a blood-red settee. Senna Young was even more beautiful than the drawing in her folder, with tight, wild curls and thick eyeliner contrasting the more delicate features of her face. A thick redhead beckoned Briar to join her from across the room, and he didn't hesitate.

Senna's gaze found Maia, studying her with curiosity while twirling a curl around her finger. Every movement was heavy with a sensuality that sent a warmth through Maia's entire body. She was far from inexperienced, but everything about Senna suddenly made her feel like she was. Dropping her gaze, Maia forced her feet forward.

"Business or pleasure?" Senna asked.

Her lace robe billowed around her as she dropped her legs to the floor. She reached up, tucking one of Maia's loose curls behind her ear and trailing a pointed nail down her arm. The goosebumps that bloomed across Maia's skin sent a shiver through her. It was terrifying how much control Senna had over her body.

Ignoring the tingle of her skin, Maia met Senna's gaze. "Business."

Her dangerous, red lips curled into a playful smile, and she flipped open an oversized feather fan, fueling the flames now in her eyes. "That's a shame."

Maia's gaze snapped to Briar, desperate for support, or at least to buffer the intensity between them. He had been watching intently as the redhead giggled, tracing the snake tattoo on his right forearm.

With some quick parting words, he joined Maia in the center of the room. "Can we talk somewhere private?"

Senna laid back on her settee, no longer interested in the conversation. "Private *conversations* are for paying customers only."

Their window of opportunity was quickly closing. They could no longer afford secrecy. "We were told you have information on Governor Shaw."

"Well, I don't."

But she did. Maia could sense it in the way the women froze in their fluid motions at the mention of the governor's name. She just needed to figure out what Senna wanted in return.

Maia's lips parted, her thoughts racing for her next words, when a crash in the adjacent room stole everyone's attention.

A clang of what sounded like metal pots and pans followed. Senna pushed herself up from the settee, while the other women slowly gathered their belongings, hesitating for only a moment before moving to the stairs.

Senna continued toward the noise, pushing open the door and pausing in the threshold. From where Maia stood behind her, she could see a woman barely conscious on the kitchen floor, a trail of blood smeared across the white tiles behind her.

"Callie?"

The uncertainty in Senna's voice was understandable. There was too much swelling and blood for the woman's face to be recognizable.

"I'm s-sorry, Madame," Callie forced through chattering teeth.

Senna rushed forward, removing her robe and draping it over Callie's trembling shoulders. A soft, warm breeze entered through the open back door that Callie had apparently stumbled through. Senna stood, peering outside before shutting it and turning the lock.

"We need to get her upstairs," Senna said, flicking shut the curtains over the windows.

Briar hoisted Callie into his arms with ease, but all eyes turned to the puddle of blood on the kitchen floor. Maia lifted the bottom of Callie's dress to find a bullet lodged in the bone of her right calf.

"We need to slow the bleeding first," Maia said, as instinct took over.

She cleared off the meal prep table, and Briar lowered Callie onto it.

"What happened?" Senna asked, taking Callie's ashen hand in hers.

"The governor—" Callie pressed her bloody fist to her mouth to keep from crying out as Maia adjusted her leg for a better look at the injury. Gritting her teeth, she continued. "The governor caught us searching his office and sent his guards after us."

Senna stepped back, crossing her arms over her corset. "Where's Adina?"

Callie shook her head, but the words wouldn't come. Senna nodded in understanding and turned away.

The bone had shattered, and Maia knew there was a high probability of infection. But if Callie were unfortunate enough to survive that, she would still require amputation.

"Can you grab that?" Maia asked, pointing Briar to a washbasin on the other side of the kitchen.

He nearly tripped over his feet, rushing to fetch it.

"Senna," Callie whispered, choking on a pain-laced sob. "He's going to come looking for me."

Maia's hand froze while dipping a cloth into the basin. If Governor Shaw was willing to kill the other woman, he would want to clean up any loose ends. Her eyes found Briar's, surprised to see a darkness within them. If the governor were here now, she was certain Briar would kill him—and it surprised her that her first thought was *good*.

"Please collect her from the table and follow me," Senna said, motioning to Briar.

Maia quickly applied a makeshift tourniquet with Senna's lace robe, and Briar lifted her from the table.

"We need to hide you somewhere he won't think to look," Senna said, grabbing a fur coat off the rack beside the back door.

She slipped it across her shoulders and continued outside. Her tall heels clicked on the stone pavers leading to the back of the building, and she unlocked a hatch to a claustrophobic crawlspace.

Callie whimpered as Briar lowered her into the tight, dark space.

"We'll come back. I promise," Maia said, squeezing Callie's chilled hand.

Shouts carried from the street, and Senna slammed down the hatch before Callie could respond, closing the padlock with a *click*.

"It appears our company has arrived." Her eyes found Maia's. "If you want information on the governor, you'll have to make sure he doesn't kill me first."

Maia nodded, understanding what Senna wanted. "We aren't going anywhere."

Smoothing her fur coat, Senna continued back to the kitchen, with Maia and Briar following close behind her. She stepped around the trail of blood and stopped at the door leading back to the front room.

"I'll try to keep them in my office so they don't see the blood. It's the only door to the left of the stairwell." She glanced over her shoulder, her wary gaze passing between them. "Let's see how much you want your information."

Easing her tense shoulders, she pushed open the door and greeted the governor.

"What the fuck did we get ourselves into, boss?" Briar asked, pushing the hair from his face. He held his bloody hands out in front of him and looked down at the stains on his clothes.

"I don't know yet." She motioned to a basket of spare clothes and rags in the corner.

He ripped off his shirt and dipped his hands in the already-blood-stained basin. "We need a plan."

Peeking through the kitchen door, Maia could see Senna casually lounging on her settee, the women protectively surrounding her.

A young man with long, blond hair and playful eyes stood over her with two guards behind him. He laughed in a light, airy way that made the hair on Maia's neck stand.

"Why don't we take this conversation to my office, Governor Shaw," Senna suggested.

He gave her a forced smile and motioned towards his guards. "Search all the rooms. We shouldn't be long."

Senna stood, eyes flickering to Maia's for a second before she continued toward the stairs.

Maia carefully closed the door, taking a second to gather her thoughts while scanning the room. A tray with decorative ceramic cups rested on the counter next to the hearth.

"Can you grab that tray of tea?" she asked, stealing one more peek through the door.

Briar carelessly picked it up, joining her. "What are we doin'?"

She glanced down at the half-filled cups rattling from his trembling hands. Maybe it was fear or rage fueling him, but she needed him to keep it together just a little longer.

"It's going to be fine, alright?" Maia assured him, giving his arm a gentle squeeze.

His jaw clenched, and he took a slow, deep breath. "Alright."

With her best attempt at a reassuring smile, she took the tray from his hands and pushed open the door to the front room.

The women sat huddled together in the entry while crashes rang from the rooms above as the governor's guards searched for Callie. Maia and Briar continued up the stairs, grateful the guards were distracted so they could move freely towards Senna's office.

"Your women tried to steal from me this evening," the governor barked.

"And what exactly did they try to steal?" Senna's voice remained confident and calm despite the chaos traveling down the hall.

"You think you're clever." His hand wrapped around her throat, slamming her against the wall. "Where is she?"

The platter slipped through Maia's hands as she reached for the dagger tucked under her jacket. With the flick of her wrist, the blade stuck in the wall an inch shy of the governor's ear, just as the tray landed on the floor with a *crash*. Senna yanked it free, resting the sharp edge just under his Adam's apple.

The guards didn't seem to hear anything over their own destruction, and Briar took the opportunity to push Maia into the office and close the door behind them.

Governor Shaw let out another airy laugh. "It appears there's been a misunderstanding," he said, raising his hands.

"I agree." Senna pushed herself from the wall. "So, let me make it clear. I don't require threats, Governor Shaw. If my girls return, you'll be the first to know."

She removed the dagger from his throat, and he stumbled back, smoothing his jacket.

"I knew you were a sensible woman, Senna."

The set of her jaw was a warning, like a rattle from a snake. "Get out."

The governor glanced around the room, his eyes pausing on the mess of ceramic and tea against the dark wood floor. A hint of a smile attempted to take hold, and he strutted toward Maia. "Did I frighten you, little fawn?"

He lifted a finger to her face, but Briar seized it, wrenching it back so hard that just a subtle flick of his wrist could snap it. "I'll show you the door, *governor*."

Shaw growled in pain, his nostrils flaring. The look in his eyes was deadly, but with Briar nearly twice his size, it seemed to be enough motivation for him to begrudgingly concede.

"That won't be necessary," he said, gritting through the pain.

Briar threw open the door, shoving him through it. "Oh, but I insist."

Senna's shoulders relaxed as the governor shouted for his guards, the three of them starting down the stairs, with Briar following closely behind. Her gaze dropped to the dagger in her hand, running her thumb across the leather hilt as if examining it.

"Who do you work for?"

"I don't work for anyone," Maia said, stepping over the tray.

Senna removed a bottle of liquor from her drawer and poured two glasses. "And now I know what you look like when you're lying."

"He killed one of your—"

"He's killed many people to get his position in Richmond," Senna said, sitting back in her chair. "I, for one, am not looking to be added to his list. Are you?"

The urgency of this mission grew with each passing moment, and Maia realized that until the rebellion had this secret, the governor would remain untouchable. "He can't keep getting away with this."

"Honey, he belongs to Portico. A carefully placed pawn in their game, and I've worked too hard to lose everything over a careless girl."

Careless. She wasn't talking about Maia. She was talking about Callie. "So, he didn't lie. You asked her to steal something."

Senna seemed to realize her slip-up. She paused in thought as Briar returned.

"What'd I miss?" he asked, trying to get a read on the room.

Maia ignored him, taking another cautious step towards Senna. "You promised me information."

"I did," she said with a sigh. "I've heard rumors the governor's... indiscretions are causing trouble for Portico." Senna slid the dagger across her desk to Maia. "There's also word he's gone to the rebels with a secret, in exchange for protection."

Maia collected her dagger, tucking it away. "He did. Which is why we need to know his secret."

"Rebels." She couldn't hide her shock. "Which means you turned him away."

"Yes."

"Then I have contacts who might be able to help." She scrawled some names onto a piece of paper and lifted it to Briar.

He hesitated. "Just tell me the names."

Senna eyed him with curiosity, and Maia yanked the paper from her hand. Now wasn't the time for him to be called out for being illiterate.

"We'll take care of it. And Callie?"

Senna waved her hand, sipping her drink. "Get rid of her. She's a liability now."

Her harsh words shouldn't have been a surprise, but as Maia glanced back from the threshold, she noticed the defeat in Senna's shoulders as her hand found her mouth. She cared more than she would allow the world to see. It was this distance that kept everyone safe, but it didn't change the pain of her loss.

Maia picked the lock to the cellar, and Briar helped her move Callie to a room upstairs before he left to meet Senna's contacts.

"Thank you," Callie said through gritted teeth, gripping the bed sheets. Maia had already given her a pain tonic, but after tending to the wound for the past hour, she was sure it had worn off.

"All I said was I would try to fix this." Maia clipped the end of the wound wrap, frustrated to see a bloom of blood already forming on the thin cloth. She handed Callie a cup of steaming tea. "This will help with the pain so you can sleep through the night."

Tears pooled in Callie's eyes. "Good people like you don't make it long in this world."

"Good and evil are just a perception of circumstance."

It was something her mother used to say about her father, but the words felt different now as they fell from her lips. Heavier, as if carrying the weight of new meaning.

Maia gathered her supplies and exited the room, surprised to find Senna waiting in the hallway.

"So, you practice healing too?"

"I was an apprentice." Maia continued down the hall toward the room offered to her and Briar.

"You realize, if she dies, it's on you now." Senna wanted to see her flinch.

Instead, Maia rubbed the exhaustion from her eyes. The adrenaline from their encounter with the governor was wearing off, and all she wanted was a few moments of sleep. "It wouldn't change if I chose to do nothing."

"I appreciate your morality," Senna said, tightening her satin robe around her. "Let's see how much longer it lasts."

Briar's heavy steps paused at the top of the stairwell. "Why the fuck did you send me to the sketchiest part of town?"

"Because that's where you get the type of information you're looking for, handsome," Senna said, running her hand down his arm.

"No. It ain't," he snapped, brushing her away. "They didn't know shit."

After everything they'd been through, they were no closer to the governor's secret. Maia turned into the room, absolutely deflated. She left the door open, and Briar entered shortly after. She was grateful for his silence as he crafted a makeshift bed on the floor with the spare blankets Senna left him. Blowing out the oil lamp, Maia drifted off to sleep the second her head hit the pillow.

"Get up!"

Briar shook her awake, his hands painfully gripping her shoulders as he continued shouting. Everything was trapped in a haze. She tried to rub it away, confused by a cloud of smoke filtering in from under the bedroom door. Was that why her throat burned?

The piercing sound of shattering glass traveled from somewhere down the hall, finally allowing her to hear Briar's shouts clearly—*fire*.

She jumped from the bed, both of them stumbling into the hallway to bang on doors. The fire had engulfed the room at the end of the hall, and Maia's stomach dropped. That was Callie's room. She wouldn't still be in there, unless... the sedative tea.

"No," she choked.

"We need to go now." Briar's calloused hand wrapped around her wrist, yanking her down the stairs and out the front door like a doll.

She collapsed onto the dirt road where the women had gathered in the street, crying on each other's shoulders. Taking in greedy breaths of fresh air, Maia watched the plumes of smoke rise above the flames, dancing against the evening sky.

"Ladies, you need to go," Senna said, her face as firm as her words. "It's not safe, and I have nothing left to offer you."

The women remained still, clearly torn between protesting and running, their eyes flickering to the shadows as if waiting for the governor to appear.

A woman beside Senna took her hand. "Promise me you'll kill the bastard when you find him."

Senna nodded, turning back to the flames as the women disappeared behind her.

It was just them now, and Maia stood, stepping into the space between Senna and Briar. "What now?"

"Portico took *everything* from me." Senna adjusted her shawl, the fire reflecting in her eyes. "I intend to do the same."

7

SECRETS

The world is filled with the bright colors of new beginning, but all I see is gray.

K. Wells – Spring 2260

Briar lit an oil lamp and placed it in the center of the table, unrolling a detailed drawing of the governor's sprawling estate. Senna glanced at him with annoyance as she removed her nail file from under the paper.

The room they rented from the local tavern was too cramped for anyone's comfort, but the tension between Senna and Briar made it unbearable. Maia was grateful all of this would be over after tonight—one way or another.

"Let's go through it again," Briar said, leaning over the drawing.

Over the last two weeks, they had found all the names on Senna's list, with each questionable character providing them just enough information to form a semblance of a plan.

Maia dropped her finger to the map, running it along the tree line surrounding the home. "We know there are two guards each on the east and west ends of the house. No one to the south." She met Briar's gaze, and he sighed, dropping into his chair, already knowing what came next. "But with the thin tree coverage and the guard posted at the back door, you'd be caught immediately."

He placed a toothpick in his mouth, a new habit he developed since Senna banned him from smoking in the room. "Ain't no coverage in the front either. Just a wrought iron fence about a hundred feet out. We couldn't even grab the bastard on his way home because of those two fuckin' guards he's always got with him."

"Not always," Senna said, filling the small space with the incessant grind of the file.

Briar frowned around the toothpick. "The only time they wait outside is when he takes someone home."

"Which is why the easiest way in is through the front door *with* the governor." She examined her nails in the lamp light before throwing a side eye Briar's way. "Like I've said several times now."

Maia was certain Senna had thought this plan through long before meeting them. She was just waiting for two people desperate enough to agree to it.

The muscle in Briar's jaw ticked. "And *I* already said I don't like Maia bein' the bait."

"She's not the bait. She's the shiny lure." Senna's dark gaze met Maia's. "You know that, right? Look, all you need to do is get into the house. Briar and I will worry about the guards in the woods."

It didn't matter how many times they had gone over the plan, a wave of dread always washed over Maia, painfully twisting her stomach. Regardless, her part was too crucial to admit she agreed with Briar.

"Then that's the plan." Maia pushed away from the table, reaching for her jacket.

"One last thing," Senna said, leaning back, her blood-red nails now sharpened to dangerous points. A warning, like the hourglass marking on a black widow. "The governor is a sadist. My girls told me he has a room filled with whips and gags he often took them to."

"Are you fuckin' kidding me?" Briar's wide eyes found Maia's, and she knew he saw the flicker of fear she didn't hide fast enough. "No. Maia ain't doin' this. We need a new plan."

"Calm down," Senna said. She shifted in her seat to face Maia directly, her back now to Briar. "That room exists to create fear. And fear is power. So, you can either give the governor the power he wants, or you can see it as an entire room of weapons at your disposal. Something he won't see coming, not from a delicate thing like yourself."

Maia's heart hammered against her ribs as if hoping to escape before her next words. "We've never talked about how we're actually getting the secret out of him."

She avoided Briar's gaze, focusing only on Senna as she swallowed the bile now creeping up the back of her throat.

"That's for me to take care of, darling." Senna stood from the table, hooking her arm in Maia's. "Let's find you something shiny to wear."

Briar cursed under his breath and leaned forward, blowing out the oil lamp.

The governor was three lagers deep before Maia caught his wandering gaze in the extravagant gambling hall. A string quartet filled the room with a rush of sound, adding tension to each side glance and raised nose that passed. The crystals of the chandeliers twinkled like stars above tables overflowing with sweet pastries and even sweeter liquors.

Despite the flashy, low-cut dress Senna had provided, Maia's scowl worked to deter the leering men in suit vests and bowler hats, faces flush from the nauseating drinks. She tugged at the pinching corset. Senna could have at least left a finger's width of room to breathe. The governor sauntered over, and Maia quickly threw back the rest of her whiskey.

"I remember you, little fawn," he said, leaning into her, the musty smell of his cologne turning her stomach. "I suppose you're looking for work wherever you can now, what with the brothel being ash and all."

Maia plastered on a fake smile as he ran a finger down her exposed arm, leaving a trail of goosebumps on her skin.

A fiendish grin crossed his lips. "I have a proposition for you. Why don't you come with me?"

He took her hand, pulling her from the safety of the crowd into the suffocating summer night.

Maia's senses remained on high alert as the wrought iron fence to the governor's estate groaned open.

"Come now," he said, sliding his hand to the small of her back and guiding her toward the towering, three-story Victorian mansion.

She tensed at his touch, and it took everything in her not to pull away. All she had to do was get into the house.

Climbing the steps of the wraparound porch with intricate filigree railings, the governor opened the large front door to the foyer, allowing Maia to enter first while his guards remained outside, just as Senna said.

The door slammed shut behind her. Shaw reached over, helping her out of her jacket. He examined her under the soft, orange glow of the entryway.

"I'll give it to Senna," he said, his penetrating gaze making her skin crawl. "She has impeccable taste in her girls. Such innocence in those big brown eyes." He motioned for Maia to continue into a room connected to the foyer. "There's a fire already going in the library. We can enjoy another drink before the fun begins."

She could still run. Her gaze flickered to the front door, but instead, she pinched her nails into her palms and followed.

A half-played chess game lay abandoned on a hand-carved wooden table, and the governor pulled out one of the gold damask chairs for her. She cautiously followed him to the center of the room, noticing the ornate chandelier hanging low from the paneled ceiling.

"I guess I shouldn't be surprised a powerful man like yourself would have such a lavish home," she said, grateful for the glass of liquor he handed her.

"I've earned every inch of it." He looked around with pride, taking a sip of his drink. "Hard work always pays off in the end."

"Are you insinuating that I'm not a hard worker?"

"We'll find out soon enough, now won't we?" Her forced smile hitched, and he laughed. "Come now, darling. People like yourself wouldn't know what to do with power if they had it."

She took a sip to allow herself a second to recover. "Most of us survive on needs, not wants."

His eyes darkened. "And what if you didn't have to?" He threw back his drink, strutting toward her. "What would you want?"

She wanted to scream, but the only way to get what she needed was to keep playing his game. "I would want to make you happy, of course."

His hand wrapped around hers, removing her glass and placing it on the coffee table. "Is that so?"

She snatched his other hand as it inched up her dress. "Why don't we go somewhere a little more... intimate?"

His eyes burned as a bead of sweat trailed along his hairline. "It's like you read my mind."

They were now moving back to the foyer and through a dark corridor towards the rear of the house.

He removed a key from his vest pocket. "I always love this moment."

The slow creak of the door sent a chill down Maia's spine as the room came into view. Perspiration and fear permeated from the carpeted walls with shackles, whips, and gags hanging on display. Nothing Senna said could have prepared her for this.

"Fear looks beautiful on you, little fawn," he whispered, nipping at her ear.

To men like him, innocence was something to steal. *Fear is power.* If she wanted to take back control, she needed to embrace his inhumanity.

Darkness washed over her, collapsing her forced smile. She approached the wall of whips in different materials and sizes, running her finger along the smooth leather handle.

"Do these hurt?" she asked, removing it from the wall.

His hands slid up her arms, but her skin didn't react to his touch this time. "Yes."

She gripped the whip in her hand and met his cold, blue eyes. "Good."

His face dropped as she swung with every ounce of her being. The strike was enough to knock the wind out of him, bending him at the waist. She didn't hesitate, shocking him with another hit directly across his cheek. He cried out in pain this time, and Maia savored the dominance she had over him.

"No one can hear you," she mocked, motioning to the carpeted walls with the whip. "But isn't that the point?"

He growled, running towards her. She didn't have time to react before he dropped them both to the ground. Frantically flipping herself over, she crawled towards the door. His hand found her ankle, and he dragged her back to him while her screams filled the room. She couldn't let him overpower her. *Use your legs. It's the only advantage you'll have.*

In one motion, Maia flipped onto her back, wrapping her legs around his neck and squeezing with all her strength. He gasped for air, scratching at her legs, his chokes muffled by the heavy cloth of her dress. She closed her eyes, the muscles in her legs spasming from the effort.

He deserved this. Her legs tightened at the thought of all the women he choked for his own pleasure.

His thrashing slowed before his arms finally fell limp.

She relaxed her legs, inching away and waiting to ensure he remained still. There was a pulse in his bruised neck, but he was out. She pushed herself onto her shaking legs, her heart rattling painfully in her chest.

There was no time to recoup. She still needed to get Briar and Senna inside. Stumbling back up the dark corridor, she found her way to the kitchen. The guard sat outside at his post, whittling a piece of wood and humming to himself.

She threw open the door with a *bang*. "The governor! He's collapsed!"

"What?" The guard jumped to his feet, dropping the knife and holding the piece of wood towards her. "Where?"

She motioned for him to follow, ensuring the back door stayed open behind them.

His face paled the second he saw the governor. "Fuck. How did this happen?"

A large shadow filled the corridor, and Maia took a measured step away from the guard. "I don't know. We were just having some fun, and then he suddenly dropped."

He started into the room when Briar's thick arm wrapped around his neck. A few quiet seconds, and the guard was now unconscious too.

"Get the pig into a chair and tie him down," Senna said to Briar as she helped Maia drag the guard over the threshold, closing the door behind them.

Briar dropped a chair into the center of the room and hoisted the governor from the floor with a grunt, tying him with his own ropes and shackles.

Maia checked his pulse and nodded to Senna. It was her turn. She lifted a whip and struck him on his lap. His eyes flew open, and he howled in pain.

Senna bent over, gripping his face, her sharp nails pinching into his skin. "Let's make this quick and painless, shall we? Why do you need the rebellion's protection?"

"I'm going to kill you, you stupid fucking—"

Senna stepped back, allowing Maia to gag him while he struggled against his bindings.

"Still think I don't know what to do with power?" Maia whispered into his ear.

He looked up at her, hatred now burning in his eyes, and a grin crossed her lips.

"Do you want to try this again?" Senna snapped the whip across his chest.

The gag stifled his screams that slowly morphed into laughter as he dropped his chin to his chest. He was either trying to hide his pain or hoping to throw them off. Senna straightened her back, reaching into the pocket of her dress.

"There's no reason to keep you alive if you won't talk," she said, lifting a pocket-sized pistol.

His laughter died with the click of the gun's hammer. Senna nodded for Maia to remove the gag.

"I'll tell you the same thing I told the rebels. I want to talk to Orion himself," the governor spat.

"That ain't happenin'," Briar said, purposefully cracking each of his knuckles. "Tell us what you know, and you might live through this."

Senna lifted a sharp brow. "I'd take that offer if I were you."

"You *fucking* whore. I can't wait to see Portico string you up."

The darkness retreated as Maia realized the governor was moments away from eating a bullet. Senna's finger tensed on the trigger, and his breath caught.

"Fine," he choked in defeat. "There's a map in the library of Old Virginia. On the back are the coordinates to *all* of Portico's coin caches."

"And why do *you* have this information?" Senna asked suspiciously.

"Because Portico's men know they have safe passage if they come through my town to get to them."

This was the secret. The secret that could change everything.

Maia tamed her excitement. "Let's see if that's true."

She opened the door to ensure the hallway was still empty before tiptoeing back to the library. The map hung inconspicuously above the fireplace. She removed it from the wall, prying the back off with a letter opener.

Five rows of numbers were written in the bottom corner.

The coordinates.

That piece of shit was telling the truth.

Maia rolled up the map and rushed back to the room. "I got it," she said, out of breath. "Let's go."

The governor laughed. "You'll all get what's coming."

Her eyes found his. There was something he was still hiding.

"That's funny. I was about to tell you the same thing," Senna said, taking aim.

"No!" Maia shouted, lunging for Senna's arm.

None of it mattered, though, as the gunshot rang through the room. Maia looked away from the governor's shattered skull, disoriented by the ringing in her ears. Unholstering his gun, Briar stepped into the hallway. His words were muffled, but the panic in his face made them clear.

Run.

8

WANTED

It took more than a week before Maia could move past the nightmares.

The governor's hand sliding up her leg.

His final words before Senna pulled the trigger.

Blood painting the hallway red as Senna and Briar ensured no one was left to come looking for them.

A success by all accounts—but at what cost?

The safe house parlor buzzed with excitement, but it sounded like a distant drone as Maia waited for Rowan to finish skimming the folder in his hand. He flicked it closed, placing it on the fireplace mantel.

"We received word from Jackson's team. The governor's information was accurate, which means..." Rowan's icy gaze thawed. "We have the locations of all Portico's coin caches."

Maia regretted wedging herself between Briar and Garcia on the loveseat as they high-fived over her head.

Even Kayla couldn't hide her smile as she dropped onto the arm of Jayce's chair, rubbing his tight-cut curls.

"Quit it," he said, shooing her away.

She leaned into his personal space, manifesting pure younger sibling energy. "Don't pretend you aren't excited."

His fake frustration broke into a laugh, and he shoved her away.

Edward removed the flask from his coat pocket, limping to his usual perch at the window. He looked as bored as Senna had since arriving at the safe house. She had turned down every attempt to form a connection, making it clear she was here strictly for her portion of the cut.

Kayla was the only one stubborn enough to keep trying.

"Mírate," Garcia said, nudging Maia in the ribs. "Following in your father's footsteps."

Taking a step forward, Senna immediately commanded the attention of the room in her shimmering gold dress with its plunging neckline. Even her wardrobe was a reminder that her role with the rebellion was temporary. "I hope credit is given where credit is due."

Rowan pinched the bridge of his nose in frustration. "Please explain to me exactly what part you would like credit for?"

"Painting the governor's brain all over his walls?" Jayce taunted.

Apparently, Rowan's moral code didn't include revenge kills, which was now a source of tension between him and Senna.

"So, how do we get these coins?" Maia asked, hoping to prevent any arguments.

"The locations are heavily guarded. We'll need to stock up on weapons." Rowan turned to Garcia. "That's where your team comes in."

"Where to?" he asked, clapping his hands together in anticipation. It was infectious, luring Jayce and Kayla forward simultaneously.

"Jamestown." Rowan handed Garcia a list of weapons and quantities. "Portico has a shipment planned in the next three days. I want you to intercept it."

Garcia nodded, passing it off to Kayla. "Consider it done."

Rowan turned to Senna next. "I need your contacts. I want to know when the next delivery to the caches is scheduled, and I want it down to the minute. You and Briar can determine the best way to get that information."

Senna's lips pursed as if biting her tongue, while Briar cursed under his breath. Not only did they have to get the information for Rowan, they also had to keep from killing each other in the process.

"Last but not least," Rowan said, his brow lifting with forewarning. "I think it's time we bring in our next recruit. He's known as The Marksman."

Senna's mouth fell open, and it took her a moment to compose herself. "So, you get upset with me for shooting the governor, but you recruit a bounty hunter?"

"A bounty hunter?" Maia's eyes darted back to Rowan.

Portico recruited murderers, not the rebellion. Or at least Maia believed they wouldn't resort to the same questionable tactics. Rowan's face, however, wasn't convincing her of that.

"Not just any, darling. The worst of them." Senna shot Rowan a glare as she passed, taking a seat in the armchair beside him. "He took an unfortunate interest in my brothel last year. Gave one of my girls the description of a man that would visit and promised her extra coin if she took him to her room. Within a week, the man arrived, and she did as she was told. Before he could even undo his pants, a bullet came through the open window. Not a sound except for my girl's screams."

"Did he pay up?" Briar asked.

Senna rolled her eyes. "Yes. Even gave her *more* than promised. She was gone the next day."

Rowan handed Maia a folder. Inside was a drawing of a man with steely eyes, a sharp nose, and chiseled jaw.

WANTED

The Marksman

Reward: 2,000 coin

DEAD OR ALIVE

"How does a bounty hunter end up with a bounty on his own head?" Maia asked, flipping through the pages. She hoped she would find something in his folder to prove this was a horrible idea.

"He went rogue." It was obvious from his tone that this was Rowan's justification for recruiting him. "And now he's on the run, last seen just outside of Williamsburg."

Dread washed over her as she reached the last page.

"So, why do we need *him*?"

"Every team needs a good shot." Rowan pointed to Kayla, a dangerous grin snaking across her lips. "Without that, you might as well stand in line for one of Portico's bullets. Plus, it's safe to assume Senna's little stunt will make this mission more dangerous."

Maia's eyes fell back to the drawing as she tried to slow her racing thoughts. Clearing out the caches could finally turn things in the rebellion's favor. Blood had already been spilled for the information, and without The Marksman, her entire team would be at risk.

Snatching the bounty from the folder, she tucked it into her pocket along with the unease it brought. If they weren't willing to fight as ruthlessly as Portico, they would never win.

"Fine. Anything else?"

"Yes." Rowan's entire demeanor shifted, making the room suddenly feel cold. "He's got Portico and other bounty hunters on his tail. If you sense trouble, it's already there."

The Marksman sat at the end of the bar, watching the door of Folly's Tavern when Maia arrived. His bounty poster had made him look harsher than reality, and the soft edges of his youthful face surprised her. He sat alone, one hand absentmindedly thumbing a pendant around his neck, the other wrapped around a glass of whiskey.

Niall did a double-take as she approached, his freckled face collapsing into a frown. "Look who found their way back."

"I'll have my usual."

She took her seat next to The Marksman while Niall grabbed a bottle from the shelf.

Folly's was surprisingly busy as a traveling theater troupe celebrated over drinks in the opposite corner. Even with their makeup smeared and their polished outfits loosened to a more casual look, they remained dedicated to commanding the attention of the few patrons scattered around the tavern.

Niall slid Maia her glass. "You know your sister—"

"Not now."

"She's been worried—"

Maia's eyes narrowed in warning. "I said, *not now.*"

Niall met her glare, jaw clenched under his bushy, red beard. She knew he was seething, but he corked the bottle and turned away, grumbling something under his breath. Her shoulders relaxed, and she noticed the man beside her tuck away his pendant.

"I thought you'd look different," she said into her drink.

They were the only two sitting at the end of the bar, but the man still hesitated.

"Is that so?" he asked in a heavy Coastal Region drawl. "More ruggedly handsome?"

She removed the bounty poster from her pocket and placed it between them. "Try slightly less murderous."

"Subtle." He yanked it from the counter, crumpling it in his hand. "You here to collect?"

"Do I look like a bounty hunter?"

His steel-gray eyes turned to her for the first time. They were endless and hollow, showing Maia nothing more than her own reflection. She could now see the man in the drawing.

"You'd be surprised." He took a slow sip from his glass. "What do you want?"

She broke away from his gaze and collected herself. "The rebellion is looking for someone with your talents."

"Killin'?" He leaned in, the smell of whiskey heavy on his breath, and she shifted uncomfortably in her chair. "As you can see, that life ain't worked out for me so far. I think I'll take my chances and keep headin' north."

"What's north?" she asked, searching for any hint of motivation she could use.

He shrugged, glancing back at his near-empty glass. "A fresh start. The Northern Territory is still untamed. Hear it's a good place to disappear."

The comment wasn't as nonchalant as he wanted her to believe. There was an emotion there he tried to suppress, and she latched onto it.

"What if you didn't have to disappear? What if there was a way to clear your bounty?"

He laughed, running his hand through his disheveled hair. "Go on."

"One job," she said, turning to him on the stool. "The rebels take Portico's coin caches, and you walk away with enough coin to start over wherever you want."

"Sounds like a trap."

She wanted to brush off his subtle jab, but Governor Shaw's warning had been lingering in the back of her mind since they returned.

"Maia?" Hannah's voice carried softly from behind her, making her stomach drop. It couldn't have been worse timing.

Without offering The Marksman an explanation, Maia slid off the stool, dragging Hannah to a corner. "What are you doing here?" Hannah's dingy clothes and limp curls made Maia take a step back. "What happened?"

Color filled Hannah's pale cheeks, and she picked at a loose thread from her jacket. "Niall's letting me stay here while I save up coin. Are you back?"

The hope in her words churned up the same guilt Maia had the last time they were together. "No... not yet. But I may have a way for us to get our home back."

A fresh start. Maia's eyes flickered to the spot where the bounty hunter had been, but his seat was now empty.

"If this has anything to do with the rebels, leave me out of it," Hannah said, starting up the stairs.

"Portico has taken too much from us," Maia blurted. "All I'm taking are some coins."

Hannah leaned forward, dropping her voice under the noise of the tavern. "Just stop and think about this without the rebels whispering in your ear. How much blood are *you* willing to spill for these coins?"

Her mouth opened to respond, but the words wouldn't come. Hannah was right. Maia had been moving the line she refused to cross ever since walking away from Briar's mother. The shift was gradual, and still so far away from the other rebels' idea of morality, that it never felt wrong. But it was the reason she was here recruiting a bounty hunter.

Hannah shook her head, eyes already glistening. "Please don't let Portico take the only person I have left." Pulling away, she continued up the stairs without so much as a glance back.

"I can make you the same offer I made Hannah," Niall said, giving Maia a sad smile. "You don't have to go back to them."

There it was again—the look of pity. The same one Mr. Thomas had given her before tossing her aside. Why did the people who knew her the most always make her feel like a disappointment?

"Thank you for taking care of her." Maia's words barely escaped the lump forming in her throat, and she rushed to the door, desperate for air. Niall didn't need to watch her break. It would be just another reason to see her as weak.

"Who was that?"

She gasped, stumbling as The Marksman stepped out of the shadows.

"No one." Maia continued walking, suddenly very aware of who she was now alone with.

"She seems important to ya," he said, tucking his hands into his pockets and falling in step with her.

"It doesn't matter." She flinched at her mistake. He didn't need to know that Hannah was important. He didn't need to know about Hannah at all. She quickened her pace, keeping her head low. "Sorry I bothered you."

"What about the offer?"

"I'll figure something else out." Every nerve in her body was now on edge.

His rough hand found her arm, and her heart sank as he yanked her to him.

"Well, look who we found." A young man with a bushy beard and greasy, black locks strolled up to them, a wad of chewing tobacco tucked in his cheek. He spat on the floor and gave them a stained grin. "You ain't very good at runnin', brother. Too easily distracted."

The man turned to Maia and tipped his newsboy cap at her with a wink.

She pushed away from The Marksman. "I was just leaving."

Another hand wrapped around her arm, and she looked back to find a middle-aged man in a Portico guard uniform had snuck up behind them. "You won't be goin' anywhere, sweetheart."

She struggled in his tightening grip, firmly anchoring her in regret.

"Come on, Micah. Let her go," The Marksman said to the man with the greasy locks. His tone was too flat and uncaring for anyone to take him seriously.

Micah turned to the Portico guard. "I ain't the one holdin' her." He pulled back his jacket, exposing the gun on his hip. A bounty hunter. Seasoned enough to bring a Portico guard to confirm the kill if it came down to it. "Let's walk."

Maia stumbled behind them as they made their way towards the woods outside of town. They were far enough away from the tavern that no one would bat an eye if she screamed. It would be too easy for them to blame her for putting herself in this situation anyway.

"We've known each other a long time, Micah, and I ain't really wantin' to kill you," The Marksman said, keeping his eyes ahead.

Micah sighed. "Cap ain't want you dead any more than I do." He rolled his neck, and Maia was surprised to sense conflict within him. "Dammit Sky, why couldn't you have just done what you were told?"

The Marksman's real name was Sky? It was too soft for the man with steel eyes, but she could see it belonging to the version of him rubbing the pendant when she arrived at Folly's.

"You know why," Sky whispered.

She struggled in the guard's grip, and he pulled up on her arm, causing her to cry out in pain.

Sky turned to them. "Loosen the grip there, big man. She ain't a threat."

The Portico guard pulled up harder, causing her to buckle over. She bit down on her lip and fought to keep her tears at bay. The pain was one thing, but she knew it was the embarrassment of how easily he overpowered her that stung her eyes.

"She seems to be good motivation for you," the guard said, twisting her arm just enough to loosen the tears.

"Watch yourself there, soldier," Micah warned. "The Marksman ain't known for askin' twice."

The guard scoffed, shoving her to the dirt. "He ain't in any position to—"

Maia's knees barely hit the ground before Sky yanked the gun from Micah, putting a single bullet in the guard's chest.

A scream pierced the night sky as she threw her arms over her head, and it took a second for Maia to realize the scream had come from her. The guard collapsed onto his knees beside her with a *thud*.

"Well, shit," Micah laughed. "Guess the show is over."

Portico's man was now sobbing as his coughs grew wet with blood.

Maia crawled to him, frantically covering the bleeding hole in his chest. His eyes found hers, and they both stared, paralyzed with fear.

He didn't deserve to go this way. No one did.

Sky crouched beside her. "Whatcha doin'?"

The guard choked on a bloody plea, and Maia looked away, dropping her hands to her sides. There was nothing she could do to save him. "Put him out of his misery... please."

She pushed herself to her feet, flinching as another shot rang behind her. The guard's body crumpled onto the dead leaves.

"I guarantee you he wouldn't have shown you the same kindness," Sky whispered, his breath on the back of her neck.

Maia shoved her bloody hands into her pockets, gripping her father's watch. "I don't care. Someone has to do the right thing."

"You that someone? Because if I recall, you offered me a fresh start and then tried to walk away from it," he said, handing Micah back his gun.

She looked between them. It was clear Micah was no longer interested in collecting Sky's bounty as he tucked his gun away, and she was beginning to wonder if he ever was.

Her gaze dropped to her boots, dotted with blood. "I can't... there has to be another way to beat Portico. I have to believe the rebels will do things the right way."

Micah laughed. "Ain't that cute. She believes she's fightin' for the greater good." He pointed to the guard's body on the floor. "This is as good as it gets. The mercy of a bullet to the head."

Maia's cheeks flushed, and she realized how naïve she must have looked to them. "I can't accept that."

Sky's piercing eyes flickered to hers, causing her to flinch.

"You're right." He walked back to the guard, flipping him over and pulling at his red jacket. "You need me. And if you're really as decent as you say, you ain't backin' outta this deal."

Her lip trembled, and she bit down on it, hoping they wouldn't notice. Sky wasn't going to let her walk away, and she didn't want to find out what happened if she tried. She remained quiet, and he nodded, handing Micah the jacket.

"What's the plan here?" Micah asked.

Sky was now struggling to remove the guard's pants. "I already gave you a body, Micah. You remember the Cirelli bounty?"

A dangerous grin crossed Micah's lips. "That's fuckin' fantastic. He *is* pretty close to your height and build." He pulled a flask from his coat, taking a sip. "I ain't the one burnin' the body though. That smell sticks to your clothes for fuckin' days."

9

Two Sides

Wher: had it become so cold? The air bit at Maia's ears, seeping into her bones as she walked behind the dead man's body. Nights like these should have numbed the senses, but at this moment, she felt everything.

Sky and Micah had waited until the early morning hours to drag the burned remains back to Williamsburg. Her eyes drifted to the body's limp, charred hands trailing in the dirt. A sudden breeze blew the smell of burnt flesh back at her. She slapped the sleeve of her jacket over her nose, suppressing a gag.

Micah sighed. "You alright?"

She wasn't. Nothing about this was *alright.* "Why couldn't I just wait in the woods?"

Sky grunted as the body caught on a rock. "You promised you'd help clear my bounty." He looked up at her. "This is how we clear it."

She swallowed words she knew better than to say out loud, and followed them past Mayor Alper's white picket fence. There were no guards perched at the entrance, like Governor Shaw's sprawling estate in Richmond. Instead, to

95

her right lay a patch of dead earth where Mrs. Alper spent each spring growing strawberries for her famous jam.

Sky knocked on the front door, adjusting his Portico jacket.

Micah stood beside him, buzzing with anticipation. He looked over, suddenly reaching for Sky's collar.

"What're you doin'?" Sky asked, slapping Micah's hand away.

"You got some blood on—"

The door opened, and all three of them straightened.

"Maia?" Mayor Alper couldn't suppress his surprise. "What are you doing out at this early hour?"

What *was* she doing? Excuses scrambled to take shape in her mind, but fell apart just as quickly. The only ones that wouldn't expose them were lies. So, instead, she stayed quiet, allowing the crickets to overcome the silence.

"She was walking through the woods, sir, when *this* man attacked her," Sky said, pointing at the body.

The mayor's face twisted with disgust. "Who is that?"

"The infamous Marksman, sir," Sky said, lifting his jaw ever so slightly.

Micah snorted, removing the bounty from his pocket and handing it to the mayor.

He took it gently between two fingers and looked it over, pulling a handkerchief from his robe pocket to hold over his mouth. "What happened to the body?"

"Fucker ran into an abandoned buildin'," Micah said, arms pumping as he reenacted his fictional chase. "Tried to smoke him out, but apparently, he wasn't gonna be taken alive."

The mayor examined the bounty closer, glancing at Sky. "Were you two related?"

There was a subtle twitch in Sky's lip. Maia held her breath, wondering if everything was about to collapse around them.

"Ya know, I thought the same thing when I saw it." Sky shook his head in mock perplexity. "Uncanny, really."

Mayor Alper's eyes flickered between Sky and Micah with uncertainty. He was stuck with an impossible decision. If his suspicions were correct, it meant he was in the presence of The Marksman, who had already killed tonight to clear his own bounty. And if he was wrong, he risked being accused of questioning the integrity of a Portico guard. So instead, he nodded. As disappointing as it was, Maia couldn't blame him.

"Yes, quite. You can bury the body elsewhere," he said, looking past them to her. "Ms. Avalos, please come with me."

Sky and Micah didn't seem bothered as she stepped into the mayor's home, continuing with him to his study.

"Trouble seems to keep finding you. I honestly don't want to know why you were wandering the woods so early in the morning. All I want to know is if you're safe."

It was her chance to tell the truth. Her eyes traveled from his worried gaze to the portrait of his family hanging slightly off-kilter behind him. He might be a coward, but he was a good man, and didn't deserve to be caught in the middle of this. It was her mess to clean up.

"I am, sir. Thank you for your concern."

He blew out a breath. "That's good to hear. Let's get these gentlemen moving along then, shall we?"

All it took was Mayor Alper's ink and pen for The Marksman's bounty to be irrefutably closed. Sky was free to wreak havoc however he pleased until his next bounty came along. The mayor removed a seal from his desk, stamping the paper with the Portico emblem.

He guided her back to the entrance, handing the signed and sealed bounty to Sky. "We appreciate you keeping our town safe."

With a grin, Micah snatched it away. "I'll be takin' that."

The mayor tensed, glancing down at Maia. "Are you sure you wouldn't like to stay here until morning, Ms. Avalos? Mrs. Alper can set up a room for you."

She couldn't hide her surprise at his offer, but quickly disregarded it as Sky's harsh eyes narrowed.

"That won't be necessary, sir, but thank you. Enjoy the rest of your day."

Maia stepped through the threshold into the cool evening breeze. The warmth of the mayor's home didn't have a chance to linger as the door clicked shut behind her.

Micah and Sky dropped the feet of the body, walking away.

"You aren't going to bury it?" Maia asked, rushing to catch them.

"We don't get paid to bury the bodies. Just to deliver them," Micah said, tucking the bounty into his jacket.

"What's wrong with you?" she hissed, well past her limit of patience. They were just as fucking awful as she imagined bounty hunters to be.

Micah ignored her, strolling casually next to Sky as if this were a normal evening for them. "You sure you know what you're doin'? This deal you got sounds like more trouble than it's worth."

They glanced over their shoulders at her.

"If it's true, it could mean a fresh start," Sky said, tucking his hands away and continuing past the white picket fence. "For both of us."

Micah sighed. "A fresh start does sound nice. Especially after all these years."

They stopped in the middle of the dirt road. A silence fell between them, while Maia leaned awkwardly against a fence post, waiting for one of them to speak.

"Well, brother, try not to get yourself killed," Micah finally said, putting out his hand. Sky looked down at it, and Maia could sense his disappointment in the gesture. A smile crossed Micah's lips, and he pulled him in for a rough hug instead. "Love ya, man."

Sky relaxed, returning the hug. Whatever their story was together, they both seemed to believe it was ending tonight. A premonition they were clearly struggling with.

"You too," Sky said, voice thick with emotion.

They pulled away, attempting to hide glistening eyes. In a quick, subtle movement, Sky rubbed his fingers together, like he had earlier on his pendant.

Micah noticed, and his face softened for a second before he looked away. "All right, I guess that's that." He pulled a crushed pack of smokes from his pocket, tapping it against his palm. "You know where to find me if you need me."

Sky chewed at the inside of his cheek, nodding in response.

With the flick of his wrist, Micah lit a match and lifted it to the smoke pressed between his lips. It immediately loosened his shoulders as he started down the road, whistling the tune of an old nursery rhyme to the shadows.

Pushing herself off the fence, Maia walked up next to Sky, watching Micah disappear. "He was never going to collect the bounty on you, was he?"

Sky motioned for her to lead the way back up the road, ignoring her question. She sighed in annoyance, starting the long walk back to the safe house in a heavy silence.

They had nearly arrived at Rowan's plantation home when Sky finally spoke.

"Micah and I grew up together," he said, ducking under a tree branch. She barely heard him over the early morning sounds of the forest, but she assumed that was the intention. "Cap took us in as kids and raised us as her own."

"Kids?" Maia's surprise was punctuated by a stumble over a root.

"We were around thirteen or so."

A chill ran through her as she allowed the information to settle. Sky was a man raised by bounty hunters. No wonder people were nothing more than targets.

"Then why kill Portico's diplomats? Why risk losing everything?"

A short, forced laugh escaped him. "Because sometimes the wrong people go too far."

"You say that as if *you* aren't the wrong people." She tensed. Her lack of sleep was loosening her tongue, which was a dangerous game to play with a man like Sky.

His piercing gaze was back on her. "There's always two sides to a story, Maia."

She couldn't help but wonder what her fathers would have been as she ran her thumb over the face of his watch.

"Fine." If he was willing to talk, she could at least offer to listen. "Then tell me yours."

She took pleasure in the flicker of surprise he quickly hid behind a cautious gaze

"Alright," he said, hesitantly. "Portico put a bounty on a man who allegedly raped a governor's daughter. Now *normally*, it's a bounty I'd be more than happy to collect on. However, Portico's diplomats were already on the job when I arrived."

"Why would diplomats be involved in bounties?"

Sky glanced at her, his face indecipherable. "How do ya think diplomats keep the peace?"

She shouldn't be surprised Portico would distort the definition of diplomacy.

"Anyway, the diplomats were too involved—too eager for me to pull the trigger. So, I did some diggin' and found out the man was innocent. A Portico scout was the one who committed the crime, and they were using the bounty to clean up their mess. So, I killed the scout. The diplomats just happened to be in the way."

Her eyes traveled to the pendant bouncing against his chest. She could almost see the young boy justifying his first kill. The struggle to maintain the good within, while being praised for the bad.

"Which is why you had the bounty on your head."

Sky nodded, suddenly looking as tired as Maia felt. "Portico makes the rules, and, in their eyes, you and I ain't any different."

They were, though. Maia would never allow herself to spiral into his darkness, even if the world already saw her drowning in it.

"You should probably take off that Portico jacket," she said as they cleared the trees surrounding the safe house. "You won't get the same warm reception here."

He started unbuttoning it, glancing around the property. "So, this is the rebellion?"

Briar sat half-awake on the porch steps with a smoke in one hand and a steaming cup of tea in the other. A shot rang from the target range, stealing everyone's attention. Kayla rolled her shoulder, cursing the kick of the shotgun.

"Who you got with you?" Garcia hollered from one of the rocking chairs.

Rowan glanced up from the chair beside him, doing a double-take as they approached.

"No shit." Garcia was now on his feet, walking over to greet them. "If it isn't The fuckin' Marksman."

Sky grinned, thumbing at his jacket. "Actually, Portico collected The Marksman's bounty in Williamsburg early this mornin'."

Rowan's lip twitched, but he quickly composed himself, suppressing whatever emotion had attempted to take hold. He looked at Maia, giving her a quick nod of approval.

How could such a simple gesture make her heart feel so full? All the second-guessing and guilt Hannah forced on her melted away. She knew she should have held onto it, even if just a drop, but instead, she wondered if her father would have given her the same look had he been there.

Briar stood, nudging her lightly with his thick arm. "Welcome home, boss."

It *was* home. The rebellion had become a place where she didn't have to hide her flaws or apologize for not living up to expectations.

"That explains the Portico outfit," Garcia said with a booming laugh. "So, what do we call you?"

"Skylar Matthews," he said, putting out his hand. Garcia gave it a rough shake, and Sky turned to Rowan next. "Sky for short."

Rowan took his hand. "Sky it is. Are you aware of the job?"

"One job to clear out all of Portico's coin caches."

The playfulness in his tone hinted that he still wasn't convinced this wasn't an elaborate setup.

"So, you're in?" Rowan asked.

Sky nodded, and Maia noticed his fingers rubbing together as if anxious for his pendant. "Wouldn't be here if I wasn't, sir."

Garcia clapped his hands together and shouted for Kayla.

"Welcome to the rebellion," Rowan said, motioning for Sky to follow him into the house. "Let's plan a heist."

Maia followed, tracing the Orion constellation etched into the wood column. She stopped and looked at it again, suddenly understanding the thin line between hope and death it symbolized.

"You're back!" Kayla said, hooking her arm in Maia's and dragging her into the house. "We weren't sure you'd make it in time to go over the plan."

The door to the kitchen suddenly swung open, and Orion burst into the foyer, arguing with Jackson. She cut him off mid-sentence, shoving a liquor bottle and glasses into his hands before rushing over to greet Maia.

"Did you miss me?" she asked, throwing her arms around Maia's shoulders.

"Not the 'getting my ass kicked' part, but yeah," Maia laughed, returning the hug.

The flush in Orion's face from the argument dissipated into a surprising softness as he watched the interaction.

"Something tells me you'd be kicking mine now."

Jackson left her arm draped across Maia's shoulder, following Orion into the parlor.

The energy of the room was contagious as everyone found their place, and Maia immediately noticed new rebels standing tall and statuesque to the side.

"Let me introduce you to my team," Jackson said, pulling her to the towering men. It was obvious they were from the Desert Region, with their gorgeous toned, brown skin and hardened, onyx eyes.

"When were you in the Desert Region?" Maia asked, hoping the flush of her cheeks wasn't too obvious as she flexed her hand to ease the sting of the men's rough handshakes.

"For most of my childhood." Jackson shrugged her bony shoulders, but there was tension laced in her words. "I can take you there once all this is over."

Maia allowed herself a moment to imagine their world after this mission. The freedom they would have to go wherever they wanted without fear of Portico's watchful eyes. They were so close. Her gaze flickered to the man beside her. He noticed, his lip tugging up in a way that made her hope she might have some time getting to know Jackson's team too.

"I like that plan."

Jackson swelled with excitement. "We're going to be so fucking unstoppable together."

An ear-piercing whistle quieted the room as Orion lowered his fingers from his lips. "Good, now that I have your attention, let's get some basic things out of the way. This mission is unlike any heist we've planned. Every pocket of the rebellion has agreed to a coordinated strike on all of Portico's coin caches two weeks from today."

"Why two weeks?" Jackson asked, straightening her back and suddenly all business.

Orion shifted his gaze to Senna.

She sat in an armchair, unphased by the sudden attention. "Portico's coin transports are scheduled twice a month for replenishment. The next one is scheduled in two weeks."

"And because once word spreads about Governor Shaw's… incident, they'll know we have his secret," Orion continued, motioning to Rowan for further explanation.

Adjusting his glasses, Rowan turned to a drawing board covered in paper sketches.

"The rebels to the north and west of the Forest Region are already heading to their cache locations, so our targets are to the east. We'll be splitting up and hitting the Newport News, Norfolk, and Chesapeake coin caches. Scouts noticed the crew delivering the coins were disguised in Scavenger clothes."

He pointed to a group of sketches, and Maia leaned forward to get a better look. The Scavenger clothing covered every inch of skin. Hands in gloves, mouths covered with handkerchiefs or scarves, hair hidden under the hoods of jackets or hats. Only their eyes were left exposed.

"Why pretend to be Scavengers?" she asked.

Sky rubbed his tired eyes. "Would *you* try to rob a pack of Scavengers?"

The sketches were enough for her to safely say no.

"So, how do we get inside?" Garcia asked, motioning with his drink to get to the good part.

Rowan flipped the board to show an enlarged chalk drawing of a bunker-like structure. "Each location has six Portico guards. Two at the entrance and four inside."

"So we take down the two outside and make our way in," Kayla said, looking almost bored.

Orion shook his head. "The door only opens from inside. If you shoot the guards outside first, you'll never get in."

"Well, the deliveries get inside," Briar said.

There was a moment of silence as everyone thought on his words.

Garcia's brows knit together. "Time the ambush with the delivery?"

"No," Maia said, looking back at the drawing. "*Be* the delivery."

"Take out the four deliverymen in the woods and assume their identities." The realization in Jackson's voice crescendoed with excitement.

Rowan and Orion exchanged a look, impressed with the idea, which made Maia wonder what the other rebel pockets had planned.

"You'll be able to walk up and wait for them to open the doors," Rowan said with a slow nod.

Anticipation grew heavy in the air as the moving parts slowly came together.

Edward turned from the window, removing his flask from his jacket. "You're walkin' us straight into the wolf's den."

His words snuffed out all the excitement, and the truth behind them tamped it firmly into the worn rug beneath his dirty boots.

"So we create some chaos," Sky said, stepping closer to the board to get a better view. "How big are the caches?"

Rowan picked up a piece of chalk, calculating the dimensions. "Approximately a thousand square feet, but there might be more below the surface."

Edward scoffed. "That's a lot of room for four people to hide."

"Smoke bombs could better those odds, old man," Sky said, making it clear he wasn't going to let Edward ruin this for everyone else. "Two should do the trick."

"I hope you have some pre-war stock hidden in the bunker," Garcia said, pulling a paper smeared in blood from his pocket and tossing it on the coffee table. "Because smoke bombs weren't on the weapons list."

As if doing a quick inventory in his head, Rowan's glacial eyes grew distant. "I do. Pre-war smoke canisters and gas masks."

Jackson reached for Garcia's list. "So, what *do* we have for weapons?"

"Only the most dangerous for you, flaca," he said with a wink.

Maia's stomach knotted as the reality of the plan sunk in. Taking out the deliverymen meant killing them and anyone else who stood in their way. If she wasn't willing to pull the trigger, she not only risked her life but also her team's.

Orion pivoted into a speech, but Maia only heard the roar of her heart as the room suddenly became sweltering.

This was always going to be the outcome. She had to fight to give a voice to those silenced by Portico... including her father's. The death of a few could bring hope to hundreds.

Why did those feel like someone else's words? When had everything become so blurred?

The others broke into groups to begin their planning, but Maia remained paralyzed.

"You have every right to be scared," Rowan said, walking up beside her.

Was she scared? She glanced up at him. "You realize what you're asking me to do?"

"There will always be casualties in war, Maia," he said, hand finding her tense shoulder. "I would prefer you not to be one of them. Don't lose sight of what we're fighting for, and what it means if we succeed. Not when we're this close."

He walked away, ending the conversation, but not Maia's racing thoughts. Hannah was right. Could she live with the person she was becoming?

The only way she'd know was if she survived.

10

DESCENT

I would die for my people, but I will kill for my family.

K. Wells – Summer 2260

The path to Newport News followed the cracked roads of the Old World. Patches of gray among the green foliage and the stench of death were the only two things differentiating it from the surrounding forest.

"What's that smell?" Maia asked, covering her face with a bandana.

She tripped on a loose chunk of asphalt, her heavy backpack nearly taking her to the ground. A decomposing foot rolled away from an unrecognizable body, and she gagged into her face covering.

"You ain't exactly graceful for someone so tiny," Briar said, pulling her back to the center of the road.

But it was too late. She already saw the eyeless bodies scattered along their path.

She had grown familiar with death as a healing apprentice, but this wasn't just death—it was cold-blooded violence.

"Scavenger territory," Sky whispered, scanning the area. "We need to move fast."

Peeling her eyes away from the remains, she joined the others as they jogged the entire way to the entrance of the city. She bent to catch her breath, massaging a stitch at her side.

The crumbling ruins of the pre-war city loomed before them. Towering buildings stretched like metallic fingers grasping for the clouds, forlornly guarding the broken streets littered with rusted skeletons of cars. A howl traveled through the shattered windows—ghostly reminders of what once was.

Light posts and street signs peeked out from under the suffocating, climbing ivy, watching them as they passed. The gluttony of the Old World on full display.

"Have you ever been to a ward?" Senna asked.

Maia lifted her bandana, hoping to make her thoughts less visible. "No. Only knew Williamsburg until a few months ago."

"I grew up in the Richmond Ward," Senna said, stepping over a shattered bottle. "This one's actually nicer."

The ward seemed endless as the buildings disappeared into a fog a few miles out. Despite its size, Maia sensed eyes everywhere. Men and women reduced to skin and bone, twitching from withdrawal or mites.

A woman paced in an alleyway, picking at a sore on her cheek while talking to a man slumped against the wall. As Maia grew closer, she noticed the rats nibbling at the tips of his fingers.

Her eyes shot to the ground ahead. It didn't matter though, she still felt the unease in her stomach and the guilt that came with it. No one lived here by choice. They were the sick and unwanted, and Senna had been one of them.

"How did you get out?" Maia asked, grateful as the crumbling buildings gave way to the newer wooden structures of Newport News proper.

Senna adjusted the straps of her bag as if it had suddenly become uncomfortable. "My mother sold me to a man for fifty coin."

It made sense now. Why she tried so hard to avoid creating connections. It was to protect herself, and Maia knew better than to keep prying into her past. "I'm sorry."

"Don't be." She gave Maia a sly smile. "At least I know what I'm worth."

Sky snorted at Senna's dark humor.

"Funny," Briar said, lighting a smoke and taking a long drag. A slowly expanding cloud leached from between his lips. "The only one laughin' is the one worth more dead than alive."

They pushed through the evening crowd of Newport News, picking pockets and stealing food from market vendors closing up shop for the night. The coin cache was still seven miles outside of town, so they continued back into the forest to set up camp.

Despite the distractions, Maia's muscles remained knotted with tension as she tried—unsuccessfully—not to think about the mission. If anyone else had the same concerns, they hid it much better than she could.

Senna tossed a few sticks onto the pile Briar was attempting to light for camp. "Do you need help?"

"No," he snapped, brushing his hair from his face in frustration. "How are none of y'all hungry right now?"

Maia sat up at the opportunity to distract her spiraling thoughts. "I can find us some food."

Briar's gaze flickered to Sky, sharing words that remained unspoken.

"I'll go with," Sky said, picking up his rifle and slipping the strap over his shoulder. "Come on."

They crept through the thicket, Maia with her dagger and him with his rifle, with nothing but an unsettling silence and the tick of her father's watch between them.

Sky pointed to a spot with two fallen trees, taking a seat on one and steadying his rifle on the other. She joined him, surprised when he tensed at their closeness.

The confidence he exuded around Micah seemed to disappear now that they were alone.

It took him a second to relax enough for their arms to touch, but when he did, even the crisp fall air was nothing compared to the chill his skin sent through her. She closed her eyes, rubbing her hands together and focusing on the sounds of the forest.

"Whatcha gonna do after tomorrow?" Sky whispered, peering through the scope.

Despite the sincerity in his voice, it was hard to imagine he actually cared.

"Use the coin to get my home back from Portico." And hopefully, make amends with Hannah.

She would never say it aloud, but since finding the map, Maia had imagined, on more than one occasion, using the coin to open a shop with her sister. Beyond that, she didn't care what it was or what they sold, as long as they were together.

"You know there's a good chance we ain't survivin' this, right?"

Her heart plummeted. Of course she knew, but the day before wasn't the time to talk about it. "I'm not backing out, if that's what you're worried about."

"It's not." He removed his pendant from under his shirt and rubbed it absentmindedly. "You *should* sit this one out."

This was why he was here—the look between him and Briar. "You think I'm a risk."

"You ever kill someone?" His gaze found hers, but it was only to confirm what he already knew. "That's why you're a risk."

A wild hog meandered into their line of sight, and Maia removed her dagger. Sky shook his head, handing her his rifle. It was too heavy, the cool metal sending a shiver through her as she adjusted her grip and placed it against her shoulder.

Rowan had trained her on this weapon, but it didn't make her any more comfortable. She drew in a breath and peered through the scope, struggling to locate the target.

"Aim first, then look down the scope," Sky whispered into her ear.

The brush of his breath lifted the hairs on her neck. "Why can't I use my blade?"

Sky moved his leg to straddle the log and leaned into her. "A knife ain't gonna win a gunfight."

His hand cradled hers, lifting the gun back to her shoulder while his other arm worked its way around her. She froze, doing everything in her power not to shudder at his touch. He aimed the rifle at the hog now rustling in the brush. Peering into the scope, she spotted it dead center.

"You see it?" he whispered. She nodded, and he clicked something on the side of the gun. "Take the shot."

Her finger itched over the trigger as Sky's hovered steadily over hers. She wanted to blame the tremble in her arms on the weight of the gun, but the buzz of panic growing inside her told her otherwise.

She couldn't take the shot.

It wouldn't be clean, and the animal would suffer

Her breath came out slowly as she hesitated, but Sky's finger pressed down on hers, forcing the decision.

The gunshot was deafening, and the animal squealed for only a second before dropping lifeless onto the dirt.

"That's why you're a risk."

Sky stood, taking his rifle and heading back to camp, allowing Maia a chance to breathe again. She rubbed the tip of her finger, the chill of metal still lingering on her skin.

It wasn't the gun she feared, though. It was the person she knew she would have to become to pull the trigger.

"You alright?"

Briar's voice startled her as he approached from the shadows. The fear on her face must have been obvious, because his entire body tensed.

"Of course," she said, forcing a soft smile.

"I'm sorry."

"For what?"

"He was supposed to give you a choice."

Maia's smile hitched. She knew Briar had done this with the right intentions, but it didn't lessen the sting of betrayal.

She shook it off, starting towards the carcass. "It's done. I'm going."

"You ain't gotta be like us, boss." His hand found her shoulder, pulling her to a stop. "I made my choice a long time ago, but you can still walk away with clean hands."

She shook her head. "It's just one mission."

It was more than that, though, and she knew it, despite the lies she kept telling herself.

"There were only two things my dad loved in this world." His gaze fell to his worn, leather boots, veiling his face in the shadows. "A lager and beatin' the shit out of my mom. I used to steal alcohol and help him cheat at poker, hoping maybe it'd make him love me too."

His confession caught her off guard. She scrambled to adjust to the sudden shift in conversation while searching for consoling words.

"I remember wondering why she always made him so fuckin' angry. But it was never about her—or me. We were nothin' to him. A punching bag and a mistake. Anyway, one day, I came home and found her cowering in a corner. I was certain he was gonna kill her this time."

He disappeared into his thoughts, and Maia wondered if they were the same tortured memories he had fought during his withdrawal.

"So, I picked up a knife and put it in his back. And you know what's the worst part? As that fucker turned to see who stabbed him, I realized he didn't even recognize me. He was too fuckin' drunk to recognize his own son."

Maia's heart shattered. Her hand found his, rubbing her thumb across his scarred knuckles. It was something Hannah used to do to comfort her.

He looked down at her hand, the muscle ticking in his jaw while his brows pinched together. His throat bobbed, as if trying to keep his emotions in check.

"You did what you had to do."

"Did I?" He pulled his hand from hers, tucking it into his pocket. "Mom cried about him for months after that. She spread a story around him losin' a fight at a tavern outside of town. But she never looked at me the same."

Maia knew she shouldn't, but she hated the woman Briar lovingly called his mother. Her heart ached only for the broken man standing in front of her.

"Briar—"

"I didn't tell you so you'd feel bad for me. I told you because me and those other two shady fuckers never stood a chance at being the good guys. But you do."

It was too much knowing how he saw himself. She wanted more than anything to be the person he thought she was, but doing that meant they were going in one person short. Could she forgive herself if he didn't come back? The thought alone made her choke on her next words.

"I can't." The gold specks in his forest green eyes lit up with hope, and she quickly shook her head. "I can't ask you to risk your life while I sit here waiting. I know what that means, and it's my choice to make."

His lip twitched with frustration, and he looked away. "Can you promise me you ain't gonna look at me any different after tomorrow?"

The cracks in her heart splintered further as he bared his wounds. Despite everything, he was still a good person, even if he didn't see himself that way. "I promise."

"Good," he said, the tension returning to his broad shoulders. "'Cause I'm gonna kill every motherfucker that gets near you. Alright?"

His promise of violence flowed through her like poison. She could hear Mr. Thomas again—feel the contempt dripping with each syllable. *Infected. Tainted. Dangerous.*

There was power in those words that she didn't understand until now. Briar's loyalty was absolute, and that alone made her realize if anyone could make her pull the trigger, it was him.

"Alright."

His shoulders relaxed, and he started towards the dead hog. "Come on, I'm fucking starving."

Morning dew hung heavy in the air as they inched along the rushing water of an overgrown creek. The Portico coin cache sat nestled between them and the woods. Maia struggled through the tall cattails, swatting at puffs of white drifting listlessly into the air.

Birds called out eagerly to one another over the deafening roar of the current. The cottonmouths alone made them each a little more cautious with their steps, but provided assurance the Portico deliverymen wouldn't sneak up on them.

They continued along the creek bed until they could no longer see the cache, tucking into the forest just as the sun peeked over the horizon. Sky bent over, examining a broken stick on the ground as Maia continued past him, spotting a scrolled *P* etched into a tree trunk.

She ran her finger over the rough carving. "Hey, I think—"

A gunshot rang through the forest, sending everyone to the ground. The birds that were just welcoming the day took off in a flighted frenzy.

Regret washed over Maia as footsteps ran in her direction. Her gut screamed for her to look back and make sure the others were still there, but her eyes remained fixed in the direction of the quickly approaching boots. They wouldn't leave her. She had to believe that. The thought didn't slow her frantic heart as a bead of sweat ran down the back of her neck.

A man burst through the trees, eyes nothing more than two bloody sockets. His wild, desperate breaths suddenly ended with a sickening crack, and he collapsed to the ground, an ax protruding from his back.

Panic crawled up the back of Maia's throat, threatening to escape. She jumped as a hand slapped over her mouth.

Sky lifted a finger to his thin lips, eyes locked on hers. A figure draped head-to-toe in ragged clothes stomped towards the man still crawling along the forest floor. Pressing a boot onto the man's leg, the figure yanked the ax free. The scream that followed turned Maia's blood cold, and the figure brought the ax down one more time, cleanly decapitating him and plummeting them back into a terrifying silence.

Maia squeezed her eyes shut, her entire body trembling as she sucked in choppy breaths under Sky's hand. The figure's heavy footsteps slowly continued towards them. It was as if he could smell the fear emanating from her. Sky pulled her to his boney chest while they remained hidden behind a fallen log, the chaotic hammering of his heart matching her own. He held his breath. The footsteps paused only an arm's length away. The world stilled as Maia waited for a hand to come down on her.

Shouts carried from the trees, and the footsteps shuffled in the tall grass. The figure returned the call, starting back.

Sky let out his breath and rolled onto his back, leaving her with the indents of his fingers on her back. "We've got a problem."

"That was a real Scavenger, wasn't it?" Her words came out choppy and breathless, her panic no longer contained.

"Yeah." Sky wiped the sweat from his face with the sleeve of his shirt and risked a glance to see if the figure was gone. With a nod, Senna and Briar now joined them.

The stories Maia's father had told her were nothing compared to what she had just witnessed. The Scavengers weren't vultures, they were predators, and vicious enough to strike fear into a man like Sky.

Senna's hands found Maia's shoulders, pulling her back to the moment as she brushed a sweat-soaked strand of hair back. "Look at me. You're fine, okay? Now we need to figure out how to get that delivery cart."

She was right. It was safe to assume the Scavengers had found it, and Maia knew better than to think they would give it up willingly.

"Senna... we'd be walkin' into a massacre." Sky's voice was gentle. Too gentle. He spoke to Senna as if cautiously approaching the queen bee's hive.

"That was *always* the plan."

She stood, brushing the dirt from her pants. Without hesitation, Senna started towards the yelling and gunshots ahead. Dropping her head between her bent knees, Maia took in a slow breath to keep from screaming. When she looked back up, she found Briar's hand waiting. He pulled her to her feet in silence as they moved to catch up with Senna.

The team ducked into the tall grass along a worn dirt path. A pack of Scavengers, all with white-painted faces, stood gathered around the last of the Portico deliverymen. He begged for mercy, tears streaming down his cheeks as he kneeled before them. The Scavenger reached for the man's face, cradling it in his gloved hands.

"You see," he said. Adjusting his thumbs, he pressed them into the man's eyes, popping them from their sockets. "Now saw."

An amulet slipped out from under the Scavenger's shirt as the man struggled to free himself.

The same amulet that Sky wore.

"Why do you have a Scavenger pendant?" Maia asked, glancing at Sky out of the corner of her eye.

Every muscle in his body hardened into sharp angles, like shards of shattered glass. "Now ain't the time for that, Maia."

His tone was laced with warning, as if she were crossing a line he had created for himself.

"You see. Now saw," they chanted as the man screamed in pain. His cry was cut short with a slash to the throat.

A Scavenger rummaged through the rags on the back of the cart and hollered, "There's more to it!"

He grunted, pulling a chest from the cart as the others joined him. One lifted their bludgeon and dropped it on the lid. The silence was suddenly deafening as they stared with wide eyes, the face paint sinking into the cracks of their raised brows before they erupted in celebration.

"Full hands. No stopping. Eye to eye?" the Scavenger with the club said to a group of three around him.

"We see the same," one said with a nod.

They lifted the chest to load back on the cart when the Scavenger stopped them with his club, shaking his head. "More here. More there."

The three nodded and worked together to carry the chest away. There were still seven Scavengers, now making their way to the cache with the delivery cart Maia and her team needed.

Sky closed his eyes, rolling his neck in frustration while Senna rushed forward, flipping one of the dead deliverymen onto his back.

"The Scavengers stole our fuckin' plan," Briar growled.

Senna struggled to pull the coat from the body, shoving it at him. Briar recoiled in disgust, but took it.

"This doesn't change the plan, it just... complicates it," she said, working on the pants next.

Maia could sense Sky's eyes on her as she stood off to the side, processing. Three men were walking away with a chest of coins. Probably enough to change all of their lives forever. It wouldn't be difficult to overtake them given the cumbersome size of the chest.

But the mission wasn't about the coins. They were just the catalyst to the shift in power that would occur if the team followed the cart to the coin cache.

Going that direction meant changing the lives of hundreds, maybe thousands, but there was no guarantee they would all make it out alive.

"You're braver than you think," Senna whispered, handing Maia a bundle of clothes. "Let's take down Portico."

11

THE HEIST

*We are the creators of our own demise, willingly
taking the bullet.*

K. Wells – Summer 2260

T he door to the cache was held open with a rock. Two dead guards were propped haphazardly against the wall—*You see. Now saw* written in blood above their heads. Gunshots ricocheted within as Maia gripped the smoke canister in her shaking hand.

Senna removed the bandana from her face and turned to Sky. "Ready?"

His eyes were steel as he loaded his rifle and slipped on his gas mask. Briar took a deep breath and did the same, aiming his shotgun at the door.

This was Maia's last chance to walk away, but standing on the precipice made her realize that, despite all the fear churning within, she was always meant to be here. This was their moment to right the wrongs of the past. To finish what her father had started.

She lowered her mask and pulled the pin from the smoke canister, tossing it through the door. The chaos within escalated as smoke languidly seeped from the opening.

Maia lifted her pistol. "Go."

Briar forced open the heavy door as they rushed into the haze, the ominous slam shrouding them in darkness.

The blinding light of each gunshot filled the room like lightning. Maia only saw flashes of bodies, alive and dead, scattered around them. The tremble in her hands slowed as she lifted her gun.

She was in control now.

The roaring in her ears drowned out the shouts and cries. Weak hands grabbed at her ankles as she forced her way forward. Her gaze dropped to the floor, and in one distracted second, a sharp, searing pain sliced through her arm.

Collapsing into a protective crouch, she pressed her hand to the burning gash. Briar fell over her, his shotgun going off, sending a shell into the ceiling and showering them in concrete.

The roaring was now ringing, punctuated by endless gunfire. Maia pushed through the searing pain, struggling to her feet, boots slipping on the debris when a hand found her collar.

"Come now, little," the figure attached to the hand said.

Her body went stiff.

The hand didn't belong to Briar.

A Scavenger now had her in his grip, dragging her across the slick floor. It wouldn't take long for him to figure out she wasn't one of them.

Images of the eyeless bodies flashed through her frantic thoughts. The ax in the man's back. The bloody words on the wall. All the brutality she'd witnessed up to this point.

This wasn't how she was supposed to die.

She dug her nails deep into his hand, raking them across it, the warmth of his blood painting her fingertips. He shouted in pain, his fingers unfurling to drop her.

The second she was free, she lifted her pistol to him.

It was him or her.

His head cocked to the side in confusion before he crumpled, a spray of blood erupting from the side of his neck.

Maia's breath escaped her with a choked gasp. Her finger had never found the trigger. She scrambled to her feet, turning into someone's hard shoulder. A flash of light exposed a scrolled *P* on the man's coat.

The Portico guard gripped her by the collar, slamming her into the wall and snatching off her mask.

"You ain't a fucking Scavenger."

They stared at each other in shock as Maia slowly pressed her pistol to his stomach. The man tensed, defeat in his eyes. It was the moment he realized he would die by her hands.

Her face quivered as she lifted her finger to the trigger.

Him or her.

A scream escaped her, and she closed her eyes, pressing her finger down. The gunshot was deafening, but it still wasn't hers. Maia's eyes shot open to find a gas mask hovering over her.

"Let's keep those pretty little hands of yours clean a bit longer," Senna said through her mask.

Sky snatched the pistol from Maia's hand, yanking off his mask to inspect it.

"For fuck's sake," he said, flipping a switch on the side and shoving it back at her. "You left the safety on."

Maia's cheeks burned. She was exactly the risk Sky said she'd be. Not even Briar could protect her from herself.

"I'm—" Sky slipped on his mask and walked away before Maia could finish. "Sorry," she whispered too late.

"Don't you dare apologize to him," Senna said, grabbing her chin. "Grab your mask, and let's keep moving."

They had cleared out the first room, and Maia took in the death around her as the smoke dissipated.

It had been a common area, with a table now flipped on its side, and a game of cards scattered across the floor stuck in pools of blood. A dartboard surrounded by bullet holes fell off the wall, bouncing off a toppled bookshelf.

Two Portico guards and four Scavengers lay motionless. The only time they would ever be at peace in each other's presence. Maia pushed past the melancholy of the moment, focusing on the fact that two more guards and three Scavengers remained hidden within.

She shook away the stinging in her eyes and reached for her mask. The burning pain shot through her arm again, and she glanced down, realizing a bullet had grazed her. It was infuriating how incompetent she felt, and she allowed that pain and anger to fuel her.

"Can you do me a favor?" Briar asked, catching his breath. He had also lost his mask somewhere in the fight, face covered in dust and blood. "Can you *try* not to run into every person lookin' to kill you?"

Her anger was now palpable, strengthening with each beat of her heart. She didn't respond, instead, slipping the gas mask over her painfully clenched jaw.

They joined Senna and Sky at the door leading to the next room. The sound of bullets ricocheting off the metal continued within.

Briar cracked the door open just enough for Senna to throw in the last of their smoke canisters. Lifting his fingers, Sky counted down.

Three. Two. One.

They burst through the door, shooting into the smoke. The room was claustrophobic, with metal bunk beds lining both walls. Maia stepped over the limbs of the fallen as the smell of blood and excrement seeped in from under her useless Old World mask.

She yanked it off, tossing it aside and lifting a bandana over her mouth instead. Their footsteps echoed off the concrete walls as they inched towards a metal door ahead. The silence raised Maia's skin—it was too quiet.

Briar suddenly cried out. They turned to find a Portico guard holding a knife to his throat.

"You ain't goin' in there," the guard said, pressing his knife in enough to break Briar's skin. "Drop the guns, and I'll let him go—I'll let you all go. No questions asked."

The fear in Briar's eyes tensed every muscle in Maia's body. She knew two things for certain: the guard had no plans to let any of them go, and if she didn't act quickly, Briar would do something desperate.

She tossed her pistol to the floor, lifting her hands in surrender. The guard's nervous gaze flickered between each of them as Maia lowered herself to the ground. She glanced up to find Senna and Sky hesitating.

"Do it," she hissed, inconspicuously unlatching a strap around her ankle.

Sky lifted his gas mask, tossing his rifle before kneeling beside her. It was enough of a distraction for Maia to remove the blade from her ankle sleeve. Senna caught the motion out of the corner of her eye, raising her chin in understanding. All Maia needed was enough of a distraction to get a clean throw.

Senna tossed her pistol and mask high into the air towards the pile. The guard took the bait, his eyes locked on the last of the team's weapons.

It was now or never.

Maia gripped her blade, sending it in one swift motion into the guard's shoulder. The man cried out, allowing Briar to grab his arm and twist it behind his back. Sky stumbled forward, seizing his rifle, and with a single shot, the guard dropped. A perfect hole between his eyes.

Briar let go of the dead man's arm, stepping over him to help Maia to her feet. His coat was torn, and she noticed a gash across his lower back. She reached for it, but his large hand wrapped around her wrist.

"You can fix me later." He adjusted his Scavenger coat to hide it. "Looks like we found what we're looking for."

They turned to the metal door with nothing but silence behind it. Maia glanced around the bedchamber, counting.

Three Scavengers and two Portico guards. If Rowan's information was correct, no one would be waiting on the other side of the door. Without another smoke canister, she hoped he was right.

They grabbed their guns from the pile and regrouped.

"Let's get this over with." Briar took a step back and kicked open the door.

Inside stood a single guard in the center of the room. A lantern hung above him, revealing his hand resting on his hip holster.

"Where are the chests?" Sky demanded.

"There's nothing here," the guard said, shaking his head with a cruel smile. "It was cleared out a week ago."

"Don't lie to us. Where are the chests?" The shake in Senna's voice betrayed her.

The guard's smile widened into something grotesque. "We knew you'd be dumb enough to take the bait."

Maia's stomach dropped, and a wave of dread washed over her. *You'll all get what's coming.* Governor Shaw's warning wasn't an empty threat. Sky was right. It was a trap.

The ring of a bullet ricocheted in the room, and the guard howled in pain, bending to the hole now in his foot. Sky reloaded his rifle and pointed it to the guard's other foot.

"Torture me all you want," the guard spat, gripping his bloodied foot. "But you're wastin' your bullets."

Sky shot at his other foot, causing him to drop to the floor. "I don't mind."

"Enough, Sky. He's not lying," Maia snapped. The man's face had gone pale, and she kneeled beside him. "If you tell us where they moved the chests, you can still get out of this alive."

The guard's unfocused eyes found hers, and he laughed. "Your *fucking* rebellion is over."

He reached for his holster and Maia stumbled back.

Not fast enough.

The warmth of the guard's blood found her face before she could divert her eyes from the mess Sky's bullet had made of the man's head.

Senna grabbed her shoulder, yanking Maia to her feet. "What do you mean he wasn't lying?"

"The chests were moved." Maia pointed to the drag marks on the floor, working their way from the center of the room out.

"You're wrong."

Senna's words were as vacant as her expression. It was as if she had withdrawn from herself to keep reality from sinking in. Maia looked away, unearned guilt washing over her. It wasn't her fault the chests were gone, but the whispering voice in the back of her mind was relentless.

You let them down. You should have known.

Sky placed the butt of his rifle on the floor and slid down the wall, wiping his worn face. All the bodies scattered through the cache. All the death. What did Portico gain from this?

Senna seemed to snap out of her stupor and stormed to the opposite side of the room, testing the walls for weak spots.

Maia looked back at the man's lifeless body, his blood still fresh on her face.

We knew you'd be dumb enough to take the bait.

They were right. Portico dropped a crumb of hope for the rebellion, and that's all it needed to draw every last rebel out of hiding. Maia was never meant to get this far.

None of them were.

That's when she realized the guard's bullet wasn't for her. It was to ensure he wouldn't be taken alive and tortured for information.

Senna screamed, kicking at a stuffed burlap sack.

Maia's focus, however, remained on the blood pooling around the man's body, stopping in a sharp line. A perfect box.

She stepped closer, running her finger along the edge. The floorboards had been cut. *If your eyes are open, the moment will always reveal itself.*

Her chest fluttered as she flipped the heavy body over, exposing a metal ring embedded into the floor around a keyhole.

She glanced around the room, noting all eyes on her.

"What if Rowan was right, and they hid something below?" she asked, digging into the dead man's pockets and removing a single key.

She nearly dropped it in her excitement as she fumbled it into the keyhole, unlocking the trap door.

The others were now hovering over her, glancing down a ladder leading into darkness. Sky kneeled, shooting into the hatch. Only silence followed.

He didn't hesitate, dropping his foot to the first rung. Senna handed him the lantern, and he started into the darkness.

The wait was excruciating, as Sky's footsteps echoed along the concrete floor below. Maia picked at the blood under her nails, trying to ignore Senna's pacing next to her.

"I found something!" he shouted. "Looks like an emergency stash."

Maia collapsed in relief, closing her eyes as Briar wrapped her in a bear hug.

"Fuck yeah," he said, laughing. "You did it, boss."

Maia bit back a smile and opened her eyes to find Senna watching them. A simple nod of approval was all Senna provided, and all Maia needed.

"These can't be real," Sky's voice called to them.

His footsteps started back up the ladder, and he rested the lantern on the edge of the hatch. Digging into his pocket, he removed a handful of coins. Gold twinkled in the orange glow of the flame.

"I thought Portico coins were only made of copper," Maia said, taking one from his hand to examine it. Her breath caught. She grabbed another to find the same amount stamped into it. "That can't be right."

"I've been paid in silver before, but those were only a thousand coin value," Sky said, his eyes locked on hers.

Senna snatched a coin from him and gasped.

"What is it?" Briar asked, eyes wide as he watched them.

"Ten… each of these are worth ten thousand coin," Senna said in a daze.

Briar froze, allowing the information to settle. "How many chests are down there?"

Sky's gaze didn't move from Maia's. "Three. And they're all full."

Briar jumped to his feet in excitement, nearly knocking over the lantern.

"You kept your promise," Sky said, the corner of his mouth twisting into a smile.

Maia's eyes fell to the coin in her hand.

If they could find them, maybe the other teams did too. She had to believe there was still a chance they would wake up tomorrow in a world where Portico no longer held all the power.

One where Maia and Hannah could find peace again. Even one ten-thousand-piece coin was enough to give Hannah and Maia everything they ever wanted.

She lifted her gaze back to Sky. "No more running."

His happiness bled into reservation. Did he know how to live without running?

"Are we getting these fuckin' chests or what?" Briar asked, lifting the lantern back to Sky.

He nodded, and they both continued down the hatch, retrieving what Maia hoped would change everything.

"Thank goodness," Rowan said when they arrived back at the safe house.

His tense shoulders collapsed in relief as Maia walked in. The dark circles under his eyes hinted it had been a while since he'd had a full night's sleep.

"I don't know what I would have done if something happened to—" He stopped as the rest of the team followed behind her.

Straightening himself, he carried on towards the parlor as if nothing had ever been said.

It was obvious what he chose to omit, which made her wonder why he said it at all. "What happened?"

Rowan took a long sip from his drink, ignoring Maia's question and joining Orion by the fireplace.

"I thought you all would be celebratin' by now," Briar shouted after him.

It had taken them longer than planned to return because of the weight and contents of the chests. They couldn't pass through towns or wards, having to take the long way through the trees.

Maia walked over to Orion, but he refused to meet her gaze. "Where's everyone else?"

"You're the only team that's made it back," Rowan said, slowly lowering himself onto the loveseat. "Our scouts have found only bodies, but there are still some missing. We assume taken at this point."

Briar dropped into the seat next to him while Senna hovered behind them, waiting.

"Garcia's team?" Maia could barely hide the tremble in her voice.

"Kayla and Jayce's bodies were found together at the coin cache. Edward's is still hanging in Chesapeake." Rowan took another sip from his drink. "Garcia is missing."

"Missing?"

Rowan rubbed at his hairline, struggling to suppress the emotions he was dulling with the drink. "Most likely captured."

Maia collapsed into the armchair across from Orion. Jayce would have done anything to protect his sister, and Kayla wouldn't have gone down without a fight. It wasn't fair that they didn't make it while she did.

"Lo que el monte nos dio," Maia whispered.

"El monte lo recogió," Rowan and Orion responded together.

Maia's guilt resurfaced as each moment she had spent with the siblings crashed down on her.

She should have said something. She could have saved them.

"It's not your fault, Maia."

She wiped the tears from her cheeks to find Orion watching her.

"You have the same look your father did the first time we failed a mission. Everyone knew the risks going into this, and they chose hope over fear."

"So, we've gained nothing," Senna said, gripping the back of the loveseat. "After everything we did, Portico has come out even stronger."

Orion's gaze dropped to the drink in his hands. "Yes."

Despite the siblings' sacrifice, nothing had changed. Maia removed the coin from her pocket, the weight of it suddenly overwhelming. Garcia's team never even made it into the coin cache if they found their bodies outside.

The blood spilled wasn't Portico's. It was rebel blood.

This wasn't what she promised Hannah. They could still get their house back and buy the shop together, but at any moment, Portico could take it all away again.

Orion returned his gaze to the fire. "We'll understand if you decide to walk away. It will take time for us to grow again... even longer before the rebellion gets another chance like—"

"How can you say that?" Maia's face flushed with anger as the words erupted from her.

Orion was the leader of the rebellion, not another scout. Their cause was even more important now. His grief and anger should have been motivation, but instead, he chose to cower in the safe house while Garcia and others were missing.

"Portico still stands," she said, her hand clenched tight around the coin, the metal pinching into her palm. "Which means we're not done."

Rowan sighed as if he had heard this too many times before. "That's not what he's—"

"Why do the rebels keep failing?" Maia snapped.

Her anger was for Kayla's and Jayce's meaningless deaths. For the life she was so close to having ripped out from under her again.

There had to be a reason for everything lost. Portico knew they would take the bait, which meant they understood the rebellion more than the rebellion understood Portico.

Rowan's face hardened, a darkness taking hold. "Why don't you tell me?"

"Because you keep allowin' Portico the advantage," Sky said, walking up beside her. "If it weren't for the Scavengers, we'd be hangin' right now too."

"Portico will *always* have the advantage!" Rowan shouted, slamming his glass on the table.

His hand trembled, and he rubbed it away, clearly hoping no one noticed. His anger was meant to hide his fear.

"Everyone has a weakness," Maia said, steady and sure. "Even Portico."

He dropped his head, rubbing his tired eyes. "You don't understand. Your father was there with me—with Orion. We know the atrocities Portico can commit with nothing more than a signature on a line. We have to play the long game."

A signature on a line.

The power one man wielded with nothing more than a pen. A power Aquila, the leader of Portico, stole.

Maia's eyes shot to Rowan's. "That signature was supposed to be yours."

Suspicion hung thick in the air, and Senna walked around the loveseat to look Rowan in the eye. "What does that mean?"

Betrayal flared in his gaze, but it couldn't outmatch the determination in Maia's.

"Can someone fuckin' say something?" Briar glanced between them, waiting impatiently for a response.

"Rowan's mother founded Portico," Maia said, glancing at the coin again. "He should have been the successor, but Aquila took it from him, offering him a place on the Council as consolation."

Questions exploded from the team all at once. Orion leaned forward in his chair to cut through the noise. "Why does Maia—"

"Even if Aquila gave me the position of Council Overseer as promised, I would still have his four trusted Council Advisors reporting to me. They'll be watching my every move, and if even one of them suspects my loyalty to Portico to be anything less than absolute, they wouldn't hesitate to hang me," Rowan said, as if he and Maia were the only two in the room.

She glanced at the others, now waiting for her response. "Then how do we get those advisor positions?"

"I'm in," Senna said, without hesitation.

Orion shot Rowan a venomous glare and stood to refill his glass.

"You asked how to gain the advantage," Maia said, jumping to her feet and tossing the coin at Rowan. It landed on the table, sliding to a stop at the edge. "*This* is it. You want to stop Portico? You'll have to destroy them from within."

Rowan picked up the coin, rubbing it between his fingers. No one spoke, waiting for his decision as the watch in Maia's pocket ticked with steady confidence.

"You have no idea how hard your father fought to escape Portico. If you decide to do this—and you survive—you won't be the same person you were walking in." Rowan's voice was quiet, his anger now a heavy sadness over something he hadn't even lost yet.

He placed the coin on the table, sliding it back to Maia.

"I choose hope over fear," she said, taking a step toward him. "You told me your mother believed that without order, there is no justice, and without justice, there is no hope. This is how we get our justice."

Briar leaned back on the loveseat, lifting his boot to his knee. "You know I'm with you, boss."

"Why would Aquila take you back now?" Orion asked, his eyes on Rowan. "You have nothing to offer him."

There was a seething hatred dripping from each of his words. Maia could almost see the damage Aquila had done to the two men. Something so ingrained in them that even the thought of being in his favor felt like betrayal.

"I think that's exactly what he wants," Rowan said in defeat. "If I return, then he knows the rebellion is over."

"It's surprisingly convenient how easy it is for you to switch sides for the cause." Orion threw back the contents of the glass and disappeared from the parlor.

Maia turned to find Sky rubbing his pendant between his fingers. "You can still head north. You've risked enough to get us this far."

His eyes searched hers. With a sigh, he tucked the pendant away. "Four Council Advisors means you still need me." He turned to Rowan. "Tell us everything you know."

PART II

ALL OF THIS OVER ONE MAN

12

GUARDED

She told him revenge is not a war against your enemy, but yourself. It's a shame we were too enraged to listen.

A. Wells – Winter 2279

Moth-eaten curtains danced against the open window as light from the moon sifted through like distant stars. Maia watched them chase each other across Hannah's peaceful face while she slept. So tranquil... for now.

The tick of her father's watch kept time with the lockpicks she nervously toyed in and out of her mother's comb. Breaking into Hannah's room at Folly's would be the easiest part of the evening.

She twirled her hair into a bun and fixed the comb in place, letting the wooden chair creak in the process. Hannah stirred at the sound, but her breathing remained slow and steady.

She had always been a heavy sleeper, something Maia used to envy. Now, she worried for her sister, being so trusting to allow herself to dream in a place like Folly's.

Maia unlatched the bag of coins from her belt, silently approaching the bed. Rowan had already made his way to Portico, but they spent the week prior to his departure reviewing mock compound layouts and detailed descriptions of the

Council Advisors. Tomorrow morning, Maia and her team would begin their journey to Portico to see if any of it mattered.

Her eyes fell to the bag in her hands. Ten thousand coin split into silver and copper pieces thanks to Senna's multiple contacts. If Hannah spent it right, no one would suspect a thing. Maia tested the weight of it in her hand, delaying the goodbye she had been dreading for weeks.

With a sigh, she dropped the coins on the nightstand with a metallic *thud*. Hannah's eyes shot open, and Maia slammed her hand over her mouth, muffling her scream. Her frantic gaze scanned the empty room, stopping on Maia with a glare.

"What is wrong with you?" Hannah mumbled, ripping Maia's hand away. "Are you trying to kill me?"

"No, but it wouldn't have been difficult if I was."

Her sister's gaze slipped into something lethal. "Is this what we're doing now? You show up to insult me every couple weeks and then leave again?"

This wasn't the impression she wanted to leave her sister with. Not today. It was her last chance to make amends for the hurt she had caused since their mother passed, and of all the things she could mess up, she refused to allow this to be one of them.

"I'm leaving, Hannah... for a while this time," Maia said, taking a seat on the bed.

Her sister's shoulders dropped in exasperation, and she rubbed her face awake. "Where are they sending you now?"

Maia chewed the raw skin on her lip. She had been so certain of what needed to be done, so angry for everything she had lost, but with Hannah sitting across from her, she realized how much she still had to lose.

"Portico."

Hannah's eyes grew wide. "No." One word was enough to steal the color from her sister's cheeks. Even her warmth had vanished as her icy hand found Maia's. "Tell them no."

"I can't. It was my idea."

Hannah didn't need to speak. The pain washing over her face as her hand grew limp in Maia's was enough.

"The heist didn't go as planned." Maia looked away, the burden of Hannah's terrified gaze crushing her. "Portico knew we were coming."

"That's not your fault."

"I told you I would—"

"I don't care about your ridiculous promise! Please, Maia..." Hannah's voice cracked with desperation. "I've lost everyone I care about... I can't lose you too. I can't."

It was the same desperation they had before their mother walked away. Maia thought the tear in her heart had healed, but the sharp pain felt fresh again. Closing her eyes, she could still see her mother's long, dark hair pulled into a tight bun and the rigidity of her back as she slid on her jacket, reaching for her healing bag.

Maia and Hannah had been crying, huddled together on the hard parlor couch, begging their mother not to go to the shantytown. She turned to them, face worn from the outbreak she had been working so hard to contain, and said, "It's my duty to do what I can to save their lives. If they die because I broke my oath, I would never forgive myself. Now please, don't wait up for me."

Maia slowly opened her eyes, lifting them to Hannah's. "We live a life of fear and powerlessness. I want to see hope in your eyes again."

Tears trailed down Hannah's smooth cheeks.

"Promise me you won't wait for me to come back." Maia's vision blurred, and she struggled to hide the tremble in her voice. "Promise me you'll take these coins and live the life we could only dream of until now. Find a man who will treat you right and marry him. Have beautiful children that you sing lullabies to each night. If you promise me that, then I can promise you I'll do everything I can to make sure you never have to worry that all of it could disappear again."

The true extent of her decision to leave for Portico settled as Maia realized she no longer saw herself in any of these moments. She refused to blink her tears free and attempted to swallow the lump forming in her throat, but both were as stubborn as she was. Maybe Orion was right to leave in search of the missing rebels. To hold on to the same barely-glowing ember of hope that had kept the rebellion alive even after her father died.

She glanced at Hannah out of the corner of her eye as her sister's tears stained the dirty sheet. No, it wasn't enough. If she was successful, these dreams wouldn't just be Hannah's—they would be everyone's again.

Maia reached for the bag of coins on the nightstand, placing it in Hannah's hands. "This is enough for you to never worry about coin again. You can get our home back and start your own apothecary. You could even buy Mr. Thomas' if you wanted."

"But I *don't* want this. I want you to stay." Hannah threw her arms around Maia, sobbing into her shoulder. "Please don't make me say goodbye."

"This might be our only chance." Maia tightened her arms around her sister, breathing in the warm scent of vanilla on her skin. It was something she could hold on to, and she wondered what memory Hannah would have of her. "I love you, Hannah. More than you'll ever know."

Choking on her tears, Hannah's nails painfully dug into Maia's back. The guilt sank deep, past the tingling of Maia's skin and the tension in her muscles, before resting in an ache that seemed to be everywhere and nowhere.

She wanted to carry all the burden she had caused, but fear took hold. One that made Maia question if she was strong enough to bear it. A reminder of the deeper fear within—that she wasn't enough.

She pulled away, knowing if she held on any longer, she would lose whatever courage she had trapped between the guilt and fear. Wiping away her tears, Maia stood from the bed, crossing to the open window and lifting one leg over the sill.

"Goodbye, Maia."

She glanced back at Hannah, but all she saw was her sister's washed-out curls against her quivering back. The evening had gone exactly as expected, but no preparation could lessen the heartbreak.

Maia had often wondered what it felt like in those last few moments of the Old World. The moment the final bunker door slammed shut while many remained outside. Those who walked hand in hand down abandoned roads or lay side by side whispering broken promises. Everything left undone. So much time wasted on things that didn't matter as the nuclear flash consumed the horizon.

Regret.

She now understood.

Sucking in a shaky breath, Maia closed her eyes. She was doing the right thing, no matter how much it hurt. If she accomplished the impossible, Hannah could live her life without worrying when the flash on the horizon would find her next. Maia climbed out the window, grateful for the bitter, numbing cold of the night.

Since walking away from Hannah, Maia couldn't seem to shake the melancholy weighing on her, like the heaviness just before sleep. The worn route leading northwest flourished with traveling merchants, couriers, and guards in marching formation, many unwitting victims of Sky's casual pickpocketing. Portico's endless iron fence stretched for miles, but directly ahead of Maia and her team stood its towering wooden gates, an iron, scrolled *P* arched over them. It was exactly as Rowan had described...

Twice a year, Portico opens its doors to potential recruits. The gathering grounds will be packed with merchants by invite-only, but within the crowd are Portico's scouts, listening and watching. Make your entrance count, or you'll have to wait until spring for another chance.

Two guards stood at attention, the brims of their hats hooding their eyes. Alone they seemed harmless, but as Maia stepped closer, sunlight exposed the glint of a gun barrel in the watchtower. Senna ran a pointed nail across a guard's cheek, giving him a wink and continuing through the gates. As if on cue, the bell tower chimed, making the guard flinch. His throat bobbed while he forced his eyes to remain on the road ahead.

The bell tower rings for three reasons: to mark the hour, to warn of attack, or to mourn a fallen leader. Once inside, you'll arrive at the Fountain of Rebirth. It's tradition for new recruits to drink from it, just as those that rose from the bunkers did when they first arrived at Portico. To the left of the fountain, you'll find a hedge maze leading to the library, training grounds, and barracks. To the right is the Diplomat Hall and ancillary staff housing.

The team continued along the white pebble walkway circling the fountain, and into the flurry of the gathering grounds ahead. Merchant booths and recruiting tables speckled the rolling hills of sharp green. Behind them stood a blinding white building with towering columns emulating Old World Roman temples. The smell of fresh-baked rolls wafted from several of the cramped stands with anxious vendors shouting praise for their products, easily luring Briar into the crowd.

Sky and Senna followed him, while Maia searched the area for the Advisors.

"Are you coming?" Senna asked, glancing back at her.

"Senna Young?"

A woman dressed in a black leather-ribbed cloak seemed to materialize next to Maia, anonymous under her hood. She took a step forward, her leather slip-on shoes silent even on the pebbles. "I need you to come with me."

Senna's red lips curled into a wry smile. "On whose orders?"

The woman lowered her hood, freeing her sleek black hair around her pale, freckled face. Death herself making their acquaintance. Maia took a shaky step back, knees suddenly weak.

Tala Cinth is the most senior council member, and someone your father and I had once called a friend. That is, until she chose Portico over the rebellion. As the Intelligence Advisor, she controls Portico's scouts and has eyes and ears everywhere. Her guile is only rivaled by her ruthlessness. She'll do whatever it takes to survive, and is the reason your father is no longer with us.

This was the woman who killed not only Maia's father, but also Hannah's parents. She stood in front of Maia, as if no different than anyone else within Portico's iron fence. Maybe she wasn't.

"*My* orders." Tala locked her hostile obsidian eyes on Senna. "I assumed that's what you wanted, what with all your contacts rushing to put in a good word for you."

Senna stepped forward, towering over Tala. "I assure you it's all true."

A dangerous smile crossed Tala's lips. Maia could imagine the same look on her face as she hid in the shadows, watching, waiting, listening for the right moment. Did Tala feel anything when the spark of life slowly faded from her father's eyes? Maia's nails pinched against her palm, breaking the delicate skin.

"I'll be the judge of that. Follow me." Tala turned to leave, but her eyes caught on Maia. "Have we met? You look familiar."

Maia's whole body trembled as a scream caught in her throat. Tala would know who she was before this was over, but for now, Maia wanted her to feel the looming dread of uncertainty.

"No. You must be thinking of someone else."

Tala's eyes narrowed, the sharp black lines around them now pointed like daggers. Her gaze was meant to cut into Maia in an attempt to bleed out the truth.

"Are we going?" Senna asked, stepping between them.

Tala turned her glare on Senna and lifted her hood, starting towards the maze.

"You've got this," Senna whispered, giving Maia's hand a quick squeeze before moving to join Tala.

She waited, watching them disappear past the rose trellis leading into the garden maze. All the tension of the moment escaped Maia in a slow breath. The deep-red flowers on the trellis were still in bloom, denying the chill that would soon overtake them. Maia needed their resilience if she was going to survive this.

She forced her shoulders to relax, turning back to the courtyard and catching Briar leaning into a curvy brunette in guard attire. Whatever document Portico required for him to sign over his life, she seemed more than willing to read to him.

Behind them stood a woman with short, platinum-blonde hair. Her heavily decorated guard uniform stood out from the rest, Portico's emblem stamped into her polished metal shoulder plate. Her angular jaw tensed as her cat-like eyes darted over the grounds, watching everything and everyone. The only softness to her face was her delicate nose, but even that had a glistening piercing through it.

General Nova Winter is the Security Advisor. She oversees the guards' training, coordinates weapons acquisitions, and manages growth strategy and security tactics. Despite the hundreds of guards rotating in and out of Portico, it takes only one sharp whistle from her lips to bring them all to attention. She's a force to be reckoned with, and has become quite influential with Aquila.

Maia jumped as a hand found her elbow, pulling her into the crowd. Rowan looked different in his red velvet coat with filigree buttons fastened to the collar. His steps were heavy, demanding authority as he dragged her along.

"Change in plans," he whispered, handing her a bag.

"What does that mean?"

"I promised your father I'd keep you safe." He nodded to a towering man in a suit vest and long coat, an unruly mess of waves sticking out from under his newsboy cap. He was easily as tall as Briar, with leaner shoulders and a narrower waist. The man lifted his strong chin in response and continued walking with Sky back towards the entrance. "This is the only way I can do that."

Maia's stomach plummeted. Was he sending her home? She lifted the flap of the bag, removing a gold name badge with the healer symbol of a sapling and *Maia Sagitta* etched into it.

You won't be able to take your father's name with you to Portico. Our names trap us in versions of ourselves that others have created. When I return to Portico, I'll be Andrew Wells again, but for you, this is your chance to become someone new. Someone capable of accomplishing things your father could only imagine.

"Not this," she whispered in disbelief. She would have rather gone home or taken any position in Portico but this one. "Don't pretend you don't know what I did... my mistake with my apprenticeship."

"It's just a research assistant position, but it *can* be a second chance as well." He scanned the crowd. "We have eyes."

Maia followed his gaze, noting the guards surrounding them. They all appeared to be having their own conversations, but she still sensed the eyes Rowan referred to, hidden somewhere in the crowd.

He continued past her, folding his hands behind his back and nodding casually at those he passed. Maia opened the bag again, hoping for something more, but all it contained were overalls and a long-sleeve shirt two sizes too big.

"What's that?" Briar asked, glancing over her shoulder.

"My ticket into Portico, apparently." She tucked the bag under her arm. "I saw you made a new friend."

"I don't think she's lookin' for a friend, boss." He winked, draping his arm across her shoulders and guiding her back towards the entrance. "You think Sky ever gets tired of being someone else?"

Sky had stopped next to the fountain, laughing at something the man in the suit vest said. It wasn't until another man in a black and gold embroidered diplomat jacket walked up, standing tall and statuesque next to them, that Maia realized who they were.

The last two Council Advisors are the twins—Aster and Rafe Calderone. Rafe is the Trade and Collections Advisor. His collectors close out debts, enforce trade agreements, and—while no one will admit it—now manage the dirty work of posting bounties. His loyalty to Portico is absolute, and he doesn't shy away from getting the tough jobs done. If you want to get his attention, you need to show you're just as capable.

The twins shared the same light brown skin and russet eyes. Aster, however, put a more deliberate effort into his appearance, with his short, black hair swept up and his facial hair neatly groomed. They were both handsome in their own way, one polished and poised while the other embodied reckless abandon. Maia and Briar stopped on the other side of the fountain, close enough to eavesdrop, and Briar removed a smoke from his pocket.

"He says he's the one who finally closed The Marksman's bounty." The favor in Rafe's voice left no question that Sky had proven himself.

"Is that so?" Aster inquired, and Maia couldn't help but appreciate his suspicion. "I have to say the resemblance is uncanny."

The matter-of-fact comment was enough to make Rafe look at Sky with fresh eyes.

A short, nervous laugh escaped Sky. "You know, the mayor of Williamsburg said the same thing." He put out his hand with confidence, but Maia could sense his growing unease. "The name is Skylar Matthews."

His outstretched hand remained empty as Aster's strong brows drew together. "Any relation to Lilian Matthews?"

The color drained from Sky's face, and his hand dropped to his side. Even from where she stood, Maia tensed at Sky's sudden panic.

"How do you...?" A slight fissure slowly spread through the persona he had created.

"No fucking way," Rafe said, jaw slack in disbelief.

"Ms. Lilian was a friend of our father's. The best trader in the Coastal Region, and the only person he ever trusted to do Portico's dealings there." Aster tilted his head as if it would help him see the resemblance. "He said she had a son about our age."

Sky's chest swelled in response, and it looked to be the only thing keeping him whole. "She... she was my mother."

"Fuck," Briar whispered. "We should go."

Maia couldn't, though. Her eyes dropped to Sky's limp, lifeless hand, drained of whatever lies had kept him going up to now. She wanted to reach out—to tell him she understood his loss and the grief that still consumed her on the nights she allowed her mind to wander, and the mornings that felt a little less bright than they once did.

Aster gave Sky a sympathetic smile. "I'm sorry. Our father was devastated when he found out what happened to her. He often wondered what became of you."

There was a moment of heavy silence between the men, but only Rafe seemed to be uncomfortable in it, the other two lost in their thoughts.

"And here you are," Rafe said, giving Sky a rough pat on the back.

Sky cleared his throat, shifting on his feet and returning to the person who had tucked her memory away. "Funny how things come full circle."

Rafe put out his hand. "We're glad to have you."

Sky shook it and muttered a thank you—still trapped somewhere between his two lives. He turned, catching Maia's gaze before walking the other way.

"Come on, let's find some food," Briar said, flicking his smoke into the revered fountain and removing the bag from under her arm.

Maia tucked her hands into her coat, allowing one more glance over her shoulder. Sky was gone, and Rafe was now harassing a guard walking by, but Aster's focus was on her.

His features darkened, and the curiosity etched between his thick brows made her wonder if he realized she was eavesdropping. Heat found her cheeks, and she told herself it was from getting caught, ignoring the sudden hitch in her breath.

Aster will be the most problematic. As Diplomatic Advisor, he's a master of lies and manipulation. Don't be fooled by his carefully crafted words and tread cautiously if he takes an interest in you. There's a motive behind everything he does, and if anyone will see through our plan, it's him. Because of this, Aquila relies on his judgment above all else. If you want to survive this, keep your distance from him.

The moment she caught him watching, he swerved his gaze away, suddenly invested in the tongue-lashing Rafe was giving the guard. She wasn't imagining the tension now cutting his jaw, and the way it twisted her stomach made her certain Rowan was right. Aster *would* be the most problematic of the Advisors.

Rowan and the four Council Advisors stood on the steps of the imposing white building known as Council Hall as the soft, orange glow of the lanterns lit up the space between the columns. Drums rolled violently as a frail man shuffled out of the building. He lifted his hands to the crowd, his long, crimson cape pulling at him in the gentle evening breeze. Not even the flames could give life to his pale, sickly appearance.

Few men were granted the luxury of life beyond sixty in this unforgiving world, and Maia wondered what he had sacrificed to evade death.

Metal chest and shoulder plates clanked as the guards clasped their hands behind their backs, all standing straight as arrows, bringing an end to the drums. Rowan remained still in subtle defiance—an action Maia couldn't help but appreciate. The old man dropped his hands, followed by the metallic clang of the guards releasing their stance.

"I am Aquila," he announced, his voice shaky and breathless, barely carrying over the crowd. "You have been chosen to join our ranks. Your oath is not just to us, but to yourselves, to bring honor to Portico by serving and protecting our people with the dignity and respect they deserve."

There was pride in the eyes of those surrounding her. Convinced they were special by nothing more than a theatrical performance. Oblivious to their insignificance as they handed over their lives.

Briar released a cloud of smoke into the air and scratched at the stubble along his jawline, while Senna and Sky whispered beside him, unphased by the deceitful speech.

"It is a privilege to wear our emblem. A symbol of pride and honor. Do not take this responsibility lightly." His wet voice sent him into a coughing fit, and he covered his mouth with a cloth tucked in his skeletal hand. "It is my sincerest pleasure to welcome you to Portico."

The crowd cheered, and Briar celebrated by lifting his middle fingers in response, his smoke resting between his lips. The personification of Maia's dangerous thoughts.

13

POSSIBILITY

The sun was barely peeking over the horizon as Maia strolled across the dew-covered gathering grounds. It had rained most of the night, the ceiling of the ancillary housing dripping onto her small cot and keeping her up. In the distance, the bell tower chimed the hour, reminding her how disgustingly early it was. She rolled up the sleeves of her oversized uniform, continuing along the pebble walkway that carved through the muted green hills toward the Agriculture and Research Building.

Harvesters were already tending to the rows of vegetable gardens and fruit trees spanning far beyond what Maia could see. Across from the gardens lay acres of open fields where horses and cattle roamed. An older woman leaned over the railing of a pen, throwing feed to the chickens while humming a nursery rhyme. The peacefulness of the morning surprised Maia after all the excitement from yesterday.

She reported in for her shift, receiving a basket and a list of herbs requested by the researchers. It was easy to pass the time wandering the forest in silence, providing a courteous wave or head nod to the other assistants walking by.

For lunch, they gathered together by the animal pens, eating meat pies lifted by the kitchen staff and fruits the harvesters had pocketed. She joined in the shared laughter of stories and sympathized with those already homesick.

Each day was like the last. Calm, quiet, tranquil even. The opposite of everything she expected, and she hated herself for enjoying it.

The late afternoon sun beat down on her neck as Maia cut a piece of her apple, tossing it to the goats. They bleated in appreciation, luring a giggle from her. Her shift had ended an hour ago, but instead of joining the others at the dodgy Game Hall on Canal Row, she decided to stay out of trouble and enjoy the grounds before the first winter snow arrived.

The sound of boots crunching on gravel straightened her back, and she turned to find Senna, Sky, and Rafe approaching. Senna looked sinister dressed head-to-toe in the black scout uniform, while Sky walked purposefully in the collector's suit and newsboy cap. They were here for business, and that alone stole the heat from the sun.

Rafe took a step forward, towering over Maia and forcing her to look up at him. "Senna has recommended you for a task. We need to obtain critical information from one of our contacts, and she says you have knowledge in both healing *and* extracting information from others. Interesting you chose a research assistant position over a scout."

"Is it?"

It took everything in her to keep from glaring at Senna. Whatever required both of those skills wasn't something she was interested in.

Rafe's face shifted from authoritative to annoyed. "Well, is it fucking true or not?"

She fought the urge to punch him square in the jaw, instead plastering a smile on her face. "It is."

He tilted his head as if expecting a different response but continued. "Our contact, Mr. Charles Foster, is a biochemist from Rocky Mount." Rafe scowled as Maia cut a piece of apple, tossing it to the goats. "There are rumors he and his partner were on the verge of a healing breakthrough before his partner passed. We want to know what it is."

He snapped his fingers for Sky and Senna to approach. There was a moment of hesitation before they stepped forward.

"They just returned from Rocky Mount and can provide further information."

Just a couple weeks in Portico and Senna and Sky were already responding to snaps.

"I suppose I'll begin," Senna said, the tightness in her voice revealing the irritation she was forced to hide from her face. "I attempted to break into Mr. Foster's Apothecary overnight, but he's currently living there. His house outside of town had nothing more than furniture and a thick layer of dust."

Senna removed a piece of paper from the pocket of her cloak, handing it to Maia. On it was a map of the town with two X's, one marking the apothecary and the other his home.

"According to the locals, his husband recently passed from somethin' sudden. Seemed to take them all by surprise," Sky said. "They say he's become a bit of a hermit since his loss, which explains why he ain't rushing to go home."

"What exactly am I looking for?" Maia asked, tucking the map into the pocket of her overalls.

Senna and Sky exchanged a look.

"They don't know," Rafe said, lip curling with contempt.

"What we *do* know," Sky retorted. "Is that his husband traveled for months on end—"

Rafe rolled his eyes. "Which means shit if we don't know where he went or why."

"Which is why we need you," Senna said, her focus only on Maia.

She understood now. The goal was to gain Mr. Foster's trust in hopes he would reveal his secret research so she could steal it. She turned to Rafe, who was awaiting her response. "Why not just force him to tell you what it is?"

He pushed back his jacket, tucking his hands into his pockets. "If it's what we think it is, the concern is that he'll destroy it before handing it over."

"And what is it you *think* it is?" Maia asked, realizing he knew more than he was letting on.

Rafe scoffed, as if simultaneously impressed and offended by her questioning. "That's not your concern."

"Feels like it is."

He forced a smile, rubbing his brow with the back of his thumbnail. "It isn't. All you need to do is find what he's hiding."

The fact he wasn't willing to tell her now made her interested. "What's the plan?"

Senna bit back a smile, as if reading Maia's thoughts. "Mr. Foster requires a new assistant."

"That's convenient." Maia cut another piece free from her apple and tossed it to the goats.

Rafe's eye twitched with annoyance. "You can thank Skylar for that."

She was almost certain she wouldn't. "And what happens once I find what you're looking for?"

"Aren't you a cocky fuck?" Before she could cut another piece, Rafe ripped the apple from her hand and tossed it over his shoulder. "Pack a bag. You leave for Rocky Mount in the morning."

Maia's long, black locks danced in the breeze as the sign for *Foster's Apothecary* creaked above her. Her hands gripped the wooden handle of her travel bag while the soft fabric of her emerald dress swept across her shins. Senna had been particular about every detail of Maia's outfit. Her loose waves embodied innocence while the lapel collar of the dress provided the sophistication needed to impress a man like Mr. Foster.

Think of it as a costume. You'll play the part of someone he should trust.

A perfectly curated lie for Mr. Foster... and herself.

With a steadying breath, Maia urged open the door to the shop. Inside was an unruly mess of wooden shelves overflowing with bottles of various herbs and tonics. Healers had expectations beyond temperament and intelligence, and among those were cleanliness and order. This was neither.

She veered carefully around the crowded displays and woven baskets of freshly pulled flora, making her way to the counter. A scale made of tarnished copper overtook the space, its coin weights scattered amongst the used mortars and pestles. Only the scent of lavender wafting from a nearby bottle provided any semblance of calm. Maia leaned over it, hoping to ease her nerves.

"Who is it?" a man yelled from the back of the shop.

Maia shot up straight, knocking her bag against the counter with a *thud*. "Um...hello? I was informed you might have an open position?"

Her question was followed by silence. She lifted herself to her toes, peering at the sliver of space between the drab curtain and door frame. With a snap, the heavy cloth revealed a short, rotund man with white hair and a handlebar mustache.

"And who are you?"

"My name is Maia, sir." She stepped forward as if proximity would ease his suspicion. "I've been told you might be looking for a new assistant?"

"How serendipitous," he said, twisting the end of his mustache with a pudgy hand.

It was true, which didn't help her with a response. She snuck a glance over her shoulder towards the door. "If you aren't looking for help, then I apologize for bothering you."

He turned, his girth still taking up most of the doorway. "Please follow me."

Trepidation sank like a stone into the pit of her stomach, but she rushed after him. Old equipment and cluttered workbenches lined the narrow hallway. A small exam room appeared lived in, with clothes draped over the guest chair and an open razor sitting beside the washbasin. Maia noted a dimly lit doorway at the other end of the hall as she followed Mr. Foster into an office.

Floor-to-ceiling bookshelves lined the office walls. Every inch was filled with an assortment of worn books, dusty boxes, and dingy glass bottles. Shoved in a corner sat a secondary desk, burdened with an old coin register and human bones—which was not unusual for a healer's office, but slightly ominous with the recent passing of his husband.

He motioned to a seat across from his surprisingly organized desk.

"My name is Charles Foster, but I believe you already know that." His smile was unnervingly discerning as she sank into the stained, cracked-leather chair. "Humor me, will you?"

Everything about his demeanor reminded Maia of Mr. Thomas. The same calm and poise. An air of superiority that came from years of practice.

"I don't consider myself particularly humorous, but I'll do my best."

Mr. Foster's smile stretched, and she was grateful he also held the same appreciation as Mr. Thomas for her smartass responses.

"The most fulfilling part of a healer's job is solving the mystery, correct? We take the facts laid out before us and ask the right questions in search of an answer. So, tell me, if you had a patient with a vague symptom of vomiting, what questions would you ask?"

And just like that, the dread of being placed on the spot during her apprenticeship returned. She pried her thoughts away from the sudden twist of her stomach. Instead, focusing only on his words. The reasons were limitless, but she needed to keep it simple.

"What did you eat last night?"

Mr. Foster's pudgy hand found his chin in an overly dramatic gesture. "You know, I can't remember."

Her stomach coiled further. The only thing worse than being placed on the spot was role-playing. "And why can't you remember?"

He crossed his arms, apparently unimpressed with her lack of enthusiasm. "Well, I was out celebrating and—"

"Was alcohol involved?"

Interruptions could now be added to her rapidly growing list of shortcomings. "*No*, my dear, I don't drink in mixed company."

"Alright, then what were you celebrating?"

"A new species of plant I discovered."

Maia straightened in her chair—interest now piqued. "What kind of plant?"

"It appears to be in the same class as privet."

Privet, a poisonous plant with a common side effect of upset stomach if ingested.

A thrill rushed through her veins, and she confidently lifted her chin. "Did you wash your hands after handling?"

His lips pressed together, but he couldn't suppress his smirk. "So, there is some truth to you. Or at least some healing knowledge and an inflated ego, which brings me back to my original hesitation. What brings you *specifically* through my door?"

He lifted a ringed finger to his cheek, waiting to dissect every one of her words. She was his mystery, and he was eager to unravel any loose thread she was careless enough to expose. There was only one way to pass his test, and her cheeks flushed at the realization.

"The truth—" Her throat grew dry, and she forced herself to swallow. "The truth is, I was dismissed from my healing apprenticeship in Williamsburg for a mistake that nearly cost a man his life. Since then, I've lost everything. How your assistant position became available is none of my concern, but I promise you my passion for healing remains. That said, I understand if you prefer I leave."

Mr. Foster's face remained expressionless as Maia nervously waited, a bead of sweat running down her hairline that she refused to acknowledge. Mr. Thomas' words slipped out of their dark corner, reminding Maia why she was here in Rocky Mount.

Healing was your mother's purpose... not yours. I'm sorry, Maia, but this is where we part ways.

She braced her heart, waiting for it to be ripped out all over again.

Mr. Foster's eyes narrowed as if reading her thoughts, and he pursed his lips. "The job doesn't pay much."

Maia sat stunned, wondering if she heard him correctly. "I... I wouldn't expect much after what I just told you, sir."

"The hours are long, and I won't provide lodging or food."

"I've been able to manage so far, sir."

His gaze fell to her white-knuckled grip on her travel bag. "When can you start?"

A wave of gratitude washed over her, and she nearly fell from her seat. "Now, sir."

"The pay is two coin per day. I won't go easy on you. Prove to me you deserve this second chance."

A second chance, just as Rowan said. From a stranger. Something Mr. Thomas, a man she had known her entire life, had refused. She pushed down the sudden desire to tell Hannah, and grief pinched her chest as she realized her mother would never know.

"Understood," she said, jumping to her feet. She thrust her hand towards him, even though all she wanted was to hug his thick shoulders. "Thank you, sir."

Ignoring her hand, he started towards the front of the shop. "Grab something to write with and follow me." He stopped in the doorway. "And leave the bag, my dear."

Tossing the travel bag on the chair, she snatched a pad and pen from his desk, rushing after him.

14

SURVIVAL

Why does loss provide a stronger bond than love?

A. Wells - Spring 2294

Mr. Foster kept his word, pushing Maia day after day to think beyond what was already known, and search for what had yet to be discovered. It was exhilarating to stretch her mind again, experimenting with new compounds for tonics. A reminder of how young their world still was with innovation.

Every day, she left his office feeling full, and only when laying in the tavern bed—the laughter of townsfolk dancing below to the string band playing each night—did she allow reality to take hold. She was here to deceive him, taking even more than what he already willingly offered.

"Where would you like these?" she asked, a basket of herbs balanced on her hip.

Mr. Foster sat at his desk, lost in the study of a specimen plated under his microscope.

"Any spot is fine, my dear."

"Well, since your desk seems to be the only spot not already occupied with odds and ends, would you like me to put it there?"

His mouth cracked into a smile, but his gaze remained fixed on the eyepiece. "If you'd like to organize the shop, there are easier ways to ask. You can use the storage space in the back for now."

"Thank you, sir."

Maia spun on her heels with subtle celebration, exiting his office. She was already imagining how she wanted the shopfront to look. Maybe he would even provide some extra coin to purchase string and resin from the market.

Wandering down the narrow hall, Maia grazed her finger along the dust-covered workbenches. Broken bottles and excess utensils littered the tabletops. A green shard of glass caught her eye, and she lifted it to the light of a filthy window.

Her lips tugged up at the corner, imagining it now part of a beautiful mosaic dish to display their tonic creations. Closing her fingers around the piece of glass, she tucked it into her pocket, excited to tell him about it later.

She reached for the closet door, jiggling the knob to find it locked. With a sigh, she lowered the basket onto a bench, removing her hair comb lockpick out of habit. The glint of a brass key hanging next to the door caught her eye.

Why was her initial thought to break in? Her fingers suddenly felt tainted by the lockpick. Or maybe it was the other way around. Yanking the key off the hook, she unlocked the door.

Inside the closet, shelves burst with unlabeled bottles in crates. She stepped forward, hopeful for an empty container. Instead, her toe caught on a box, and she nearly took down an entire shelf. Cursing under her breath, she tried to steady herself, knowing Briar would have something to say about her clumsiness.

The lid of the box had shifted, exposing stacks of Old World books and loose papers. She bent to close it, when a familiar drawing violently yanked her back to reality.

Portico sent her for a reason, and she had found it.

"I'm famished. Would you—"

Maia jumped at Mr. Foster's voice behind her, hitting her shoulder on the bottom of the shelf. "I'm sorry. I was trying to find a place for the ingredients and tripped over this box."

"That doesn't explain why you proceeded to read the papers within." His words laced with accusation, making her flush in response.

"I didn't know."

He lifted a bushy brow. "But now you do?"

Her eyes dropped to the drawing again. Identical to the one in W. Wells' journal, documenting his experimentation with bio-weapons. "This is an Old World disease. An attempt at using it for... something."

"Not Old World, but similar, and it was merely an attempt at the impossible," Mr. Foster said, turning back to his office. "A cure for red lung."

Healing is magnificent in that it can cure as easily as it kills. It was something her mentor, Mr. Thomas, taught her long before her mistake. Her mind worked over the word *cure.*

She could still see her mother gasping for air, her lips stained with blood too bright for her pale face. The desperation in her eyes for it all to be over, and Maia couldn't help but allow the dangerous thought of, *what if?*

She took a seat in the worn leather chair. "What did you discover?"

Mr. Foster closed his eyes, sucking in a shaky breath. An action that looked practiced. "Death. As did everyone else my husband tested his so-called cure on."

The pain he forced himself to contain mirrored hers. She had numbed it with liquor—muted it with noise from the crowded taverns or her restless thoughts—but it was always there, barely restrained under the surface.

"I'm sorry, sir," she whispered. "My mother died from red lung too."

His eyes found hers, searching in silence, either for words of comfort or understanding. Neither of which she wanted. Maia dropped her gaze to her tightly wrung hands.

"She was a healer. And most likely the reason for my unhealthy relationship with curiosity." Mr. Foster snorted, drawing a small smile across Maia's lips. It had been too long since she smiled while talking about her mother. "I knew what red lung did to the body, but it didn't make it any easier to watch."

Her voice broke as memories rushed back. The rasp of her mother's forced breath. The blood stains on her once white nightgown. The smell of stale sickness that lingered in her bedroom for weeks after she passed, despite the days Maia spent scrubbing the mattress and walls.

"I did what I could, but there comes a point where the only mercy left is death."

Maia paused, watching a small bloom of blood form on the edge of her nail where she had picked it raw. Old wounds opened all over again. And while she couldn't see it, the sting of her eyes told her the tear in her heart had done the same.

She braved a glance at the broken man before her, and Mr. Foster quickly wiped tears from his cheeks.

"My poor child, there's nothing you could have done. In all my years as a healer, I've never witnessed such a gruesome death."

"I know." She did, but it didn't stop the endless wondering.

What if she had been the one to answer the door the night they came asking for her mother's help?

Found the right words to convince her mother not to go?

Had the cure?

"Why would your husband risk everything if he didn't believe in even the slightest possibility of a cure?"

Mr. Foster's sadness deepened as he sank into his chair. "Peter did believe in it. We just don't have the technology needed to achieve the same healing advancements as the Old World. We remain decades away from even the most elementary Old World healing."

She could still see the drawings in her mind, both the hopeful cure and the deadly weapon. "All that knowledge right in front of us, but still out of reach."

"As if by design." With a sigh, Mr. Foster leaned over to open a drawer, removing a dusty bottle of wine. "Peter and I were saving it for a special occasion, but..."

Old World wine was nearly impossible to come by, but its rarity was nothing compared to the sudden change in Mr. Foster's gaze.

Their shared tragedy had transformed her from an apprentice to an equal. She should have thanked him for his kindness and tucked it away, but the warmth of it tempered the cold she hadn't been able to shake for months.

"But now we honor him," she said with a gentle smile.

His nod was pained again, but his eyes held a different sadness. He poured two glasses into clean tonic bottles, lifting his for a toast. "To those we've lost, and those newly found."

She tapped her blood-colored drink against his. The bitter and sweet hit simultaneously, and her face twisted in surprise. She rolled it over her tongue, savoring the black cherry and woodsy flavors. It tasted like death. The bitterness of loss and sweetness of peace. Beautifully melancholy.

Mr. Foster's cheeks immediately flushed from the drink, and his eyes glazed over in thought.

"Why didn't you continue Peter's research?" Maia asked, wondering if that's where his thoughts had gone.

He took another sip before meeting her gaze. "Because I never believed in it. Or rather, I didn't *agree* with it."

"What do you mean?"

"I didn't agree with the way he was going about his research. He used Scavengers as test subjects, believing them to be dispensable creatures. Something less than human, while in actuality, they're just different." Mr. Foster swirled the drink in his glass, examining it. "Either way, it would have never worked on them."

"Why not?"

"Scavengers are the descendants of those who left the bunkers first. Their bodies were exposed to the radiation when it was still too much, creating sores and burns all over their skin."

She thought back to the coin heist, their bodies covered head-to-toe in cloth. It wasn't for intimidation. It was to hide their disfigurements. "Why wouldn't they just go back?"

"They tried, but the people inside were too scared to allow them in. Scared they'd bring in a disease that would kill them all."

"So, they left them to die?"

"Sacrifice is the key to survival," Mr. Foster said with a sigh. "It was something Peter used to say."

"Which is why he tried the cure on himself." Even if she'd never met him, she was beginning to understand who Peter was. "But how did he do it?"

"The Old World called it an inoculation. A way to build immunity through controlled exposure of the disease by introducing infected blood serum through cuts to the skin. You would then place the subject in close quarters with the infected to determine if it worked." Mr. Foster's face twisted with guilt. "He refused to test it on me, despite the countless times I offered. Our rudimentary technology made it impossible to truly replicate the Old World process. Most didn't survive the inoculation... including him."

Mr. Foster sat healthy and flushed in his chair. Would it have worked differently on him? She thought back to the time spent curled up next to her mother as she wilted away in her arms.

"Why them and not us?"

Mr. Foster raised a bushy brow.

"Did you care for Peter while he was dying?"

"Yes."

"I cared for my mother as well," she said, feeling the rush of hope take hold. "So, how are we still alive?"

Mr. Foster slowly lowered his wine glass, his eyes wide in realization. "Now *that* is the right question, my dear."

They spent the rest of the evening poring over Peter's paperwork and finishing the rest of the wine. It wasn't until their eyes hung too heavy to read that they finally called it for the evening.

Maia pushed open the door to the tavern, the noise hitting her like a wave. Her toes caught every other step as she climbed the stairs to her rented room, fumbling with her key. The lock finally clicked, and she stumbled inside, surprised to find Sky sitting by the window. His boot rested on his knee with a book she borrowed from Mr. Foster sprawled open in his lap.

Of all the nights for him to show up...

She straightened her back, lifting the key to the door hook. It hit the floor with a deafening *thud*. Ignoring it felt like the only way to salvage her dignity as she maintained his gaze.

"Good evenin', Maia," he said, steel eyes creasing at the corners in amusement.

"How did you..."

Of course he would know where she was. It wouldn't even surprise her if he had convinced someone downstairs to just let him in.

"Did Portico send you to check on me?"

Maia gripped the dresser for balance, attempting to slip off her boots. Apparently, she had taken extra care lacing them that morning.

She plopped down on the edge of the bed and bent over, immediately regretting the movement as the room spun, sending her stomach into her throat.

"They did."

Sky snapped the book shut, walking around the bed to stand in front of her. He looked different. The polished vest of his collector's uniform contrasted his rolled-up sleeves in a way that transformed his sharp edges into something more refined. He lowered himself to his knees, tracing his icy fingers up the back of her leg as he unlaced her boots.

"They wanted to see if you found what we're lookin' for."

Her stomach barely returned to its rightful place before launching back to her throat. Mr. Foster trusted her. Looked beyond her mistake and saw something Mr. Thomas either didn't, or chose to ignore. The truth meant she would take the only thing he had left of his late husband, but a lie left her open to retaliation from Portico.

Knowing that didn't change what she knew deep down was the only right answer.

"No," she said, choking on the consequences of the single word.

Sky looked up at her from under his newsboy cap. "You sure?"

He was offering her a chance to change her mind. She wasn't just putting herself on the line. Saying *yes* put Sky in danger too, which meant she had to choose. Protect him or Mr. Foster. The alcohol made everything feel slower, heavier. She wasn't in the right mindset to make that decision.

"I just need more time."

His face flickered with disappointment as he lifted himself to leave. Conflicting emotions churned her stomach as he reached for his jacket. Embarrassment for being in this state. Guilt for disappointing him. Desperation to make things right.

"I forgot," she blurted.

He paused in the doorway. "'bout what?"

"I forgot what before was like. The memories of my mother were fading, but being here, with Mr. Foster... I can see her clearer than I have in months. Her smile. Her laugh. The smell of her hair when she'd lean over to kiss me goodnight. All the things I'd forgotten."

Her words made her feel exposed and raw. She pulled her arms protectively to her stomach. With a sigh, Sky walked over, taking a seat beside her. His hand hovered between them before squeezing into a tight fist.

"This ain't real, Maia. It's a con. An unnecessarily messy one right now, but still a con. And that man is a target. Nothin' more. I need to know if you found what we're lookin' for."

She should have let him walk away, but he was beside her now, asking her to choose. Her eyes welled. "I don't want to hurt you... but I *won't* hurt him."

He tensed beside her. She expected him to storm away, but instead, he lifted his hand, grazing her burning cheeks. Her eyes traveled up his face, past the sharp tip of his nose and the pepper of freckles on his cheeks, all the way to the crease between his brows, twisted in conflict.

"Portico will find what you're hiding, and when they do, they'll kill us all."

She choked on a sob as he tucked a strand of hair behind her ear, pulling her to him. The scratchy wool of his jacket was rough against her cheek, but she was desperate for his comfort. She needed to know he could forgive her.

"I'm sorry, Sky."

"Therein lies the problem. I ain't gonna watch you hang over some ridiculous loyalty to a stranger. I knew you weren't ready for this."

Maia's breath caught, and she pulled away. His doubt burned at her skin like a brand. She thought back to the last time they had been alone together. He had done it differently, harsher, forcing her into a corner. All choreographed moments to get exactly what he wanted.

"Please go."

A forced laugh. Mock surprise. A quickly faded façade as he realized she saw right through him. "I ain't leavin' until we have what Portico sent us to get."

She wiped away her openness and laughed at her naivety. Maybe the softness in his face or the gentleness of his touch was real, or at least a version of real, but in the end, he only understood survival.

"Sacrifice is the key to survival," she whispered.

It was true, beyond just physical survival. Maia had bled her truths to Mr. Foster to gain his trust. She'd have to do it again to keep him from losing everything he had left.

Sky's hand found the pendant around his neck. "Give I. Live we."

The words combined were foreign, but something about them felt familiar. Maia's eyes traveled from his pendant to the faint pink on the tips of his ears.

"It's a Scavenger saying," he said, shifting uncomfortably under her gaze. "Sacrifice is survival."

"Is that what the pendant means?"

He stood from the bed, shaking out his jacket. "You've got twenty-four hours, Maia. Figure it out, or I'll figure it out for you."

She waited until the door closed behind him before allowing herself to fall back onto the lumpy pillow. The thaw of his fingers against her skin remained. A gentle reminder of exactly who and what Sky was willing to sacrifice to survive.

15

COLLATERAL

Maia shuffled into Mr. Foster's office the next morning with a splitting headache and eyes still swollen from tears. The crisp fall air had plummeted into a biting chill overnight. A hint that the first snow would soon arrive.

Mr. Foster sat at his desk, elbow propped on the arm of his chair, while he rubbed at his temple. A warm cup of tea sat waiting for her, and she swelled with appreciation. She took a careful sip, the gentle kiss of steam comforting against her cheeks. Curling her fingers around the delicate teacup, she soaked in its warmth.

"Good morning, my dear," Mr. Foster said, glancing up from his book. "I hope your evening went better than mine."

Her face dropped.

"Distractions help," he continued, plopping a stack of papers in front of her.

Returning her cup to the table, she scanned the pages, hoping he was right. A distraction was exactly what she needed. Something to keep her mind off the dread sitting like a lead weight in the pit of her stomach. She had spent her night curled up in a chair, staring out the tavern window and playing out each potential scenario.

No matter the outcome, they all began with her admitting her deceit. Over and over, she imagined telling Mr. Foster the truth. And each time, the grip around her throat and ache in her stomach forced her into a tighter knot of limbs.

She focused again on the words scrawled across the page, and discovered Peter already had a theory on immunity—the idea that certain people had formed a tolerance to the virus. As she continued thumbing through the pages, she watched his research shift in that direction.

It was clear he had hit a wall in his testing, but it wasn't because of the lack of advancements. The idea was simple, but required more resources. Something Portico would have.

She paced the cluttered office for hours, forgoing meals and breaks, lost in Peter's writing. All she needed was one reason not to hand this over to the enemy. Proof that what Peter had found wouldn't give them the power to choose who lived or died.

Mr. Foster stood from his chair and stretched, slipping on his jacket. "I believe we've done enough for one day. Would you care to join me for dinner?"

She was out of time. Dread gripped her throat all over again as she lowered the papers to the desk, pressing her hands to the polished wood. The words played out in her mind. She could see them—feel them forming on her tongue—but panic took hold. She just needed one more hour, minute... second.

"Thank you, but I wouldn't want to impose."

"Nonsense. I'd appreciate your company, and the house is far too quiet now."

She pulled her hands from the desk, a film of fear leaving an imprint behind, and reached for a new stack of papers. "We still have so much to—" Her eyes stopped on the word *weapon* scrawled in Peter's scattered writing, dropping the floor out from under her.

"Is everything alright, my—"

"I need to tell you something." The hammering of her heart thundered in her ears, rattling in her chest so hard she thought it might explode.

He remained quiet, and she forced her eyes from the word she hoped not to find, to his look of concern she didn't deserve.

"It's about how I found this position, sir."

Concern shifted to suspicion, and he sank into his seat.

She took in a deep breath, but it did nothing to ease the tightness in her chest. "It wasn't by chance. You were right. I was sent here."

His mustache twitched. "By whom?"

Her eyes returned to the word. She knew what had to be done. "Portico."

Pain. Grief. Anger. All of it flashed across Mr. Foster's face, but it was the look of betrayal that remained. "For Peter's research." She nodded. "And now you have it. Was that the plan? To take it tonight and disappear?"

"No." She grabbed at the papers, packing them haphazardly into the box. "Take it and run before they get here."

His face flushed with anger and bewilderment. "I'm just supposed to believe you've—"

She shoved the box towards him. "They know you have something, but not what it is. I'm truly sorry. You're a good man, and you don't deserve any of this."

Mr. Foster looked at the box, drumming his fingers on his desk, lost in thought. "And what happens to you if I leave?"

"Ya ain't goin' anywhere, Mr. Foster," came a voice from the shadow of the doorway.

Maia and Mr. Foster jumped as Sky stepped forward, pulling back his jacket to reveal the pistol on his hip.

"You don't know what it is. I won't—" Maia jumped towards him, sliding to a stop as he lifted his gun.

He wouldn't shoot her. It was another act to get what he wanted. A show to force Mr. Foster to choose, just like he did with Maia the night before.

Mr. Foster lifted his hands as if trying to placate a wild animal. But Sky wasn't an animal. He was the cold-blooded hunter.

"Stop, please!" Mr. Foster begged. "There's no need for this. She didn't mean what she said. We've had a long day, and—"

"Maia always means what she says. It's an unfortunate weakness of hers."

Mr. Foster turned to Maia, tears in his eyes, and his shoulders collapsed with resignation. Her heart shattered.

It was supposed to be *her* sacrifice, not his.

"He won't shoot," she choked out.

Sky cocked back the hammer of his pistol. "Don't test me, Maia."

She hated him for putting her in this position. Sky could protect himself against Portico. Blame it all on her if he wanted. But Mr. Foster didn't deserve to be caught in the middle.

"Sir, I beg you. Take it and go."

Mr. Foster searched her pleading eyes and slowly stood, grabbing the box from his desk. "I'll go willingly to Portico with my research, but only if whatever you overheard stays between us."

Her head fell in defeat. Portico would get what they wanted. A potential cure they could give only to those they deemed worthy. Even worse, if they found Rowan's journals, they would have everything needed to ensure complete dominance.

Sky holstered his gun, gripping Maia's elbow. She wouldn't fight. He'd already won, even if it meant everyone else lost.

"Fair enough." Sky tucked the box under his other arm. "Welcome to Portico, Mr. Foster."

The trip back to Portico was one of silence, heavy with words trapped in tormented thoughts and leery gazes. Sky refused to allow anyone else to hold the box of research papers, and Mr. Foster refused to let Maia out of his sight. Neither broached the subject of her betrayal. Their distrust remained solely on each other when it should have been directed at her.

Staring into the campfire, she lost herself in moments. Each regret recounted ad nauseam, as they had since leaving Rocky Mount. Reciting interactions with Mr. Foster. Weaving complex webs of even more *what-ifs*. A reminder she was never the spider, but forever the fly in the game.

Mr. Foster cleared his throat and stood. "I'm going for a walk. Maia, would you—"

"Enjoy your walk, Mr. Foster," Sky snapped before he could finish.

Mr. Foster hesitated, looking between them.

"Don't make me say it again," Sky warned.

Pursing his lips, Mr. Foster balled his pudgy hands. Maia shook her head before he grew brave, and after one more second, he begrudgingly stormed off.

Sky poked at a log, shifting it farther into the fire and sending a cloud of smoke into the air.

"You have no idea what you did," Maia hissed.

He sighed, as if expecting this very conversation. "I saved us all from the gallows."

His oblivious confidence was infuriating. "You're handing them an unstoppable weapon."

"Stop!" The bite of his tone made her back snap straight. "Stop lyin' to me, Maia." Despite the harsh lines on his face, hurt laced his words. "I snuck into his office last night and read through the paperwork. It's a cure for red lung, not a weapon."

"How did you—?"

He reached into his pocket, removing her mother's black comb. She clenched her fist to keep from reaching for her hair. His hug made sense now. None of it was real.

Maia walked to him, ripping her comb from his hand.

"You realize if they have the means to weaken red lung, they have the means to strengthen it too, right?"

Sky returned his gaze to the flames, remaining quiet.

"They don't deserve the cure. It belongs to us. To the rebellion."

He scanned the clearing, grabbing her hand and pulling her next to him. "You do realize there's a lot more on the line than just this box of papers, right? The only way to get close enough to destroy the Council is by gainin' their trust. I need you to tell me you know that."

Despite everything within her screaming that this was wrong, if they succeeded with their mission—their true mission—the cure would be theirs. For now, it would have to be a sacrifice, along with Mr. Foster. The line of morality moved just a little further.

"I understand," she responded through gritted teeth. The weight of her decision sat heavy on her shoulders as she stood. "Don't ever point a gun at me again."

"It wasn't loaded."

Her glare was as sharp as her dagger.

"He needed motivation," Sky said, unphased by her fury.

"He had no reason to protect me after everything I'd done."

"And yet he did." He lifted a brow, looking up at her with his steel gaze. "Just like I knew he would."

"Now you're the one lying."

He rubbed his fingers together as if itching for his pendant, but knowing it would draw attention. "I haven't lied to you yet. He protected you for the same reason I do."

There was something hidden between his words that made Maia grow cold. If this was how he showed he cared, she was terrified of what he'd do if he didn't.

Portico's guards stopped them at the gates, escorting them to the Trade and Collections office. Blown-out windows exposed abandoned floors with Old World furniture falling victim to the elements. The worn, gray entrance was flanked by stone, obelisk monuments on each side with a flag pole in between. An oversized Portico flag waved in the breeze, tattered and worn from its once vibrant red to a muted pink, as if it had yet to be replaced from the first day it was hung. A woman stood smoking out front, the collar of her coat lifted to shield her from the cold.

"These the ones we've been waitin' for?" she asked, lifting the smoke to her bright red lips with a trembling hand.

Sky nodded, pulling open the cracked glass door of the building. The woman eyed Maia with curiosity before entering, motioning for them to follow.

Shaking off the cold, she marched them down a series of crowded halls. Maia glanced into a room as they passed, catching an artist working on a drawing, emulating the sketches seen on bounties.

"Nah, his nose is crooked from a break," one of Portico's collectors said, leaning over the artist's shoulder. "Trust me, nearly broke my fist on that honker."

A woman carrying a stack of papers nearly knocked Maia over as she exited a room. Inside, people sat at rows of desks, scrawling on more slips and stamping them before placing them into trays.

The woman continued down the hall, opening the door to a room booming with shouts. She handed the slips to a man in front of a collections board, while others sat at tables counting Portico coins. The door swung closed behind her, and Maia glanced back at Mr. Foster's flushed cheeks as he struggled to keep pace.

"Can someone please explain what's going on?" he begged, swatting at the cloud of smoke trailing behind the woman.

She ignored him, stopping in front of a wooden door with a gold placard labeled *Council Advisor*, and knocked twice before pushing it open.

Rafe sat with his polished shoes up on his desk, glancing past his paperwork at them.

"I told you no fucking smoking in the building." He dropped his feet to the floor, pointing to the corner of his office where Aster sat with a book, head propped against his hand.

"Shit, sorry, sir. I didn't know he was here." She snuffed her smoke on the metal case, tucking the butt away for later.

Aster didn't seem to notice the interaction, his eyes catching on Maia's royal-blue scoop-neck dress. Another one of Senna's picks for the con, which accomplished its desired effect. Unfortunately, it was from the one person she didn't need to be garnering attention from.

"It's fine," Aster said, dragging his gaze across the rest of the group to the box under Sky's arm.

"She ain't the one stuck listenin' to you wheeze for—"

"Mr. Charles Foster," Aster announced enthusiastically. He walked over, putting out his hand. "It's truly a pleasure to make your acquaintance, sir. We've heard so much about you. My name is Aster Calderone, Diplomatic Advisor."

"I..." Mr. Foster hesitated, looking almost disoriented by the sudden civility.

Even towering over him, Aster's confident smile eased the frustration etched between Mr. Foster's bushy brows. The lingering moment of trepidation faded, and he took Aster's hand.

"Mr. Calderone, can you please explain to me what's going on?" It was obvious from his tone he was grateful to find someone reasonable to speak with. He took a protective step towards Maia, which didn't go unnoticed by the room, and pointed to Sky. "This man arrived at my office claiming to represent you and threatening my—" There was a pause as Mr. Foster's gaze flickered to Maia, conflict holding him in his thought. "My assistant. She said you may be interested in my research."

"Did she?" Rafe asked, walking around his desk to stand beside his brother. They held the same curious gaze on her, forcing Maia to drop hers to her feet, hoping they couldn't see the heat their attention brought to her cheeks. "You three can go. Aster and I can take it from here."

The woman gave him a two-finger salute, eager to escape the escalating situation, while Sky handed over the papers.

"Show her to the housing quarters," Rafe said, nodding in Maia's direction. He took the box from Sky and gave him a commending pat on the shoulder. "She can have the empty room across from yours."

"Yes, sir," Sky said, flinching at his touch.

Mr. Foster snuck a final glance at Maia, giving her a reassuring smile. Her guilt returned tenfold as Sky guided her out of the office. Mr. Foster chose to protect her over his husband's research. Whether it was right or wrong, they would all soon find out.

Once outside, she followed Sky along a path wrapping around the back of the building where the housing quarters were tucked away. They were the only two buildings still fully intact along the Old World road, the others in varying stages of collapse. It was obvious Portico's grounds weren't intended to stretch this far, which made her wonder if the collectors were a second thought in Portico's original plan.

Sky wrenched open the lopsided door, dragging it across a line etched into the floor. He rubbed his tired eyes, waiting for her to enter.

"What's the plan here?" Maia asked, plunging her hands deep into her coat pockets and passing the threshold into the dingy lobby.

Whether it was fatigue or the fact his job was done, the harshness faded from his eyes. "Now, we wait."

Paint chips hung like crystalized butterflies from the water-stained ceilings as they continued up a set of broken stairs. It wasn't until they reached the second floor that the musty odor dissipated. They stopped at the end of the hall at a broken window overlooking the encroaching trees.

Sky pushed open a door, leaning against the frame and thumbing his pendant. "Listen, I forgive you for choosing him over me."

Maia refused to meet his gaze, knowing all her excuses and justifications would only make it worse.

"But don't *ever* lie to me again." His tone was sharp as glass, the gooseflesh rising on her skin. He pushed himself off the doorframe. "Get some sleep."

Without waiting for a response, he crossed the hall to his room, closing the door behind him. The forceful click of his lock allowed her shoulders to relax, and she walked into the room Rafe had apparently made hers, grateful to have it to herself. She needed space to process everything without the guilt of Mr. Foster or Sky hovering over her.

Walking into the small room, she noticed it was nearly identical to the ones she'd become accustomed to in the taverns. Tightly tucked sheets and a clean basin of water on the vanity. She frowned at the collector's uniform neatly folded on the dresser. If this was Rafe's informal way of offering her a position, she had no problem informally turning it down. She walked over, throwing open a drawer and tossing the uniform inside.

Crossing the room, she collapsed onto the vanity chair and hesitantly glanced into the mirror. The version of herself staring back was a lie of Senna's creation. Still, somewhere hidden behind the wind-kissed cheeks and the long, loose braid of black hair were the splintering cracks in her disguise. Selfishness consumed her—guiding each of her decisions in Rocky Mount. Pieces of her true self slipping through in her weaker moments.

She pushed away from the vanity, dropping onto the bed and curling into a tight ball. She didn't deserve Mr. Foster's empathy or Sky's forgiveness. She didn't even deserve the collector's uniform she'd so easily discarded.

The destructive thoughts took hold, pulling her deeper and deeper into an endless darkness.

She was so tired. Tired of the regret—of the fear.

So, she surrendered to the darkness, allowing her eyes to flutter shut as her guilt followed her into her nightmares.

16

THORNS

Shooting up in the bed, Maia gasped for air as she slowly settled back into her terrifying reality. The morning sun crept into the room, slowly exposing the shadows. She jumped as the light found Tala sitting in the vanity chair, her feet resting on the edge of Maia's bed.

"You're a surprisingly heavy sleeper," she said, dropping her slippered feet to the floor.

Maia fought the urge to press herself against the headboard, every inch desperate to create distance between them. Instead, she untangled herself, ignoring her muscles screaming in protest from spending hours locked in place.

"Why are you in my room?"

"Is this your room now?" A contemptuous smile crossed Tala's lips as she watched Maia. "Rafe is so easily impressed."

"What do you want?"

Tala removed a blade from her cloak. The tension was now suffocating in the confined room. Was it the same blade she'd used on Maia's father?

Her stomach turned, and Tala's grin deepened as Maia shifted uncomfortably. It was the reaction she was looking for.

"Sagitta," Tala said, rolling each letter across her tongue. She turned in the chair, etching something into the wooden vanity top. "Such a curious surname. Yet, for some reason, it sounded so familiar. Do you know why?"

Maia inched around the bed, stretching for a better view over Tala's shoulder. "No."

"Sagitta is a constellation. It means *the arrow*. Or, more specifically, the arrow that killed the god-like eagle, Aquila, according to ancient myths."

Maia's body grew stiff as Tala's work came into view. A constellation of five stars in the shape of an arrow. The sudden knock on the door made her nearly jump out of her skin.

"Unfortunately for you, Aquila is a paranoid old man, certain that rebels have infiltrated his compound," Tala continued, slipping her blade under her cloak and leaning back to admire her art. Another knock sent a shock to Maia's heart. "Do you know the coward who started the rebellion chose the name Sagittarius?"

Maia remained quiet—the tick of her father's watch tucked away in her pocket suddenly deafening.

Tala scoffed. "Even if that traitor had known who his true target was, he would never have been brave enough to shoot. Which makes me wonder if his arrow found its own way?"

Maia's hands trembled at her side, itching for the blade hidden under her skirt. She should have known her nickname had meaning. A breadcrumb her father had left behind for her to follow. *We're stronger than we look, my little Sagitta.*

Tala was testing her, ensuring Maia understood she wasn't safe. Another knock broke their gaze, and Maia threw open the door.

"Good morn—" Aster's smile dropped at Tala's presence. He took a step forward, filling the doorway. "Aquila has been asking for you."

She pursed her lips in amusement. "Did he finally tire of you buzzing in his ear?"

Every muscle in his body had tensed, but he remained controlled, forcing Tala to break first.

As she moved to the door, she stopped beside Maia. "I don't read much into these things. Let's hope no one else has reason to either."

It wasn't until Tala was no longer in earshot that Maia finally relaxed, only to find Aster watching her.

"My apologies, Ms. Sagitta—"

Her stomach plummeted again, and she kept her eyes from flitting towards the vanity. "Maia, please."

Curiosity pulled at his brows. "Of course, Maia. I wanted to formally introduce myself."

She could see him analyzing each of her words. Every shift in her stance. The flush of her cheeks as the tension slowly seeped into the room once more. She needed to get him as far away from that symbol etched in the vanity as possible.

"I know who you are, Mr. Calderone. Care for some fresh air?"

His eyes searched hers, and she hoped he didn't find whatever he was looking for. "Yes, that sounds wonderful. And you can call me Aster."

Maia released a breath and grabbed her coat from the back of her chair. When she looked back, his dark gaze had found her vanity. "Ready?"

With a soft smile, he stepped aside so she could exit the room. The subtle scent of bergamot and cloves surrounded her as she passed, and that alone seemed to deceptively warm the space between them. With one more glance into the room, he closed the door behind them, following her down the hall into the chilled morning air.

"I hope you managed some rest before Tala arrived."

He tucked his hands into his coat pockets and glanced down at her out of the corner of his eye. Despite the cold, he seemed to be forcing his shoulders to relax.

"I did, thank you."

He nodded, but remained quiet as they turned down the road leading to the main gates. The distant chimes of the bell tower filled the silence.

The twins might have shared the same confidence, but they couldn't be any more different. Where Rafe was the flash of lightning, Aster was the slow and sure roll of thunder that followed.

"So, you didn't want the new clothes left for you?"

She felt his gaze again and realized his questions danced around what he was truly searching for. He wanted to know why Tala was there, and why Maia would turn down Rafe's offer. So instead, she followed in Aster's carefully planted steps.

"They didn't fit."

Amusement played across his face, tugging his lips into a dangerously alluring smile. "And here he thought he sized you up well."

She chewed on her lip, ignoring the sudden warmth weaving through her like ribbons pulling her to him. Aster played his part well. Despite their height difference, he had slowed his pace to match hers, walking side by side as if with an old friend. There was something soft and welcoming about him that made her comfortable, even when she knew she shouldn't be.

"I imagine there's a reason for this stroll that goes beyond small talk," she said, using her words to put a wall between them.

He noticed the shift and dropped his smile into something more disciplined, continuing past Portico's gate.

"Why did you take the time to gain Mr. Foster's trust, when all we requested was his research?" The dance was over. He asked the question he wanted the answer to. And even if she chose to lie, she knew he'd see through it.

"All I did was tell him the truth. He deserved a choice." Even if he didn't get one.

"So, it wasn't your idea for him to come to Portico?"

The suspicion in his tone made Maia wonder how Mr. Foster had spun things. "It was his. Sky just provided some... motivation."

They passed under the rose trellis leading into the garden maze, and Aster pulled one loose, twirling it between his fingers. "I don't get it."

"What?"

As if by reflex, he held the rose out to her. She jerked away. This had to be one of his tactics of manipulation.

"The guilt you have when you look at him," he continued.

It was unnerving how perceptive he was. Maia carefully took the flower, focusing on the delicate petals while formulating the right response.

"I didn't deserve his kindness," she said, lifting the petals to her nose. Another desperate attempt to create a wall between them.

There was another moment of silence as they continued strolling through the maze. A question plaguing her since returning with Mr. Foster now rested on the tip of her tongue. She knew it was dangerous—really any questioning here was—but she had to know.

"What do you plan to do with his research?"

Her question pulled Aster from his thoughts. "It seems he has a potential cure for red lung, which I believe you already know. If it's true, we could save thousands of lives."

His response was disarmingly sincere, but she knew better than to believe anything that came from his mouth.

"I'll be curious to see who Portico decides is worth saving."

Aster stopped, his face suddenly twisting with confusion as they found themselves at a dead end. He rubbed the back of his neck, glancing behind them as if trying to figure out where he had taken the wrong turn. Maia continued into the secret alcove towards the lone bench.

"You look lost," she said, taking a seat on the cool stone.

His cheeks darkened, and his entire demeanor shifted to the same poised and stoic man he had been with Sky by the fountain. "Mr. Foster asked for you to be assigned as his personal assistant going forward. Rafe, however, has rejected his request, believing you would be better suited to join—"

"No." Maia jumped to her feet, the word escaping her in a desperate plea.

Her outburst surprised him, and it took a second for Aster to respond. "Then what would *you* prefer?"

The lift of his brow told her there was weight to this decision. She looked down at the already-wilting petals of the flower as if time moved faster in this lost corner of the maze. He knew she would turn down the collector's position, which meant the choice was between gathering herbs or joining Portico in their search for a cure.

Even if it was a test, the gratitude filling her from Mr. Foster's request made her choice easy.

She stepped forward, noting the way his body suddenly grew rigid. "I'd like to continue working with Mr. Foster."

He nodded, but his expression remained detached. "I'll inform Aquila accordingly in my briefing. Thank you for your time, Ms. Sagitta."

He turned to leave, but his step wavered. "Aquila holds his advisors to certain expectations, and Tala's threat towards you goes against the oath we took when accepting our positions. I'll ensure Aquila is informed so he can address it with her. I hope the rest of your day is not nearly as eventful."

With that, he disappeared from the alcove, allowing Maia's panic to take hold. If he told Aquila about the threat, he would have to explain the arrow carved into her vanity.

Unfortunately for you, Aquila is a paranoid old man, certain that rebels have infiltrated his compound.

That was why she had threatened Maia in front of him. Aster had Aquila's ear *and* his trust. They had fallen right into her trap, and now Aster would plant the seed of suspicion without Tala having to say a word.

The rose slipped from Maia's hand, and before it even hit the ground, she was running.

Maia took the stairs two at a time in the collector's housing, slamming the door to her room shut and locking it. Ripping the blade out from under her skirt, she stabbed it into the wooden top of the vanity, marring the etching of the arrow.

How could she have been so blind to Tala's plan? Aster's smile suddenly flashed through her racing thoughts. The warmth that seemed to surround him. She dug her knife deeper into the wood.

She needed to warn Rowan before Aster found Aquila's ear. The local mayors had arrived last night, which meant Rowan would be stuck entertaining them all day at Aquila's manor. The most heavily guarded place in Portico. She needed a disguise.

Closing her eyes, she braced against the edge of the vanity, trying to slow her thundering pulse so she could think. With a slow breath, she glanced up at the mirror past her blanched face to a cloth hanging haphazardly from one of her dresser drawers. The collector's uniform.

She pushed away, quickly changing and rushing back across the Portico grounds before she could change her mind.

Aquila's manor was a two-story plantation home located behind Council Hall. Freshly painted black shutters matched the iron gate entrance with a *Councilor's Manor* placard anchored to the stone wall.

Guards stood at the entrance, a bright red Portico flag casting waves of shadows across them. Behind the gate was a gravel walkway and fountain circled with deep-red rose bushes. More guards patrolled from the flat roof with eyes on all corners of the perimeter.

She adjusted the vest of her collector's uniform, ensuring her hair remained tucked beneath the newsboy cap. A group of guards marched past, and she cut through their formation, disappearing into the trees next to the manor. Walls surrounded the garden with a single entrance door. A server walked through it with a tray of dirty plates and cups, revealing her way in.

She waited for the next server to arrive, opening the door with a key and disappearing into the garden. Maia stopped the door with her foot and allowed a second before following him inside.

The guards on the roof and balconies watched the festivities below with vacant eyes, unaware of Maia's entrance. She continued onto the crowded brick patio where diplomats, guards, and collectors walked around socializing with the guests, laughing loudly, and toasting each other.

The cellist started a new song, transforming the ambiance of the garden from a quick, vibrant tempo to something more haunting. Maia casually removed a glass flute filled with a golden drink from one of the serving trays. Taking a spot under the porch, she searched the crowd for Rowan.

A laugh behind her made her jump, and she glanced through the window to see another crowd inside. She took a sip from her glass, scanning the garden one last time. Her nose scrunched at the sweetness, and she abandoned the drink on a patio table before slipping inside.

White upholstered furniture sat on a red and gold rug spanning the entire parlor. The men and women gathered in elegantly dressed groups, too involved in their conversations to notice Maia. Her stomach dropped as she caught sight of Aquila standing next to the fireplace, whispering with Aster. She was out of time. He must have walked straight here from their conversation.

Maia hid her face, tucking into a hallway. She pressed herself against the wall, trying to slow her racing heart. All she needed was a second to think, but whispers from farther down the hall stole her attention.

She inched forward, slipping into a room and peering around the doorframe. Tala returned a book to a shelf in Aquila's library, while a hooded scout hid a letter under their cloak.

"Get caught and you'll be swimming with the fish in the canal," Tala warned.

The scout nodded, and Maia tucked herself back into the room, waiting for the two sets of footsteps to walk past.

"Where the fuck have you been?" Maia immediately recognized Rafe's hostile voice.

"Briefing a scout." Tala's words were calm and measured. "What do you want, Rafael?"

Maia's back straightened against the wall. Tala was hiding something from Aquila and the other Advisors.

"*I* don't want anything, but apparently you pissed off Aquila. He wants to talk."

Tala scoffed. "So he sent his errand boy. Run off now to your next pointless task. I know where to find him."

Rafe mumbled something under his breath, and they both walked away.

Once they were far enough, Maia crept across the hall to scan the shelves. Removing a random book, she thumbed through it, unsure what she was looking for.

"What are you doing?"

The book fell from her hands, hitting the floor with a deafening *thud*. She spun on her heels to find a red jacket emerging from a hidden passage in the wall. It was the first time she was grateful to find Rowan's narrowed gaze on her.

She clutched her chest, slowing her heart and letting out a breath. "I was looking for you."

"In a book?"

Rowan joined her at the shelf, removing a different book and gently running his fingers across the pages.

Maia peered over his shoulder, noticing indents around certain words from marks that had been erased.

"What did you find?"

"I don't know yet." He slammed the book closed. "Why would you risk coming here to find me?"

"Did you know Sagitta means 'little arrow?'"

"No." He returned the book to the shelf.

"Did you know that, according to ancient myths, Sagitta was the arrow that killed Aquila?"

Rowan froze, looking down at her. "Where did you hear this?"

"From Tala."

"Fuck." He pinched the bridge of his nose. "Does anyone else know?"

"She threatened me in front of Aster, but he doesn't know why."

Rowan's face hardened. "I told all of you to stay away from him."

"He came to me." Her words were forceful, but sounded more like an excuse than an argument. "I know to keep my distance."

"Good. I'll take care of this mess." Rowan adjusted his red Overseer coat and started towards the door. "Use the passage to leave so no one sees you."

"Did you bring your journals?"

His shoulders tensed, and he turned back to her. "Why?"

"The man they sent me to find in Rocky Mount has similar research to the weapon drawings in your journals."

"Then it's a good thing no one else knows about them."

It wasn't the answer she was looking for, and he knew it. He resigned himself, walking back and placing his hands on her shoulders.

"Your mother was right. You're too much like your father. Do what you're told, nothing more—nothing less. Things like this will cause suspicion you can't afford." Maia opened her mouth to argue, and Rowan smiled, already expecting a fight. "He would have been proud of you."

He stole the argument from her lips as she realized his words were from his own admiration. Even his gaze felt different. It was protective in a way that went beyond their alliance. The same way she was protective of Hannah. She nodded, allowing Rowan peace of mind, and before he was out of sight, Maia was already closing the passage door behind her.

17

CONFIDENCE

It was never about having hope. I realize now that to change the world, you have to give hope.

A. Wells – Fall 2294

It had been weeks since Tala's threat, and Maia took Rowan's advice, doing exactly what was asked of her. No more, no less. It was suffocating, constantly trapped under the watchful eye of Portico's scouts.

Every movement, word, even breath could be the one thing that gave her away. She spent so much time and effort forcing herself to appear loyal that, somewhere along the line, truths and lies blurred into a new reality where both—and neither—were absolutes. Each morning, she arrived at the lab as scheduled. Her white coat crisp and ironed. A pastry and tea always waiting as she and Mr. Foster reviewed research notes or cut into fresh cadavers of red lung victims, depending on what the day brought.

A woman named Juliana took an interest in their work, offering her expertise in Old World microbiology. It was her precise hands that harvested red lung cells from the cadavers, and her quick thinking that suggested the storage of the petri dishes in rows of ice chests.

With the help of the other researchers and days huddled over Old World texts, they discovered how to cultivate the virus from the dishes. Maia recognized the instructions from W. Wells' journals, and while she celebrated with the others, she couldn't help but feel the looming dread of what could easily come next. It didn't take long for word to spread about their achievements. Within days, Mr. Foster was called to Council Hall by Aquila himself to present their findings.

Maia's footsteps echoed off the checkered tile floors of the Council Hall rotunda, following Mr. Foster and the other researchers being escorted by a guard. A cracked and dismembered full-body statue guarded the entrance. Around them, forgotten men forebodingly stared down from wall niches, immortalized in the form of chipped-marble busts.

Rowan and the four Council Advisors sat behind a curved wooden podium at the front of the Council Chambers. The engaged columns and domed glass in the coffered ceilings surrounded them in Old World architecture. It was too extravagant for their New World, all of it reeking of corruption.

Rowan did a double-take as Maia entered, glaring with suspicion. She had to admit she wasn't exactly sure why Mr. Foster insisted on her joining them either. Taking a seat at the end of an extended table, Mr. Foster lowered himself next to her.

He placed his worn leather healing bag on the floor between them and folded his hands on the table. Only the anxious bounce of his legs gave away his thoughts. The tension radiated uncomfortably from him, quickening Maia's pulse. She searched the room for a distraction, only to find her gaze now on Aster.

He sat at the end of the podium, pen gliding across the pages stacked in front of him. The afternoon sun filtered in through the window, highlighting the bronzed peaks of his cheekbones, and warm amber of his eyes. His pen paused on the page, and as if sensing her from across the room, his liquid-gold gaze found hers.

She sucked in a breath, grateful that at that exact moment Rowan stood, stealing their attention as he made his way across the room to a side door. Aster was a dangerous distraction she didn't need, but she couldn't deny the way the warmth of his gaze weaved under her skin.

Aquila hobbled through the door, sending Council to their feet. He struggled to lift himself to the podium behind the Advisors, stepping on his cape and collapsing into his chair. Maybe the stupid fucking cape would be what finally ended his reign.

The Advisors hesitantly took their seats again, while Rowan stood beside Aquila unbothered.

"Thank you for coming on such short notice," Aquila said, gasping for air despite the short walk. "I've been told you've made progress on the cure for red lung. I apologize you won't have much time to celebrate, but we have a time-sensitive request."

Tala stood, and despite her small stature, she conveyed an authority Maia would have envied had it been anyone else. "We've received word there's been an outbreak of red lung in a shantytown just a few miles south of our compound. There are concerns it could find its way beyond our walls."

"We would like to use this opportunity to test the cure," Aquila said, trapping Mr. Foster in his yellowed gaze.

"I want to be clear," Mr. Foster said, glancing down the table at the others. "What we've found is *not* a cure. We believe we've attenuated the cultivated cells enough for possible inoculation."

Juliana straightened in her chair, lifting her sharp chin. It wasn't Mr. Foster who had discovered this—it was her—and she clearly didn't appreciate him using the collective *we* in this situation.

"Is that a yes or no, Mr. Foster?" Tala's question hinted that there was only one right answer.

"No," Juliana answered, her cheeks flushing to match her flame-red hair. "If the cells aren't attenuated correctly, it could kill the subjects. It would be wrong to test it this soon."

"Then, when?" Aquila asked, leaning over his podium with the most authority Maia had yet to see him muster. "You should know, they're dead with or without your help."

Conflict seeped from Mr. Foster's pores, making Maia shift uneasily in his silence.

"Fine," Aquila snapped. "General Winter…"

The General's lips were razor sharp lines that matched her lethal glare now pinned on Juliana. She trailed her cat-like eyes to Aquila, but seemed to already know what would come next.

"Send your guards out immediately," he ordered. "Eradicate the area. We cannot risk red lung finding its way into Portico."

Eradicate the area, not the virus. Maia shot a glance down the table at the researchers, disgusted to see the relief on their faces. It wasn't about people dying. It was about maintaining a good image. Before she could stop herself, her hand was on Mr. Foster's.

"We don't have to promise them a cure, sir," Maia whispered. She knew how desperate she looked, but she didn't care. "They just need a chance at hope."

His knee stopped bouncing for the first time since they arrived, and clarity seemed to wash over him. "A chance at hope."

His eyes grew distant in thought as he nervously twirled the end of his mustache. The softness between his brows made Maia wonder if he was thinking about his husband.

He turned to Aquila. "We'll test the inoculation."

Juliana snapped forward, glaring at him. "You'll be able to sleep with their deaths on your conscience, Mr. Foster?"

Maia's blood boiled at the hypocrisy in her question. "Will *you*, Juliana?"

"You shouldn't even be here!" she spat.

Mr. Foster slammed his fist on the table. "She is *exactly* the person who needs to be here. She understands what this could mean to them."

Juliana's lips pursed, and she stood, pressing her hands firmly on the table. "If she's so willing to risk the lives of all those innocent people, then why don't we test the cure on her first?"

"Enough!" Rowan shouted, drawing the attention of the room again.

Maia had almost forgotten about their audience, and shrank at the attention. Rafe had leaned forward, elbows on the podium, apparently enjoying the spectacle. General Winter's face had softened, her thin lips hitched with respect. Tala's dark gaze was unreadable, while Aster's hand hovered just over his lips, patiently waiting for what would come next.

Aquila, however, was livid.

"You will mind your place in these chambers, Overseer," Aquila warned.

"Sir." Rowan's voice was tight, as if moments away from snapping. "Respectfully, if this fails, then we've willingly released red lung to everyone behind our gates."

Aquila's harsh gaze traveled back to Maia. "I'll allow this, but you leave tonight. And if you fall sick, you will *not* be allowed back in. Do I make myself clear?"

She thought about the Scavengers, realizing how easy it must have been to turn them away at those bunker doors.

Mr. Foster gave her a small, encouraging smile.

While she appreciated it, she didn't need it. She already knew her answer. Her gaze met Aquila's. "Understood."

"This is madness," Juliana said. "I refuse to take part in this. I hope you can live with whatever happens next, Mr. Foster."

He straightened, making it clear he wouldn't back down. Juliana shook her head in disappointment. Without another word, she started for the door, the other researchers joining. It slammed shut with a deafening *bang,* sealing them in the moment's tension.

Mr. Foster reached for his bag, placing it on the table and removing its contents.

"It's as we discussed," he said, holding a scalpel over the flame of a lighter. "Two tiny cuts to the forearm. Just enough to create immunity, but not infect."

She knew, but it didn't slow her racing heart as she struggled to swallow. What if Juliana was right? What if it was too soon?

"Aquila, please reconsider," Rowan said, and Maia wondered if she imagined the tremble in his voice.

Mr. Foster's eyes bore into hers. "You'll be fine, my dear. I promise."

Despite his confidence, they both knew he couldn't be certain of this. Still, she survived exposure once. She had to believe this would be no different.

Biting down on her lip, she rolled up her sleeve. If she believed, then Aquila would believe. "I trust you."

He cleansed her arm with alcohol and dipped the cooled blade into a vial of the attenuated red lung cells. The scalpel hovered over her arm with a second of hesitation before puncturing her skin in two red lines. She watched the drops of blood lazily trail down her arm, mesmerized by how insignificant they appeared. Naïve of their potential.

The silence in the room was deafening as Mr. Foster covered her cuts with a cloth.

A victorious smile seemed to breathe new life into Aquila. "Excellent. General Winter, prepare your guards for travel," Aquila said, turning to his Advisors. "Mr. Calderone, please assign a diplomat to the group."

"I'll go myself," Aster replied, turning to Aquila.

"It's too much of a risk. There are—"

"I insist, sir." Aster's gaze was firm. "It's important we control the message, or we'll only make things worse."

Aquila twirled a thick ring around his bony finger in hesitation. "Fine. I trust your judgment." He sighed, looking back at Maia and Mr. Foster. "Expect resistance. Rebels have been impersonating Portico guards and attacking shantytowns, making us look rogue. Give these people a reason to trust us again. Good luck."

His warning was a shock, and she forced herself not to glance at Rowan. Rebels wouldn't attack shantytowns. Even if they were impersonating guards, it would still mean attacking those they risked their lives to protect.

A sudden sharp pain in her arm derailed her thoughts. Her eyes dropped to the bandage as her father's watch slowly ticked away in her pocket.

They would soon know if Juliana was right.

The shantytown looked the same as the ones outside of Williamsburg. Women sat outside the run-down structures, their dirt-covered hands stitching tattered clothes, while the men gathered in groups gambling for smokes. Wild dogs rummaged side by side with children through piles of garbage on the edges of the dirt road. A man broke away from a game of dice, following behind them. It only took one to draw the attention of the others.

Aster lifted his hands to the growing crowd. The gold embroidery of his diplomat coat glistened in the sun, making it obvious he didn't belong. Mr. Foster stood next to him in his white lab coat, something Aster advised him to wear in an attempt to build the people's confidence. Maia was grateful to be safely hovering off to the side, leaning against a wooden post and taking in the spectacle.

"My name is Aster Calderone, and Portico has sent us to assist with your red lung outbreak."

"And how you plannin' to do that?" a man up front asked, sending a wad of tobacco-stained spit to the dirt.

Aster responded with a flawlessly confident smile. It seemed reserved for moments like these, where the master of lies and manipulation could shine. He made it look effortless. A reminder of exactly who she was up against.

"I'll allow our esteemed healer to answer that question," Aster replied, turning the attention to Mr. Foster.

With a hesitant step forward, he cleared his throat, kneading the handle of his leather healing bag. "We've been working on an inoculation that could potentially create immunity to the disease."

The crowd remained silent, unaffected by his words.

"Boss?"

Maia's heart skipped at the familiar voice, and she spun around to find Briar grinning back at her. He rushed over, crushing her in a hug, and she squeezed back just as hard. Being in his arms made her heart ache for the moments they'd missed while apart.

"I shoulda known you were the one everyone's been talkin' about." He pulled away, looking down at her. "How you feelin'?"

"Just a little sore from the cuts. I'll survive."

Briar seemed to appreciate her choice in words as they turned back to the crowd.

"What he means is that we think we've found a cure for red lung," Aster said, giving Mr. Foster's shoulder a reassuring squeeze.

Realization traveled through the crowd.

"How so?" the man up front continued.

Aster motioned for Maia to step forward. "Just two insignificant scratches."

She hesitated, and Briar nudged her forward. Despite her plain clothes, the crowd still eyed her with suspicion as she rolled up her sleeve.

The man laughed, crossing his arms. "No way. You ain't cuttin' me. Portico ain't known for helpin' nobody."

"You're right," Maia said, and the man's eyebrows shot up in surprise. "There's no guarantee it will work on everyone. All we're here to offer is a *chance* for those willing to take it."

"And if we don't?" the man asked, taking a confrontational step forward.

Briar was at her side in less than a second, towering over the man. "You'd be wise to back the fuck up."

The man's face was now bright red, and Aster stepped in. "If you decide not to take this opportunity, you'll be placed under quarantine until the outbreak has passed. Those are your choices."

The man had been trying to create a scene the second he opened his mouth. But it was Aster's words that broke the dam.

"You can't keep us prisoners here!"

"We ain't givin' in to your threats!"

"Portico's gonna kill us all!"

Mr. Foster lifted his hands to the deafening crowd. "We understand you're scared. We just want to help."

The crowd didn't back down. General Winter stepped forward, her fingers placed between her lips as an ear-piercing whistle made everyone pause. "If you ain't lookin' for our help, then go back to what you were doin'," she warned.

With the snap of her finger, her guards slowly corralled the crowd back towards their shacks. Maia's shoulders relaxed, but she still felt the adrenaline of the man's hostility coursing through her veins.

"Well, that went exactly as expected," Mr. Foster said, wiping a sheen of sweat from his flushed face. He looked up at Briar. "Thank you, sir, for stepping in."

"Mr. Foster, this is my good friend, Briar Harper," Maia said, shielding her eyes from the sun as she glanced up at him. Despite their short time together, she realized Briar was one of the few people she could truly call a friend.

He beamed at his introduction, and the two men exchanged a handshake.

"So, what do we do—" Briar removed his water canteen from his hip and jumped, finding a young girl standing next to him.

Her brown hair was tied back in a messy braid, and her dirty dress had holes worn at the knees.

She looked at the bottle longingly before her eyes broke to Maia's. "Mama has a question for you."

Maia exchanged a look of surprise with Mr. Foster. "Sure. Where is she?"

The girl led them to a small structure made of an assortment of wood and metal. She opened the door to reveal her mother sitting at a table, bouncing a baby on her lap. The only thing in the house was a wood-burning stove in one corner and a filthy mattress resting on the dirt floor in the other.

"Good evening, ma'am. Your daughter said you had some questions for us," Mr. Foster said with a trained smile.

She jumped to her feet. "I apologize. I have nothing to offer you but a seat."

"You don't need to offer us anything," he continued.

"Please, let me at least give you that," she begged. Her face fell with embarrassment, and Briar removed his hip belt, dropping into the chair. Her shoulders relaxed, and she continued. "What you offered out there sounds too good to be true."

"Again, we can't guarantee you anything, but there's a chance it might help."

The woman nervously bounced her baby in her arms and turned to Maia. "How likely of a chance?"

She wanted the truth, not the talking points she expected to hear from Mr. Foster in his white coat.

"I'm the only person it's been tested on," Maia started, and the woman's face dropped. "But I'm here, standing in front of you. That has to mean something."

The little girl took the other seat at the table, feet dangling as she swung them back and forth. She was so tiny sitting next to Briar, but they looked like kindred spirits as a childish grin crossed his lips. He slid the canteen to her, and Maia nearly melted as the girl's face lit up. She eagerly snatched it, taking a sloppy swig and wiping her face with a dirty sleeve.

Holding it back out to him, he shook his head. "Keep it, kid."

The woman's face looked pained as she watched the interaction, and she turned back to Maia. "I only want to do what's best for her."

Her? Maia's stomach dropped as she realized the woman wanted the inoculation for her daughter. It wasn't something she considered back in Portico, but it changed everything. What if it didn't work? What if it was too much for a child? The uncertainty made her lightheaded as she realized what it meant.

What if she died because of Maia's rash decision?

Mr. Foster stepped forward, placing a hand on Maia's shoulder. "If that's what you want, we'll prepare the supplies."

Tears pooled in the woman's eyes. "Hope's strong. She can fight it."

With an encouraging nod, Mr. Foster lifted his bag onto the table. "Maia, I'll need your assistance."

Briar made room for Mr. Foster to work, moving towards the doorway where Aster stood, quietly observing. He gave Maia a soft smile, thawing some of the fear freezing her in place.

"Hope?" Maia asked, dropping to her knees in front of her. The little girl nodded, her feet still swinging. "That's a pretty name. Mine is Maia. How old are you?"

She held up one full hand and two small fingers.

"Seven?" Briar said with over-the-top surprise. "I've never met a seven-year-old as badass as you."

Maia shot Briar a look, but Aster was already elbowing him in the gut. Hope giggled, dissolving the tension in the room.

"Can you show me how strong you are?" Maia asked, flexing her arm. "Roll up your sleeves and do this for me."

The little girl pushed up the sleeves of her dress and scrunched her face, like Maia's must have looked, as she flexed.

"I think she might just be stronger than you, Briar," Aster said, behind them.

Maia could only imagine the look Briar responded with based on the size of Hope's grin.

Mr. Foster waited for the scalpel to cool. Calm and confident, just like her mother. A fresh tear opened in Maia's chest as Mr. Thomas' words finally made sense. Mr. Foster was here to do what they promised, just as her mother would have. Their confidence needed to keep the hope of the people alive.

Mr. Foster handed Maia a cloth soaked in alcohol, and she cleaned the film of dirt off the girl's arm. "It'll hurt for only a second, but afterward, you'll be even stronger."

Hope's eyes grew wide at this, and Maia trusted it was out of excitement and not fear.

"Ready?" Mr. Foster asked, and Hope nodded. "One, two, three." His scalpel drew two short lines on her skin. "All done."

"That wasn't so bad," she said with a shrug, but her eyes had grown glassy.

"Hope," Briar said, and she turned to him, chewing the inside of her lip. "You're *definitely* stronger than me now."

She laughed as Mr. Foster covered her cuts with a thin cloth. "Keep the area clean until it scabs over," he advised, turning back to her mother. "We'll check on her daily for the next week to make sure she's okay."

The woman nodded, and before they could pack up their things, Hope was already dragging Briar outside to show off her new bandage.

She was the only brave one that day.

18

HEROES

Weariness shrouded the camp in silence while General Winter's guards picked at scraps of food around a fading campfire. She had pulled them from their post with no sleep or warning of what they were walking into. Still, there were no complaints.

Just silence.

Briar sat across from Maia, a smoke balanced between his lips as he shuffled a deck of cards. Why him? Why these five guards? He dealt the cards, gifting Maia another good hand, and she couldn't help but think maybe all of it was just the luck of the draw.

Unable to focus, she stared at the cards while her thoughts remained trapped in the shantytown. She should have stayed to watch Hope overnight. The fear of not knowing made it impossible to think of anything else. They tossed bets into the center of a shield flipped into a makeshift table. What did she throw in? Obviously, nothing that would prompt questions.

Mr. Foster cleared his throat, and Maia snapped back to the moment, revealing her hand.

"Fuck," Briar groaned, dropping his cards. "That's the best fucking hand in the game."

General Winter tossed her hand into the pile. "You could have picked us all clean."

"Lack of strategy has worked so far," Maia said, detached.

Aster gathered the cards into a neat pile, handing them to Mr. Foster. Even the dying light of the fire couldn't hide the subtle tug of his lips. Maia's gaze lingered on them, grateful for the distraction. Would they feel as soft as they looked? Taste like his warm scent of cloves? Numb her to all of this?

Her stomach dropped as dread washed over her. No. They would destroy everything. The same lips that could condemn her to hang in the courtyard. She forced her attention back to her meager winnings, wondering if the fact she should stay away from him was part of the reason she couldn't. Another dangerous rebellion that she struggled to resist.

"How ya feelin', Maia?" General Winter asked. She leaned back into a deep stretch, her muscles bulging against the sleeve of her shirt.

The question captured Briar's attention, his gaze burning as bright as the tip of his smoke.

"Fine." It was true, but she drew out the word with insecurity.

"The flush of your cheeks says otherwise, my dear," Mr. Foster said, dealing out the cards. Maia removed her fingerless glove, pressing the back of her hand to her cheek. "I'll check you after this hand. You may have a fever."

"I'll keep an eye on her tonight," Briar said, his focus back on the game.

Maia sorted her cards, suddenly aware of how hot she felt despite the steady fall of snow around them. She had been too concerned about Hope to notice the change.

"Thank you," she mumbled, wishing she didn't need all the sudden attention.

General Winter laid a rough pat on her back, nearly knocking her off the stump. "Chin up, back straight. A little fever ain't gonna be what does you in."

"No need to test your theory, Winter," Aster said, glancing at her over his hand.

Their look held a whole other conversation, measured in a way only those proficient in politics could maintain.

Winter broke it first with a nod. "No harm in getting checked though."

"What do you think will happen tomorrow?" Maia's desperation to change the subject came out as forced as it felt.

Mr. Foster twisted the end of his mustache. "I suppose it depends on what happens tonight."

"For fuck's sake." Briar flicked his cards to the table. "Hope's gonna be fine, just like Maia. I'm gonna grab more wood for the fire before we all fuckin' freeze to death."

Briar snuffed out his smoke, storming into the woods.

"He'll be fine," Winter said, adding her cards to the mix. "Harper ain't known for controlling his emotions, but he cools off just as quick as he heats up."

"He has a right to be angry." Mr. Foster paused, as if second-guessing himself. His eyes found Maia's, giving him whatever confidence he needed. "We all do, given the position we've been put in."

Winter raised a sharp eyebrow, her nose piercing glinting in the moonlight. "You had a choice, Mr. Foster, remember? You *chose* to cut those two lines into Maia's skin."

"And Briar?" Maia asked, keeping her head low. "Did he have a choice? Or is he just another sacrifice to the cause?"

The silence around the table made Maia regret her words, and she hoped they didn't read into it. If they knew what she was willing to do to protect Briar, they could easily use it to their advantage.

"I *chose* him and this group because they were the right ones for *this* job." Winter's words were strong, but not harsh. She leaned forward, bracing her elbows on her knees and forcing Maia to look into her cat-like eyes. "Most people think my position makes it so I only know how to follow orders. It couldn't be further from the truth. What makes me so good at what I do is that I'm not afraid to *question* orders. I respect what you did for these people. Which is why I chose the team I did. I know better than to underestimate you, Maia, and I would appreciate if you'd grant me the same courtesy."

The way she changed her words and tone to match Maia's made it clear she considered her equal—far from a puppet.

Maia nodded in understanding.

With that, Winter pushed herself to her feet, adjusting her uniform. "We'll stand beside you tomorrow *regardless* of what happens tonight."

She gave Mr. Foster one last look before joining her guards.

"I'm going to grab my bag," he said in a whisper. "Have a good evening, Mr. Calderone."

"You as well, Mr. Foster."

Fatigue washed over Maia, making her suddenly feel heavy. Still, the last thing she needed was to be left alone with Aster, so she stood. "I'll go with you, sir."

A gunshot rang through the trees, sending Aster to his feet and Maia to his side, her grip tight on his arm. He looked down, surprised. The fear in her eyes hardened his face protectively as he gently pulled her behind him.

Winter, however, wasn't as kind, yanking Maia back by her coat and dragging her behind the guards.

They had already kicked out the fire and drawn their weapons, aiming at the now-silent tree line. Maia's heart thundered in her ears. Briar was still out there. Why wasn't he back yet? She refused to allow any of her racing thoughts to take root. He was okay. He had to be okay.

More gunshots punctured the foreboding stillness, followed by shouts that made Maia's entire body tense. Footsteps rushed in their direction, and she reached under her coat, unlatching her dagger with a trembling hand. Winter raised a tight fist, readying her guards for her order. They held a collective breath.

Heavy steps slid into the clearing, and Maia nearly collapsed with relief as Briar stumbled towards them.

"A group of Portico guards just invaded the town," he said, bending over to catch his breath.

Winter cursed, dropping her hand. "It's those fucking rebels impersonating us again. They chose the wrong *fucking* town." Her voice was closer to a growl than anything human as she shoved a rifle into Briar's arms. "Let's go!"

Winter pushed forward into the trees and Maia followed, earning a nod of respect. Could Briar ever carry himself with the same authority Winter held so naturally? Maybe they were making the wrong decision overthrowing her.

A single shot from Winter's gun and one shrouded figure was down. Moving in a swarm, they continued past the trees onto the dirt road. A second figure ran from behind a stack of crates, falling from another bullet. They continued to the center of the town, where a small crowd stood with weapons drawn.

"Thought you said you were here to help," the confrontational man from earlier snapped.

Winter lowered her gun as a sign of peace. "They're not ours. Just rebels dressed as us."

"Fucking rebels." The man spat on the dirt. "Looks like they were trying to poison our well."

Maia's stomach dropped. It was the same tactics Portico used. What did the rebellion gain from poisoning a shantytown?

"How do you know?" she asked.

He pointed his gun at a body lying next to the well. "That asshole was holdin' this."

Maia took the vial from the man's hand, removing the stopper. The musty, urine-like smell turned her stomach. It was one she would never forget from her apprenticeship.

"Poison hemlock."

She closed the vial, tucking it into her pocket as she made her way to the body. The guards searched the perimeter while the townsfolk started back to their shacks. Maia checked the man's pockets and pulled up the sleeves of his jacket, hoping not to find what she was looking for. Her heart plummeted. She lifted a string with a small metal disk from around his neck.

Orion's symbol. Aquila wasn't lying.

Dropping the necklace, she stood to find Winter and Briar hovering behind her.

"You look disappointed," Winter said in the same measured tone as before.

Maia wiped her hands on her coat, starting back up the road. "He deserved what he got. They all did."

The rogue rebels lying face down in the road weren't worthy to wear the symbol. Briar followed silently, giving her shoulder a comforting squeeze. The attack wasn't about restoring hope. It was nothing more than petty retaliation. She gripped the vial in her pocket. They fucking deserved it.

They returned bleary-eyed early the next morning. Hope skipped over, reaching for Briar's hand.

"Mama said you kept us safe last night."

Briar picked her up, throwing her over his shoulder as she giggled infectiously. "Couldn't let you show me up."

The bond that seemed to blossom between Briar and Hope filled Maia's heart while simultaneously shattering it. In a different life, she could imagine him with a family of his own, surrounded by all the love he deserved.

They stopped. A crowd now stood before them, as if eagerly awaiting their arrival. The man who had been arguing with them the day before rolled up his shirt sleeve.

"You said just two cuts, right?"

Mr. Foster glanced at Maia, unable to contain his excitement. "Yes. Precisely." The crowd erupted, thrusting their dirty arms towards him. "Please, there's no need to worry. We have more than enough for all of you."

Before the day was over, they had inoculated five families, an older man, and a group of mineworkers. The guards kicked a ball around with the children while Aster sat with a group of townsfolk, appreciative to share their stories with someone eager to listen.

More stepped forward with each passing day, and the praise for Portico's philanthropy grew. Maia found herself getting caught up in the excitement. Toasting lagers around the campfire with men and women who should have been the enemy. Speculating if word would spread to other shantytowns about the cure. Imagining crowds standing outside of Portico's gates, waiting for their chance at hope.

It wasn't until she lay down to sleep, Briar snoring beside her, that she forced herself to think of the rebellion. It was the reason she was here, but the longer she spent in Portico's presence, the more she had to remind herself of that.

The next evening, Maia made her final pass for the night, knocking on an elderly man's door.

"Mr. Kline," she said, through the rusted aluminum. "Just checking to make sure you don't need anything before we leave."

The silence wasn't like him, and she knocked again. Still, no response. She pushed the door open, finding him curled up on a dirty pile of clothes in the corner.

Fear gripped her chest. "Mr. Kline?"

"Leave," the old man managed between wet breaths. "I ain't well."

She continued forward, kneeling beside him and placing a hand on his frail shoulder. "It's okay. I can—"

The blood-soaked cloth tucked in his trembling hand stole the words from her lips.

It didn't work.

"Please, go."

Another fit of wet coughs shook his body. Maia ripped off her jacket, placing it over him. What did they do wrong? She thought back to the two lines she cut into his arm. She had sanitized the scalpel. Cleansed his arm. Done everything right. *Infected. Tainted. Dangerous.* She shook away the words.

"I'm not leaving you."

A knock on the door made her jump. She spun to find Mr. Foster peering inside. He didn't have the cuts, and she couldn't risk him getting sick. Her eyes pleaded for him to leave as she shook her head.

His face dropped with understanding. "I'll be outside if you need me."

Shifting back to Mr. Kline, she propped a pile of rags under his head to help with his rattling breath—just as she had for her mother. His symptoms were too far along, and she wondered if he had already been sick, the inoculation only making it worse. It didn't matter. His lines were by her hand, which meant she would be with him until the end. She wiped his feverish forehead and rubbed his ice-cold hands.

The door opened again, and she glanced over her shoulder to find Aster holding a bowl in his hand, his posture tall and sure.

"Hope's mother asked me to bring Mr. Kline some soup."

Maia's heart broke at the kindness of the woman who barely had enough for her own family. She stood, taking the dish from him. "Please tell her thank you."

Aster's eyes searched hers. "I can stay."

"He's too sick." She forced an appreciative smile. "Thank you though."

"I have the inoculation too. I asked Mr. Foster to do it the night of the rebel attack."

"You didn't..." Maia struggled to find words, looking up at him in disbelief. Why did he risk the cuts before knowing they were safe? And why offer to stay for a dying stranger? "You don't need to."

The worry etched between his brows softened. "I want to."

She didn't care if it was a lie, or some attempt at manipulation. Aster's presence somehow made her feel more in control as she forced down her fear. Returning to Mr. Kline, she carefully lifted his head. He took sips of soup between coughs, and Maia wiped his mouth each time he spat it back up. Tears ran down his cheeks as he apologized, but Maia reassured him she didn't mind. Despite the watch in her pocket, it wasn't her time ticking away.

His breathing grew shallow as the night progressed. She held his cold and clammy hand, humming a nursery rhyme her mother used to sing. Aster removed his jacket, resting it on Maia's shoulders as Mr. Kline's breaths grew short and quick. She lowered her head, recognizing the pattern. The same breaths her mother took just before she passed. His grip loosened around hers, and with that, he was gone.

She sat in silence—lost in it—searching for an emotion or thought to ground her. His hand now lay open, cold and infinitely empty, and she stared at it until it no longer held meaning. Her breath caught, refusing to move from where it lodged in her throat. This was her fault. Guilt rested heavy on her chest. She was going to die, if not from her barren lungs, from her pounding heart. She had been so certain the cure was the answer without thinking about what the consequences truly looked like. They looked ashen and worn. Frail and stiff.

She closed her eyes and bit down on her trembling lower lip as her breath forced itself out in a gasp. Time was the only thing holding her together, but the seconds of numbness were slowly running out. A warmth found her hand. It was almost painful, thawing the ice crystalizing in her veins, and flooding her with a comfort she didn't deserve.

"I'm sorry, Maia," Aster whispered.

Her fingers closed around his, too tight, too desperate to hold on to something that wasn't even real. His kindness was to someone who didn't exist. A story created to make him trust her. Who was really the master of lies here?

It didn't matter though. In that moment, she needed him. His resolve. His warmth. And she was selfish enough to take it.

"What am I going to tell them tomorrow?"

The shake in her voice betrayed her as she desperately grabbed for the slowly shattering pieces of herself.

"Nothing." Aster tightened his hand around hers. "That's what I'm here for."

"I didn't mean to—" She choked on an emotion forcing its way to the surface.

The pain was so real, so visceral, that she wondered if somewhere deep inside she wasn't hemorrhaging from self-inflicted wounds.

Aster lifted her chin, his face as pained as she felt. "This isn't your fault, Maia." His warmth was so close, she ached for it to surround her so she didn't have to hold herself together anymore. "People here forget what hope looks like... how it *feels*. You gave that to him. Most people aren't that lucky."

Aster's words loosened the tears pooling in her eyes, and she dropped her face as his thumb gently brushed them away.

"I'm sorry." Her words felt heavy and empty at the same time. She slipped her hand from his and stood, allowing herself one last parting glance at Mr. Kline.

Tonight, she would mourn him, but tomorrow she would stand beside Aster as he spun the carefully crafted lies they needed to remain the heroes of this story.

19

SACRIFICE

One day, the ripples of our actions will catch up to us, and we will finally understand the consequences of what we've done.

A. Wells – Winter 2294

Aster Calderone had a talent for beautiful lies. He stood, face worn, eyes heavy, as if carrying the town's grief on his shoulders. While the crowd gathered to mourn, Aster recounted the stories they had told him about Mr. Kline.

A day that should have been one of tears turned into a celebration for a man loved by his community for his kindness, contagious laughter, and outlandish stories. Maia didn't know that version of Mr. Kline, but by the end of the day, she felt like she had.

Still, even with smiles on their faces, a heaviness lingered in the air—one the fear of mortality often brought. By the end of the week, the unease of those who had been inoculated had passed. Maia and the team said their goodbyes, burdened with gifts they didn't need, but couldn't deny.

Expecting a grand welcome when they returned to Portico, they were surprised as the guards posted at the front gates turned their weapons on them.

"Aquila says you're to be quarantined until cleared," the young guard squeaked, clearly second-guessing his orders as he looked up at Winter.

"Where is he?" she asked, gently dropping her hand on his shoulder.

The guard lowered his weapon, trusting whatever threats he received wouldn't be enforced. "The regional merchant representatives arrived this afternoon for discussions."

"I'll ensure he knows you did as he asked."

He bowed his head in appreciation, stepping aside. As they continued across the busy gathering grounds towards Aquila's manor, Maia noticed each of the salutes and nods of respect directed towards Winter and Aster. They might have been Aquila's pawns, but they were still regarded as leaders in their own right.

The iron gates of Aquila's manor swung open without question. Winter's boots crunched with authority on the gravel walkway surrounding the fountain. She forced open the wooden front doors, barging into the foyer. The crowd of merchants gasped, faces filled with shock, and conversations suspended in the heavy, hot air.

Tala, however, froze. Her hooded scout quickly tucked a paper into their cloak pocket. It was only a second, but Maia saw fear flicker across Tala's face. Whatever she was hiding, Maia needed to uncover. It was the only way to balance the scales and no longer be at Tala's mercy.

Tala stalked forward, parting the crowd. It was as if they feared the darkness she exuded might stain their lavish attire. "Aquila ordered your useless guards to—"

Winter continued past her into the parlor, Maia and Aster at her sides. The scout, face shadowed in anonymity, attempted to sneak past unnoticed. A slight bump of their shoulders, and Maia was tucking the letter from their cloak into her pocket.

Perched in an armchair, Aquila sat, frail and delicate, watching them with veiled annoyance. "I see you've returned."

Winter eyed Aster. They no longer needed her brute force, but his finesse. He stepped forward with his captivating smile. "It worked, sir. Portico now holds the key to eradicating red lung."

Maia shifted uncomfortably at the buzz of whispers surrounding them.

Aquila, however, fed off it, a wicked grin slithering across his lips. "Excellent work, my boy. Mr. Foster, would you please explain what this means to our esteemed guests?"

His face flushed, but he nodded. "Yes, of course, sir. It appears to be the solution to preventing future outbreaks. We obviously need some further—"

Aquila stood, lifting his arms to the room. "This is a momentous day for the future of our New World. With this discovery, you and your families will no longer need to fear the gruesome death of red lung. Please join me in applauding the expertise, courage, and devotion of this exceptional group."

Maia appreciated the contrast of her ratty travel clothes against the brightly dressed crowd, lifting sparkling glasses in praise of something they didn't understand. Aquila's boney hand found her shoulder, and she looked up, surprised at his fleeting gaze of approval, before he disappeared into the crowd.

Winter released her guards to enjoy food and drinks before heading to the barracks.

"Come on, boss. Let's grab some fancy grub," Briar said, nudging Maia with his elbow.

She smiled, but was acutely aware of Aster's presence beside her. "I'll be there in a minute."

Briar nodded, flinching as another guard hooked his arm around his shoulders, dragging him to a group of women eyeing them from across the room.

Maia should have walked away, kept her distance from Aster like she was told, but between them was an inexplicable pull that held her hostage at his side.

A server walked by with a tray of drinks, and Aster took two, offering Maia one. "Care to join—"

Aquila called to him from across the room. The flicker of irritation looked foreign on Aster's face, and he quickly replaced it with a forced smile and apology.

If his kindness had been nothing more than manipulation, it worked, and she hated that she couldn't tell the difference with him. She threw back the drink she didn't want, ignoring how cold the room suddenly felt as Aster walked away.

"Maia," Mr. Foster beckoned, pulling away from a group. His eyes held the same sadness she had seen back in Rocky Mount. A longing for moments that would only ever be memories. "I wanted to say thank you. Being in that shantytown... I understand now why Peter couldn't give up on what he believed."

She forced down the voice in the back of her head, reminding her that Mr. Foster was here because of her betrayal. Everything he gave up to save her when it was him in danger the whole time.

"I will never stop missing him," he continued, his bushy brows pulled tight. "But the anger is fading."

She gave him a weak smile, grateful that despite everything she had taken, there was something she could offer him in return.

"I hope one day you'll be able to let go of that anger too, my dear." His eyes were hopeful. If only he knew—anger was the only thing keeping her fear at bay. Fulfilling the same dark need as each glass of whiskey at Folly's.

"Just remember, this is *your* work, sir, not Portico's," she said, her gaze flickering to Aquila. "*You* decide what's done with it, no matter what they say."

He tried to read her face, but as he looked away, she wondered if he decided it was best not to know. "This is *our* work now, and I imagine you'll know before I do what needs to happen next. Have a good night."

Mr. Foster struggled through the crowd as they aggressively shook his hand and landed strong pats on his back. Rowan ignored him as he passed, his eyes only on Maia. The flames gleamed off the golden buttons of his jacket as he stood next to the fireplace, waiting for her to join him.

She sighed, reaching into her pocket and removing the letter she picked off the scout. Her fingers teased the folded edges, but it wasn't until she was at Rowan's side that she was brave enough to open it.

"Congratulations," Rowan muttered into his cup. "Your little stunt worked."

Holding the paper up to the fire's light, she stared at the letters scrawled across the page arranged in no discernable order. Why would Tala hide this? She flipped it over to find the other side blank.

Rowan glanced over her shoulder. "What is that?"

"I don't know yet," she said, echoing Rowan's words from the library.

He tensed beside her. "What did you do?"

Before Maia could tuck it away, Rowan snatched it, holding it over the flames.

"We won't get a second chance to find what she's hiding," she said, voice tight with bridled panic.

Rowan's hand hesitated for too long, and Maia's shoulders collapsed with relief. He had given into his weakness of protecting things he shouldn't. Folding the paper, he tucked it away, glancing around the room to ensure no one noticed.

"Go to Canal Row and wait under the eyes of the owl. I'll be there as soon as I can leave unnoticed."

Canal Row was the last place she wanted to be, especially at night, but Rowan walked away before she could argue. Grabbing another drink from a tray, she threw it back, grateful to escape into the cool winter air.

Banquet tables filled with food from the visiting merchants sat along the crowded gathering grounds. Roasted chickens, pigs, and lamb could not compete with the intoxicating smell of the freshly baked breads. Maia's stomach growled in response, and she wished she would have followed Briar.

Past the ancillary housing, just outside of Portico's marked territory, awaited the dingy bars, game halls, and brothels of Canal Row. A place known for supplying guards with contraband and allowing them to indulge between posts. Ancillary staff often risked their day's earnings for a chance to double or triple it at the game halls, and even the respectable diplomats changed into commoner clothes, giving in to their more carnal desires.

Canal Row existed outside of Portico's law and order, where the only rule was to not get caught. Cheating and stealing often led to bans or broken bones. But in Portico, if someone disappeared, there was a common saying—they were *swimming in the canal.*

Maia shoved her hands deep into her pockets, keeping her head low as she turned onto the crumbling walkway, the rushing sound of water beside her. Darkness had only just claimed the sky, and men already sat passed out under bridges, faces and knuckles bruised from fights they wouldn't remember. Maia could almost see Briar in their broken faces.

Men and women emerged from the brothels, faces skillfully painted, wearing clothing of delicate fabrics to justify the prices of their broken bodies. They reached out, grazing Maia's jacket, but never meeting her eyes. Canal Row wasn't about creating connections. Without the promise of anonymity, it wouldn't exist.

The buildings were basic, wooden structures, built as quickly as they could be taken down. Searching the signs and posts, Maia had yet to spot the owl eyes Rowan had mentioned. She was about to turn around when a rickety Old World bridge appeared in the distance through the snow flurries.

Graffiti peeked through overgrown foliage bursting from a shell of a building across the canal. It was exactly the kind of place Rowan would pick to meet. Maia tested the stability of the bridge with her boot. With a glance over her shoulder, she continued across the rushing canal to the concrete cavern, her footsteps echoing under rusted steel beams twisted with vines. The light of the full moon illuminated the dark space, catching two wary, yellow-green eyes from a dark blue mural of an owl.

Now she waited. Leaning against the wall, she lowered herself to the cool ground, pulling her knees to her chest. Clouds passed over the moon, shrouding her in darkness as a rat scurried into a patch of green stubbornly growing through the concrete. The hairs on her arms stood as she realized how alone she was. A sitting target. Like a rat in a cage. The sound of footsteps approached, and her hand trailed to her hip, unlatching her dagger.

"At least no one can sneak up on us here." Rowan had changed into commoner clothes, his pants the same dirt-stained pair he wore the night she joined the rebellion. He removed the letter from his jacket, waving it at her. "You realize Tala has no issue killing you for this, right?"

She blew out a breath and stood, brushing the dirt from her pants. "Let's hope exposing her to Aquila will force him to get rid of her first."

Rowan unfolded the paper, holding it under a shaft of light. "It's a cipher. The key is to focus on the smaller words to spot consistencies." His finger ran across the page and stopped on an *N*. "These are most likely *I*'s or *A*'s."

Maia scanned the tunnel for something to write with. Grabbing a stick, she walked to a patch of snow near the water, drawing dashes for each letter of the note. "What do you think it is?"

His eyes grew distant in thought. "Tala would keep something like this vague. Let's go with *A*'s."

Maia wrote *A*'s over the dashes and turned back to Rowan, surprised to see a sad smile on his face. "What's wrong?"

He glanced back at the mural. "This is where your father started the rebellion."

Maia followed Rowan's gaze back to the owl eyes. Her father had been here. His footsteps echoed against the same walls as hers. Whispered in the same darkness about things far more dangerous than the letters scrawled in the snow. The eyes felt different now—watchful, protective.

"Come on, let's get back to it before someone drunkenly wanders this way," he said, angling the paper under the light.

They continued with the code as the cold took hold of the night, exposing their breath.

She can't be trusted. Her actions counter any traction made and suggest she may be actively working against the cause. Give the word, and I'll cut this loose end before it's pulled.

Maia's teeth chattered as she glanced down at the message, arms folded for warmth.

"She's talking about you," Rowan whispered.

"I know." She knew from the first sentence. "This isn't to Aquila, though. She's working with someone behind his back. Do you think it's another Advisor?"

Was it coincidence Aster knocked on her door the morning Tala visited with threats? A shiver ran through her, and she tightened her jacket. Could all of this have been a setup?

Rowan kicked away the message, tucking the letter back into his pocket. "This was a mistake. We need to plant the letter on someone and get back to Portico."

"No. Aquila needs to—"

Rowan grabbed her arms, pulling her to him, his teeth bared. "You don't get it. Someone *will die* because of this. I'd prefer it not be you."

Her stomach dropped, and she shrunk in his grip. It was the first time she was terrified in his presence. "I'm sorry."

"I'll take care of it," Rowan said, loosening his grip. "You head out first, and I'll follow. Go straight to the collector's housing. Don't turn around, especially if you hear footsteps following. Do you understand?"

She should have said *no*, taken the letter and the consequences that came with it. Instead, she stayed silent, face burning with shame. This wasn't about survival, no matter how she twisted it. She nodded, refusing to meet his gaze.

"I'll fix this, I promise." Rowan's voice softened, and Maia dared a glance. The knit of his brows was for her, not for what he had to do. "Meet me here again tomorrow—same time—and we'll figure out our next steps."

The owl's eyes watched in disappointment as her echoing footsteps started back to Canal Row. *Someone will die because of this.* Because of her.

She reached the other end of the bridge, collapsing against the wall of a brothel. The knots in her stomach forced her to double over in pain. This couldn't be the person she was becoming. She promised herself she wouldn't give in to the darkness. Regardless of the consequence, she needed to make it right.

Gunshots rang from behind her, wrenching Maia's attention back to the tunnel.

"Rowan?" Her voice was barely a whisper, forcing itself past the grip of fear around her throat.

The men and women hovering outside of the brothel slowly moved back into the building, leaving Maia alone in the dead winter silence. She closed her eyes, trying to block out the horrifying scenarios her mind was creating, and held her breath, slowly counting down until her heartbeat matched the dwindling numbers.

Three, two, one.

Maia jumped to her feet, rushing through the shadows back to the tunnel. She peered around the concrete opening. Rowan kneeled in the center of the tunnel, his skin a ghostly shade of white under the light of the moon. He held a deep gash above his left hip. Two of Tala's scouts lay motionless on the floor, while the other two argued.

Maia unlatched the sheath of her dagger, nudging a rock loose with her toe. If she could just draw one of them out—

"What are you—" The man's voice trailed as she spun, meeting his hooded gaze. Another one of Tala's scouts. She didn't even hear his footsteps in the snow. They both remained frozen, staring at each other. Her heart stopped as a scream caught in her throat. A single blink was all it took for the world to collapse around them.

The man rushed forward, his blade swiping at her gut, but catching her jacket. She turned to run. Not fast enough.

He tackled her to the ground, knocking the wind from her lungs. Flipping her onto her back, he pressed his knife against her throat.

"Why are you here, Sagitta?" he growled.

There was no time for strategy as she frantically squirmed under his weight. It made her sick how weak she felt as his knees dug painfully into her arms, pinning her down. She spat in his face, and without thinking, he lifted the knife from her throat to wipe his cheek. This was her chance.

Her knee found his groin, and he choked on a cry, rolling off of her. Maia flipped over, pushing herself back to her feet. The wet snow slid out from under her.

Get up.

A sob escaped from deep in her chest as she pushed herself up again. Her toe caught her other boot, dropping her back onto her hands and knees.

GET UP!

Her heart collapsed as the man's grip found her ankle, yanking her back to him.

This wasn't how she would die.

Not alone in the cold.

Not on Canal Row.

She removed her dagger, stabbing it into a dead patch of grass and dragging herself forward. He pulled back harder. Tears blurred her vision as she gripped the handle with all the strength she had left. He was going to kill her. Her incompetence would be her downfall. The metallic *clink* of a gun hammer echoed in the night.

It was him or her.

She pried the dagger from the dirt and spun, thrusting it forward.

His face hovered only inches from hers, mouth wide in surprise as his hood fell. Blemishes ran along the hairline of his youthful face and patchy beard. He was a kid, no older than Kayla had been. Eyes searching hers, he kneeled in silence, mouth still gaping. His hands dropped to his sides, the gun slipping from his loose fingers. She wanted him to scream, to curse her, to say anything—but his mouth sat open, hollow and endless.

What had she done?

He fell backwards, taking her blade with him. Her hand trembled violently, suspended between the person she was, and the one she had become. His eyes fell to the dagger in his chest, fingers grazing the handle. A wet sob escaped his lips as he winced in pain.

She felt it... everything.

His fear, his pain, his hopelessness, and she deserved it all.

The tremble in her hand seized her body, tightening her chest. She couldn't breathe.

She didn't deserve to breathe.

Maia squeezed her eyes shut, sending tears down her cheeks as she tried to remove herself from their cold world. Her blood-soaked hands covered her face, the sickening metallic smell surrounding her.

Don't you dare look away.

She dropped her hands, meeting his grieving gaze. Blood pooled in his mouth, trailing down the side of his graying face. She wanted to reach over and wipe it away, just as she had done for her mother. But she was trapped in her fear.

His breath rattled as the blood filled his lungs. The sound was too familiar. Too close. It wouldn't be long before he drowned in his own blood. Just like her mother.

With clipped breaths, he lifted his hand, reaching for her. He had every right to want to put it around her neck, but in his last moments, all he wanted was someone to hold it. Maia reached out to him. Not fast enough.

His hand dropped into the snow as he gasped his final breath.

He was gone, and the world fell silent. Too still and calm, as if holding its breath to allow him a moment of peace. She remained frozen, taking in every feature of his face. It would never be far from her thoughts.

A howl from the woods broke the silence. Maia leaned over and threw up, her ears ringing so loud it made her lightheaded. She swayed on her knees, trying to keep herself conscious as she took in her blurry surroundings.

Canal Row was bustling again as if in a different world than hers, and she suddenly remembered why she was here. Swiping the boy's gun, she stumbled to her feet, peering around the edge of the concrete wall. Rowan was gone, only a trail of blood left behind. If they took him back to Portico, he could explain what happened.

She leaned back against the wall, closing her heavy eyes. The boy's gaping mouth waited for her. Her eyes shot open with a gasp, only to find his lifeless body in the snow. Her bloodied fingers gripped her hair as she slid down the wall, a horrifying wail escaping her. The sound was so feral, using its sharp nails to crawl out from somewhere deep within her. She allowed herself to feel everything.

Until she felt nothing.

A hollow shell all over again.

She stared at the lifeless body for what felt like days. Unmoving. Unblinking. When she finally stood, her pants had soaked through from the snow, and her muscles ached from the tension.

Without order, there is no justice.

She walked over to the man, pulling her dagger from his chest. The surrounding snow was stained red. Just like her mother's white gown. Something stirred in her chest, but she pushed it back down.

Without justice, there is no hope.

She cleaned her dagger on his coat and tucked it away, lifting the collar of her jacket as she continued back to Canal Row.

What do you sacrifice to become the wolf?

She now knew the answer to Hannah's question.

Everything.

20

REFLECTION

No one met Maia's empty gaze as she drifted back to the collector's housing. Her heavy feet guided her up the stairs to the door across from hers. She didn't remember knocking, but as the door opened, her hand still hovered in the air.

Sky's brows knit together with confusion, eyes heavy with sleep. The dark, malevolent gaze of his amulet stared back at her, making her shift uncomfortably in the doorway. Its darkness felt infinite, like the night sky against the inky-black ocean.

"What happened?" he asked, immediately snapping awake.

Despite the dark circles under his eyes, he reached for her, taking a quick glance down the hall. She didn't fight as he pulled her past the threshold into his room. There was a reason she ended up outside his door. He helped her to his bed and grabbed the water basin from the vanity.

"Who did this to you?" he whispered with so much violence it made the air still. His knuckles blanched around the washcloth while he carefully wiped the blood from her face.

Her hand rose to his, and her mouth moved, but everything felt detached. She had splintered into pieces, each one now struggling to survive on its own.

"It's not mine."

He stilled at her touch, and his steel eyes softened to a storm-gray as he looked at her. Or at least a version of her.

"Whose is it?"

She glanced at the shadows and nearly laughed. The ones to fear in Portico didn't need to hide.

"It was him or me."

The color drained from Sky's face, and his fingers found his pendant. Whatever he had fought to hold on to was gone. Was he mourning the person she had been the last time he saw her?

She took the rag and water basin from him, walking back to the vanity. Her hands trembled as she violently scrubbed away the blood. They hadn't stopped shaking since her dagger had found the boy's chest. She couldn't blame it on the cold or fear anymore. Catching sight of her reflection, she stopped.

The person staring back at her was unrecognizable. They were someone else's eyes.

Distant. Empty. Cold.

She nearly rubbed them raw, daring another glance. Dark circles made her look sickly and dangerous. Blood streaked her face and matted her hair. This was the person she had become. Her heart slowed, and she looked away, terrified of who she now saw in the mirror. Instead, she focused on the cloth, dabbing at the blood under her nails.

His blood.

A flash of his face. The blood pooling in his mouth. She saw him even without closing her eyes. Her chest ached, hands bracing the edge of the vanity. Panic slithered its way from her knotted stomach. She gasped for air that wouldn't come, as guilt constricted itself around her.

It was him or me.

The boy's face twisted in pain.

It's just a memory.

He raised his hand to her.

It's not real.

Another wave rolled her stomach. She choked as if his blood was now filling her lungs. He held out his hand—scared, desperate. She reached for it. So close. Not fast enough.

His hand went slack. She would never be fast enough.

He took his final breath all over again while she held her own. She slid to the floor, tears now streaming down her cheeks.

You deserve this...

Sky was beside her, cradling her in his arms as he brushed the bloody strands of hair from her face.

"It's okay, Maia. It's okay."

It wasn't. No matter how many times he said it, it wouldn't be okay. She curled herself painfully against his boney chest, the amulet pressing into her cheek. He whispered words she needed to hear—but didn't deserve—until her body refused anymore tears.

Sky lifted her onto the bed, his pained gaze lingering on her worn face. She could almost feel his walls falling between them, but instead, he pushed himself away, blowing out the oil lamp and trapping them in darkness. The mattress shifted under his weight, and she hated how cold he felt beside her. She tucked her trembling hands under the pillow, waiting until she could trust her voice.

"He was just a boy," she whispered, hoping he didn't hear.

His silence stole her breath, making her twist with guilt. She pinched her eyes shut and saw the boy's face. Felt his fear. *Your fault.*

Sky closed the space between them, wrapping his icy arms around her. "You can torture yourself all you want, but his age doesn't change anything. Trust me."

She thought about the boy Sky once was, justifying his kills. The man he had become with the soft edges as he sat alone with his thoughts.

That was why she was here. She saw him in the boy she left in the cold. Hoped his forgiveness would ease the burden of guilt burrowing deep into her being, but it didn't. The boy's death was now part of her. A shadow she would never escape.

Tears spilled onto the pillow. "It was him or me."

Sky's sharp nose pressed into her hair, and he pulled her closer. "I know."

His arms felt heavy. Suffocating.

Tonight would remain her purgatory.

Time passed slowly as Maia's panicked thoughts numbed into something far more terrifying than fear. Emptiness. A nothingness that made her grow cold and stiff. An unpolished, blood-covered stone.

Shadows reached for her as dusk threatened to banish them to their corners. Maia slipped out from under Sky's arm. His eyes opened, following her around the room as she gathered her boots and coat.

"I won't let anything happen to you," Sky said as she reached for the door-knob.

His promise was too late. She deserved whatever consequences waited beyond the door. Her grip tightened on the knob, and she forced down the panic building in her chest.

"I know."

Closing the door behind her, she pressed her back against the wood. She needed to pull herself together, but Sky's cold made her desperate for warmth. The same warmth that could easily destroy her, and yet she was willing to risk it. Pushing off the door, she crossed the hall to change out of her blood-stained clothes.

The low haze of dawn stretched lazily across the gathering grounds as Maia passed through Portico's gates. Six chimes from the bell tower died on the still air, and her gaze flickered towards the Council Hall. She shouldn't have been searching for Aster. He was the enemy, and it was becoming dangerous how often she had to remind herself of this. Still, her eyes lingered. A glint reflecting off the bright-white snow caught her attention.

Her body froze, refusing to allow her another step closer as she noticed something hanging from a wooden structure between the columns of Council Hall. A pair of glasses peeked from a chest pocket, catching the dulled sunrays. They were familiar to her the same way the pants with dirt-stained knees were. A black hood covered a head held up by a thick rope.

Anonymous. Erased.

Rowan's body gently swayed in the morning breeze as a crowd slowly formed around her. The emptiness inside her filled with something dark and volatile, slowly spreading over her bones. A viscous oil waiting for a spark.

"Lo que el monte nos dio," she whispered.

Orion's mark branded Rowan's chest, searing itself into the back of her eyes. *These stars... they're a target.* Edward warned her back at the safe house. Something she didn't want to believe until now. All she could do was hope they burned the stars into his skin after hanging him.

Her teeth ground at the whispers from those who stood dangerously close.

"Let 'em rot where they hang."

"Fucking traitor got what they deserved."

"One less rebel to worry about."

The cowards wouldn't even speak his name. He was a symbol now. A warning to traitors. Portico's *justice* was nothing more than propaganda. Maia touched her chest, as if the brand was already there.

"Looks like Aquila found his rebel."

Revulsion slithered up Maia's spine, settling on her tense shoulders as Tala emerged beside her.

"Let's hope this is a warning for any other traitors who might be hiding." Tala's words dripped with venom, forcing Maia's hands into tight fists, her nails puncturing her palms.

All the hate and anger she had before coming to Portico returned to her in a flood. Would things be different had she felt this sooner? She shook away the thought. She needed the anger, not the guilt.

This wasn't a long game anymore. If she was next, Maia would make sure everyone hidden behind Portico's gates knew the truth about the role they played in this New World. It was time to stop hiding and treat each of the Council Advisors as the targets they were. If she was going to end Portico, she needed to be just as ruthless as them.

"It doesn't worry you that Aquila not only allowed a rebel onto the grounds, but also gave him the second-highest position?" Maia lifted her chin, hoping her voice would carry over the whispers. "He had the power to manipulate anyone, including the Council."

Eyes were now on them, and Tala took a second to collect herself. "Good thing we caught him before any of that happened."

Maia's lip curled. "Let's hope."

Council's power was from the trust of their people. But Aquila's lies were nothing more than precariously balanced cards. All it took was a strategic nudge for everything to crumble around him.

He bred devotion with meaningless speeches, conning his people into believing their world was better because of him. Convincing them to trust only his words and not their eyes. And they were willing, because lies kept them safe and unburdened. The truth would mean that every fucking one of them were wrong.

Maia turned to leave when Tala's grip clamped around her wrist, pulling her close. Her lips grazed the shell of Maia's ear. "I know it was you who stole the letter. And I know you put the dagger in Caleb by the canal. You have both of their blood on your hands."

Caleb. His face appeared again, but felt different now. Familiar.

Maia tried to push away, her hand catching on Tala's cloak. She flinched as the grip around her wrist tightened.

"But that letter was nothing compared to the journals we found hidden in that traitor's room."

Her obsidian eyes bore into Maia's. Could Tala feel her skin go cold in her grip? Hear her thundering heart?

A soft, nasally laugh escaped Tala, and she nodded as if realizing something she should have known. "You should be very clear about what side you're on, Sagitta. Our Overseer seemed to have forgotten his allegiance." Tala's grip loosened, and she glanced back at Rowan's body. "But he won't anymore."

Maia tucked away the dagger she picked from Tala's cloak. The same shifty hand that stole the letter might as well have wrapped the rope around Rowan's throat, and handed the journals to Portico. At least Tala couldn't stab her in the back as she walked away.

Turning into the crowd, Maia noticed Sky and Briar behind her.

"We should get out of here," Sky said as Maia approached.

Briar pulled her protectively to his side, continuing past the crowd towards the garden maze. "I hate to say it, but he's right. We ain't got a plan anymore."

"Yes, we do," Maia said, passing under the still-blooming rose trellis. Senna stepped out of the shadows and lowered her hood. She didn't have to say anything, her confidence in Maia reflected in the way she stood waiting for her to continue. "We came here for a reason, and I think it's time we finish it."

Senna's gaze ignited. "So what's the plan?"

Maia removed Tala's dagger from her pocket. It was painted flat black from hilt to point, except for a *V* engraved in the metal just below the handle. "It would be *detrimental* to Portico if their people began to question the Council and Aquila's judgment. Allowing a rebel to infiltrate their halls could be all it took to sway them."

Senna's lips twisted venomously. "The things a rebel could have planted in Aquila's delicate mind. I'll see if the scouts can do some digging."

Sky tucked away his pendant, not hiding his frustration. "Fine, the collectors can look into the books. Missing funds could be getting routed to the rebels."

It was all they needed. Rumors and suspicion. None of it had to be true. Maia, however, had a bigger problem to solve. Keeping Rowan's journals out of Aquila's gaunt hands.

"What the fuck am I supposed to do?" Briar asked, glancing between each of them.

"You'll figure something out, handsome," Senna said, lifting her hood as they each walked their separate ways.

Portico would know the truth. If they wanted to make Rowan's death a symbol, Maia would give it the meaning it deserved. And if Tala would regret anything today, it would be not hanging Maia beside him.

21

FLAMES

*There's beauty in seeing the exact moment tinder ignites—
even if it leads to nothing more than destruction.*

A. Wells – Fall 2279

I t only took a few scattered seeds for the whispers and rumors to spread like weeds. General Winter confiscated dozens of drawings of Aquila as a senile old man, now a pawn of the rebellion. But no matter how many times she reprimanded her guards, there were always more. As for the collectors, Rafe was in over his head with his unbalanced books. Only Tala and Aster seemed to remain untouched.

Each morning since Rowan's death, Maia would cross the gathering grounds towards the lab, sensing eyes everywhere. Mr. Foster busied her restless mind with tasks, while the other researchers maintained their distance. They weren't quick to forgive her for undermining them in front of Aquila and his council. It was easier for Maia to know she was hated—there was a familiarity to it. The same familiarity as the suffocating loneliness she felt since finding Rowan.

Portico had suddenly become small. Once invisible behind its gates, she was now surrounded by whispers she wasn't sure were for or against her. As she made her way to the collector's housing each evening, there was comfort in knowing she would find Caleb waiting for her in the darkness. Still, after two tiring weeks expecting Tala to retaliate, she wondered if something far worse was brewing in the silence.

The door to the lab opened, and Maia straightened as Aster entered. His eyes found hers before anyone else's, and the weight of his gaze dropped her stomach like an anchor, forcing her to look away.

"Good afternoon, Mr. Foster," Aster said, now standing beside her. "Maia."

He said her name softly, like a secret between them. She hated wishing it was. Chewing her lip, she gave him a quick nod.

"Mr. Calderone, to what do we owe the pleasure?" Mr. Foster asked, twirling the end of his mustache with curiosity.

Aster removed his heavy coat, draping it over the back of a chair—a gesture she was certain he had learned to make himself appear more casual. Unfortunately, it didn't hide the tension rolling off him in waves as he gripped the edge of the table.

"What's wrong?" Maia asked.

He stilled beside her, his gaze burning into the side of her face. "I..." There was a moment of hesitation before he straightened his back, as if trying to maintain the formality of the entire room. "I'd like for you and Mr. Foster to join me this evening in the Diplomat's Hall for a... private matter."

The lab grew quiet around them, and Maia realized she had drawn attention to something he hoped to keep discreet.

"Of course, Mr. Calderone. We'll be there," Mr. Foster said, trying to slow the build of suspicion.

Aster thanked him and picked up his jacket, his arm brushing hers as he passed, leaving her with the smell of bergamot and the lingering warmth of his touch.

"Are you okay, my dear?" Mr. Foster asked, reaching for a vial sitting in the rack. "You look... unsettled."

She rubbed her arm and turned back to her paperwork. Whatever the secret was, it was enough to rattle the confidence of a man like Aster, and it terrified her that it could be any number of her lies.

The Diplomat Hall was a faded gray building with a red terracotta roof, looking longingly up at Council Hall. Maia and Mr. Foster waited as a group of diplomats passed under one of the columned entrances, making their way home for the evening. Their shoulders sat low from leather bags and thick books in hand, while their hooded eyes fought off fatigue.

Taking their time, Maia and Mr. Foster wandered the many empty halls of the building until finding Aster's name placard on the wall. The large double doors were already open, and a fireplace cast an inviting orange glow throughout the office. Overstuffed crimson armchairs and a loveseat sat in front of it. A plush fur rug and a dark walnut coffee table filled the space between. Everything needed to create the illusion of comfort.

"Lower your voice," Aster hissed. Maia gripped Mr. Foster's arm, holding him back from entering the office. "I don't need to explain myself to you, Rafe."

The twins were arguing, and she tiptoed closer to eavesdrop. Mr. Foster's eyes grew wide, glancing down the hall with uncertainty, but he remained quiet.

"This isn't like you. Since when do you go against Aquila's orders? He told you to ask Mr. Foster for help, not *her*."

"He trusted her before. He will again."

"Are you really willing to risk your life on that? What the fuck is going on with you?"

A chair creaked, followed by the slam of what sounded like a heavy book. "You have bigger things to worry about. Your collectors are shaving coin in transit. The books are perfect. It's the delivery that doesn't match."

She rubbed at the pocketful of coin Sky had given her earlier that week.

"Don't change the subject. You need to be careful with her, she's—"

Maia took a step into the doorway, gently knocking. "Are we early?"

The twins straightened simultaneously, as if pulled by the same string.

"No," Aster said, handing a leather-bound book to Rafe. "He was just leaving."

Rafe's lips pressed together with indignation, and he yanked his jacket from the back of a chair. Mr. Foster whispered a weak *good evening* as he passed, receiving a grumble in response.

"Please, come in," Aster said, walking over to close the door. Maia unbuttoned her coat, surprised by the light graze of his fingers as he helped her out of it. "You can take a seat by the fire. I apologize for the secrecy earlier, but it wasn't something I could discuss in front of others."

Draping her jacket over his arm, his hand found the small of her back, scorching her skin through the cloth of her dress. Her body betrayed her, straining to lean into him.

She forced herself forward, focusing on the intricate hand carvings of his wooden desk and walls of neatly organized books. Her gaze stopped on Mr. Foster, a crooked smile tucked under his mustache as he watched.

Maia slipped into the loveseat closest to the armchair Mr. Foster chose.

"Thank you both for joining me this evening." Aster unbuttoned his diplomat jacket with two quick flicks, easing into the other armchair. The crisp, white shirt under his jacket hugged his chest, loosening slightly at the taper of his waist. Another dangerous distraction. "Aquila asked me to review the late Overseer's journals. However, there are things that appear more suited for a healer over my Old World history and war knowledge. I was hoping you might provide your expertise?"

Rafe's argument now made sense. She wasn't a healer, and Aster was intelligent enough to understand the significance of the journals on his own. Which made her wonder why she was there. The three journals sat in the center of the coffee table, a vase of roses resting between them and the fire.

"Of course, Mr. Calderone. We're happy to assist," Mr. Foster answered for both of them.

"I appreciate that, sir." Aster handed Mr. Foster the journal embossed with *A. Wells*. Maia's stomach dropped as he reached for *W. Wells* next, handing it to her. "I believe with the three of us working together, we should be able to determine this evening if these journals are truly as beneficial as Aquila hopes."

"I apologize, but I'm just an assistant," Maia said, surprised by the shake in her voice. Her instincts were telling her to leave now. "I don't know how helpful I'll be."

Mr. Foster's head cocked with suspicion. "My dear, we're well past the point of modesty. And don't pretend you have something better to do this evening."

Aster rubbed his finger across his lips, his shadowy gaze finding hers. She pulled her eyes away to center her thoughts.

"I'm not a healer, sir."

"And yet here you are—brilliant, inquisitive, and determined despite that," Mr. Foster said, his words holding more meaning than he let on. She was here despite Mr. Thomas' decision, right or wrong.

Maia bit the inside of her cheek in conflict. "You don't have to—"

"He's right," Aster said, the glow of the fire emphasizing the sincerity in his brown eyes, transforming them into a stunning amber. "About all of it."

Maia's cheeks heated, and Aster stood before she could find a response.

"Would either of you care for a pour?" he asked, walking to a cabinet.

"Yes," Maia and Mr. Foster said together, and with that, the tension in the room suddenly lifted.

Aster bit back a smile, pouring drinks and handing them each a glass before taking his seat again. Maia took a sip of the whiskey, the taste of caramel, vanilla, and honey balancing out the subtle burn. It was smoother than anything she'd had in the taverns, and the thought brought back memories of Niall and Folly's.

The first time she'd met Rowan. The last time she'd seen Hannah.

All the reasons she was here. She took another sip, wishing the burn was stronger. Aster would know the truth about the journals soon enough, and if he was willing to give the blueprints for the bioweapon to Aquila, she had to be willing to stop him.

Flipping open the journal, she focused on the scrawled handwriting just enough to not appear suspicious. The tick of her father's watch drowned out the comforting crackles of the flames, and Maia timed the turn of her pages to stagger slightly behind Mr. Foster's.

Apprehension took hold as the sky blackened the office windows. Mr. Foster was now skimming pages, and Maia slipped off her shoes, tucking her feet below her to keep them from nervously fidgeting. She snuck a glance at Aster to see if he noticed, surprised to catch him watching. He dropped his gaze back to the book in his lap, taking a casual sip from his glass.

"Have you already read these journals, Mr. Calderone?" Mr. Foster asked. "You've been surprisingly distracted this evening."

Aster's cheeks darkened, causing Mr. Foster to purse his lips in response. "I have, sir." He closed the journal and sat up. "Read the journals, that is."

He'd been watching, waiting for her reaction when she finally found the pages with the bioweapon. The room was suddenly sweltering, and she looked away, finishing her glass.

"I see," Mr. Foster said, his gaze flickering back and forth between them. "Apologies, but I believe the drink has gotten to me. Maia is more than capable of reviewing the rest of the pages herself."

"Sir—"

Mr. Foster stood, grabbing his jacket from the back of his chair and giving her the same crooked smile he had earlier. "I hope you both enjoy your evening."

She looked at him in disbelief, his wink confirming what he thought was going on. With that, he was gone, leaving Maia and Aster alone in a heavy silence. The tick of the watch was deafening, and Maia shifted again on the loveseat, aware it would do nothing to ease her tension.

"Another glass?" Aster offered, walking over and grabbing the bottle.

She nodded, relief washing over her. He refilled their drinks, leaving the decanter on the table.

"May I join you?" he asked, motioning to the confined space beside her.

The sudden pounding in her chest should have been for what she knew waited just a few pages away, but it wasn't. It was for something she refused to allow herself to acknowledge. That the idea of him being so close was enough to ignite every nerve in her body.

"Of course."

The cushions shifted from his weight, pulling her to him, and he draped his arm over the back of the loveseat. She didn't dare steal a glance, instead continuing to flip through the unread pages.

Her body hummed with awareness as his hand rested just behind the nape of her neck. The tick of the watch slowed. She'd found the dreaded drawings. They both finished their drinks as she closed the journal.

"W. Wells had some interesting ideas," he said, lowering his glass to the table. "Especially on those last few pages."

"Why am I here, Aster?" She glanced at him out of the corner of her eye.

"Aquila asked—"

"Tell me why I'm really here?" She wouldn't play games. Not about this. Not with him.

He met her gaze, searching her eyes for something before nodding. "I needed someone I could trust to tell me the truth."

Trust? One word was enough to make the world spin, even as she sat still.

"The truth about what?" She wanted to hear the words from his mouth.

He leaned forward, scrubbing his hands down his face before dropping them between his knees. "I need to know if it's what I think it is. There are pages of weapon schematics that we're decades, even centuries, away from replicating.

But one…" He took a deep breath and looked up at her. "One looks like the framework to make red lung into a weapon."

She met his gaze straight on. He had wanted to see her reaction, to catch her in a lie, and now she wanted the same. "It is."

His head dropped, and his shoulders collapsed around him. She would have given up everything for a second of his thoughts. If he chose to tell Aquila the truth, she would have to destroy the journals. And if she did that, Aster would have to be the one to take the fall.

Despite the repercussions, Maia couldn't tell him what to do. He needed to make that decision on his own, or she would be the one taking his place in the noose.

"I can't," he finally said, his voice fractured and vulnerable. Her heart stilled, as if holding its breath with her. She couldn't have heard him correctly. He turned to her, brows drawn tight with conflict. "No one should have this knowledge, Maia. Not even Aquila."

She wanted to believe they were lies. A desperate attempt at manipulation, but she had become so proficient at both that she knew this was his ruinous truth.

"If Aquila finds out, you'll be marked as a traitor," she whispered.

A rebel. For a split second, she allowed herself to imagine what it would be like to tell Aster the truth. To be near him without the fear of one slipped secret compromising everything.

"There's already too much death without the existence of this weapon. I can't—I *won't*—willingly hand it over." He finally broke her gaze, as if not wanting to influence her response. Despite the consequences, he didn't ask her to lie for him or keep his secret. She was here as a witness to his betrayal. The arbiter of his fate.

He trusted her, which would either save or destroy him.

"Tell me what you want me to say."

The weight of her words tensed every muscle in his body, and his eyes pinched closed. This wouldn't just be his betrayal now, it would be theirs. If only he knew.

"You don't have to say anything. I'll tell him we found nothing."

Her hands ached to touch him, and she forced them into fists in her lap. "We found nothing."

As if reading her thoughts, he glanced at her knotted hands and reached over, wrapping his hand around hers. Vulnerably entwined. Reckless with trust.

Seeing him so casual and open made her self-conscious of her stiff posture beside him. Every inch of her felt cold and pulseless despite the frantic beat of her heart.

His hand tightened, and he looked up at her through his dark lashes. She nearly shattered at the burn of his gaze, the intoxicating scent of bergamot and cloves surrounding her. His eyes seared with the reflection of the flames, chasing away the shadows slowly encroaching on her since the night everything changed.

Their secret allowed his walls to crumble around them, leaving him exposed and breathtaking in a way that his poised façade could never attain.

"Am I interrupting?"

They jumped away from each other as Tala stood in the doorway, arms crossed. Maia's fingertips still tingled from his lingering touch. She balled them into a tight fist, nails pinching her palm to ease the sudden ache.

"What do you want, Tala?" Aster's voice came out low and husky, and he quietly cleared his throat as he stood.

"Where's Mr. Foster?" she asked, stepping into the room and eyeing Maia suspiciously.

Aster picked up the glasses and bottle, moving them back to the cabinet. "He had a little too much to drink and excused himself about an hour ago."

"The old man is as foolish as he looks," Tala sneered. "Aquila asked me to do the morning briefing."

"If that's what he desires, then I'll be there," he said, stacking the journals on the table and reaching for Maia's coat.

She remained still, knowing that every one of his movements mirrored his anxious thoughts.

"*Both* of you can be there at 0800," Tala said, turning away.

"Maia won't be needed."

Tala's lip curled. "Oh, but I *insist*."

Aster didn't speak, but Maia didn't need him to. She stood, straightening her back and locking glares with Tala. "I look forward to it."

Tala's eyes sharpened to black points. "As do I, Sagitta."

The second she was down the hall, far enough from earshot, Maia felt Aster behind her. He lifted her jacket, and she slipped back into it, his hands lingering on her arms.

"You don't have to do this."

She glanced up at him, the anxious beat of his heart exposed in his neck. "It's the right thing to do."

It was impossible to think of him as the enemy when his dark brown eyes held so much warmth. The soft tug at the corner of his lips melted her in a way that blurred the line between right and wrong.

"Thank you." His voice was a low hush, reminding her of their hidden alcove in the maze, while his thumbs grazed her arm, comforting in a way she didn't deserve.

She pulled away, plummeting back into the harsh cold coursing through her. "Goodnight, Aster."

He tucked his hands into his pockets, as if restraining them. "Goodnight."

Maybe one day she would deserve his warmth. But for now, he would have to get the version of her she allowed him to see. The version that lied with every shaky breath she took.

22

TRAITORS

The Strategy Room waited ominously down a long corridor below Council Hall. Elaborate white trim encased two tall, wooden doors that Maia stared at impatiently. Adjusting uncomfortably on a bench, the frenetic tap of her foot echoed down the endless hall. It had been too long since Aster was called inside. Long enough for her to question every word whispered between them.

The door creaked open, forcing Maia to her feet as Tala stepped out. Her face was as rigid as the buffs in the rotunda above. Aster exited behind her, chin lifted a little too high, revealing the fissures in his usual confidence.

"Ms. Sagitta," he said with a nod. He looked desperate to say more, with depths to his gaze that she couldn't quite place while he continued past. She would know soon enough if Aster truly was the master of manipulation.

Maia followed Tala into the windowless, circular room. Yellowed, map-covered walls surrounded them, illuminated by the orange glow of wall sconces. Blue- and red-tipped pins marked different locations, some denser in one color than the other. Tala hovered over a massive round table, the flame of a candle dancing as she exhaled sharply above it.

"What did you find in the journals?" Her gaze was low and menacing in the candlelight.

Maia's throat grew thick as a sudden tremor of fear rolled through her. One word stood between her and a noose.

Her heart clenched. It was time to find out if Aster would be Portico's undoing or her own. With a calming breath, she met Tala's gaze.

"Nothing."

Tala's lips curled into a terrifyingly calm smile. The world disappeared from under Maia's feet, and every muscle tensed to keep her from collapsing.

"Fucking useless," Tala whispered. "How could you both find nothing?" She slammed her fist on the table, causing Maia to jump.

He wasn't lying. Aster had betrayed Aquila and the Council. Placed his life in Maia's cold, blood-stained hands to keep the weapon a secret. A burden she no longer had to carry alone.

"Get out," Tala snapped. "Get out of my fucking sight! I'll review the damn journals myself."

There was desperation in Tala's outburst. She knew more about the journals than she was letting on.

"It was *you* who chose to do this briefing, not Aquila." The words tumbled from Maia's lips as realization set in. "You think Rowan was hiding something from you."

Tala's eyes narrowed, her darkness overtaking the light of the flame. "Careful with your words, Sagitta."

The measure of her tone told Maia just how precariously she stood, balancing on the tip of Tala's blade.

Maia took a dangerous step forward. "That's why you hanged him."

Tala's eyes were murderous, her hand reaching under her cloak when the door suddenly swung open, filling the room with air again.

"Apologies, I wasn't aware you were in a meeting," Senna said, not hiding the fact she wasn't sorry, or as unaware as she claimed.

"What is it?" Tala asked, keeping her eyes on Maia.

Senna continued forward, tossing a paper onto the table. "My contact located the rebel you've been looking for."

Maia's heart skipped at the drawing before her.

WANTED

Theodore Garcia
Rebel Conspirator

Reward: 3,000 coin

DEAD OR ALIVE

The last time she heard his name, Garcia had been captured, or worse. Yet here he was, looking up at her with the same mischievous grin, and very much alive... for now.

"Perfect timing," Tala said, her lips snaking into a wicked grin. "Tell me, Sagitta, what would you do with this rebel bounty?"

Portico would want him dead, and capturing him could be even worse, unless she could find a reason they would keep him alive. Her thoughts raced, and she hoped Tala was as desperate as she seemed.

"Let me go to him. If those journals hold rebel secrets, maybe he'll know what you're looking for."

He wouldn't, but it could buy them all some time.

Tala cocked her head with suspicion, but nodded. "Fine. One last test of your true allegiance."

"If that's all I have left."

"Let's see what you decide." Tala pushed away from the table and walked towards the door. "Tell her where she's going, Senna."

"My contact is waiting for *me* to return, not a stranger." Senna's tone made it clear Maia wasn't going alone.

Tala's face twisted the same way Orion's had when Rowan offered to return to Portico. Any trust she had in Senna dissipated like the smoke from the flame still dancing on the table.

"Then I guess you both get to prove your allegiance."

Maia didn't say a word, continuing out of the room with Senna. As the door slammed shut, she was certain the decisions now trapped in that room would be the beginning of the end for them all.

The tight, leather scout uniform transformed the way that Maia felt as she walked beside Senna. Everything about it made her confident, back straight and steps sure. It was dangerous how easy it was to give into the power. She was in control of each prying eye. Not just of what they saw, but how they felt in her presence.

A grin crept across her face, hidden beneath the hood, while she thumbed Tala's dagger tucked against her hip. Something was changing inside her, shaping her into the person her mother had warned her about, Hannah had feared, Rowan had nurtured, and Portico had forged.

She was becoming the person needed to finish what her father started.

"Tala knows who you are."

Senna's voice was calm, like a purr. Hearing her say it so nonchalantly muted the shock of her confession.

"Why do you say that?" Maia asked, following her down an alley in Richmond Ward.

"Because I read the letter you stole." She walked the maze of streets with ease, as if no time had passed since she'd called them home. "It was moving hands west towards the Desert Region before I swiped it. I recognized the code from a letter Rowan asked me to decipher. There's a book in Aquila's library he told me to use. *Both* of the letters were about you, and neither of them were complimentary."

Despite the eerie silence, Maia could sense eyes on them from the blown-out walls and shattered windows of the tall, gray buildings surrounding them.

"So, she's working with someone from the Desert Region?" Maia said, suddenly remembering Jackson's promise from what felt like a lifetime ago.

They were going to go together to the Desert Region where she grew up. When they were still hopeful of what the heist meant to the rebellion. Those few moments when they truly believed things could be different. Maia's chest suddenly ached as the loss splintered a fresh fissure in her heart.

"Maybe," Senna said, her thin brows pulled tight. "But why wait to expose you to Aquila? She could have hanged you with Rowan, but she swapped the letters."

Maia jolted to a stop. "What?"

Expecting the response, Senna continued. "Which makes me think she either *can't* because of someone else's orders. Or she's planning something else for you entirely." Her eyes slowly traveled to Maia's and, for the first time, there was fear in them. "Something only her and the person on the other side of those letters know."

Her fear was in the uncertainty, and knowing that made Maia's body grow cold. Senna always had a contact, a way of knowing what would happen next. Even Governor Shaw burning down her brothel was predictable. But Tala was a wild card. She had the perfect chance to kill Maia, and she didn't, and Maia had to wonder what Tala thought was a worse fate than death.

"You knew I'd come with you to find Garcia." Maia said, realizing she was yet again falling into Senna's carefully laid out plans.

"You're about to need all the allies you can get, darling," she lifted her nail, tucking a loose wave behind Maia's ear.

She was no different from Sky, using touch to get what she wanted, and right now Senna wanted Maia to understand the danger she was in.

Her red lips slipped into a soft smile. "Also, Garcia is refusing to talk to anyone but you. According to my contact, he arrived with two other men, beaten and bloodied. Hasn't said a word about what happened, and the innkeeper is getting nervous that trouble might be following."

She continued down the alley, pushing open a nondescript door tucked between stacked crates and boxes. Maia followed Senna inside, tracing her finger over Orion's symbol etched into the doorframe. People laid strewn across the floors and stairway on threadbare mattresses and dirty wool blankets. A cacophony of coughs and throat clearing cut through the stench of sickness hanging heavy in the air. Maia lifted the thin scarf of the scout uniform to keep from breathing in the disease.

"You're back." A mousy, skittish-looking man sat behind the counter looking disappointed by Senna's arrival. He had wisps of wiry, brown hair, and his bloodshot eyes kept darting towards the stairs. "Your guy is still up there, but the others left this mornin'. They were arguing about not waitin' for Scavengers to find them again."

"Thanks for keeping an eye on him," Senna said, dropping a bag of coin on the counter and continuing towards the stairwell.

"I ain't keepin' an eye on no one. I want all of you gone tonight. Ain't lookin' for no trouble with the Scavengers, ya understand?"

"Understood."

They carefully stepped over the emaciated bodies, tiptoeing down a dark hallway. Pushing open the door at the end of the hall, Senna allowed Maia to enter first. Garcia stood in front of an open window, moth-eaten curtains swaying in the breeze. The light of the full moon bathed his face in a grayish glow, revealing a swollen eye surrounded by deep purple bruising. He had wrapped a dirty makeshift sling around his arm, his swollen hand missing a pinky.

Sensing their presence, he spun—pistol drawn—squinting with his good eye. "Maia?"

"You look like shit," she said, lowering her scarf and pulling back her hood.

She wasn't prepared for the emotions she felt seeing him again. He had been alive all this time, and only Orion took the time to look for him. She wanted to rush over and hug him, but her guilt held her in place.

His face collapsed in relief as his booming laugh filled the room. "So, the stories are true."

Limping forward, he wrapped her with his good arm in a heartfelt hug. She was careful, returning it but keeping her distance. Not just because of the way he flinched as her arms pressed around his ribs, but also because of the new panic washing over her. If the rebellion didn't know about Rowan's death, they would now. And, eventually, the role she played in it.

"What stories?" Senna asked, taking a seat on the edge of the sheetless, blood-stained cot.

Garcia pulled away, confused. "Sagitta." He glanced between them as if that alone should have explained it. "The rebel traitor."

Maia's heart plummeted. It was a trap. Someone was spreading lies and turning the rebellion against her. Tala's letter. *She may be actively working against the cause.* Maia thought it was Portico's, but Tala never said *her* cause. Which meant Maia had nowhere left that was safe.

In one swift motion, she slipped Tala's dagger from her hip, pressing it against Garcia's stomach. "Who told you that?"

His eyes grew wide, and he lifted his hand as Senna placed the barrel of her gun against the back of his head.

"Espera, espera. ¡Carajo! Orion has marked us all traitors." His trembling hand slowly lowered, pointing to his jacket pocket.

"Bullshit," Senna snapped, causing Garcia to flinch.

"What do I gain from lying to you?" he yelled in frustration. "I lost *everything* in the heist! *All* of them! I hoped it was true—that Maia turned. Because if it was, then their sacrifice could mean something." His eyes found Maia's, pleading. "I *need* it to mean something."

The pain from his loss caused Maia's suspicion to falter, and she loosened her grip on the dagger. Reaching into Garcia's pocket, she removed a folded piece of paper.

WANTED

Maia Avalos
Rebel Conspirator

Reward: 30,000 coin

"How do you know this isn't Portico's?" She already knew the answer, though. If Portico knew, she'd already be dead. Which meant Orion wanted her alive. The realization sent a chill down her spine like winter's first breath.

Garcia shook his head, his eyes filled with apologies he didn't owe her. "Because we survived the heist when we shouldn't have. Orion thinks you had something to do with it. He's been working with Scavengers to hunt us down one by one."

Orion had been smart enough to use the word conspirator. A traitor to the rebellion. An enemy to Portico.

"Did he do that to you?" she asked, lowering her blade, her gaze lingering on the bloodied wrap around his hand.

He nodded, but the tension remained in his shoulders. "The Scavengers caught us stealing weapons and bullets from a rebel boat. We've been on the run, trying to build up a cache to overthrow him—restore the rebellion to what it was supposed to be. What your father had wanted."

Senna laughed. "So, you *are* a fucking traitor."

"He's lost his way, Maia," Garcia said, his face twisted in anguish. "Vivir sólo por venganza es pensar sólo en violencia. ¿Entiendes?"

She understood. Garcia believed Orion's need for revenge had clouded his judgment, turning him into a monster no better than Aquila. If it were true, then everything lost, and still left to lose, would be for nothing.

"I'm sorry, Garcia," she said, breaking their gaze and moving to the window. The gentle snow flurries soothed her burning cheeks. She closed her eyes, taking in a slow breath. "I don't believe you."

Garcia was the traitor, not her. She could explain this to Orion—fix whatever damage the lies had caused. The rebellion was all she had left. Her only chance to make things right.

"Then you can see it for yourself." Garcia walked up behind her. Too close. "I'll tell you where it is, and you can see what he's done to your father's legacy."

Garcia knew exactly what to say to convince her, which made her doubt him even more. She was beginning to wonder if there was any truth left within any of them. "Then show me."

"We can't go alone," he said, motioning to his mangled arm. "The only reason I'm still alive is because of dumb luck."

Maia leaned back on the windowsill. He was certain of his lies, and she could feel her anger growing. "Fine. Then we'll use Portico's army."

Another booming laugh. Maia didn't flinch, and he stopped. "You can do that?"

"You're already a traitor," she snapped, pushing off the sill. He took a step back, sensing the escalating tension between them. "If what you say is true, then Aquila will send Portico's army himself."

He shook his head, eyes wide. "How can you guarantee they won't kill me the second I step foot on their grounds?"

"I can't." Maia continued slowly stalking towards him. "You'll be the one to decide that. What are you willing to tell them for their protection?"

Garcia swallowed audibly, looking to Senna for support he wouldn't get. His gaze dropped to his hand again, and his jaw clenched tight. "Just get me to Aquila and I'll prove to you I'm not lying."

Maia wanted him to back down, to admit it was all a lie, and her heart sank at his resolve. It was clear that, regardless of what she wanted, the truth would be revealed through bloodshed.

23

SAGITTA

There was power in his name. A promise of
things to come.

A. Wells – Fall 2274

They had become shadows. A darkness in a world suddenly too bright. Portico's guards didn't ask questions as Garcia limped behind Maia and Senna, his mangled hand reeking of infection under the filthy, blood-stained wrap. He wasn't the same person she had met—eyes now hardened in the same way as Sky's. The look of someone who understood the fight was never theirs to win. That each shot needed to kill.

Two of the guards seized Garcia by the arms and followed. A stain of hooded scouts stood arguing with the diplomats at the bottom of the Council Hall steps. The finger pointing was seconds away from shoving as the collectors watched impassively through the haze of their smokes.

They embodied the change in their leaders, the cracks slowly spreading in Portico's foundation. Maia adjusted the hood of her scout uniform, shielding her eyes from the blinding light reflecting off the building, and continued towards Aquila's manor.

The guard at the entrance crossed his arms as they approached, making it clear he wasn't in the mood for whatever they were bringing his way. "The Advisors are in a meeting."

"Noted," Senna said without breaking her stride.

She pushed open the door and trailed her finger on the circular mahogany table in the foyer, plucking a rose from the black vase resting in the center.

Shouts echoed down the hall, and Senna slowed her pace as they approached the doorway to the library. The guards hesitated, holding Garcia back. The argument happening on the other side of the wall wasn't for their ears, and they knew how dangerous it was to know things they shouldn't.

"He's lying!" Tala shouted. "There's something in those journals, and he's keeping it from you."

"Accusations of treason require evidence, which you have yet to provide," Aquila warned. "According to your briefing, Ms. Sagitta also found nothing in those journals. Is that correct?"

"It is, sir." The flames from the wall sconces flickered as Maia stepped past them into the room.

Tala hovered over Aquila, sitting propped up behind his desk and looking more worn and jaundiced than before. She straightened as Maia lowered her hood, her raised brow daring Tala to say otherwise. General Winter lay sprawled across a white chaise along the back wall, one boot on the floor and an arm draped over her eyes. She lifted her arm at the sudden silence, watching Maia cross to stand beside Aster.

He glanced down at her, a flicker of a smile crossing his lips. There was power in the balance between them. She had thought his warmth was there to temper the harsh cold coursing within, but they were never meant to dull each other. His gentleness only sharpened her jagged edges. Her defiance only strengthened his steady pulse of confidence.

She knew he felt it too, his stance widening beside her before he turned back to Tala. "You were saying..."

Tala's fists clenched, but she remained quiet, walking behind Aquila's desk. His tufted leather chair nearly hid her in the shadows, and it was the first time she had ever seemed small.

"Where the fuck have *you* been?" Rafe asked, leaning against the wall beside the door, legs crossed at the ankles and arms folded over his chest.

"She didn't tell you?" Senna asked, her penetrating gaze raking over Tala. "Now who's keeping secrets?"

Rafe rubbed his brow with the back of his thumbnail in annoyance. "That's not a fucking answer, Senna."

She leaned into him, running the soft petals of the rose down the side of his face. "Then I suppose it's a good thing we don't owe you one." With a snap of her fingers, the guards shoved Garcia into the room. It was empowering to see how quickly Senna had gone from responding to snaps to wielding them.

"Pinche cabrón," Garcia mumbled, adjusting the sling around his shoulder.

Aquila's yellowed eyes narrowed. "Aren't you supposed to be dead?"

Garcia froze, eyes wide. There was a deafening second of silence before he pressed his lips together with a nod. "The welcome I expected from Portico."

Senna smashed the rose into Rafe's chest and sashayed across the room, flicking Garcia's ear as she passed. He flinched, his good hand shooting up to ease the pain.

"Play nice, Theodore," she warned, continuing to Maia's side.

Rafe grinned, enjoying the power Senna seemed to have over the situation. He shifted against the wall, hooding his mouth with his hand. A mannerism the twins seemed to share.

"Maia, would you care to explain why you brought a rebel into *my* home?" Aquila's voice remained measured, but his patience was waning.

"Theodore Garcia is a traitor to the rebellion, sir. Isn't that right, Garcia?" He shifted uncomfortably at her directness, but nodded. "He offers information for refuge."

Curiosity seemed to breathe new life into Aquila as he straightened in his chair. "What *kind* of information?"

All eyes turned to Garcia, the color sinking from his brown cheeks into his full, black beard—a small patch of gray peeking from the sharp angle of his jaw. It was no longer about convincing her. If he didn't convince Aquila, he wouldn't survive the night.

He cleared his throat twice before he could speak. "I have the location of a large shipment of weapons and Old World ammunition stolen from the rebels."

General Winter's heavy boots dropped to the floor behind them, steps thundering as she approached. "How large of a shipment?"

She towered over Garcia, her broad shoulders blocking the light from the wall sconces. Garcia took a step back. His eyes flickered to her hand, casually resting on the pistol at her hip.

"About five thousand rounds of ammunition, a crate of grenades, and four transport boxes of rifles and pistols."

Winter gripped his shirt collar, yanking him back to her. "You're telling me the rebels had *all* of that?"

Garcia's chest heaved frantically, as if knowing his next words would only upset her more. "That... that was just one shipment."

A hush fell over the room as Winter's grip went slack. Her almost translucent brows knit with unease while her eyes grew distant. The news was a surprise, and Maia couldn't help but wonder who had the upper hand now.

Aquila steepled his hands together, his eyes finding Aster's. They were calculating. Assessing Aster the same way Maia watched each of her patients after the two cuts on their arms. He was waiting to see what would come next.

Aster stepped forward, casually taking a seat on the corner of Aquila's desk and crossing his hands over his lap. "What else are you willing to offer in exchange for protection?"

A soft, almost fatherly smile crossed Aquila's lips as he watched Aster with pride. It was human and vulnerable. Even tyrants had their weaknesses.

Garcia took a deep breath and lifted his chin. This was it. The moment where he truly turned, and he understood once it happened, he could never go back.

"Rebel camp locations, ally names, and the next area Orion plans on converting."

"And you're willing to give us all those rebel secrets?" Tala's eyes darkened.

"Not just me," Garcia said, taking a small step forward, his voice barely suppressing his desperation. "Orion's been torturing anyone he deems traitors. I escaped, but there's dozens more that are still prisoners. If you free them, they'll talk too. I'm certain of it."

"Orion is torturing his own?" Aster gripped the edge of the desk, but his face remained composed, like a bronzed mask.

Garcia nodded, his eyes dropping to his bandaged hand. Rafe cursed under his breath, pushing himself from the wall to join Winter.

"Why?"

Maia appreciated Aster's steady calm in the growing chaos. Garcia's gaze flickered to her. He knew better than to give up her cover, so she nodded for him to continue.

"The coin heist... the consequences of it created a rift in the rebellion—an 'us vs. them.' To Orion, anyone part of the heist who survived... Well, we became 'them.'"

"He thinks you knew it was a set up." Aster said, and Garcia confirmed with a nod. "Where are the other survivors?"

"Hopewell. It's a heavily guarded Scavenger camp."

"And the weapons?" Winter asked, commanding Garcia's attention back to her.

"An abandoned bunker in Weyanoke along the James River. The only ones watching the area are survivors too."

The Advisors turned to Aquila as he sat lost in thought. His face collapsed and Maia couldn't tell if it was defeat, sadness, or guilt. Whatever it was, it weighed heavily on him.

"It appears Orion has lost his way." He clenched his tremoring hand. "I offer you protection if you pledge your allegiance to Portico *alone* from this day forward."

Garcia let out a breath. He was safe. For now. "Yes, sir."

"Let me be clear," Aquila continued, struggling to push himself to stand. "If any of your information proves to be false, you will hang."

There was only one acceptable response. "Understood, sir."

Aquila motioned to the guards. "Take him to a holding cell until we receive confirmation that what he said is true, and station additional posts outside his door. Aster, prepare your diplomats for Weyanoke. Winter, Tala, and Rafe—I want all of you to gather teams for Hopewell." His gaze turned to Maia, studying her the same way he had with Aster. "Ms. Sagitta, if this information is accurate, this could bring an end to the rebellion. The significance of your decision is immeasurable. I'd like you and Ms. Young to join the others in Hopewell."

If Garcia's information was true, then the rebellion was already over. Maia nodded, turning on her heels, with Senna and Aster by her side while the others followed.

War was a beautifully choreographed dance, with each person flawlessly executing what Portico trained them to accomplish. An expectation—routine.

It was the way Tala and Senna's blades quietly found the throats of those lazily wandering the perimeter. Not a sound as their bodies fell.

The way Sky's perfect shot dropped a man dead center of a crowd outside the bunker. A distraction and signal for General Winter's guards to attack from the flanks.

The way war blurred the world into different shades of red against the bright-white snow blanketing the ground. A canvas of death.

"It's time," Sky said, standing in the tree line and adjusting the gun strap over his shoulder.

The world felt slow and heavy as Maia stood, Sky and Rafe beside her as they descended into the chaos. She didn't reach for her daggers—she didn't need to.

Briar and Senna emerged from the crowd, disposing of anyone standing in their way. Maia's long coat billowed over the fallen bodies as they moved through the center of the battle, the ebb and flow of her heartbeat drowning out the metal clangs and pops surrounding them. Her sight locked on the door ahead.

Inside the bunker remained one Scavenger, guarding the cells. He stood as tall as Briar, wearing rags and chalky, white face paint. Sky rubbed his amulet, assessing the situation. With a quick nod, he lifted the gun and shot out the guard's knee, dropping the massive man to the floor with a deep guttural howl. Rafe and Briar pulled him into a chair, tying the guard down as Maia drifted forward.

"Call yourself," Sky said in Scavenger tongue, lifting the man's chin with the barrel of his gun. The guard remained silent. "You half-tongued or full-weight?"

Maia scanned the room of barely conscious prisoners lying in their own feces and reeking of infection. Many were missing fingers, and some struggled to stand on broken limbs. They were treated worse than caged animals, and all dejected eyes were on her. Waiting.

Despite what she wanted to believe, she already knew why the man in front of her wouldn't speak. Her hand moved towards the chain around his neck, and he tensed at her touch. Orion's symbol was etched into the round metal piece. The world fell out from under her as she ran her thumb over the rough punctures. Garcia was right.

The guard spat in her face and within seconds Senna's blade was resting against the frantic pulse in his neck, while Sky and Briar's guns were at his head.

"Give me one fuckin' reason to keep him alive, boss," Briar growled.

Maia took in the man's face, quivering with rage. He had no idea how alike they were at that moment. Everything she had fought for—everything given up—had been for nothing. If the rebellion won, nothing would change. Just another tyrant silencing anyone who wasn't them.

She slowly lowered the barrel of Briar's gun. "Because he doesn't deserve a quick death." Removing her jacket, Maia laid it on another chair by the door. "What lies did Orion tell you?" Maia slowly rolled up her sleeves and unlatched Tala's dagger from her hip. "That you gave a voice back to the people?" Her dagger slowly moved around the room, heavy with silence. "What about these people?"

His lip curled with disgust. "I won't tell you a *fuckin'* thing, Sagitta."

Her head tilted as she realized Sagitta meant something different to each person. But each of them knew it.

"You don't need to." She pressed the tip of the blade against his arm, feeling the pop of his skin as a drop of blood bloomed beneath it.

He would know Sagitta as pain.

"I already know the answer. A tally for each voice you've silenced in these cages."

The prisoners hollered from their cells, shaking the bars violently as Maia added line after line to his arms.

A line for each rebel who died for nothing.

A line for each lie Orion fed her.

He remained perfectly still, fists clenched as she slowly worked up his arms. Just enough for him to feel the pain, but not enough to bleed out. Her thoughts remained focused on the hate, anger, and task at hand. Orion had taken everything from her.

Her father's legacy had now warped into the exact thing he had fought against.

The chance at hope she had promised Hannah.

Every death and sacrifice... meaningless. Jayce and Kayla... Rowan.

She could sense Caleb's presence beside her, watching each one of her carefully placed cuts.

"We need to—" Tala skidded to a stop on the concrete floor, pulling Maia out of her trance.

When had it grown quiet? The prisoners stared at her with a mix of respect and fear as the man in the chair trembled in pain, his arms and chest covered in tiny cuts. She stepped back, noticing Rafe shift uncomfortably on his feet. Sky and Senna watched with dark eyes while Briar's focus remained on Tala alone, his hand hovering over his gun.

"Loyal to the end," Tala sneered, lifting her gun and shooting the man in the chair. The force of the hit sent him to the floor.

Rafe cursed, wiping the man's blood from his face. "What the fuck is wrong with you, Tala?"

She stepped towards Maia, whispering in her ear. "You've crossed a line you can't come back from." The threat in her words raised the hair on the back of Maia's neck. "You better hope you're as indestructible as you think, Sagitta."

Tala holstered her gun and turned to leave. "Reinforcements are coming."

Briar waited until Tala disappeared before lowering his hand. "What now, boss?"

Maia dropped to her knees, digging in the man's pockets as he moaned in pain. She threw Sky the keyring. "We need to unlock the cells... fast."

Sky started around the room as Senna helped Maia to her feet. "That's not what Briar's asking," she said, nodding to the prisoners. "They're looking to you."

The weight of their desperate eyes was suddenly suffocating, and every muscle in Maia's body tensed. She closed her eyes, trying to focus. "I don't know what to say."

"Yes, you do." Senna's hand found Maia's chin, and she gently lifted it to meet her gaze. "What you're doing isn't defined by a cause, Maia. It's the spark of hope that somehow endures in a world constantly trying to destroy it. That spark is what they see right now. Like moths to a flame."

There was something in Senna's eyes—in all of their eyes that fed the spark within. Maia sucked in a shaky breath and turned to the prisoners. "Orion has marked you as traitors. Even free from this prison, you won't be safe without protection."

"We go where you go, Sagitta," a prisoner said, struggling to hold up another. Senna was right. To them, Sagitta meant hope.

She noticed Rafe watching, as if trying to figure out what he had missed when they first met. Briar walked over, giving her shoulder a gentle squeeze, a reassuring smile hitching his lips as Sky unlocked the last of the cells.

None of them would survive without Portico's protection, and Maia realized her next words solidified what Orion feared.

Her gaze returned to the crowd. "Then I suggest you follow us back to Portico."

They huddled together, stumbling past the mass of rebel bodies left behind, and into the dense trees surrounding the bunker. There was a dangerous desperation that developed when the only thing left was survival. It forced irrational and reckless thoughts. Created weakness by removing the predictability of actions, leaving everything to the mercy of chance.

But this wasn't about survival. It was about revenge. The cold, calculating assessment of causal sequence and probability. The art of anticipation. If Orion had doubts about her loyalty before, there would be no question now.

He would know Sagitta as the villain.

Part III

SO, WE RISE

24

ENDGAME

On the rare nights Christian Avalos would come home, he spent his evenings patiently teaching Maia the game of chess. He would carefully arrange the rough, hand-carved pieces on the wooden board. One white and one black pawn hidden in his hands for her to choose. She giggled each time he revealed the white, cursing under his breath and mumbling not to repeat it in front of her mother.

Nothing more than chance. She was too young then to understand, so all of it was chance.

Even now, as the pieces slowly took their positions on the board around her, Maia still remembered his first lesson.

You'll never know what your opponent is thinking, only what options they have. Your advantage is knowing they'll always choose the move to end the game.

In one move, she would have him in check, and just as quickly, lose everything. A lesson she didn't understand until now. She sat with Mr. Foster, exhausted from the hours spent tending to the sick and dying rebels who survived the arduous journey back to Portico. Two cramped rows of metal cots lined both walls of the infirmary. Sheer curtains were drawn to allow the patients a semblance of privacy while they cried themselves to sleep.

It was then that Maia realized their bruises would fade and their bodies would scar long before they healed.

The wooden chair creaked as she leaned back from the desk, allowing herself a dangerous moment alone with her thoughts. No matter how many times she thought back to her last meeting with Orion, even knowing he didn't agree with Rowan returning to Portico, none of it could have prepared her for his betrayal. She now understood why her father had cursed each time she drew white.

Orion had the advantage of the first move, which meant she had to figure out what options came next. Closing her eyes, she rubbed the tension building in her forehead. She needed Rowan, and hated herself for being the reason he was gone.

What would he think of her decision to bring the deserters here? What would her father think of his daughter being one of them?

The door to the infirmary groaned open behind her, and she glanced over her shoulder to find Rafe crowding the threshold.

"Aquila is looking for you," he whispered, hesitating to step any farther into the room.

She glanced at Mr. Foster, chin tucked into his chest and eyes closed. With so many injured, they had been covering moonlight shifts in the infirmary. This wasn't worth waking him. He deserved his peaceful sleep. Grabbing her jacket, she followed Rafe outside.

"Whatever the traitor told Aster's team worked. They secured the weapons and more deserters," Rafe said, bathed in the orange glow of the lantern hanging above the door.

"He's back?" she asked, wondering why Rafe was here instead of him.

"Yes, went straight to the manor for debriefing, like he was told."

The harsh bite of winter nipped at her ears, and she lifted the collar of her jacket. "Is that what I'm supposed to do now?"

"That's protocol. Not that you care," he said, removing his gloves from his jacket and offering them to her.

She looked down at them suspiciously. "What are you doing?"

There was a moment of hesitation before he pulled the gloves back, striking them against his palm in thought. "I'm *trying* to be nice, but I'm second-guessing it now."

The conflict in his kindness tugged at the corner of her lips. There would never be a day they weren't at each other's throats, and there was comfort in that. "It's probably for the best."

He sent her a side eye, but seemed to appreciate the sarcasm. "Aquila's probably gonna give you a medal or some shit anyway."

"I can add it to my wall."

A snort escaped him, and he shook his head. "You're fucking insufferable."

"The feeling's mutual," Maia said, turning on her heels and starting towards Aquila's manor.

The guards nodded to Maia with the same respect given to General Winter just weeks ago. She pushed open the doors to find Aquila sitting alone across from the parlor fireplace. He looked up, motioning for her to take one of the gold-laced, high-back chairs.

The hard cushions forced her shoulders to uncurl in a way that felt vulnerable. So instead, she leaned forward, resting her elbow on the carved-mahogany armrest and picking at a hangnail.

"What made you choose to join Portico, Maia?"

The hairs stood on the back of her neck. His question felt like an accusation she couldn't afford. Panic took control of her thoughts, making it impossible to form an acceptable answer.

But as her gaze roamed from the heavy bags under his eyes to the tremoring glass of whiskey in his hand, she realized he no longer had the strength for strategy. This was nothing more than curiosity. Something she understood too well.

"To right some wrongs from my past, sir."

"And have you succeeded?"

Him still breathing meant she hadn't. "I'm beginning to think it might not be possible."

"I believe you're right." He turned to the marble fireplace, twirling a thick ring around his bony finger while lost in thought. "I've made powerful enemies in my time, and have many regrets. But the young man I found in a shantytown years ago will always be my greatest. Christian Avalos was someone I truly believed would one day lead Portico, but instead, he chose to form a rebellion against me. His betrayal is a wound that will never heal, and his death hangs over me like a blade."

Hearing her father's name from the man who ordered his death turned her blood into venom. The poison spread through her, making her lethal.

She imagined the look on Aquila's face as she stuck her dagger deep into his hollow chest.

The jaundice of his skin fading to white as she whispered her true name into his ear.

The moment he realized *she* was the blade.

She gripped the armrest of her chair, a temporary antidote to the hatred churning within.

"As you said, some wrongs you cannot right, and Orion is one of them. He's as ruthless as Tala—two of the most blood-hungry people to pass through my gates. He only knows intimidation and violence. Even his wife feared him, which is why I sent Tala to destroy him. Had I known then what she was truly capable of ...”

Until now, Maia could only imagine the extent of Tala's ruthlessness. The words Aquila left unspoken would confirm it.

“What did she do?”

“There are things far worse than death, Maia. Tala killed Orion's wife and daughter before she got to him, and unfortunately, he escaped. The only person to ever survive her blade. For now, his rage fuels him, but I always knew it would eventually consume him.”

Tala must have been the reason for the scar on Orion's throat. A reminder of everything Aquila took from him. His hatred and rage were as justified as Maia's, and her stomach knotted as she realized Tala wouldn't hesitate to do the same to Hannah.

“Why are you telling me this?”

“Because there is change in the air.” Aquila finally met her gaze, a surprising sadness in his yellowed eyes. “I believe the execution of our Overseer has expedited what's to come. As such, I've taken the appropriate precautions and drafted my letter of succession.”

She knew the choices Aquila had. If he wanted to destroy the rebellion, he would need someone as merciless as Orion. The strategic choice was Tala.

Maia's heart stopped. The crackle of the fireplace was drowned out by the terrifying silence hanging in the air.

“I have named Aster as my successor.”

She collapsed, her breath escaping her in a sigh of relief. An approving smile curled Aquila's lips, and he returned his gaze to the flames.

“He's a good, honest man, and the leader Portico needs to survive what's coming. There are many who won't agree with my decision. Claim I wasn't in the right mindset. Try to overrule it. They'll fear the change he'll bring.” His eyes found hers again. “I'm glad I was right to assume you wouldn't be one of them. He'll need people like you by his side. People he can trust.”

"What are you asking of me?"

"You've shown you're willing to fight for what you believe. So, I ask, do you believe in him?"

She did. But it was for all the reasons Aquila shouldn't.

The two cuts, now dark scars on his arm.

His treasonous whispers that only she knew.

The hope he still had in their broken world.

Maia lifted her gaze, suddenly imagining Aster sitting across from her instead of Aquila.

If your eyes are open, the moment will always reveal itself.

Orion had lost his way, but imagining Aster taking Aquila's place on the board somehow changed everything. He was already a traitor to Portico, which meant he was the ally Maia needed to still succeed. With Aster, she saw hope again. The dangerous thought that she could still keep her father's legacy alive, as well as her promise to Hannah, if she played the game the same way her father once did.

"Yes. I believe in him."

"Then I need you to *fight* for him, Maia." Aquila clenched his anemic fist. "Our late Overseer was to be my successor until Tala conveniently found the rebel letter on him. A lie I couldn't expose in time. She's now using the journals as threats of treason against Aster. I need *you* to find proof of her lies before Aster ends up in the same position. Do you understand?"

She did. She needed to find who was on the other side of Tala's letters. "Consider it done."

The chair creaked as Maia stood, starting back to the foyer. Destroying Tala would be the only common ground she and Aquila would ever find.

"Be careful, Maia. I fear when the transition of power occurs, a veil will fall, and the rebels who have infiltrated Portico will reveal themselves. I hope to expose them before my end, but if I don't succeed, they will seek to destroy you too."

She looked back at Aquila, his eyes hooded with fatigue from the conversation, and she finally realized Portico's weakness. Aquila. An old man desperately looking for permanence before he took his final breath. Delusional enough to believe after everything he'd done, he could still be the hero. She continued out the door, removing her father's watch, comforted in knowing that each second slowly ticked closer to Aquila's demise.

Portico organized a celebratory festival the next evening, with rivers of flickering lanterns winding across the gathering grounds and converging in front of Council Hall.

Food booths with deep-red awnings encircled a wooden dance floor, now crowded with guards and staff. The string band seemed to be paid per song, hastily bouncing from one jig to the next. It was exactly what the crowd wanted. The dancers were almost buoyant as they laughed and spun, brushing sweat-soaked hair from their faces, unbothered by snow lazily falling around them.

Beside the dance floor, the rebels sat huddled together at tables overflowing with food and drink they eagerly devoured. Maia leaned against one of the dozens of wooden poles assembled solely to hang red cloth streamers. She caught one in the wind, twirling it around her finger. The red against her palm made her freeze as she saw Caleb's blood on her hands again.

She was back at Canal Row. Her dagger in his chest. His mouth wide in surprise.

She dropped the cloth, stumbling back into an icy grip.

"Everythin' okay?" Sky asked, scanning the space around them as if trying to find the source of her distress.

"Yes." She rubbed her hands together, grounding herself back in reality. "Just tripped."

He caught her movement, and she wondered if he saw her attempting to wash the blood away again. Forever stained.

"Come on, the others are up there," he said, nodding towards the Council Hall steps.

The click of Sky's polished collector's shoes punctuated the silence between them as they climbed the steps. She glanced at him, catching the subtle bounce of his amulet under his shirt.

"You spoke Scavenger in that prison."

His jaw clenched as he glanced up the steps. The others were still too far to overhear. "I did."

It was the most he had ever offered, and she latched on to it. "And your pendant?"

They stopped close enough to the crowd to drown out their conversation. "They call it the Rancor." He freed it from under his shirt, running his thumb over the smooth lacquer glistening in the moonlight. "They believe emotions passed through gazes can heal or poison the soul. A loving gaze heals, while this talisman protects against the more poisonous ones."

"Who gave it to you?"

"The Scavenger who killed my mother." He glanced towards the others again. "When he found me hidden in the trees, I was sure he'd kill me too... but he didn't." He paused, and Maia could almost see him hesitantly choosing which walls to temporarily drop. "Back then, I often wished he had. Instead, he took me in. Fed me. Gave me shelter. Did everything he could to make things right. But it was impossible. I couldn't forgive him. So, when I left with the bounties, he gave me his amulet and said *mistake not, forgive not*."

"What does it mean?"

His eyes softened to an overcast gray. "You only understand what forgiveness means when you're the one needin' it."

It was the version of him she had seen with Aster and Rafe the day they arrived. The one she had wanted to reach out to. So this time she did. "I'm sorry."

He looked down at their hands entwined, rubbing her palm like he would his pendant. "It was a long time ago, Maia." With a sigh, he let go. "I understand now how much forgiveness means to people like us."

Us.

That's what changed—why he was now willing to share his flaws. In his eyes, she was now his equal. She had become the darkness she promised she wouldn't succumb to when they first met.

He started up the stairs again, and Maia slowly followed, her steps suddenly heavier.

"What shitty thing did you say to her now?" Briar asked as they approached.

Sky took a seat on the step ahead of Briar, propping himself on his elbows. "You always gotta assume the worst of me."

"You ain't proved me wrong yet," Briar said, taking a sip from a flask and offering it to Maia.

She gratefully took it, stepping behind him to sit between Senna and Garcia. Senna had discarded her scout uniform for a blue-patterned dress with a plunging neckline. Intricate gold earrings grazed her shoulders, making her look far too glamorous for the celebration.

"That color looks nice on you," Maia said, avoiding Senna's gaze as she took a sip from the flask.

Briar leaned back into Maia's legs, the nape of his neck resting on her knee. "She's already made us tell her that."

That wasn't a surprise. And neither was the soft brush of Senna's wild hair against Maia's cheek as she leaned in to whisper, "It looks nice on you too, darling."

Senna had picked the same color for Maia—the one that caught Aster's attention. Maia turned to her, seeing the flames reignited in her gaze. But she had changed. This time, it didn't flush her cheeks, instead fueling her and twisting her lips into a dangerous grin. Only Senna could make her feel beautiful, powerful, and dangerous all at the same time.

Sitting on the steps of Council Hall, bathed in a peace as soft as the glow of the lanterns above them, felt surreal. Inevitable. As if everything had somehow been leading to it.

"I'm sorry I didn't believe you, Garcia," Maia said, watching General Winter carrying fistfuls of lagers to the table of rebels. She landed a rough pat on one of the rebel's shoulders, sloshing her mug as she raised it to them.

Garcia laid back, eyes lost on the sky above. It was the first time he looked relaxed since arriving.

Aquila had released him from holding as soon as they returned with the rebel deserters and weapons. He was even gifted a room in the lush diplomat housing as a show of gratitude.

"Trust me," he said wistfully. "It took a long time for me to believe it too."

"I think about Kayla and Jayce often." Her hand found Briar's shoulder, as if holding him close would keep him from the same fate. He dropped his head to rest on it. "I can't even imagine your loss."

"Believe it or not, Edward is the reason I survived." Garcia tucked his good hand under his head, the other still trapped in a slightly cleaner sling. "The old bastard jumped in front of me when they ambushed us. By the time I could run, Kayla and Jayce were already down. I still don't know how I got out of there alive, but Edward died a damn hero."

She wondered if he'd found redemption in his last moments. Thinking back, though, Edward didn't seem like someone who would allow himself that kind of peace.

Guilt gripped her chest as Garcia quickly wiped away a loose tear. She should have said something. The confession of Governor Shaw's warning rested on the tip of her tongue. If they knew the truth, would they blame her as much as she blamed herself?

She decided it wasn't worth finding out. "What are we going to do about the bounty Orion put on me?"

"Luckily, he wants you alive," Sky said, resting his arms on his knees and glancing at her over his shoulder. "I'll talk with Cap, the head of the bounties. She can clear it for us."

"And what about the rebels?" Senna asked, nodding towards the crowd below. "They know who Maia is too."

There was a moment of silence before Garcia finally answered. "I'll take care of them until the bounty's clear."

"Then what?" Senna pressed.

"Then we head North. Start over." The certainty in Sky's answer made it sound as if it were something already decided.

"All of those rebels are looking to Maia," Garcia snapped. "If she leaves—"

"I'm not." He was right. She couldn't walk away, not after everything. "I'm here to finish this."

Her eyes scanned the crowd, finding Aster and Rafe laughing together with Mr. Foster. She couldn't walk away when she was so close to fulfilling her promise to Hannah.

"That said," Maia continued, toying with the cap of the flask. "I understand if you all decide to leave."

Sky's face darkened. "They're gonna fuckin' hang you, just like they did to Rowan."

"Watch yourself," Briar warned, suddenly filling the space between them.

"You know as well as I do she isn't any safer out there, Skylar. Not with the rebellion and bounties hunting her." Senna turned to Maia. "I trust you have a plan."

"I do." Maia couldn't hide her gratitude as she reached for Senna's hand.

"Well, it's a good thing I have a dangerous soft spot for you." Senna gently squeezed it, giving Maia a wink. "I'm with you to the end."

"Thank you. But don't stay because of me."

"You don't get it, boss." Briar swiped the flask from her. "We didn't come here for Orion or the fucking rebellion. We came here because we believed in you."

His confession filled her heart, making her feel whole in a way she never knew possible. There was weight to his words—a promise. They were in this together until the bitter end.

Tears welled in her eyes, and she cleared her throat, glancing towards the stars. Orion's constellation hovered above, watching them. "Then we finish this."

Garcia sat up, a smile tugging at the corner of his lips. "Just like your father."

"Orion will regret making an enemy out of you," Senna said, offering Maia her hand.

Her words weren't a warning, but a reminder of what Maia was now capable of. They started down the steps, no longer needing to hide in the shadows as they took their positions on the board.

25

HIDDEN

Allegiance was nothing more than a tactic of
manipulation.

W. Wells - 2132.09.21

Secrets bled from the traitors like open veins. New information feeding the excitement still heavy in the air days after the celebration. Infectious in the same way as Garcia's laugh, and as dangerous as red lung.

The tension resting on the Advisors' shoulders remained hidden behind the closed chamber doors. Maia only saw it after her late shifts in the infirmary as Council, weary from hours of deliberation, made their way to their quarters for the night. A welcome distraction that allowed Maia's plan to go unnoticed.

Senna shadowed Tala and her scouts, searching for clues to the person on the other side of her letters. The collectors covered for Sky's absence as he worked to clear her bounty. Briar and Garcia kept the rebel deserters quiet, training them separately from Portico's guards. Everything and everyone moved in their respective directions, while all Maia could do was wait for Aster to take Aquila's place.

Restlessly twirling a pencil around her finger, Maia chewed a raw spot on her lip, staring at, but not reading, the words written in the patient's folder. There were only a few left in the infirmary, but they were the most complex. Each one slowly drawing closer to the point of no return.

The door opened with a bang, jerking Maia from her wandering thoughts. She straightened in the desk chair—eyes wide as Mr. Foster stormed in.

"What's wr—" Maia's next word dissipated as she realized exactly what was wrong.

"I need to know what you've found," Tala hissed behind him. She paused in the doorway, frozen in Maia's icy gaze.

Mr. Foster dropped his leather bag on the chair with a *thud*, leaning over his desk. "I've already told you. I don't have time to read those journals. Aquila asked me to focus on our patients, which is what I'm doing."

Tala wasn't giving up on the journals, and now Mr. Foster was caught in the middle.

"I don't give a shit what Aquila said," Tala snapped.

Scarlet red crawled across Mr. Foster's cheeks, his hands trembling as he pulled paperwork from his bag. Tala could threaten Maia all she wanted, but she would regret intimidating Mr. Foster.

Maia's chair slowly scraped across the floor, and she moved into the space between them. "I already told you there's nothing in those journals."

"Stay out of this," Tala warned.

"No." Maia pushed forward, forcing Tala back a step. The only thing Tala understood was fear. Without it, she no longer had power over Maia. "Threaten me all you want, but it doesn't change anything."

Tala's face grew menacingly blank, hiding the thoughts within. In one quick motion, her dagger was now pressed under Maia's chin.

"You will *not*—" Mr. Foster shouted.

"I know you're lying." Tala's eyes remained locked with Maia's. The point of her blade broke the skin, but Maia remained still.

It didn't matter what Tala thought, and that alone made Maia feel powerful again. A smile curled her lips as she leaned forward—her voice nothing more than a whisper. "Prove it."

Had Maia blinked, she would have missed it. Just a flicker of respect in Tala's gaze before she lowered her dagger. "I suggest you find time to read those journals sooner rather than later, Mr. Foster."

"We don't answer to you," Maia called out as Tala stormed back to the door.

She paused, glancing over her shoulder to look Maia in the eye. "For now."

There was a certainty in Tala's response that made Maia's blood go cold as the door slammed shut.

Aquila no longer had control over her—if he ever did. Mr. Foster lifted her chin with his still trembling hand, assessing the damage from the dagger.

When he seemed satisfied it didn't require attention, he gripped her shoulders, eyes firm. "You knew. That's what you were warning me about."

"Yes."

He took a deep breath, his thick shoulders collapsing around him. "Our knowledge makes us capable of annihilation, my dear. I could never forgive myself if I played a role in it."

Her heart broke at the defeat in his voice. It was exactly what she had feared the moment she saw his husband's research. "I won't let that happen. I promise."

The knit of his bushy brows told her he already knew.

"I need you to keep those journals safe and as far away from Tala as you can," Maia said, grabbing her winter coat from the chair. "I'll figure out how to get rid of them."

She started for the door when Mr. Foster whispered, "Maybe one day you'll tell me who you really are in all of this."

Fear locked her in place. It was only a matter of time before he knew. Before they all knew. "That will be for you to decide, sir."

She continued out the door, knowing better than to wait for a response... or worse, the silence that might follow.

Clouds lazily drifted across the gray winter sky as Maia laid on the lone bench, tucked away in the hidden alcove of the hedge maze. There had been so many opportunities for her to destroy the journals. So many chances to do the right thing, even if Rowan wouldn't. And yet, they remained.

Because, unlike Rowan, who kept them to honor his family's legacy, she couldn't destroy them because of fear. Fear of the consequences, first with Rowan's threat, and now with knowing someone would hang for her actions. All she could hope was that this time, it would be her.

Footsteps approached, and she shielded her eyes to the sun, watching Aster enter the alcove.

"Lost again?" she teased, sitting up and dropping her feet to the floor.

A smile twisted his full lips as he twirled a rose between his fingers, effortlessly navigating its thorns. "I can safely say I'm not. This was actually my secret spot until I absentmindedly brought you here that day."

She leaned forward, propping her arms on her knees and rubbing the melancholy from her face. "It's a good spot."

He took a seat beside her, but remained quiet. So close, but somehow miles away. She hated the ache blooming with each beat of her heart. The tingle of her fingertips desperate to reach for his. It was reckless to stay, regardless of what she wanted.

"I should go."

His hand floated towards hers, resting beside it on the cool stone. He had reached out to her before, but this time, he hesitated.

Did he sense the danger too, or did he just need to know the fire between them was burning her too?

Her instincts screamed for her to walk away, but instead, she remained painfully still.

"I'm beginning to wonder if there's a right side to all of this." Voices carried over the hedges, and he paused. His words were for her alone, and knowing that set off every nerve within her, one by one, racing just under her skin. "Portico has always tried to right the wrongs of the past, but it's imperfect. The rebellion was an important reminder of the progress that could still be made."

"It doesn't have to stay this way." She tightened her grip on the lip of the bench. The amount of effort it took to fight the pull her arm had to his was enough to make her muscles sting. "There's still a chance to make things right."

"Orion's forgotten that rebellions aren't about destroying something, but making it better." There was a restrained passion in his voice that only strengthened his allure.

She loosened her fingers from the bench, discreetly hooking her pinky around his. "Orion is just a man out for revenge. He isn't the rebellion. Rebellions are the quiet acts of courage, despite the consequences."

Like destroying the journals.

She closed her eyes, dropping her chin to her chest. There would be consequences to destroying a piece of history—in erasing the mistakes of the past—but the alternative was hoping no one would use this knowledge for their own gain. Only Aster proved it a possibility.

Never let fear guide your decisions. It was the right thing to do. Something worth dying for.

Aster tucked his hand under hers, wrapping it in his warmth. It was soft and tender in a way that made hers feel calloused and burdened.

She glanced at him, grateful to find him lost in thought, allowing her a moment to see him without being seen. Soft worry lines had creased into the space between his windswept hair and brows. His neatly groomed stubble shadowed his strong, tensed jaw. He was breathtaking, with his beautiful high cheekbones that drew her eyes to those full lips she thought of more often than she should.

She entwined her fingers with his. "You gave hope to those people in the shantytown. You chose peace over power. A person who does the right thing regardless of their allegiance can change the world."

Aster turned to her, their faces only inches apart. She could feel the whisper of his breath on her lips as his eyes searched hers. "You know..." The words escaped him like a sigh of relief.

"Aquila chose the right successor."

His gaze seemed to melt at her words, eyes now a stunning liquid amber. "You'll be one of the few who thinks that," he said, thumb gently stroking the back of her hand.

"Then let what you do change their minds."

"I hope to." The smile that tugged at his lip was so dangerously tantalizing she had to bite down on her own to keep her wants in check. "And I'd like you with me when I do."

The final piece of the plan. Council would be theirs, but as she took her place on the board her heart stuttered. In his eyes she saw the same want igniting every inch of her.

"Rafe told me what the rebels said in Hopewell. They don't believe in our cause right now, but they believe in you."

This was the reason she should have walked away. The reason why, even hidden away in secret alcoves, she had to maintain her crumbling walls. All these rebels needed was one word from her lips to turn on Portico. She was here to destroy them, and her heart twisted painfully, knowing that could mean having to destroy Aster too.

She didn't deserve his warmth when she had none to give in return. She didn't deserve his honesty when even her name was a lie. He would know the truth about her one day, and the weight of that alone would eventually crush her.

And she would deserve it.

"You don't need me," she said, pulling her hand from his. He opened his mouth to argue, and she quickly stood. "But as long as I'm still standing, I stand with you."

"I promise you, Tala won't be a threat anymore once this is done."

"I'm not asking for your protection." She couldn't hide the frustration in her voice as her head and heart warred within.

Aster was on his feet, his long stride quickly closing the space between them. He reached for her, but she took a step back. That single step somehow put miles between them as he froze in front of her.

"Then tell me what you want, Maia."

"I'm asking you to remember the words I've said," she swallowed, forcing her next words, "Instead of the ones I can't."

He slowly nodded, and she could almost see him analyzing every interaction they'd had up to this moment. If only she could tell him the reason for her walls. The distance she wished she didn't have to create. The secret she struggled to keep from him, even knowing it could be her last.

"I won't ask, but whatever it is, I'm here if you don't want to go through it alone," he said, confirming he cared for her in the same ruinous way she cared for him.

She felt his words settle slowly around her shattered heart, tugging at its jagged edges. She didn't owe him anything for his openness, but as they held each other's gaze in silence, all she wanted was a moment of connection with him. A moment where she didn't have to pretend.

She knew she shouldn't, but she thrust herself onto her toes, wrapping her arms around his neck. The smell of bergamot and cloves surrounded her, making her feel impossibly light, as if she only remained upright from the air itself.

"It's not fair for me to ask for anything more, regardless of what I want," she whispered.

There was only a second of surprise before he wrapped his arms around her, lips grazing her neck. She shivered, despite the heat between them.

"I'm not asking for fair, Maia."

Her hand raked through the short hair on the back of his neck as she melted into him. Dangerous confessions rested on the tip of her tongue.

Why she found her way through Portico's gates. Her father's legacy. The reason Tala was no longer the threat that kept her up at night.

She could feel the fissures slowly spreading in her resolve, as delicate and deadly as a black widow's web.

"I'm not..."

Her throat closed around her words. Tala was already using the journals against him. If he knew the truth about Maia and kept it from Council, it would be all Tala needed to hang him next.

Dread washed over her. Was this what Tala was waiting for all along? She lowered herself and slowly pulled away. He seemed unable to let go, taking her hand and running his thumb across her palm, easing the burden tucked within.

"I'm not someone you should be found alone with right now."

His thumb stopped. The softness of his face sharpened with awareness and he straightened, tucking his hands deep into his pockets. She had become his death sentence.

"I'm sorry, Aster."

She started towards the exit, struggling against the pull drawing her back to him. Portico had created a new kind of torture. One that allowed her to be close enough to the only person who calmed her heart and thawed the ice in her veins, but far enough away that she could only yearn for that kind of peace and comfort.

⟵⟶

Maia returned to the infirmary for her evening shift, grateful for the distraction from her racing thoughts and the smell of bergamot. The night was quiet, allowing her time to focus on the lists left behind by the healers.

Tonics that needed refilling.

I'm not asking for fair, Maia.

Wound dressings that needed changing.

The softness of his lips against her neck.

She clenched the list in her hand, forcing down the need blooming in her chest, and went to work.

As she chipped away at her tasks, her thoughts wandered back to Orion and the prison. Anger still flowed within her, like the sting of a dead arm waking. She ground her teeth to steady her hands as she changed the dressing on a rebel's gangrenous foot. His eyes were focused on the ceiling—blank, emotionless. As dead inside as the rotting flesh slowly spreading outside.

Orion had destroyed him, all of them. Taken the fragile idea of hope and spent the time to clean and polish it into something that could shine again, before shattering it against the cold prison floor. Maia hated him for making her carry the burden of cleaning up the broken pieces he left behind.

You think you're better than him? She froze as Caleb's presence hovered beside her, his cool breath on her ear.

Saving these lives won't absolve you from the ones you took. Who cleans up the pieces you leave behind?

Maia's throat grew tight, as if his icy hand had wrapped around it.

There is no redemption for you. Only a reckoning.

"Maia?"

A hand found her shoulder, anchoring her back in the sterile reality surrounding them. She jumped, gasping for breath as if resurfacing from underwater.

"What's wrong?" Senna asked, desperately searching Maia's eyes.

Caleb's words turned her stomach, and she knew better than to say them out loud. They didn't belong to him, but the truth she had been trying so hard to bury deep within her. Senna shook her head forcefully, wiping tears from Maia's cheeks.

When had she started crying? The thought of losing control of her body was not nearly as terrifying as the realization she might be losing hold of her mind.

"We're so close, Maia. You just need to hold on a little longer." Senna pulled Maia's trembling body into a hug.

"I'm sorry," Maia whispered.

"Don't *fucking* apologize. Tell me you're okay."

Maia forced her eyes shut, taking in a shaky breath. Her heart slowed as Caleb faded back into the dark corners of her mind, the ominous curve of his blue lips promising her it wouldn't be long before he resurfaced. Pinching her nails into her palms, she nodded, locking him in place.

"That's not enough. I need you to say it, Maia."

With another slow breath, she focused on the muffled tick of the watch in her pocket. *We're stronger than we look, my little Sagitta.* She met Senna's gaze. "I'm okay."

Her shoulders relaxed, and she rubbed Maia's arms. "Good. Because Aquila's dead."

Maia nearly laughed. "You're joking."

"The bells have been ringing for over an hour." Senna's thin brows pulled tight with worry.

The bell tower rings for three reasons: to mark the hour, to warn of attack, or to mourn a fallen leader.

"Come on," Senna said, holding out Maia's jacket. "The Ascension Ceremony is about to start."

Maia allowed a moment of hope to carry her away. She would be safe again—could almost see the door of her childhood home open with Hannah waiting on the other side. So close to no longer having to keep secrets. To watch the journals burn, once and for all.

This was finally their chance at a new beginning.

26

UNVEILED

The slow ring of the bell tower solemnly cast itself like a shadow across the crowded grounds. It had never been so quiet, a nervous energy filling the space where words couldn't. Maia fed off their unease, feeling it heavy in her chest as if her heart suddenly hardened to stone. She hoped it would prepare her for whatever came next.

Senna spotted Briar towering over the surrounding group and started towards him. The tiny hairs on the back of Maia's neck stood on end, sensing eyes in every direction.

"Has anyone said what happened?" Senna asked, squeezing between Garcia and Briar.

Garcia stood wide, cringing as a group of guards encroached. It was clear he wasn't comfortable in the congested space. "Se jodió," he said, eyes focused on the guards beside him.

"What does that mean?" The low roll of the drums announced the beginning of the ceremony, drowning out Senna's question.

"It means who fucking cares." Briar shouted, dropping his smoke to the floor and snuffing it out under his boot.

Garcia pressed his lips together, impressed. "Close enough."

Two guards pulled open the large Council Hall doors. The Advisors emerged dressed in dark red ceremonial robes with satin shoulder capes and gold piping. Aster and Tala confidently led them through the towering columns while General Winter scowled, exuding nothing but resentment for the too-tight outfit hugging her muscular physique. A slight sheen of sweat glistened on Rafe's forehead under the glow of the torches. He tugged at the collar of the robe where a row of gold buttons ended.

Aster raised his hands to the crowd, and the drumming drew to a close. There was a powerful silence—a collective holding of breaths—as they waited for him to speak. *There are many who won't agree with my decision.* The confident gaze of the spectators suggested Aquila's concern might have been for nothing.

"It is with a heavy heart we announce Aquila's passing." Aster's voice traveled over them, strong and steady, softening the worried creases on the surrounding faces. "Let us have a moment of silence in honor of our fallen leader."

Everyone dipped their heads in honor, including the rebel deserters. Regardless of what they believed, there was still respect to be paid to the man who provided them refuge.

Aster lifted his head and continued. "Aquila was a man who understood the fickleness of power. The importance of using his influence to shape our new world into one that doesn't focus on the destruction of our past, but on the new beginning that emerges from it. There are roses just outside the garden maze that serve as a constant reminder to me of who we truly are. Because even the harshest of winters are incapable of muting their resilience. We will overcome our loss and grow stronger together. We will continue the legacy he created."

The hesitation had all but vanished, as the crowd swelled with the same pride she noticed the day Aquila welcomed the new recruits to Portico. A camaraderie that formed from knowing everyone else felt it too.

"Prior to his passing, Aquila named his predecessor."

Maia's heart seized at the subtle, almost pained hitch in Aster's smile. Something was wrong. He turned away from the crowd as if ashamed by what he was about to reveal.

"Tala, please step forward."

The world fell silent as the winter chill seeped under Maia's skin. Her eyes traveled to lips hovering beside ears in the gathering, but heard nothing. Senna's hand found her arm, but she felt nothing.

She disappeared into the void of her own irrelevance. Nothing more than a pawn in Tala's game. But none of it mattered at that moment.

The moment she realized they were all fucked.

"Get Mr. Foster out," Maia whispered. "Make sure he has the journals with him."

Tala lifted her chin with certainty while Aster seemed to be willing himself to continue. "Tala, Aquila has selected you to carry on his legacy. As the new leader of Portico, you must bear in mind that your successes are that of the people, but your failures are yours alone to carry. Your decisions can strengthen our power, but just as easily expose our weakness. Your influence may gain followers, but it will also draw enemies. You have the potential to shape our world for better or worse. Do you accept this honor and burden?"

Tala's lips twisted with satisfaction, sending a shiver through Maia. This was her plan all along. Everything she did was carefully coordinated in preparation for this moment. Tala's threat echoed in the back of Maia's mind. Was she the reason for Aquila's sudden demise?

"I do."

"Maia, this isn't—" Garcia started.

"I know." Maia's plan hinged on Aster being in power, which meant they had no plan now.

Senna gripped Maia's arm, her nails pinching painfully into her skin. "We need to go. *Now.*"

Aster scanned the crowd as he removed a yellowed scroll from his robe. His eyes met Maia's. For a moment, in all the chaos, it was just them. His lips moved slow and silent, warning her to *go*. Unrolling the scroll, he continued.

"Tala, do you swear to serve the people with the honor and respect that is rightfully theirs?"

"I do."

No. This wasn't how it ended. Tala took the move she thought would end the game, without realizing she left herself open. Somewhere there was proof she stole this position from Aster. It could be enough to create a rebellion within Portico's gates. The distraction needed to quietly take it all. She just had to find it.

"Do we know who she's writing to?" Maia asked, eyes still focused ahead.

"She's going to kill you," Senna hissed. She looked to Briar for support, but he remained strategically quiet, his face not hinting at who he agreed with. "No. There wasn't enough time."

The darkness within continued to spread like poisoned vines hidden just under Maia's skin. "What book did Rowan tell you to use to decode the letters?"

Senna shook her head, but defeat washed over her face. "*Understanding the Enemy*. Third shelf from the right of the passage. The page number was on the top corner of the letters, if there's any left to find. She'll keep them close, so you'll want to search her room. The code itself is easy to crack once you have those two pieces."

"Do you swear to do all things with honesty and integrity?" Aster continued.

"I do."

Garcia adjusted his sling, leaning into her. "Senna and I will take the healer to the—"

"Don't tell me," Maia said, finally meeting his gaze. "Just promise me you'll keep him safe."

"I promise." Garcia took her hand. "Rumor says Sagitta can't be killed. Let's hope they're right."

Briar tensed beside her as she gave Garcia a weak smile. Senna, however, pulled Maia into a forceful hug. She didn't speak, but the way she held Maia exposed her inner turmoil.

Brushing away a rogue tear, she composed herself, squeezing Maia's hand. "Send word when it's safe to come back."

Despite her anger and frustration, Senna still held the same confidence in her.

"Do you swear to protect those you serve with your life?" Aster asked.

"I do."

Maia closed her eyes, and Senna's hand disappeared.

"Tala, please announce your new name."

Maia's eyes fluttered open again, the world now tinted a vengeful red as Tala stepped forward. Her small frame stood sharp and lethal in her red robe. "From this day forward, you will know me as Scorpius."

Names were never chosen without purpose, and Maia wondered what Tala's meant. The guards, staff, and diplomats cheered, but the rest of the audience remained silent. Tala scanned them as if noting who would have to be punished later.

"Council now recognizes Scorpius as the new sworn leader of Portico," Aster announced. "And so, as one ascends to the sky, the next descends to the earth."

A fire ignited on the gathering grounds behind them. Aquila's body lay on a wooden platform over the flames, sending him back to nature as his ashes swirled up into the clouds of smoke. The assembly dispersed in two directions. The rebels were willing to pay respect for the fallen, but refused to celebrate his legacy.

"It should have been you up there, Sagitta," someone whispered in passing. A flicker of gratitude lit within Maia, but she quickly extinguished it, keeping her eyes low and knowing better than to meet their gaze. They risked everything to speak those words. Another person willing to hang for her.

Briar's silence was deafening, and she wondered if he was contemplating the reality of what came next.

Even if they found the proof to expose Tala, there was little chance they'd get out of this alive.

He lit another smoke, watching the fire before them, trapped in a world where time held no meaning. Minutes were hours, transforming the flames into embers.

"Maia," Rafe said, stepping beside her. He was no longer in the ceremonial robes, hands tucked in his pockets. "Care to join me for a walk?"

"No."

The muscle in his jaw ticked with annoyance. "The question was rhet—"

"She said fuck off." Briar pushed his hair from his face, fatigue resting heavily under his eyes.

General Winter's hand dropped onto Briar's shoulder, causing him to flinch as the metal plates of her uniform clanged with authority. "Keep it in check, Harper. We ain't here for trouble."

"What do you want?" Maia asked with a sigh.

"Aquila's death was from natural causes. It seems surprisingly fortunate it happened while he still had his letter of succession gripped in his hands."

Maia met Winter's measured gaze. It was the same look she often gave Aster. The one Maia believed was a conversation only they understood. It wasn't though.

It was never about the words spoken, but the person speaking them. She understood Winter now, and her piercing green eyes told Maia they were certain the letter was planted.

"Don't seem so fortunate for him," Briar said, crossing his arms. "Where you goin' with this?"

"We need to make things right." Rafe was almost docile with his response, as if playing nice in hopes of her and Briar doing the same.

Maia's eyes drifted back to the embers still burning. They wanted to expose Tala too—which meant a new rebellion had begun.

"I'll need a book from Aquila's manor called *Understanding the Enemy*. Do you know how to access the passage to the library?"

"All the Advisors do," Winter said. Her pale brow lifted. "And apparently you."

"Third shelf to the right. Bring it to Tala's room."

Winter nodded, shoving her way through the crowd.

Maia glanced up at Rafe. "You both could hang for this."

"Well, there's comfort in knowing you'll be swinging right there next to us."

The scout's housing was a hauntingly gothic building looming behind Council Hall, with four pointed towers as sharp as daggers. Oxidized green lamp posts guided them towards the unwelcoming granite entrance. A heavy cast iron lantern hung over the two arched double doors that creaked open in the deafening silence.

Within awaited a burst of clashing colors. An arcaded gallery of gold and white arches surrounded them in the sky-lit atrium, with chipping columns of intricate blue and green details. Tarnished chandeliers hung over muted green doors, leading them to a blood-red staircase that continued up three more dizzying floors.

Everything about the building was unsettling as their footsteps echoed across the checkered, underlit floor of blues and greens like sea glass from the Coastal Region.

Rafe gripped Briar's shoulder, pulling him to a stop. "Keep watch down here in case we have company."

"Fuck that," Briar said, shoving Rafe's hand away.

In a blink, they were now standing nose to nose.

"It's okay," Maia said, gently laying her hand on Briar's arm.

His glare remained locked on Rafe, but his shoulders relaxed at her touch. "Anything happens to her and I'll tear you limb from limb," he warned, taking a step back.

Rafe smoothed his vest. "Understood."

Briar's gaze flickered to Maia, telling her he would be here if she needed him. She gave him an appreciative smile before following Rafe up the steps.

"You already knew the letter of succession was forged, didn't you?" Rafe asked when they were no longer in earshot. Maia remained quiet, which he seemed to take as a yes. "Who told you?" he continued.

"Aquila."

He paused on the step. "Did you kill him?"

Maia rolled her eyes. "You give me too much credit."

"You forget, I saw you in Hopewell," Rafe said, catching up with her. "Why are you here, Maia? The real reason."

"I'm here to find the letter needed to get Aster into power."

"I've dealt with Aster's half-answers long enough to know when someone is fucking with me."

She followed him down a hall on the third floor, heading to a door at the far north end, tucked under the clock tower.

"It doesn't matter anymore what brought me here." Her eyes darted around the eerily quiet hall. "Just know we want the same thing."

Rafe leaned against a doorframe Maia assumed to be Tala's. She removed her hair comb, unpinning the lockpicks and dropping to her knees.

"So were you sent to stop Tala?" he asked, hovering over her. She ignored his questions, trying to focus on the lock. "Is that why you were with the Overseer the night she caught him with the letter? My contacts on Canal Row saw you there."

She removed the picks from the lock and rubbed her eyes, her frustration growing with his hovering and questioning. "Tala is hiding something, Rafe."

"Which is why I didn't say anything, or you would have hanged with him."

"I'm going to guess that was more Aster's decision than yours." She returned the picks to the lock, closing her eyes so she could focus.

"You're dodging the question."

"If we can find proof, then we'll know who's helping her."

"And then what?"

"Why don't we figure this out first?" The lock clicked, and Maia turned the knob, pushing it open.

Rafe's gaze narrowed. "Seriously, who the fuck *are you*?" he asked, putting out his hand and pulling her to her feet.

Another question for her to ignore as they walked into the room. He shut the door behind them while she flicked open the curtains so the moonlight filtered in.

Rafe pushed his unruly curls from his face, scanning the massive room with dark walls and a towering matte-black canopy bed. "Where do we start?"

"Look for false walls or floorboards."

Rafe nodded, starting towards the corner of the room while Maia wandered into the bathroom.

"You know, you're the first person Aster's trusted since our father passed," Rafe said from the other room. "Fuck, it's been five years now."

She froze. Her deceitful reflection looking back at her in the mirror. Dropping her gaze, she checked for loose tiles or anything tucked behind the clawfoot tub before returning to the main room.

Rafe had torn apart the bed with pillows and sheets strewn everywhere.

"Everything needs to look untouched."

His face hardened, and he tossed the pillow to the head of the bed. "I know you don't want to hear it, but I'm tryin' to tell you somethin' here."

"Then fucking say it already."

He balled his fists on the sheets, taming his frustration. "People used to take advantage of Aster's compassion, and it drove our father up the fuckin' wall. He was awful to him, absolutely berated Aster until he became the untrusting and impenetrable person he is now. Then you show up, and I think he saw the version of himself our father had destroyed. Something he wanted to protect."

She saw it. The curated image he portrayed. The carefully chosen words he spoke. It was all to mask the person she saw that night in his office. The man who handed her the rose as they strolled through the maze. The reason she needed him in power instead of Tala.

Rubbing the tension building in her shoulders, she scanned the room, her eyes catching on the red brick fireplace.

Rafe dropped onto the edge of the bed, his shoulders caving in around him. "She's going to kill him, Maia."

That's why he wanted her to know Aster's weakness. He hoped she would help keep his brother safe.

"Not if we find what we're looking for," she said, running her hand over the rough bricks inside the firebox.

"What if it isn't enough?"

"It has to be." She nudged the log rack aside, her finger tracing the missing mortar around a loose brick on the raised hearth.

Using Tala's dagger, she pried it free, placing the brick to the side and searching the space where it had been.

"What's this?"

Rafe removed two pieces of paper tucked inside the hollowed-out brick. The rush of her heartbeat suddenly filled Maia's ears. She pushed the brick and log rack back in place before brushing the soot from her hands.

Rafe had moved to the light of the window, where she joined him. The first letter was the formal letter of succession, naming Aster as the next leader of Portico.

"You fucking found it!" he said, slapping the page.

The door to the room suddenly opened, and they both spun to the door, eyes wide with fear.

General Winter's nose piercing glinted under the light of the wall sconces, and she lifted the book to them. "Found it."

Rafe blew out a breath, turning back to the window. "Is this code?" he asked, scanning the second letter, his thumb grazing an ink splatter at the bottom.

Maia tried to calm her racing heart. "Yes. The same type of coded letter found on the Overseer."

This was the proof Aquila wanted. All she needed to do was decipher it, and Tala's reign could be over as quickly as it started.

"I need something to write with."

Maia took a seat at Tala's desk, finding the page number in the top corner of the letter and flipping to it in the book. She already deciphered three letters before Rafe found a pen, and the rest fell into place within minutes.

Don't do anything rash until I return from the Desert Region. She's the key to our success. Not just for the weapon plans and healer, but to stop the bleed of deserters. Put the plan in motion, and hand over the loose thread. I'll make sure it unravels.

It wasn't an ink splatter. At the bottom sat Orion's symbol. Which meant...

Bile worked up the back of Maia's throat as she pushed away from the desk, crossing the room and throwing the window open for air. Her heart rattled in her chest so hard she was certain it would explode. Planting her hands onto the windowsill, she gulped in deep breaths, trying to keep the world from spinning.

"Tala's working with Orion," Rafe whispered.

No. It wasn't true.

Tala was the personification of Portico's corruption and manipulation.

"The hidden rebel Aquila was worried about." Winter's words sounded like a distant echo.

If Tala was with Orion, that meant Orion now had control of Portico. The rebels that were promised refuge were prisoners all over again. And if Maia exposed Tala as the hidden rebel, it would only strengthen Portico against the rebellion. Maia's *and* Orion's. She ran her hand through her hair, gripping it to keep from screaming.

I fear when the transition of power occurs, a veil will fall, and the rebels who have infiltrated Portico will reveal themselves.

It didn't make sense. Tala single-handedly killed Maia's father, Orion's wife and daughter, and Rowan. All of these things could only benefit Portico.

"We need to expose her. She should be hanging right now!" Rafe shouted, joining Maia at the window as if looking for her support.

"Keep your voice down," Winter hissed, walking to the other side of Maia. "We're the only three people who know, which means only three bodies for Tala to dispose of. If we give this up too soon, we lose any chance of getting Portico back."

"The weapon plans," Rafe said, scanning the letter. "Is Orion talking about the journals?" Maia's eyes grew wide, and he scoffed. "You're not the only one Aster confides in."

"That's why Tala wouldn't drop it." Maia's thoughts raced for a connection, and her heart sank. "With the weapon, no one would risk overthrowing them."

The sound of feet dragging along the floor captured their attention. Rafe quickly folded the letters, tucking them into his pocket. His thick brows furrowed as he exchanged a look of fear with Winter.

"I'm sorry," he finally said to Maia.

Someone needed to take the fall for this, and Rafe chose her. She didn't have time to react before his hand gripped her hair, pulling her head back and yanking her towards the center of the room.

Tala and Aster were arguing when they appeared in the doorway, with Briar in tow. The four scouts holding him had fresh-looking injuries on display. A string of drool fell from the corner of Briar's mouth, his eyes dilated and struggling to stay open. They had dosed him.

"Tell us what you're doing in here!" Rafe shouted at Maia for show.

"What's going on?" Tala asked, her obsidian eyes narrowing at Maia.

"Don't *fucking* touch her," Briar growled, thrashing against the scouts. A kick across his face dazed him as he fought to remain conscious. Winter balled her fists so tight her knuckles cracked at the pressure.

"We were heading towards the training grounds and noticed her sneaking into the building," Rafe said, tightening his grip on Maia's hair.

She bit down on her lip to keep from crying out as she dug her nails into the back of his hand. It was dangerous to appear this weak and exposed, but that's what she was.

For Council to keep Tala's trust, this needed to be believable, which meant she was at their mercy. Which was a terrifying place to be.

"She hasn't said what she was looking for, but we'll get her to talk."

"There's no need," Tala said, eyes flickering towards the fireplace for only a second before she moved into the room. "There's a more pressing matter at hand."

Dread washed over Maia. The letter was true. Maia and Tala were the same.

Both rebels.

Both traitors.

Both leaving a trail of blood in their wake.

The only difference was that Tala had won, and now Maia had become the loose thread to unravel.

The queen had stepped out from the shadows, taking her place on the board.

Check.

Rafe shoved Maia to bow at Tala's feet and stepped away. "Back off," he warned, voice tense enough for Maia to lift her gaze. He had Aster by the collar, pushing him back to the door. "She brought this upon herself."

"Where's Mr. Foster, Maia?" Tala asked, tone as sharp as her dagger.

"I don't know."

Tala crouched, lifting Maia's chin to meet her gaze. "That won't bode well for you."

With a nod, two scouts stepped forward. One pulled Maia to her feet, while the other's fist found her stomach. A cry escaped her, and she bent in pain.

"Enough!" Aster's voice was so forceful it caused Tala to flinch as he broke out of Rafe's white-knuckled grip.

Tala's dagger was drawn, softly pressing against Aster's neck. Maia froze as the entire room fell silent.

A wicked smile slithered across Tala's lips. She reveled in the fear she was creating. "My scouts found witnesses that believe they saw Mr. Foster heading east. They'll take you, Briar, and Maia to interrogate them."

There was only one reason Tala would send them together. She had a plan to get rid of them all at once. Rafe's eyes grew wide, and he stepped forward, reaching for his pocket.

He was going for the letters, hoping it would be enough to save his brother. The desperation to protect him was something Maia understood, but she couldn't let him do it. Three bodies would now be five, and Tala had gotten rid of much more than that with the *accident* she coordinated to kill Maia's father.

"You're just as pathetic as that fucking dagger you think looks so powerful," Maia spat.

"Careful, Maia," Tala taunted. "You answer to *me* now."

"Your title means nothing." Maia's defiance earned her a punch across the face.

"Stop!" Briar struggled against the scouts, and two more jumped onto him, tackling him to the ground. Maia nearly broke as his anger turned into wet sobs, his face pressed against the dirty floor.

"Please, stop hitting her." Briar's muffled words were saturated with desperation, and Winter stormed over, throwing a scout so violently off him, they slid somewhere past the doorway.

"Get up!" she shouted, yanking Briar to his feet. Her grip tightened around his waist to keep him from collapsing. "I'll take him to get ready to leave."

The scout dropped Maia's hands, and she massaged her sore wrists.

"I told you to pick a side, Maia. You picked wrong," Tala whispered, raising the hairs on the back of Maia's neck.

Rafe gripped Maia's shoulder, pulling her from the room. She struggled to keep pace with his long stride as he rushed to create as much distance between them and the room as he could.

"Winter and I will work on getting a group together to find you. We just need time to get them out of here without being noticed."

Maia nodded, "I'll do what I—"

Aster's hand clamped down on Rafe's shoulder, nearly knocking him over with a punch to the face. Maia stumbled back in shock. Before Rafe could recover, Aster shoved him into the wall, their faces only inches apart as he trembled with rage.

"Don't you *ever* fucking touch her like that again!" he shouted, as Rafe struggled in his grip.

Tala's scouts rushed forward, pulling Aster off his brother. Before Maia could process her thoughts, her dagger pressed into the back of the scout holding him.

"Let. Him. Go."

The scout dropped Aster's hands, lifting his own in truce. Aster collected himself, straightening his diplomat jacket as Maia returned her dagger to its sheath. Everyone kept their distance as the scouts continued with them down the hall.

She snuck a glance over her shoulder to find Rafe wiping blood from the corner of his lip. He gave her a quick, reassuring nod. There was trust that this wouldn't be the last time he saw his brother alive.

27

SCARRED

Alone cabin rested peacefully in a clearing of snow-dusted pines just north of Williamsburg. Off in the distance, a conversation between two barred owls traveled across the dark-velvet sky. A moment too serene as Tala's scouts shoved Maia forward. Briar growled behind her, earning a jab in the ribs with the butt of a gun. Aster remained quiet, as he had since they left. Smart enough to keep his mouth shut to avoid bruises and injuries.

"Knock twice and do as they say," a scout ordered. "We have no trouble shooting if any of you decide to run."

Up to now, the scouts had refused them even a step without someone by their side. Which made Maia wonder what was waiting for them in the cabin that changed that?

Aster continued confidently towards the soft wink of a candle in the cabin window. Welcoming in the same way as the wind chimes at Rowan's safe house. He stopped in front of the door, giving two quick knocks, just as he was told.

A chair scraped across the floor inside, and Maia hesitantly joined him, scanning the exterior for any exits. Her eyes stopped on Orion's symbol etched into the doorframe. Realization pulled at her stomach like an anchor. The rebellion was about to collect their bounty.

Maia straightened her back as the handle turned. There was nowhere left to run. A man with frosty-blue eyes stood before them, noting Briar and Aster towering beside her.

His hand twitched for the blades at his side before his eyes fell on Maia. "You ain't nearly as impressive as the stories make you out to be, Sagitta."

Flicking back her jacket, she tucked her hands into her pockets. The motion would have been more threatening if her daggers were resting on her hips, instead of at the bottom of a scout's bag. "We'll see about that."

Aster and Briar tensed as if preparing for a fight, while Maia held her glare on the man.

He smirked, tugging at a piercing on his bottom lip. "I guess we will. Make yourself at home." He lifted his long, blonde hair into a messy bun and started for the center of the room.

Aster's heavy boots commanded attention as he stepped in first, with Briar behind them. The entire cabin was a single room. To the right, a man with waves of greasy, black hair stood with his back to them, pouring himself a drink at the wooden counter and gazing out a dusty window.

In the other corner, a cot rested against the wall with stuffing spilling from the mattress. An old man sat on it, sharpening his blade and admiring his work against the soft glow of the fireplace. Positioned in the center of the room was a single wooden table with ropes resting on chairs.

The door slammed shut behind them, and Maia's heart plummeted. Another rebel back from the dead. The matted, long, blonde hair knotted with colorful strings and beads should have been a welcoming sight. But as Jackson turned the lock of the door, Maia flinched at the deafening *click*.

"You have some explaining to do, Maia," she said, leaning into the door.

The blue-eyed man gripped Maia's shoulder. She wasn't going down without a fight. In one motion, she pulled the dagger from his hip and swung, cutting him across the cheek. His mouth gaped as his piercing fell to the floor with a clatter.

"You fucking bitch!" he shouted, blood spilling through his fingers down his chin.

A sickening *crack* made Maia stagger as a searing pain shot across the back of her head, turning her vision black.

Moments of lucidity attempted to take hold as Maia flickered between consciousness.

The soothing crackle and warmth of the flames from the fireplace.

The metallic taste of blood mingled with the sour of a cloth gag.

Her eyes fluttered open, scanning the room, vision blurring on the edges in time to the throbbing in her skull. Aster was bound beside her, while Briar sat gagged and unconscious in the center of the room, a large bruise blooming on his cheek.

"Well, shit, look who's finally awake." The old man stood by the fire, holding his knife over the flames.

Dread's icy hands gripped her shoulders as she struggled against the rope scratching at her wrists and ankles. He removed the blade from the flames and blew on it, a dark glint in his eyes. Hobbling over, he lifted her chin with dirt-crusted fingers.

"We're gonna toughen up that baby face of yours. Give ya the same cut ya gave Hawke."

The oniony stench of his body odor made her eyes water. She tried to pull her chin from his grip, bile crawling up her throat. The sour taste of the gag now made sense, and she closed her eyes, swallowing her vomit.

"You should have done it while she was passed out," Jackson said, rolling her eyes and tugging on a teal bead in her hair.

"Nah, I wanna hear her scream." His rotting teeth hung loose, dancing with each word.

"I promise if you give us time, we can locate Mr. Foster for you." The panic in Aster's voice made every muscle in Maia's body tense.

She tugged at the ropes, but they only cut deeper into her skin. The old man's eyes darkened at the fear in hers, and he pressed the scorching blade into her cheek. Red overtook her vision, even with her eyes closed, and she screamed into the gag.

"Stop! We'll give you whatever you want," Aster shouted, thrashing in his chair.

Jackson turned to Maia, wide-eyed. "He doesn't know, does he?"

Maia collapsed as the blade finished its path, attempting to numb herself from everything while struggling to remain conscious. A cackle escaped the old man, and he leaned back to admire his work.

"What don't I know?" Aster asked, his eyes hesitantly moving from Maia's to Jackson's as Jackson sauntered over to him.

"And here we thought you were the smartest of the Council Advisors, Aster Calderone," Jackson taunted, running her thumb along the curve below his lip.

At that moment, Maia could have killed her herself. Aster jerked away, earning an amused grin from Jackson before she forced a gag into his mouth. "Move him with the other one, Hawke."

The blue-eyed man stepped forward. The cut on his face was bright red and poorly stitched, but it didn't seem to deter him from his mission as he struggled to drag Aster to the center of the room.

"Play nice," a man said from behind Maia, forcefully pulling down her gag.

His voice was familiar, but she couldn't place it until he walked around the table. Maia's head dropped in defeat.

Micah, the bounty hunter she ran into with Sky, had the same tobacco-stained smile as he did the night they burned the Portico guard's body.

She wasn't getting out of this alive.

None of them were.

"You wouldn't happen to know where our healer is, would you, Maia?" Jackson asked, propping her head on her hand.

She didn't, but pretending she did could help buy them time. "Give me a reason to tell you."

Micah's eyes darkened behind his greasy locks as Jackson leaned back in her chair, crossing her arms. "I'm disappointed in you. I thought it would be you and me leading the rebellion one day. What promises did Aquila make to convince you to betray your blood?"

"Open your eyes! Orion lied to you, to all of us! Do you even know what you're fighting for anymore?"

"I'm fighting to end Portico's tyranny! I'm fighting to bring hope back to our world. *You're* the one who's forgotten."

The old man hooted from the fireplace, thriving on the growing tension, while Hawke's hands moved to rest on the blades at his hips.

A loose string from Maia's binding grazed her finger, and she tugged at it. "By killing them? Making them fear the rebellion as much as they once feared Portico? Tyranny by the rebels is still tyranny."

"Those weren't rebels. They were traitors to your father's cause, Maia *Avalos*." Jackson took her time enunciating each syllable, a cruel smile tugging at the corner of her lips. "*You*, of all people, should understand that."

The building tension of the room now snapped painfully against Maia's chest, stealing her breath. Her eyes flew to Aster's as he sat eerily still in the palpable silence. Watching and listening with a calculated gaze.

"Well, shit," Micah said. "Daughter of Taris himself. That explains a lot."

On restless nights, when her torturous thoughts denied her sleep, Maia would dream up countless apologies and excuses for this exact moment. All of them combined didn't feel like enough anymore. Aster deserved every raw and vulnerable truth she was too scared to speak until now.

"It's no longer my father's cause," Maia said, turning back to Jackson. "The fall of the rebellion will be on Orion."

Jackson's brow lifted in surprise. "I see."

"No. You don't."

Maia laid her neck against the headrest, suddenly exhausted. Despite the conviction in her voice, she knew men like Orion never took the fall. Not when there was someone like her to blame. She closed her eyes, carefully working the ropes as they loosened around her wrists.

"You know, the stories say that those brave enough to travel to the Desert Region never return. It's true, but not in the literal sense."

The calm, strategic shift in conversation made the room grow cold. Jackson had prepared this speech. A prologue to the proviso.

"You see, the Coastal Region is made up of muted blues and grays, and the Forest Region is browns and greens, but the Desert Region... it's every color imaginable. Rows of clay homes, in different shades of sunset. There's beauty in survival, an energy that emerges from chaos."

Maia stilled. The dirt and shadows of the old man's face transformed into a dark anticipation that sent a chill through her.

"The Desert Region creates survivors. So, while people may return, they're never the same person they were when they left. That's what Portico's done to you. Which is why I'll ask one more time. Where's the healer, Maia?"

Briar groaned, slowly coming to. His eyes grew wide, and he shouted into his gag, fighting against his binds.

"Let them go, and I'll tell you where he is," Maia said.

"You know I can't just let a Council Advisor walk away." Jackson removed her dagger, testing the point with her fingertip. She gave Hawke a quick nod, and he lifted a can of kerosene, pouring it on the floor around Briar and Aster's feet. "This could have been so much easier. Orion *will* get you to talk. One way or another."

They were out of time.

"You're right. This could have been much easier." Maia pulled the rope loose, and it fell to the floor behind her. Gripping the seat of her chair, she kicked the table forward with all her strength.

Jackson gasped, taking the hit directly in the chest. There would only be seconds before the pain and shock wore off. Briar threw himself into Hawke, knocking the matches from his hand. They both fell to the floor, smashing the chair under their weight, and now wrestling for the matchbox. Maia stumbled for Aster when a stabbing pain shot up the back of her leg. She cried out, dropping to her knees. The old man cackled from the other side of the room, his knife protruding out of the back of her leg.

She closed her eyes, sucking in a slow, controlled breath. The darkness coursing through her veins hardened like tar, numbing her to the pain. Gritting her teeth, she yanked the blade free, and the old man's smile collapsed. He shouldn't have given her a weapon.

With the flick of her wrist, the dagger stuck into his stomach, forcing him back a step. There was no surprise or disappointment on his face. That asshole knew he would go this way.

Gripping at the air, his hand brushed a lantern off the fireplace mantel. It exploded on the floor, lighting up the oil spilling from the shattered glass. The smell of kerosene hung heavy like a storm cloud. It was only a matter of time before the flames found it too.

A *pop* of bullets outside made them all freeze.

"Who is that?" Jackson demanded, aiming her gun at Maia.

There was another click of a hammer as Micah pressed the barrel of his pistol into the side of Jackson's head. "No hard feelings darlin', but this one and I have history."

He gave Maia a wink, and she realized Sky had come through yet again.

Jackson's entire body trembled with rage as she lowered her gun. Smoke filled the room while the flames slowly engulfed the old man and the cot in the corner. The sound of wheezing carried over the chaos. Maia glanced over her shoulder to find Aster struggling to breathe. Gripping the back of her leg, she staggered to him in the haze, cutting away at his bindings.

"Briar!" she cried out, collapsing under Aster's weight.

A second of distraction allowed Hawke to land a punch, splitting Briar's lip. It was all it took for Briar to go feral. Grabbing Hawke by the shoulders, he head-butted him with a sickening *crunch*. Maia lost count of how many punches he threw, finally seeing the version of Briar that Rowan had recruited.

Hawke stumbled back as blood poured down his face. Briar was now at her side, pulling Aster to his feet while more gunshots rang from the trees. Sky was clearing out the scouts for their escape.

"Get off of me!" Jackson shouted as Micah slammed her hand against the wood floor, trying to release her grip from around the pistol.

Maia rushed for the door when Hawke's arm wrapped around her neck, dragging her back into the room.

"Let go of her!" Briar roared.

Hawke wasn't a large man, but he was smart. Jackson's pistol had been knocked free, and Hawke lifted it to Maia's head, stopping Briar in his tracks. She scratched at his arms, leaving tracks of raw skin, but Hawke only tightened his grip around her neck, forming stars on the edge of her vision.

"Dammit, Sky! Take the fucking shot!" Micah shouted.

The glass shattered from a window, and Hawke's arm went limp around her. They both fell to the floor as Maia gasped for air. She looked down to find a bullet hole in the back of Hawke's head.

Behind her, Micah cried out in pain as Jackson's knee found his groin. He rolled off her onto the floor. Within seconds, Jackson was on her feet, climbing through the broken window.

The wooden ceiling beams groaned in protest. It was about to come down. Micah rushed to her, yanking Maia from the floor. The beams snapped as they ran, clearing the doorway just as the building collapsed in on itself.

"What happened in there?" Sky barked, gripping Micah by his collar.

Briar held a handful of snow against his busted lip, rubbing Aster's back as he desperately gasped for air. "Come on, man. You gotta breathe."

"Are you fucking kidding me right now?" Micah shoved Sky away. "We almost died because you stalled on the shot."

Maia tried standing, but the world went black. Her thoughts screamed for her to stay conscious just a little longer. She sucked in a deep breath and closed her eyes.

When she opened them again, the world was back in focus. Crawling to Aster, she lifted his face to hers. She had seen fear in his eyes before, but nothing like this.

"You're going to be fine. Look at me."

He forced shallow, hungry breaths, eyes pleading as they found hers. Desperate. Terrified.

"Breathe with me, Aster."

She took a slow, deep breath and held it, waiting for him to follow. His breathing quickened with his panic. It was only a matter of time before he passed out. She slowly exhaled, and his breath escaped him in a fit of coughs. He pulled his face away, tears leaving streaks down his soot-covered cheeks.

You're going to lose him. Caleb's voice crept from the dark corner of her mind. *This is your fault. Again.*

"You said you'd give a signal," Sky continued arguing behind her.

"The fucking building burning down wasn't enough of a signal?" Micah's voice cracked with incredulity.

"I couldn't see shit through the smoke!"

Maia steeled herself, placing her hand on Aster's chest and resting her forehead against his.

"Come on, Aster. Stay with me. Please," she whispered.

She took another slow breath in and out. His heart pounded under her palm, and he gripped her wrist, eyes closed tight as he focused on a slow, desperate breath.

"Good," she choked out, finally allowing her tears to escape. "One more. I'm right here."

He took another deep breath, followed by a long wheeze. His hand loosened on her wrist, and she pulled her forehead away as his eyes fluttered open. The fear was still there, but exhaustion was taking over.

She wiped the loose tears from his cheeks, smudging the soot. "You're okay. Everything's gonna be okay."

Micah and Sky had grown quiet behind her, and she jumped as Sky's cold hand found her shoulder. "We need to go, Maia."

Her eyes remained on Aster. He took another slow breath and tried to stand on his own, collapsing from fatigue. Briar didn't hesitate, placing his arm around Aster and lifting him to his feet.

"Tell me you have a plan, boss," Briar whispered.

"We need to get him to Williamsburg."

"What's in Williamsburg?" he asked, adjusting his hand around Aster's waist.

"A healer." Maia wished her words didn't feel so much like betrayal. Sky put out his hand, and she struggled to her feet, her vision blurring on the edges. "My sister."

He caught her before she fell, grunting as he lifted her into his arms. "The blonde from the tavern?"

She nodded, closing her eyes and resting her head against Sky's sharp shoulder.

"He'll make it there?" Micah asked hesitantly.

It didn't matter who he was asking, there was only one answer. "He has to."

28

HOMESICK

Just as nature returns us to winter, so our lives return
us to our coldest, darkest moments.

W. wells – 2163.08.26

White specks of dust hovered in a shaft of light, filling the room with warmth and pulling Maia from her nightmares. Sky sat fast asleep in a wooden chair, his head resting on his hand, elbow on the armrest. Maia's eyes drifted across the room to the light-blue vase on the dresser filled with fresh white peonies. Neatly arranged bottles of perfumes and makeup sat in brightly colored dishes on the vanity. Sighing, Maia pressed her face into the pillow, inhaling the scent of vanilla surrounding her.

She was home.

Running her hand over the soft quilt, she lifted the sheets. The sight of a tight bandage wrapped around her bare thigh caused the numbness to wear off, and she suddenly felt everything.

The burning cut on her face.

The raw sting trailing down her leg.

Pressing her head back on the pillow, she pinched her eyes tight, fingers aching from the iron grip she had on the sheets. She tested the injury, bending her knee and feeling the tightness of stitches under the gauze. The damage felt different—permanent—and she wondered if her luck had finally run out. She let out a slow breath and relaxed her grip, forcing the pain back down.

"Looks like the tonic wore off," Sky said, removing a vial from his pocket. He lifted it to her, but not far enough for her to reach without moving.

Maia grit her teeth to keep from crying out as she sat up. There was a second of hesitation before her fingers wrapped around the glass bottle, half-expecting him to hold it back.

"Thank you." The hush in her voice delicately balanced her gratitude with the burden of debt it now held.

"Told you I wouldn't let nothin' happen to you." He picked up a shallow mason jar on the vanity and moved to the bed, taking a seat next to her. "You do, however, make it difficult to keep that promise."

The smell of honey wafted from the open jar, and he dabbed it with his finger, gently applying it to her cheek.

"How's Aster?" she asked, picking at a loose thread on the quilt. Her concern shouldn't have twisted her stomach with guilt, but Sky's sudden tension forced it to.

He lowered his hand, rubbing the residual honey between his fingers. "Sleepin'. Your sister gave him something to help with the whistle in his chest. She said to change your bandage when you woke."

Leaning over, he placed the jar on the chair and lifted the sheet. The possession in his gaze made her feel small and powerless as he examined the bandage. Still, sitting next to him in nothing but her underwear somehow felt less exposed than the night in Rocky Mount.

His icy fingers trailed up the inside of her thigh. The chill numbed the pain while he positioned her leg in his lap, allowing him to unwrap the gauze.

"Do you remember what you said back in Rocky Mount?" he asked, as if reading her thoughts.

She remained quiet, terrified of where the conversation was going.

"I couldn't say it then, but I knew what you meant about findin' someone who feels like home." He swallowed audibly as he applied honey around the stitches, his storm-gray eyes refusing to meet hers. "Someone you ain't gotta pretend around."

The ice from his touch spread over her skin, dropping the temperature of the room. He tied off the fresh gauze, his hand lingering on the bare skin below it.

"There's a reason you came to my door that night and not his. You knew I could never judge you." His eyes finally met hers, and she wished they hadn't. "He will. They always do."

His words hit her like a slap to the face. "Why would you say that?"

"People like us—people broken beyond repair—all we do is hurt the ones we love. They're better off without us, Maia."

Her heart ached, remembering how quickly she had caused Hannah's life to spiral. All this time telling herself that everything she did was to make their world better. That it would be worth it in the end if she finished the fight her father started. But none of it was true.

She destroyed everything in search of something to fill the hole in her heart. He was right. Hannah had been—and would always be—better off without Maia. But hearing it made the world violently shift under her.

"You know what I'm sayin' is true. Walking away from them is the only way to keep them safe."

Sky knew exactly how to break her, and the worst part was that all he did was tell the truth. His words slithered through her icy veins, constricting around her heart and driving their deep fangs into the black, pulsing flesh.

"You're right," she said, steadying her breath as she adjusted to the new poison coursing through her. The one that would no longer apologize for the person she had become. The poison that made her feel as dangerous as the serpent who bit her. "They are better off without us, but we're both selfish enough to continue to love despite the pain we cause."

His edges sharpened to dangerous points, contempt radiating from him. He removed her leg from his lap and stood, placing the jar of honey back on the vanity. "Don't come knockin' on my door when he refuses to love you back."

Panic took hold as he moved to leave. She hated the shallow graves of doubt he buried in her. What if he was right and Aster never looked at her the same? What if Hannah wanted her to leave now that she was better? What if Sky's cruel love was the only love left that she deserved?

"I won't leave without saying goodbye," Maia said, defeat weighing down each heavy word. Sky stopped in the doorway, hesitating for a second before gazing at her over his shoulder. "Just let me have tonight. We can leave first thing in the morning."

His eyes softened, and he nodded. "I'll let Micah know."

She had walked away from Hannah once, and while it nearly broke her, she knew she had to do it again. All she could hope was that Aster would be easier.

She lowered her feet to the floor, testing the weight on her leg. The pins and needles remained constant, now a part of her. Pushing herself up, she limped to the oak armoire in the corner. Inside was overflowing with Hannah's colorful dresses. She removed a thick, gray robe before continuing into the parlor.

Micah lay sprawled on the couch, his loose waves slightly less greasy, and face no longer darkened from dirt and soot. He looked different, clean and vulnerable, with his arm hanging over the edge. She couldn't help but wonder who Micah and Sky could have become if they had been as fortunate as Hannah when they were younger. Sky kicked the foot of the couch, causing Micah to jump and draw his gun.

"Grab a drink with me," Sky said, lowering the barrel.

Micah rubbed his eyes with the back of his hand, still holding his gun, and spotted Maia out of the corner of his eye. "Fuck. What now?"

She pressed her lips together. Even a man like Micah dreaded the chaos surrounding her. Steeling herself, she continued across the parlor and pushed the kitchen door open.

Briar and Hannah sat huddled together at the table, whispering over cups of steaming tea and freshly baked biscuits. Seeing Hannah again after saying their goodbyes at Folly's pulled all Maia's buried emotions back to the surface.

Her sister's golden hair hung in shiny ringlets, framing her full, healthy cheeks. She looked just as Maia remembered before Folly's—radiant. Briar seemed to notice as well, dragging his captivated gaze from her to the cup in his hand, ears dusting with pink.

"Maia." Hannah said, face tight and gaze distant, confirming Sky's venomous words.

Hannah's welcome was Maia's doing. Still, deep down, she had hoped it would be different.

Maia dropped her gaze to the floor, crossing her arms over her chest to ease the new tear in her heart. "Sorry for showing up unannounced like this."

Hannah stood, placing her cup on the counter. "Are you staying?"

"We'll be gone in the morning," she said, steadying herself on the back of a chair to take the weight off her foot. "Unless you prefer we leave sooner."

"Don't be ridiculous. This is your home as much as it's mine." Hannah walked over, gently turning Maia's face to get a better look at the cut. "Did you cauterize this yourself?"

"The cut was from a hot blade." Watching Hannah up close, Maia now saw the cracks in her façade. Despite the glow surrounding her, the blue in Hannah's eyes was now faded and melancholic.

Hannah lifted the sleeve of Maia's robe, her fingers grazing the two purple scars on her arm. "Was this from a hot blade too?"

Maia soaked in the comfort of Hannah's touch, wishing it didn't twist her heart so painfully. "A scalpel."

"The diplomat in your room has the same scars," Hannah said, her beautiful, soft brows knit with sadness.

"Those are from the red lung cure." Briar took a bite from a biscuit, leaning back in his chair. His swollen lip had gone down, and the bruising around his eyes and broken nose had turned a sickly green. "Maia was the first to test it."

Hannah's eyes shot to Maia's, searching. "Cure?"

"Inoculation," Maia corrected, sliding the sleeve of the robe back down.

"So, the rumors are true." The measure in her voice hinted at the hundreds of questions she was sorting through. "A Portico healer really figured it out."

Maia nodded, ignoring the lift of Briar's stitched brow.

"They said a young woman helped the healer save a shantytown from an outbreak." Hannah's words hung heavy between them, holding the question Maia knew she wanted to ask.

"All I did was help give inoculations."

"Fuck that," Briar snapped. "*Maia* convinced the healer to join Portico. Cut open dead people to help him create the cure. Risked her life for strangers that ain't had nothin' to give in return. Don't fuckin' act like what you did wasn't important, boss."

Hannah's wide eyes collapsed under heavy brows. "Because of mom." She took Maia's hand, rubbing her thumb across her knuckles in the same comforting way she used to. "I didn't realize—"

"You were right, Hannah," Maia whispered, eyes focused on the softness of Hannah's hands in hers. "About all of it. The rebels aren't the good guys."

"Is that who did this to you?"

"There's nowhere safe for me anymore." Maia's words grew thick with emotions she tried to keep in check.

Hannah tucked a loose curl behind Maia's ear. "If that were true, you wouldn't have come here."

Maia nearly collapsed as Hannah pulled her into a hug, tears spilling down her cheeks, stinging the still-raw cut. Maybe Sky was wrong.

"I'm sorry, Hannah."

Her sister's arms tightened around her. "I love you too."

With a sigh, Maia pulled away, knowing if she continued to hold on, she'd never be able to let go. Hannah gave her a soft smile, her blue eyes glassy, as if seeing an old friend again.

"We'll figure this out together, okay? I have a couple appointments this afternoon, but I'll be back in time for dinner. Promise me you'll still be here?"

Wiping away her tears, Maia nodded. "How's Aster?"

"He had wheezing in both lungs, but his fever broke," she said, handing Maia a bottle from her dress pocket. "Two drops of butterbur under the tongue every six hours. You should wash up and then go check on him. He was asking about you."

"I smell that good?" Maia teased, ignoring the disorienting plummet of her heart. How could he possibly care after what she had done?

Hannah smiled softly, grabbing her coat from a rack beside the kitchen door and reaching for the knob. "I missed you, Maia."

Silence fell in the room as the door closed behind her.

"You alright, boss?"

She took the seat across from Briar, dropping her head into her hands. "We shouldn't have come here."

"I don't wanna know what would have happened if we didn't."

With a sigh, she met his gaze. "If Orion finds us…"

"You ain't givin' her enough credit." He picked at the crumbs scattered across the wooden table. "You know, she didn't ask one damn question when she saw you. Let a bunch of fuckin' liars, thieves, and murderers walk right in, just to keep you safe. What you have here—family—that's what's important in this fucked up world. I ain't gonna ask why you left, but this is the life you deserve. Not whatever bullshit lies Rowan promised you."

There was heartache blanketing his words, and Maia leaned forward, taking his hand from across the table. "Briar, you're just as much my family as she is, and you deserve all of this too."

His soft, green eyes found hers. "Hearin' you say that makes me think it might actually be true." He gave her hand a gentle squeeze and pulled away. "You do smell like shit though."

"Alright, I get it." She pushed herself to her feet and started towards the bathroom.

Briar removed a smoke pack from his pocket, tapping it against his palm. "Love ya, boss."

His words surrounded her with the same comfort as his hugs. Maia regretted a lot of things, but she would never regret meeting Rowan that night at her mother's tree, because any other choice meant she wouldn't have Briar in her life. "Love you too."

The smile tugging at the corner of his lip melted Maia's heart, and she wondered how long it had been since anyone had said those words to him.

She continued into the bathroom, throwing a towel over the mirror and pressing her hands to the counter. If Sky was wrong about Hannah, maybe he would be wrong about Aster too. With a sigh, she grabbed a washcloth, cleaning the blood from her hands all over again.

Wringing her hair dry with a towel, she returned to the kitchen to find it empty. The kettle sat on the wood-burning stove, and Maia lit it with a match. She took her time, cutting ginger root into small pieces and dropping them into the cup, pouring the steaming water over it. Her chest grew tight. She couldn't procrastinate any longer. Grabbing the tea, she pushed open the door to her room.

It looked exactly as she had left it. The flowers in the vase were long dead—dried petals littering her desk. Her sketchbook sat open on a half-finished drawing of a little boy feeding ducks by the pond. The only thing new was Aster, asleep on her small childhood bed, his bare feet hanging off the end.

She ran her finger along the gold stitching of his diplomat jacket hanging on the back of her chair. Everything about him was too grand for her tiny room. A man who grew up under the protection of Portico, into one with an extravagant office wearing gold-stitched clothes. She had lost herself in his world, forgetting who she really was before all the lies.

Pulling open the drawer to her dresser, she removed the bottle of whiskey tucked away. The cork quietly thumped as she popped it open, clearing the petals off her desk and dropping into the seat. Taking a sip from the bottle, she looked closer at the sketch.

A young boy played gleefully by the lake, now watched by her mother's tree. She picked up her pencil, tapping it against the page, but whatever she saw in that moment was long gone. Ripping it from the book, she crumpled it in her hand, throwing it towards the waste bin. Aster twitched, nearly waking himself as he flipped onto his side, facing her.

She pressed the soft eraser against her lip, waiting to see if he woke. Instead, his chest continued its steady rise and fall, a splay of hair clinging to a sheen of sweat from the fever. She turned her chair towards the bed, resting her sketchbook in her lap.

For a man who took great pride in his appearance of control, it was unsettling to see Aster lose that. His normally meticulous hair was now carelessly tousled, and her fingers ached to tame it. Instead, she focused her desires into the soft lines of her pencil against the paper. The defined cut of his clavicle, the thick veins of his arms, and the smooth curve of his waist. She took her time on his long, dark lashes and full lips, just slightly parted.

Aster's body shook from a sudden coughing fit, startling Maia and causing her to drop the pencil. Tossing the book onto the desk, she grabbed the cup of tea and leaned towards him. He groaned, curling into himself as he braced his stomach in agony.

Maia dropped to her knees beside the bed, gripping his arm, desperate to ease his pain. "Drink this. It'll help with the cough."

His strong brows twisted in confusion as he struggled to open his eyes. "Maia?"

He cleared his hoarse throat, wincing. It took him a few seconds to orient himself, but when he did, he pinched his eyes closed again, as if fighting a new wave of pain.

Maia's grip loosened. It wasn't pain—it was hurt. He must have remembered where he was and why.

Pushing himself up, he took a cautious sip as she stood. "Thank you. Can you hand me my shirt?"

Maia glanced around the room, finding it neatly folded on the dresser. It was something so trivial, something Hannah probably didn't even think about as she did it, but the action made Maia's heart ache.

Aster deserved someone who didn't have to try so hard to be good. She forced her hand forward, grabbing his shirt and trading it for the cup. He pulled it over his head, dropping his feet to the floor and scrubbing the sleep from his face.

Maia held out the bottle of butterbur. "I'll give you some space. Two drops under the tongue before you go back to sleep, and again in the morning."

"I don't need space, Maia." He gazed at her through his thick lashes. "I want answers. Can you give me that?"

She braced herself. "They won't be what you want to hear."

"We'll see," he said, jaw clenching in preparation. "Are you really the daughter of Taris?"

There it was again. Hurt hidden in the directness of his question.

"I am."

"That explains the arrow Tala carved into your vanity." Aster paused, as if trying to piece things together. "She knew all along."

Maia's throat tightened, so she nodded in response instead.

"Which is why it wasn't safe for us to be seen together. Why you had to keep it from me."

"She was looking for any reason to hang you, just like she did to Rowan... the Overseer."

"That's what doesn't add up," he said, shaking his head and pushing himself up from the bed. "Why threaten you if you're both on the same side?"

Maia thought back to the morning she woke up to find Tala in her room. The cure should have gone to the rebellion, but Maia walked Mr. Foster through Portico's gates instead. Her actions looked like betrayal from the start.

How long had Tala been plotting and laying the groundwork needed to overthrow Portico, for Maia to come in and create ripples with stones that should have never been thrown?

"We weren't part of her plan."

"But you *were* part of the Overseer's plan," Aster said, inching closer.

Maia shook her head, refusing to break his gaze. "It wasn't his plan. It was mine." Aster's surprise was overshadowed by his curiosity as his eyes searched hers. "I convinced him to come back to Portico."

The realization hit her, causing her voice to catch. She had been Rowan's executioner long before she stole Tala's letter. She looked down at her hands, calloused and graphite-stained. The blood was still there, even if she couldn't see it.

"Why?" Aster took another step forward, now towering over her and forcing her into the desk.

She lifted her chin. He deserved to know every vengeful thought that brought her to him. "To destroy Portico from within. Take each of the council positions one by one, starting with Aquila's."

Her confession hardened his face into his harsh bronze mask. "Was every-thing you did for Portico just for show then?"

"I never did anything for Portico. I did them because they were the right things to do."

His eyes fell to her sketchbook, and he reached across her, turning it to him. "Was I your target?"

"No." Maia didn't move, her heart pounding at the tension radiating between them. His questions were now dancing around the answers he wanted, just like he did the first day in the maze. "Rowan warned me to stay away from you. Said you would be... *problematic.*"

Every muscle seemed to tense under his thin shirt, and he leaned in just a little closer. "Is that so?"

"He was right."

Aster's gaze returned to hers, hesitant and soft. "In what way?"

Maia dragged her eyes from his, knowing it was time for their dance to end. She slipped past him, creating the distance she needed for her next words. "It wasn't fair for me to ask anymore of you then, and it isn't now. Every secret and lie, mistake and regret, will eventually catch up with me. It's best for everyone if I leave before anyone else gets hurt."

He sat on the edge of her desk. "And what if I want you to ask for more?"

Her breath caught, and she bit down on her raw lip. Aster's eyes caught the movement, and he reached out, fingers grazing the outside of her hand. She took a dangerous step towards the one person who could destroy her in every way. His hands slid to her hips, pulling her between his legs.

"I don't deserve someone like you. Not after everything I've done."

His grip tightened on her, eyes longing for the same thing she had tried so hard to bury. "My feelings for you were never something you needed to earn, Maia."

There was safety tucked away in his depths, soft and vulnerable with promises of something she refused to allow herself until now. Her body ached with want as they held each other's gaze, straddling the fading line between them.

His eyes traveled to her lips, and he lifted her chin. "They're yours, if you want them."

She never knew herself to be someone who needed another's touch, but the way his set her skin on fire made her give into the moment, allowing it to consume her.

Gripping his shirt, she pulled him to her, their lips colliding. Nothing existed outside of this moment. Nothing mattered except for him and her. Each touch burned more than the last as his arms wrapped hungrily around her.

A low rumble rose from his chest as his lips moved along her jaw to the delicate skin on her neck. Her fingertips tingled as they ran through his short hair and down the taut muscles of his back. She was desperate for more.

For all of him.

She closed her eyes, feeling everything. The erratic beat of his heart. His soft breath against her skin. The powerful press of his fingers against her back. It was too easy for her thoughts to travel to all the other places she wanted to feel his touch.

He took in a slow, ragged breath and rested his forehead against hers. "It's been torture being so close, but just out of reach from you."

"I know the feeling." She took his hand, pulling him towards the bed.

Lowering himself, he looked up at her, eyes burning with want.

Her hand ran over the rough stubble of his jaw, and she grazed her thumb over his lower lip. "This has been torture," she said, desperate to kiss the tantalizing smile that took hold of his face.

Instead, she trailed her fingers down the front of his shirt, slipping them under the hem, and pulling it over his head. Running her palms over his chest, she relished the goosebumps forming on his skin. "And this."

His hands couldn't remain still any longer as they found her hips again, pulling her towards him. She lifted her leg, straddling his, when a sharp pain nearly dropped her.

Aster's grip tightened, worry extinguishing the flames in his gaze. "What's wrong?"

She grit her teeth, pinching her eyes shut. "I think I just popped a stitch."

"Should I get Hannah?" he asked, as Maia collapsed onto the bed next to him.

She shook her head, pressing her fists against her eyes to keep the tears at bay. "She won't be back until dinner." Her hand plunged into her pocket, removing the pain tonic, and she took another long sip. "I'll be fine."

Aster stretched himself out beside her, running his hand across her stomach. He was quiet now, and even with her eyes closed, she could almost see the furrow between his brows as he lost himself in thought.

"The last thing I wanted was to hurt you, Aster," she said, glancing at him out of the corner of her eye. "I'm sorry... for everything."

"I know, Maia." He pulled her to him, kissing her softly on the forehead.

His warmth surrounded her, and she nestled into his chest, surprised by how long it had been since she felt this safe. The tonic kicked in, and she wondered if she might have taken too much. Her body somehow felt simultaneously heavy and light as her heart steadied to match her slow, shallow breaths.

"You have no idea how much I wanted to tell you."

He tightened his arm around her, sighing into her hair. "You have no idea how many times I wanted to hold you like this."

The soft smell of bergamot and cloves still lingered on his shirt, washing over her as sleep took hold.

29

WARRING

Maia woke to the slow and steady beat of Aster's heart. She laid curled up against him, head resting on his bare chest. She had held, and been held by others before, but with him it felt different. Soft and delicate, like a rose petal.

The thought reminded her of the way he twirled the rose stems between his fingers, effortlessly navigating around their thorns. Her uninjured leg was draped over him, the warmth of his hand resting on it, and she wondered if he had learned how to avoid her thorns too.

With a deep breath, he turned into her, their bodies pressed tight as his hand slid farther up her leg. Closing her eyes, she melted into him, soaking in the moment. Regardless of what happened next, she at least had this.

"Good morning," he whispered, voice low and husky with sleep.

"Morning." Her hand skimmed the dip of his waist, inching up his back. "Sorry to cut things short yesterday."

His fingertips pressed into her leg, confirming the want between them still burned as hot as the day before. "We have plenty of time to pick up where we left off."

A giggle traveled from the kitchen, and Maia froze, wondering if it was just her imagination. It had been too long since she heard happiness in these walls.

"Everything okay?" he asked.

She untangled her legs from his, rolling onto her back to hide the sad smile taking hold. "It's nice to hear my sister laugh like that again."

He remained still beside her, eyes softening as if adjusting to her vulnerability. "Let's go help with breakfast."

The room suddenly grew cold as he shifted away. Too soon. Would it ever be enough?

For now, all she wanted was to feel his lips one more time before they left their hideaway. Just one more moment before the truth of their situation came crashing down again. Her hand slid up his arm, pulling him back to her.

"I don't think I'm ready yet."

A beautiful, lazy smile crossed his lips as he allowed her to guide them softly against hers. It was different this time. The hunger was still there, but they savored it. Discovering each other with a slow and tender touch. The sharp curve of his bicep as he held himself over her. His fingertips burning a trail from her hip up her side.

A bang from the kitchen, followed by Briar's string of profanities, ended their moment too soon.

Aster pressed his forehead against hers, closing his eyes with a sigh. Nothing more than a tease—just a taste of one another so they could crave more.

He rolled over, sitting up and slipping his shirt over his head. The shift of each tight muscle in his back made Maia internally curse Briar herself. The movement loosened a cough from deep in Aster's chest, and Maia sat up, rubbing his back as he braced himself.

"I'll make you some more tea," she said, pushing herself to her feet.

The pain in her leg anchored her back to reality. It was the reason they were here, and each minute they remained hidden away in these walls put Hannah at risk. To the rebellion, everyone Maia cared about was disposable, and once they realized she lied about knowing where Mr. Foster was, she would be too.

Maia pulled open the door as Aster slid on his diplomat jacket. His hand found the small of her back, pressing a soft kiss to her temple before they continued into the kitchen.

Briar towered over Hannah in the cramped room. In one large hand, he held a wooden spatula while the other skimmed her cheek where a smudge of flour kissed it. She flushed under his thumb and bit back a shy smile, catching sight of Maia and Aster out of the corner of her eyes.

"Good morning. Did you both sleep well?" she asked, turning back to the batter she was mixing for griddlecakes.

A playful grin overtook Briar's swollen face as he stirred the pan of eggs he was cooking beside her.

"We did. I can't thank you enough," Aster said, his usual charm back on full display. "Is there something we can help with?"

"No, please Mr. Calderone, you're a guest."

"Call me Aster." The confident smile he reserved for winning over crowds was now on Hannah.

Maia squeezed past them to Briar.

"Mornin' boss," he said, nudging her gently with his elbow. His hair was slicked back and shirt tucked in as if he had put extra effort into looking his best for the day. Still, his face remained heavy with fatigue beyond the bruising and swelling. "Wondered where you disappeared to last night."

She lifted the kettle, pouring two cups. "Did you get any sleep?"

His hand stilled, and he avoided her gaze. "Kinda lost track of time talkin' last night."

Picking up the mugs, she gave Briar a soft smile, whispering as she passed. "It's been a long time since she's found someone worth staying up for."

Briar finally met her gaze, pink dusting his ears again. "She wanted to hear about you."

"From you. Not me."

His brows knit, and he lost himself in thought as she continued back to Aster and Hannah. They were still in the middle of their conversation when she returned, handing him his cup. She took a sip, surrounded by the soothing smell of elderflower and honey.

"The embroidery on your jacket is beautiful. It gave me some dress ideas for Maia."

"I don't need a dress, Hannah, but thank you," Maia said, realizing it was pointless to argue. Hannah was already scanning her for measurements.

"Nonsense. A woman saving the world needs a dress as powerful as she is. One that commands the attention of a room without a word."

Her argument stunned Maia. The last time she saw her sister, she was nothing more than a criminal. When had she become the hero in Hannah's eyes?

Briar glanced at Maia over his shoulder. "You know Senna would agree with her."

"I can't wait to see it," Aster said, his hand slipping around Maia's waist. The carefully crafted smile he wore for Hannah shifted into something more mischievous as his gaze found hers. "But Maia seems to have that power in anything she wears."

Hannah smoothed her apron and gave Aster a nod. "She does."

The burden of being seen as a hero instead of the villain twisted Maia's stomach, ruining her appetite.

"We'll help set the table," Maia said, reaching past Hannah to the cupboard.

There were apologies in her sister's eyes that Maia tried hard to ignore. She shouldn't be the one apologizing. Not after everything Maia had put her through.

"That would be wonderful, Maia. Thank you."

Hannah started back to the stove where Briar was now removing the eggs from the heat.

"My mom used to make a big breakfast like this when I was younger," he said, leaning against the countertop. "She used to make fun shapes and drizzle honey on top."

Maia wondered if his mother was even capable of such kindness, or if he just remembered it that way.

"What was your favorite shape?" Hannah asked, looking up at him.

He laughed, rubbing the back of his neck. "That was a long time ago—"

"Don't be silly. You don't forget those kinds of things," Hannah said, turning back to the pan. "Maia's was always a flower."

Briar beamed at Maia. He fit in a way that made the walls around them feel like home again, and it tightened her stomach further as she helped Aster set the table.

Returning his gaze to Hannah, he was no longer shy about his answer. "I liked when she made hearts."

The softest of smiles touched Hannah's lips, and she carefully poured the batter into the pan. Maia took a seat while Aster busied himself spooning Briar's eggs into a bowl, skillfully adding herbs and spices. She eyed him suspiciously as he set it on the table.

"I look forward to seeing your reaction when I make a full meal for you," he whispered, taking a seat next to her and draping his arm along the back of her chair.

"I might have broken sooner if you said you knew how to cook," she teased.

A playful smile lit up his face. "So, you *do* have a weakness."

Maia bit back a smile, resting her head against his arm the same way she wanted to back in his office. There were so many more words resting on the tip of her tongue, but it was another moment she couldn't see herself in. The realization made her throat grow tight, making it almost painful to force the words back down.

The kitchen door swung open, and Micah and Sky stormed in.

"Mornin' Miss Hannah, breakfast smells amazing," Micah announced, dropping into a chair. He grabbed Maia's cup of tea, took a sip, and spit it back out. "I thought that was liquor."

"Why?" she asked, pushing her cup away.

"Because he assumes everything is," Sky said, picking it up and dumping the tea to pour her a new one.

Hannah slid a plate of griddlecakes onto the table, placing two flower-shaped cakes on Maia's plate. "Thank you, Micah, but flattery won't make up for you using my vase as a spittoon."

Micah stole a cake from the plate, shoving the entire thing in his mouth as he spoke. "To be fair, they do look deceptively similar."

Briar dropped into the seat next to Hannah's, noticing four heart-shaped cakes already on his plate, each drizzled with honey. His wide chest swelled, and he lifted his hand to his mouth to hide his smile.

"The horses are waitin' outside," Sky said, glancing at Maia.

His eyes stopped where Aster's thumb stroked the back of her arm, excitement fading into the same hurt she had seen too many times before.

"What does that mean?" Hannah's face immediately hardened to polished stone.

"I told you last night, we can't stay. It's not safe for you." Maia reached for her sister's hand, but she pulled away.

"For *me*? You weren't even conscious when they brought you here. Look at you! You're skin and bones, covered in cuts and bruises, and can barely walk. Where are you going to go?"

All eyes were now on her, and each wanted a different answer. She straightened her back, lifting her chin with feigned confidence. "Back to Portico, to end this."

"Maia, can we talk?" Sky asked, pushing away from the table.

"She don't look like she wants to talk," Micah said, taking another cake from the plate. "Sounds like she's made up her mind."

"I was never going north, Sky, but I won't judge you if you do. We know what's waiting for us outside these doors, and there's no guarantee any of us will survive," Maia said, forcing her voice to stay as calm and sure as Aster's grip on her arm.

"That's not fair," Sky whispered, dropping his head to avoid her gaze. "You know damn well we won't let you do this alone. That's the problem with your choices though. They always end up with someone else dead."

"You're such a manipulative asshole," Briar growled, his hands balled on the table. "She ain't askin' you to stay. If you wanna run, no one's stoppin' you."

"I'm going with you," Hannah said. "I was too scared the first time you left. It nearly broke me the second, but I know this time I can be helpful."

There was uncertainty in Hannah's eyes. The same fear Maia had known for too long. The fear that she wasn't enough. Sky's gaze found Maia's. He wanted her to argue with Hannah—to tell her all the reasons she shouldn't go. Make her question if she was making the right decision.

Instead, Maia nodded. If anyone would survive this, it would be Hannah. Maia would make sure of it.

Hannah sighed with relief, her face softening with appreciation. "Thank you."

Aster sat quietly beside her, watching the conversation unfold around him, before finally leaning forward, filling the small space with his presence. "You told me rebellions are the quiet acts of courage, despite the consequences. I should have known then," he said, reaching over and wrapping Maia's hand in his warmth. "Let me stand by your side as you burn it all down."

Micah removed a flask from his jacket, half-heartedly lifting it to her. "To the greater good and shit." He took a swig, but Sky snatched it, storming out of the kitchen. "Come on, man. What the fuck?"

A crash sounded from the front room, and Maia sighed, pushing away from the table.

"You don't owe him anything," Briar said cautiously. "You don't need him, either."

He already knew all the lines Sky would use against her, and she was certain he learned it from his father. She gave Briar a sympathetic smile and nudged the door open to the parlor, freezing as it swung shut, hitting her in the back.

A shattered lamp lay on the floor at Sky's feet while Jackson held him at gunpoint.

"You'd be wise to play nice this time," she warned.

The sound of a fight broke out from behind the kitchen door as Hannah's scream filled the air.

Tendrils of fear crawled down Maia's spine. She lifted her trembling hands, taking a step forward. "I'll do whatever you say."

Jackson's lips curled into a dangerous grin. "That's what I thought."

Maia traced the jagged *x* carved into the table in the center of Folly's Tavern. There was comfort in the familiarity. An appreciation of the cyclicity of the moment as Niall nervously polished a glass, grabbing her favorite bottle off the shelf.

Tala's scouts stained the surrounding seats, quietly hidden under hoods of anonymity. She hated how vulnerable she felt in commoner clothes, like the other rebels scattered throughout the room. Carefree, talking amongst themselves as if they had just stopped by for a drink.

"It's been a long time, Maia," Niall said, placing a glass of whiskey in front of her.

She took a sip, savoring what might be her last pour. "I should have taken your offer."

He gave her a sad smile. "Now ain't the time for regrets. Not with so much at stake."

Glancing over his shoulder, she followed his gaze to a corner table where Aster and Hannah were being held by rebels. Her sister's hair was now tousled, and makeup smeared down her face. Aster, however, looked as calm and poised as always. There was an air of control around him that kept the rebels alert.

On the other side of the room, Maia could hear the anxious tapping of Briar's boot. A few tables away, Micah sat leaned back in his chair sipping from a drink she was sure didn't belong to him. Jackson, however, kept Sky beside her at the bar, still at gunpoint.

All of them far enough away that if they tried to help, the rebels would kill them long before they got to her.

"You need to leave," Maia whispered to Niall, taking another sip from her glass.

He shook his head. "Your father told me the same thing when they caught him, and I was dumb enough to listen. I ain't runnin' this time."

"Hannah and the man beside her are getting out of this alive, you understand?" Maia glanced at him, and he nodded, uncorking the bottle and refilling her glass. "They survive this, even if no one else does."

The door swung open, a beam of light piercing the dimly lit room. Two men entered in heavy black coats, the first catching sight of Maia, his lip curling with disgust as he continued towards the bar. It was the same man she had tortured in the rebel prison, his left arm stiff from where Tala had shot him. *Loyal to the end.*

She should have known then what side Tala was on. So many moments where she had slipped and Maia—too blinded by fear or rage or a deadly combination of both—missed it.

The second man removed his hat, lowering the collar of his coat and revealing the thick scar on his neck. Orion.

Despite the painful twist of her stomach, she kept her gaze locked on his. He wanted to see her fear—use it like a weapon. But it was the only thing left in her control, and she refused to allow him to take it from her.

Niall squeezed her shoulder. "I understand."

He made his way back to the bar as Orion took his seat across from her.

"Maia," he said with an exasperated sigh. "It's good to see you again."

He was different—or maybe it was her—but he wasn't nearly as intimidating as she remembered. His broad shoulders and hooded eyes hung low with fatigue. Even the scar on his neck no longer held the meaning it once did. She thought she understood his need for revenge, but he was never brave enough for that. The one person he should have dedicated his life to destroying was his greatest ally.

She couldn't hide the pity from her smile. "Can't say the feeling's mutual."

"I see," he said, in the same way Jackson had in the cabin. Maia glanced at her, noticing the same dark gaze in her eyes. "I hoped that bringing you back to Folly's might remind you why you joined the cause."

"I never forgot." Maia swirled the whiskey in her glass. "But it seems you did."

"I've dedicated my life to the rebellion," he snapped, slamming his fist on the table. Tension thickened the suddenly quiet room, while Maia took a sip from her glass. "Because of my alliance, we've nearly won. We're just missing one vital piece."

He was talking about Mr. Foster. The weapon that would make them a threat to anyone refusing to join their cause. "What is it you think you've won?"

A door opened upstairs, and the mousy innkeeper who had been hiding Garcia appeared, gun exposed on his hip. The stars etched into the inn's door frame were just another target. The man's eyes fell on Maia as he peered over the balcony.

"Rowan told me he found you here. Said how pathetic you looked, tucked away in the corner, lost and alone. How scared you were of the world." Orion leaned forward, folding his hands on the table the same way Rowan had. It was a move meant to exude power, and she took note. "You aren't that person anymore, are you, Sagitta?"

He was right. She was no longer the little fawn Governor Shaw had seen. She knew exactly what needed to be done with the power she had.

"You didn't answer my question." She glanced around the room again at all the hooded scouts. A glint of light caught her eye from under one of the hoods. "Tala is the one in power, not you."

"A temporary placeholder until I have what I need."

"Does she know that?"

Orion's jaw ticked as he watched her. "Where is Mr. Foster?"

Garcia was right. Orion's pursuit of power had no limit. To him, victory was the only thing that mattered anymore. Not the mass casualties that would come from the fallout. Maia had done enough wrong to realize the rare times she did something right.

She finished her glass of whiskey and leaned forward, folding her hands on the table. "Let my team go, and I'll tell you."

"That's not how this works. If you're willing to cooperate, I'll let you decide what happens with his research. I still believe we can succeed together."

Her stomach dropped. Had she known where Mr. Foster was, could she have taken his offer? Avoided all the bloodshed yet to come? It would mean trusting him to honor his deal, and he had proven to be far from honorable.

Regardless, she didn't know where Mr. Foster was, which meant there was only one way out of this. Her pulse steadied as the world slowed around her, grip tightening around the glass.

In one desperate motion, she threw her arm back, sending the glass towards the bar. Niall ducked just in time for it to miss his head, shattering the oxidized mirror behind him. It would be her only distraction.

Chaos erupted around them as the room sprang into battle. Maia flipped the table towards Orion, and the scouts hurtled forward to protect him. Gripping her chair, she smashed it into the rebel seated behind her, stealing his gun and shooting at two men lunging towards her.

Her shots missed, but Sky's didn't as both rebels dropped to the ground. She scanned the room for Hannah, surprised to find Orion fighting against the scouts, dragging him away. Aster grabbed a rebel by the coat, punching him across the face while Hannah smashed a pint glass into the side of another's head.

Sky's steady shots paused as Jackson trapped him in a headlock. Maia pulled a blade from a dead scout, sending it into Jackson's shoulder. Taking advantage of the hit, Sky kicked away from the bar, sending both of them to the floor.

A barrage of bullets sprayed across the room, and Maia dropped behind the flipped table.

Briar and Micah collapsed beside her, loading their guns while catching their breath.

"What's the plan here, boss?" Briar shouted, pushing his hair from his face.

Micah glanced around the table, cursing as a bullet whizzed past him. "It better involve findin' some better cover."

Maia rubbed her throbbing leg, noticing the dead eyes of a fallen scout staring up at her from under his hood.

"Isn't that one of Winter's guards?" she asked, the man's blood slowly inching towards them.

Briar followed her gaze, and his eyes grew wide. "Yeah, that's Keenan. He was with us at the shantytown."

With another quick glance around the room, Maia suddenly realized why they were still alive. The scouts were fighting the rebels, and Maia caught the glint of General Winter's piercing as she struggled to keep Orion pinned to the door. Portico's guards were here to save them, just as Rafe promised.

The explosion of a shotgun shook the room. Peering over the table, Maia found Niall struggling with Jackson for the gun.

Briar leaned his head against the table, taking a deep breath. "We'll give you cover."

She nodded, counting down on her fingers before slipping out of hiding. The pain surged through her leg, fueling her as she ran, while Briar and Micah's bullets took down anyone too close.

Jackson dropped the shotgun and pulled her pistol, turning it on Niall. Throwing herself over the counter, Maia knocked him to the ground. Jackson's bullet found the bottles above him, sending shattered glass down around them. Niall winced in pain from where he landed on his arm.

"You okay?" Maia asked, reaching for him.

He pulled away, protecting his arm as he sucked in a pained breath. The way it hung made it clear it was broken, which meant he would only be in the way.

Sky slid under the flip-up counter, shooting with calm precision. "We're running out of bullets," he warned, reloading his weapon.

A new set of shots filled the air, and she followed the sound to the balcony above them. The rebel's gun was pointed in Aster and Hannah's direction, and Maia's stomach lurched.

They were making it out alive, even if no one else did.

She shook the glass from her hair and picked up Niall's shotgun. He covered his ears, and Sky turned away as she pointed the gun straight up.

Pressing her finger on the trigger, they ducked as bloody wood showered down around them.

When Maia glanced over the counter again, Aster was being dragged towards the door by Winter. He thrashed against her, shouting words Maia couldn't hear over the ringing in her ears. His gaze found Maia's across the room, transforming from panic into something on the verge of feral.

"Go!" Maia shouted.

Micah and Briar provided cover so Winter could shove Aster through the tavern door.

Dropping back behind the counter, Maia let out a breath. Sky was right. They were running out of bullets, and Hannah was still lost in the chaos.

"I need you outside, Sky. You won't get a clean shot in here. Take him with you," Maia snapped, shoving Niall toward him. Niall started to argue, but she grabbed him by the collar. "This is your last chance to get out of this alive. I can't keep you *and* Hannah safe."

He scowled, shoving a box of rounds into her hand.

Sky didn't move, his face hardening at her demand. She couldn't hear his words, but as he shook his head, his hand finding hers, his lips said, *'Don't be a hero.'*

She knew better. If she wanted to survive, she needed to be the villain.

Sky dragged Niall out the back door, and Maia popped two more shells into the shotgun with a trembling hand. As the ringing dulled, she realized how quiet the tavern had grown.

"Briar?" Silence. "Hannah!"

Her heart twisted painfully, and she held the gun tight to her chest. With a deep breath, she pushed herself up, pointing the shotgun at the few left standing. The bar was littered with dead and dying. If any of General Winter's guards had survived, they had left with her.

Jackson stepped over the bodies, reloading her gun, while Briar struggled against the grip of the man Maia had tortured. Orion stood in the center of the room, holding Micah and Hannah hostage.

"All you had to do was cooperate," Orion said, jaw clenched and shoulders tight.

"You can still get out of this alive. Just let them go," Maia warned.

"You're in no position to make demands," Orion said, pointing his gun at Hannah. "Do you really want to test me?"

Maia's chest tightened, making it difficult to breathe as tears streamed down Hannah's trembling face. Briar shouted, taking a hit to the stomach, while Micah watched Maia patiently. She needed to stay focused. See beyond the red. It couldn't end like this, not after everything they had been through. She closed her eyes and placed the shotgun on the counter, raising her hands.

No one moved, making Orion snap. "Someone get the fucking gun!"

One brave, reckless boot took a cautious step forward. Then another, each thud heavy with uncertainty against the wooden floor. They were close now. Close enough.

Maia's eyes fluttered open, and she snatched the shotgun, taking aim. The shell exploded into the rebel's chest, and everyone staggered back, allowing her a second to lift the flip-up counter and take aim at Jackson.

"No!" Orion shouted, his large hand suspended in the moment.

"I will kill every fucking person in this room if you don't let her go," Maia said, her voice as even and dark as Micah's gaze.

Orion's face twitched with rage. Jackson was important to him. But Maia didn't realize *how* important until he took a step back.

"Fine." He pulled Hannah to him, whispering into her ear.

Maia watched the color drain from her sister's face as she went still. Whatever he said stole the tears from her eyes, now terrifyingly blank.

"Just tell him what he wants, Maia." Hannah's voice was tight, as if forced to contain her emotions in each word.

Her sister was on the verge of shattering, and Maia felt a fresh tear open in her heart. Her brows twisted painfully as she dropped her gaze from Hannah's. She could have saved them all if she knew where Mr. Foster had been taken.

"Maia, watch out!" Hannah screamed, and before she could react, she was knocked to the floor by Briar's heavy body, a bullet lodging in the wall behind them.

Orion's gun was still pointed where Maia had stood. He looked down at the blood now splattered against his shirt and face, before dropping his gaze to the dead rebel crumpled at his feet. Glancing around the room, he noticed the hole in the window where Sky's shot had come through. The rebel must have stepped in the way of Sky's shot in all the chaos.

"Cover the windows!" Orion shouted. "The Marksman is out there!"

All of it had been enough of a distraction for Micah to take hold of Hannah and run.

Maia's head fell back against the floor in relief. Jackson picked up the shotgun, now abandoned in the space between them, and turned it on Maia.

"It didn't have to go like this," Orion said, kicking Briar in the stomach. "Now, we do things the hard way."

Jackson lifted the gun, bringing the butt down on the side of Maia's head.

30

BROKEN

A steady drip from corroded pipes kept in time with the watch resting in her pocket. The musty smell of mildew hung thick in the air as Maia watched water trail down the gray walls. Memories from the last few days had become a prison, even worse than the cold room she woke in. Perched on the tattered mattress, springs digging into her hips, she felt the cold seep under her skin into her aching bones.

Think.

She just needed to think. Closing her eyes, she rubbed at her throbbing temples. Distant screams traveled through the piping. Screams punctuated by profanities that belonged to Briar. She took in a shaky breath and opened her eyes, scanning the room.

Think!

The absence of windows made it impossible to grasp any concept of time. Resting beside the door was a single metal chair, and in the opposite corner, a water basin on a stone counter with a cracked mirror hanging above it. An erratic pattern of light reflected off it—the flame of a candle struggling to survive the looming darkness. A tightness pinched deep in her heart as she saw herself flickering with it. All it would take was a whisper to blow both of them out.

Ripping a piece of dirty bedding, she limped to the basin, catching her reflection in the mirror. The serrated scar on her face followed the jagged crack, splitting her into the two versions of herself she'd become. A seeping gash from the butt of the gun marred her left cheek, while her right remained soft and rounded—innocent.

Naïve. Weak. When had its meaning changed?

Pressing her hands against the stone countertop, she leaned in, focusing on the coldness in her eyes. The set in her jaw. The violence in her countenance.

She wasn't the flame. In following her father's shadow, she had willingly become her own form of darkness. A darkness people feared as much as they respected. She was the hushed whisper that could extinguish them all. Dipping the torn cloth into the water basin, she lifted it to her cheek.

Briar's screams stopped, and Maia straightened her back as heavy footsteps approached. She pushed herself from the counter. She would overcome whatever was waiting on the other side of the door. The smooth slide of metal and two loud clicks were followed by a slow squeal.

The man she had tortured stepped into the room.

No.

There was a price for the fear and respect she now had, and it was watching her in the mirror, a crooked smile crossing his cruel lips. If she was innocent, she wouldn't be hiding her trembling hands.

He rolled up his sleeves, revealing rows of tiny silver tallies like distant stars twinkling in the candlelight. Marks she had carved mercilessly into his skin. He wasn't here to make her talk. He was here for retribution, and even though she deserved what was coming, it didn't change the panic clawing up her throat.

Maia's stomach plummeted, taking all the blood from her body with it.

No, no, "No!" she screamed, gripping the counter in desperation as he grabbed her legs, yanking her to the floor.

She knocked over the water basin and candle, condemning them to her darkness.

Maia stood at the water basin, dabbing at the rows of tiny cuts on her arms. With torture, there comes a point where the body no longer feels pain. The mind loses a sense of self, allowing the physical form to become nothing more than a shell.

Maia had been there before. It used to terrify her—the emptiness she felt. The hollowness in her chest where her heart should have been, but this time she was grateful. Disappearing into herself, she could watch the knife puncture her skin, appreciating the sharpness of the blade, the unnatural straightness of the cut. How frail the human body truly was, as each red line of blood seeped to the surface.

She dipped the rag, watching the red bloom in the water like one of Aster's roses.

You've crossed a line tonight that you can't come back from.

Tala was right. Morality wasn't a single line to be moved—there were rows of them. Each one, now carved into her skin.

How many deaths were on her hands? She thought of all the bodies scattered around the tavern. A cut for each of them. Tallies, to remind her of all the things she had done to get to this moment. It was terrifying to realize they were enough to disgust even someone as dangerous as Tala. All under the guise of virtue.

The smooth slide of metal and two loud clicks from the other side of the door made her tense. Orion stepped inside, grabbing the metal chair and scraping it across the concrete floor.

Cringing at the sound, she gripped the edge of the counter. "I have nothing to say to you."

The smell of bread wafted towards her. Gaze drifting to the chair, she spotted a tray with a bowl of cornmeal and a roll.

How long had it been since she last ate? The sound of Hannah's laughter. The smell of elderflower and honey. Flower-shaped griddlecakes. A sharp pain in her stomach made her flinch as she pulled her eyes from it.

"Did you know Tala killed my father when you formed an alliance with her?" Maia asked, focusing on her cuts.

Orion walked over, leaning against the wall beside the mirror. "Tala and I had plans long before your father came along. Aquila was always weak, and your father knew how to fuel the flames of discontent."

His answer was too quick—voice too sure—for it to be a lie.

"Are you saying he was just a pawn in your plan?"

There was a pause this time before he answered, and she braced herself. "Your mother made him question the cause. Extinguished that flame of passion he once had, making him as weak and lost as Aquila. Lena nearly destroyed the rebellion."

That wasn't her mother. Yes, she was analytical and poised, but in that came an endless curiosity and calm that allowed her to look beyond what everyone else saw. Her mother had seen where the rebellion was headed. If Tala hadn't killed her father, would her parents have been the ones to end the rebellion?

"She was right to make him question it."

Orion's jaw clenched, and he pushed himself off the wall, grabbing at the tray. "If you aren't going to eat, then I think we're done here."

Maia chewed the inside of her cheek, eyeing the bowl. Starvation made resolve a fickle beast. She lunged for the tray, tearing into the bread. Her stomach groaned in appreciation and she closed her eyes, devouring the rest of the roll.

"You have your father's passion, Maia. It's something people swarm to like moths to a flame. Do you understand what that makes you?"

She ignored his question, plunging her hand into the bowl and scooping greedy handfuls to her mouth. The sweetness on the back of her tongue made her eyes well, and she fought to keep her tenuous emotions in check.

"Either our greatest ally or our most dangerous enemy," Orion continued. "I can't allow you to ruin everything when we're this close to succeeding."

Maia's hand hesitated over the bowl as the sweetness on her tongue turned bitter.

"Do you know how your father died?"

A sharp pain in her stomach stole her breath as she curled into herself. She should have recognized the taste of privet. The berries were deceptively sweet, just like a good poison should be. Another stabbing pain loosened the tears from her eyes, and she desperately shoved her fingers to the back of her throat, her entire body heaving.

"Aquila thought it would be poetic to use the same poison your father refused to use on the shantytown. The one that started the rebellion." Orion seemed unphased as Maia emptied the contents of her stomach at his feet. "Hemlock is a slow, painful death that starts with an overpowering weakness, followed by an incurable sickness. All the while, the poison is slowly eroding away at everything inside you. You know you're going to die, but it won't come soon enough."

But it wasn't hemlock, because he needed her to survive, so he could continue to make her suffer. He stepped forward, grabbing her chin. Her heart pounded as she fought through each painful wave of nausea. Panic took hold, making it difficult to breathe. She tried to focus on steady breaths, but each time she closed her eyes, she saw her father over the chessboard. The game of strategy he thought he was playing when it had been sabotaged from the start. He didn't deserve to die so callously, but it was all Orion and Tala understood.

"You would be wise not to remain an enemy, Sagitta," Orion growled.

He threw her face away from him, and she gagged at the sudden motion. He pounded on the door, signaling for them to unlock it, and leaving Maia trembling on the mattress. Her stomach heaved, tears streaming down her cheeks.

It had all been a lie. Her father wasn't a hero. His death was the fuel needed to strengthen the flames of the rebellion again. *All of this over one man.*

There were no heroes here. Only those who survived to tell the stories.

Death was a kindness Maia didn't deserve as she writhed in endless misery. Orion believed she held the key to the rebellion's success, and the privet was just enough to make her wish she did.

Her eyes fluttered open as she lifted her cheek from the cool stone floor. The ache in her stomach and burn in her throat was punishment for all her lies, each one delicately placed over the last, precariously swaying on her teetering sanity. She pushed herself up on shaky hands, but stopped when she noticed Orion seated in the corner, lost in the shadows.

"That scar on your face suits you, Sagitta. It seems the girl Rowan found in Folly's died a long time ago, lost somewhere in the trail of blood you've left behind."

"Monsters like us are known for the scars we carry." Maia's voice was as rough as gravel. "Did Tala forget your alliance when she gave you yours?"

"Tala never betrayed me. My wife did," he snapped. "Offered to hand me over to Aquila to save herself and our daughter." Orion looked away from Maia's glare, running his hand across his neck, his thick finger grazing his scar. "Tala found me just in time and helped my daughter escape to the Desert Region before Portico could use her against me too."

When were you in the Desert Region? For most of my childhood.

Maia's eyes grew wide as realization violently took hold. That's why Orion took a step back in Folly's. Why Jackson believed she and Maia would lead the rebellion one day. Everything she did—the person she was—now made sense. *If your eyes are open, the moment will always reveal itself.*

Jackson was Orion's daughter, and she would do anything for his approval.

Everything about him was a lie. Orion never lost his wife and daughter for the rebellion. He gave them up for it.

"Your family would have been better off without you." Maia wanted her words to hurt as much as his betrayal did.

Orion stood, and in two long strides, his hand was wrapped around Maia's throat. She didn't flinch, instead matching the rage in his eyes.

"Is this the game you want to play, Maia?"

Her vision blurred, and she fought to hold on. With a growl, he released his grip, knowing he'd get nowhere if she passed out. Maia gasped for breaths that wouldn't come fast enough. The burn of her throat fueled her, and she clenched her fists against the floor. Glancing up at Orion, she was surprised to see Caleb hovering behind him, his dead, hazy eyes watching her.

He can't break you. He needs you.

He was right. She still had the upper hand.

"It's the same game you've played with me," she whispered. "Don't ask me to steal for you if you don't want something to go missing."

Orion's jaw ticked, and he folded his arms tight across his chest. "You're running out of time. We have leads on where your healer is hiding."

Caleb's gray lips twisted into a smirk. *More lies.*

A laugh escaped Maia, and she pushed herself onto shaky legs. "Don't fucking lie to me and expect me to tell you the truth."

"How many more lives are you willing to sacrifice for your own selfish reasons?"

Caleb's face fell, and he remained silent. The time for her guilt had come and gone. She took a step towards Orion and he lifted his chin, but took a cautious step back.

"Don't call me selfish for the blood on my hands when you ask me to kill for you." Caleb's icy presence fell in step beside her as they stalked forward to the tick of her father's watch. Lifting her hands to him, she could still feel the warmth of blood on them even if she couldn't see it. "It's just as much on yours, you fucking hypocrite!"

Orion stumbled over the chair, his gaze locked on hers. She gripped the flimsy metal headrest and threw it across the room, hitting the mirror. No one blinked as it shattered on the floor.

Orion spun, banging on the door, shouting for it to open.

"You're just as weak as Aquila," she taunted. "Pathetic. Insignificant. Unworthy."

The door cracked open, and Orion slipped behind it. "I warned you, Maia. What happens next is on you."

He slammed it in her face, followed by two clicks and the slide of metal. Maia's head cropped to her chest, her adrenaline escaping her in a sob.

Infected. Tainted. Dangerous.

The regret sitting in the pit of her stomach wasn't for the awful things she said to him, but for what would come of it. There was a reason Briar was brought in with her.

Maia turned, tripping over the metal chair and landing hard on the shards of mirror scattered across the floor. She cursed, carefully pulling the sharp pieces from her palms, stopping as she caught her fractured reflection. Picking up a shard, she stared at the broken person she had become.

Caleb appeared in the reflection, his sympathetic eyes studying her. *What will you sacrifice to become the wolf?*

Maia's hand clenched around the shard. If she wanted to win this dangerous game, she had to embrace all her darkness, sacrificing whatever light was left in her.

Grabbing the dirty cloth from the countertop, she wrapped it around the jagged piece of mirror, slipping it into a hole in the mattress. If she wanted to win, she'd have to make Orion regret letting her live through the night.

Maia didn't sleep anymore. The pain from starvation had faded, but now began the struggle to not disappear with it. *We're stronger than we look, my little Sagitta.* Each time she drifted towards the unknown, the thought of the door opening pulled her back. When that moment finally came, she would only have one chance to do what needed to be done.

Shouts filled the silence outside, and she tensed on the mattress. The voices moved away before disappearing completely. She closed her eyes again, only to feel the world shake below her. Her eyes shot open, staring at the gray wall as if she could see through it if she concentrated hard enough. Gunshots approached, and Maia held her breath. This was it.

The door flew open with a deafening thud, followed by the grind of metal scraping against concrete.

"It's fuckin' over, you piece of shit," Briar shouted as the legs of the metal chair slammed down.

"Time's up, Maia," Orion said, out of breath from dragging Briar into the room. "Tell me where Mr. Foster is or Briar dies."

She closed her eyes, remaining still, her hand slowly inching towards the hole in the mattress. Only fractions of an inch forward with each tick of her father's watch.

Another explosion shook the floor, followed by a light snapping of a finger.

"I'm gonna kill you," Briar snarled, voice tight from pain. "What did you do to her?"

"Silence won't work anymore, Maia."

Another snap. Briar muted his yell through clenched teeth, but she remained still, her fingers grazing the hidden rag.

"Maia! Why ain't she movin'?" Briar spit out through a sob.

"We need to go now, sir!" someone shouted from the doorway. She could hear the tremble of fear in their voice, and she closed her grip on the piece of mirror.

"Get up, Maia!" Orion's footsteps thundered towards her.

"If you fuckin' killed her, I will—"

Orion's hand found her shoulder, flipping her onto her side. He stilled as she dug the jagged shard into his stomach, the warmth of his blood running down her hand.

"Checkmate," she whispered.

Orion stumbled back, clutching his wound. The rebel at the door rushed forward, dragging him out while another explosion traveled down the hall. Maia crawled to Briar as the gunshots drew closer. Using the bloody piece of mirror, she cut his bindings.

As soon as his hands were free, he had her wrapped in his arms. Neither of them said a word. Nothing would change what they had just been through. Her fingers grazed the scabbed tallies covering his skin. He didn't deserve any of them, another consequence of her reckless actions that someone else had to endure.

General Winter's booming orders echoed off the concrete walls just as two guards appeared in the doorway. They hesitated, taking in the scene. A sob escaped Maia, her heavy eyes refusing to stay open any longer.

You can sleep now, Caleb whispered.

31

ANCHORS

Maia gasped as her eyes shot open. The needle in Hannah's hand fell to the table under the soft, orange glow of an oil lamp.

"It's okay," Hannah said, wrapping her tight in her arms. "You're okay now."

Maia's panicked gaze raced around the room, searching the shadows. It was familiar, even down to the cobwebs in the corner, untouched despite all the time that had passed. They were back at Rowan's safe house.

She needed this to be real, but her mind was too fragile to trust. Slowly lifting her hands, she hesitated before gently resting her fingertips against Hannah's back. Maia collapsed in relief. This was real. Hannah was safe.

The smell of vanilla surrounded her as the ache in her leg returned. She dug her face into her sister's soft curls, fingers gripped painfully around the cloth of Hannah's dress.

Hannah pulled away, checking the pulse in Maia's wrist. "You need to relax."

Her innocent words shredded into Maia, leaving her trapped between laughing and crying. Instead, she closed her eyes, focusing on steadying her breaths and taking inventory of her injuries. The cuts on her arms and hands no longer burned, and the sharp pains in her stomach had dulled to an ache.

"How long was I—"

"A few days here," Hannah said, words clipped and tense. "Too long with Orion. They should have found you sooner."

It worried her that Hannah wouldn't say exactly how long. "What happened after you escaped?"

"Skylar brought us here." Hannah's gaze dropped to her hands. "There were only a few of us who survived the massacre."

Maia's stomach dropped. That's exactly what it was. A massacre. By her bloody hands. "What did Orion whisper to you at Folly's?"

The color drained from Hannah's face, and she shook her head. "It doesn't matter." She reached for her bag, removing a stethoscope. "You're safe now."

But she wasn't. None of them were. Orion was still out there, and Tala still had control over Portico.

Hannah lifted her stethoscope, but Maia pulled away, looking her sister in the eye. "Tell me what he said."

They stared at each other as if waiting to see who would break first. Hannah dropped her gaze, removing the earpieces. "He said—" her voice caught, and she forced herself to swallow. "He said he would send you back in pieces."

Maia could still see the jagged mirror shards on the prison floor, and she realized he didn't lie. He had broken her more than anyone could ever understand.

Hannah's thumb grazed Maia's knuckles. "Don't," she said, as if reading Maia's thoughts. "I forgot how powerful it felt to walk next to you. But ever since they carried you back, that power ripples through this house—and through the hundreds of people camped outside ready to fight."

"I can't handle any more blood on my hands," Maia choked. "I feel like I'm drowning in it."

"If you need forgiveness, I'll give it to you. I forgive you for everything you had to do to make things right." Maia tried to look away, but Hannah followed her eyes. "But it doesn't matter what I say, because eventually, you'll have to forgive yourself too."

Maia's heart ached at her sister's words. "I'm not nearly as forgiving as you."

Hannah stood, smoothing her dress. "Good and evil are just a perception of circumstance, Maia." Her eyes flickered to the mound of black cloth on the table. "Those people out there believe you're the good in this, even if you don't. I'm going to find you some food."

The door closed behind her sister, and the silence that followed was terrifying. Maia stood, grateful for the pins and needles in her foot, anchoring her back in reality. She ran her fingers over the soft, black velvet bunched on the table, and lifted it.

Her jaw clenched as she took in the dress. Gold embellishments were stitched along the high neck and wrists of the long sleeves, like armor. This would have taken weeks to make, and a sob escaped Maia as she realized how long she had been imprisoned.

She fought the urge to rip it to shreds, allowing the fabric to slip from her fingers. The dress was an expectation she hadn't realized until now. Despite being shattered, she was supposed to look powerful. To pretend she wasn't the darkness she now embraced. Hundreds were gathered outside, trusting her to have the answers. Tendrils of dread crawled around her chest as she realized what was at stake if she failed. If she wasn't enough.

Turning away, she bit down on her lip to keep from screaming. A vase filled with peonies sat on the vanity. Hannah's way of saying she missed her. She didn't deserve Hannah's forgiveness. Not after the things she had done to survive.

Maia stormed forward, pushing past the ache in her heart, and gripped the vase. Unleashing a violent scream, she smashed it against the wall. Her arms flung across the vanity, sending the bottles and paperwork onto the floor next, before smashing the mirror with her fist.

The door flew open and Sky stood, weapon drawn, in the doorway.

"What happened?" he asked, searching every dark corner of the room. Briar stumbled in a few seconds behind him, followed calmly by Senna.

"Nothing, I just need a minute," Maia said, trying to tame the embarrassment, rage, and adrenaline flooding her.

Senna took inventory of the destruction, closing the door behind her. "Put your gun away, Skylar."

She eyed him like an exasperating child, picking up the waste bin and gathering the flowers from the floor. Sky seemed to realize what Senna already understood. He stalked forward, his face reflecting the same sharp edges Maia now saw in hers.

"This is *enough*!" He shoved Maia into the wall, pressing his arm against her neck.

Senna's hand found Briar's shoulder, keeping him from interfering.

"Are you fucking done yet?" Sky growled, face inches from Maia's. "Or do you *want* him to kill you so you stop feelin' guilty?"

"You can't say I don't deserve it," Maia spat. "You, of all people, should know that."

She wanted her words to be just as venomous as his, and they were. He threw her into the vanity, and she winced as her hip met the wood. There was a click, and the room stilled.

He pressed his gun into her temple, and for a terrifying second, she wanted him to pull the trigger. He saw it in her eyes, and that alone seemed to change everything.

"You think this is brave?" His voice cracked, steel eyes transforming into storm clouds, welling to match.

She had broken him. His walls now lay crumbled at his feet. He lowered his gun and reached for her, his thumb gently brushing away her tears. She wanted to scream that he was just as much of a coward as her, but the words wouldn't come.

Instead, she dug her nails into his arm. The anchor she needed to push through the guilt stabbing her heart.

"We all deserve a chance at redemption, Maia. A chance to be better than what anyone, includin' that voice in the back of our minds, tells us."

The drop in Senna and Briar's gaze confirmed the sad truth. Sky's confession was something they all wanted to believe.

His hand trailed to the back of her neck, and he pulled her tight to his boney chest, his amulet digging into her cheek. "What's brave is fightin' to be better than the person you were yesterday," he whispered, his breath soft against the shell of her ear. "Because eventually the pain dulls, and that voice quiets, and you realize that this darkness was nothing more than a moment."

He pressed his icy fingers possessively into her back and neck, tempering the rage within her. It was the first time his touch didn't feel suffocating. His need to keep her safe was his attempt at redemption, and the tragedy was that he chose her.

He pulled away, wiping his tears with the back of his hand. "When the light finally breaks through, it'll be so much brighter than it ever was. You'll see. I promise, Maia."

Sky turned for the door, and Senna caught his hand as he passed, exchanging a knowing look. He composed himself and gave her a nod before continuing out the door.

"I'm sorry I didn't ask if you were okay," Senna said, putting the waste bin down beside the vanity.

Maia collapsed onto the edge of the tabletop. "I would have lied anyway."

"You forget, I know what you look like when you lie." She took Maia's hand with a weak smile. It wasn't the look of pity that Maia had expected, but an apology. "Which is why I knew you weren't."

Chewing the inside of her lip, Maia wondered if she was that transparent to everyone else. Briar lifted the dress from the floor, carefully laying it across the bed and taking a seat beside it.

Senna reached for one of the thick dreads Maia's hair had become while a prisoner. "I thought if I kept telling you that you were—if I made you say it enough—that you'd overcome whatever was slowly shattering inside you."

"I wish it would have worked too." It was the truth. Without Senna's confidence in her, all of this would have destroyed her so much sooner.

Her nail trailed along the scar on Maia's cheek. "He's right about the darkness, darling. But I need you to know you're never alone in it." Her eyes finally met Maia's with the same fire and passion she'd had since the first day they met. "The war they're planning downstairs is nothing compared to what you've already survived. You're so much stronger than you think, and you'll be unstoppable when you finally believe that for yourself."

Senna gently squeezed Maia's arms, and she looked like she wanted to say more, but instead, she turned, following Sky from the room.

It was quiet again, and with Maia's adrenaline dissipating, exhaustion took hold. She no longer had Sky's anger or Senna's passion fighting the surrounding darkness. With a sigh, she glanced at Briar.

He remained still on the bed, eyes focused on his splinted fingers. The candle flickered on the table, a soft glow against his sharp cheekbones. She saw it—the light the blind man at the tavern had seen in Briar. The steady beacon that cut through the storm within her, calling her back home. She walked over, sinking into the mattress next to him. Her heart calmed as his arm slid around her shoulder, pulling her tight to his side.

"I'm going to kill him for what he did to you."

"No," she whispered, suddenly terrified at the thought of losing his light to the war awaiting them. "I need you to make me a promise, Briar."

His body tensed. "Please don't ask me to sit this one out, boss."

"You can't shoot with your splinted fingers, and I need to know Hannah's safe." She glanced up at him, matching the defiance in his face. "Promise me—no matter what happens, you'll keep her safe."

Red crawled up his neck, and the cut of his jaw told her he wanted to argue, but his defiance slowly turned into dejection, as if already mourning her.

"I won't let anyone fuckin' near her," he said, tightening his hold around Maia.

She curled into him, shoulders relaxing. "Thank you," she said, closing her eyes and drifting back into her darkness.

The smell of freshly baked biscuits greeted Maia as she staggered down the grand staircase the next morning. Garcia's booming laughter traveled from behind the kitchen door, and she readied herself to pretend to be okay.

With a step forward, she sensed Aster before she saw him, sitting alone beside a burning fire in the parlor. His boot rested on his knee, finger running across his lip, lost in thought. Despite the worry knit tight between his brow, seeing him again took her breath away.

She moved towards him when the door to the kitchen opened.

"He's probably still fuckin' sulking over—" Rafe stopped in the foyer, eyes wide in surprise. "Maia." He glanced into the parlor before tucking his hands into his pockets. "Uh, how you feelin'?"

Senna smacked his arm. "What's wrong with you?"

"What the fuck are you supposed to say in this situation?"

Winter shoved him towards the parlor. "We're glad to have you back," she said, giving Maia a sympathetic nod. "Now, let's talk."

Senna linked her arm with Maia's, easing her limp as they walked into the parlor. Maia dared a look at Aster, slowly lowering herself into the seat across from him.

He leaned forward, as if trying to close the space between them. "You were asleep when I got back last night. I didn't want to wake you."

His fingers twisted anxiously, eyes searching hers. She wanted to reach for him, but he had seen the blood she spilled at Folly's, and she didn't know if that changed things.

"I know why you've put this conversation off, Aster," Winter said, her heavy boots stopping beside his chair. "But we're quickly losing the advantage of surprise."

Aster closed his eyes, dropping back in the chair with an exasperated sigh. His finger was back to his lip, gaze lost in the flames. "Surprise isn't an advantage if your soldiers aren't ready."

"Don't pretend to know my guards better than I do," she said, her voice tight in warning. "If I say they're ready, they're ready."

He turned to her, poised and confident in the same way he had been in Portico. Maia appreciated that sitting across from her, Aster filled the chair in a way Orion never did. Everything was different now. Everything but Aster.

"And the rebels?" he asked. Confusion twisted Winter's translucent brows before she lifted her chin in understanding. "They're under your command now, and there's nothing to talk about until they're ready too."

"Our contacts on Canal Row confirmed Orion is now hidden behind Portico's walls," Rafe said, rubbing at his temple, elbow propped on the armrest of the couch.

"Does that change things?" Aster's gaze passed between Rafe and Winter, allowing them a chance to decide.

Winter balled her fists as if fighting with herself. "No. It doesn't."

"If Orion is in Portico, then Senna and I can pull Mr. Foster from hiding. The rebels should also be back in a couple days with more weapons from a nearby cache," Garcia said, hovering behind Maia's chair. "We should at least wait until we see what they've found."

Senna brushed Rafe off the armrest and took a seat on it. "My contacts confirmed support in the Coastal Region and Rocky Mount. I have more, closer to Richmond, but they aren't as easily influenced without some sort of incentive."

Micah removed a flask from his jacket, taking a sip and handing it to Sky as they stood by the same window that had once been Edward's perch.

"I'll give them some fuckin' incentive," Micah scoffed, resting his hand on his pistol.

Senna rolled her eyes. "If we can gain their support, we would have Tala and Orion surrounded."

"You're right. Let's discuss what we're willing to negotiate." There was respect in Aster's gaze, and Senna nodded with appreciation.

"What about the bounties?" Rafe asked, snapping his fingers for Sky and Micah's attention.

"Is this motherfucker snapping at us? Nope," Micah said, yanking the flask from Sky and wandering out of the room.

Sky sighed, rolling his neck. "We'll know by the end of the week."

"Tell me you've at least prepared your speech?" Winter asked, glancing at Aster out of the corner of her eye.

"How's he gonna have a speech if we ain't even got a plan?" Briar dropped into the seat beside Rafe, both of them taking up the entire couch.

"They're not lookin' for a plan, Harper," Winter said. Her gaze softened as it met Briar's. It was protective, like a mother with her child. She cared about him—about all her guards—and the situation seemed to be chipping away at her armor. "We know what we signed up for. We just need to believe what we're riskin' our lives for is important."

His gaze dropped to his splinted fingers. She didn't know he wasn't fighting.

"The rebels aren't here for Aster," Garcia said, hand now resting on Maia's shoulder. "They followed her."

She tensed, panic slowly building in her chest. "No, they followed an idea. I'm not who they think I am. Not after everything I've done."

Pinching his lips together with annoyance, Garcia stepped forward. "You need to stand together, Aster."

"Don't you dare talk about Maia like she isn't here," Senna snapped.

Gripping her knees, Maia fought through her racing thoughts.

The bottle of tonic gripped in her trembling hand.

Hannah begging her not to go to Portico.

Hope's infectious giggles, and Mr. Kline's final breath.

Rowan's body swaying in the breeze.

All her memories and regrets swelled painfully in her chest.

The argument continued, but it sounded miles away. She forced a slow, shaky breath, but it did nothing to fill her lungs. She gripped the arms of her chair. Why couldn't she breathe?

"He's right," Winter said. "You two are stronger together."

Garcia's pleading eyes were back on Maia. "They need you right now, even if—"

She could no longer hear him. He blurred before her, and all she could hear was her heart raging behind her bruised ribs. She already knew what he wanted—what all of them wanted.

Everything felt heavy. The weight of things done, and those still to come. The burden perched on her shoulders. She could give them every broken piece of herself, and they would still want more.

With a shaky breath, her eyes met Aster's. She knew he could see it—the anxiety gripping her so tightly she could no longer breathe, the fear of dying from the erratic thrashing of her heart, the unraveling of every ounce of strength she had left.

"I need a moment," he said, standing and offering Maia his hand.

She forced herself to move, wondering if she could even make it across the room on her unsteady legs. She was so fucking weak when they needed all her strength.

Aster tightened his grip around her trembling touch, lengthening his stride to hurry them from the suffocating room into the kitchen. The second the door closed behind them, he pulled her into his chest, allowing her to unleash.

Tears streamed down her face as she gasped for air, fighting to hold on to what little grasp she had on her broken thoughts. She had survived so much on her own. Pushed herself through everything that should have destroyed her, all for what?

Her legs grew weak, dragging them onto the white marble floor.

"It's okay," he whispered. "You don't need to be strong right now."

She choked on a sob, her white-knuckle grip on his jacket as she shattered in his arms. Every raw emotion she hadn't allowed to heal, ripped itself from her all at once, leaving her terrifyingly vulnerable.

Another shock of panic rolled through her, taking her breath away. Aster's warm hands were rhythmic, slowly caressing up and down her tense back to the slow and steady beat of his heart.

"I can't do this." Her words slipped through chattering teeth. She was shivering despite the sweat on her palms. "I'm so tired."

"Then let me carry this for you."

It was exactly what she wanted to hear, but the guilt took hold. "I can't ask you to do that."

She pinched her eyes closed, fighting another wave of panic. Her vicious thoughts had consumed every painful inch of her body, and Aster tightened his arms, fighting them with her.

"You don't have to." His voice was steady, his heart calm, like the low crash of waves on the shore, taming the storm within her. "Maia, I would carry all of it for you if it meant giving you even one moment of peace."

The warmth of his steady hand, his arms wrapped tight around her, slowly eased the tension in her muscles. She took in another shuddering breath, pressing her forehead into his chest.

"We promised to stand together." His thumb grazed her cheek. "Sometimes that means holding each other up."

"So you can fall with me?" She shook her head, loosening her grip on his jacket. He needed to walk away from her, and she hated herself for not having the strength to do it for him.

He lifted her chin, his eyes open and vulnerable. "If I need to fall with you to help you back up, I will, because the thought of not standing beside you makes everything else feel unbearable."

Maia stilled, his words stopping her heart completely. He waited, a hint of uncertainty now flickering in his gaze. Despite war looming like a cloud over them, she slid her arms around his neck, kissing him softly, choosing to weather it together.

"As long as I'm still standing," she whispered, forehead resting against his.

His shoulders tensed as the significance of her words settled. There was a good chance she wouldn't be when all was said and done. That neither of them would.

"As long as *we're* still standing, Maia."

32

RECKONING

T he clearing outside of Rowan's safe house was quiet, allowing the soft crackling of the campfire to set the tone for the evening. Hundreds of men and women were gathered together wearing everything from dirt-stained pants to gold-embellished diplomat jackets. Each one of them traitors to their causes.

Raised tents expanded farther and farther from the safe house with each week that passed, as more support arrived from Senna's contacts, Sky's bounties, and Garcia's rebels. Despite those numbers, they all knew it was nothing compared to what awaited them behind Portico's gates.

Which is why Aster stood in the center of the crowd, quietly watching, a buzz of anticipation in the air for what would come next. Maia couldn't help but appreciate the beauty and terror of those few moments before he spoke.

With a deep breath, he lifted his chin. "We shouldn't be here... but we are. We find ourselves prepared for war in a world still healing from the last. Those in power have lost their way. They forget that without our trust, they stand alone."

He paced in front of the flames, each person standing a little straighter as he met their gaze. Leadership felt different meeting them on the same ground they stood.

"Revolution spreads slowly until it happens all at once. A single moment that has the ability to change everything. They have used fear and manipulation to tear us apart. Keep us prisoners to the status quo. You stand here because you see through their lies."

He swept his hand toward Maia, this was now *their* rebellion. She stepped forward, whispers adding to the hum in the air. She wanted to shrink under their gaze, but as she scanned the crowd, she caught sight of Mr. Foster. His face lit, and he gave her a nod of encouragement, pride radiating from him.

Maia smoothed the dress Hannah made, feeling the power it promised. "There is a fire within each of us, bright and all-consuming. Fueled by the lies we've been told, the injustices we've endured, the helplessness we've been forced to accept. Let it fucking burn, because within that fire—what gives it life—is hope."

She had carefully scrawled her speech, carving out pieces of herself—the shame and pride, tragedy and joy—finding the balance of all she had been through and transforming it into words. They deserved the raw and vulnerable truth, regardless of how terrifying it was, and in turn, they raised their chins in respect as she continued.

"It burns in spite of the cold hand of loss that has touched each of us, shrouding our world in gray. You stand here because you fight to hold on to even the faintest light."

"*That!*" Aster shouted, his voice transforming from the slow rumble of thunder to the crash of lightning. "That is worth fighting for. We fight for peace, and that alone makes all the difference. We may stumble, but we will hold each other up. There are no walls we cannot tear down together."

He moved to Maia, his skin a beautiful bronze and eyes a polished amber in the flames. His hand wrapped firmly around hers. The poise and power he radiated was something to admire, even as his hand shook around hers.

She tightened her grip, turning back to the crowd. "You stand here because each scar, each fall, each loss has only made you stand taller, more confident in what you're capable of. Because you know that each of these battles you've already won has prepared you for this moment. *Our* moment."

"They have deemed us traitors, but our legacies will speak the truth. Our battle cry will be their reckoning. In a world divided, we rise as one!" Aster lifted their hands together as the crowd erupted in celebration.

No amount of planning could prepare them for what was to come, but as Maia took in the faces surrounding them, there was no fear or uncertainty. Winter had been right. Within each of them was a glow of confidence that only hope brought. They understood that no matter what happened on the battlefield, change would come. No matter how fleeting, there would still be a moment of peace. And if they died, it would be with honor.

It was well into the morning hours, and while the crowd outside had ended their celebrations, inside the safe house the bottles of liquor circulating helped to ease the nervous tension.

Senna had draped herself across the small loveseat in a fiery-red dress, while Rafe sat tucked in the other corner. He adjusted the dangerously high slit, so it no longer exposed her entire leg, before lazily resting his arms across her.

Earlier in the evening, he had complimented her dress, only to be given a single word answer of *no*. But now, with her bare feet propped on his lap, it seemed she decided tonight wasn't one to push away kindness.

Winter snored in a chair by the fire, her boots hanging over the armrest, while Hannah and Briar were tucked under a blanket together in front of her. Hannah's head nuzzled into Briar's shoulder, a sweet smile tugging the corner of his lips.

He pulled her closer to him, their attention drifting back to a story Micah was reenacting in front of the fireplace. His messy waves bounced as he waddled, pretending he was running with his pants around his ankles. Garcia's booming laughter only added to the ridiculousness of it all.

Maia felt lighter sitting curled up on Aster's lap, laughing with them, despite having no idea what they were laughing about. Aster's hand tightened on her hip, and his surprise softened into a look of pure adoration.

No one had ever looked at her like that before, and it flooded her with a warmth that pooled just below her navel and flushed her cheeks even more than the liquor. She dropped her gaze, lifting the blanket to hide her smile, and caught Sky watching from the floor in front of the loveseat.

Where she had grown used to seeing pain, his storm-gray eyes now held loss. He snatched the half-empty bottle hanging loose in Garcia's hands and took a swig, dropping his head back on the cushions. With his story now finished, Micah dropped down next to Sky. He reached for the bottle, which turned into an argument that quickly led to them wrestling over it on the floor.

Sky could make her feel guilty for choosing Aster any other night, but not this one. Not when it could be their last.

Unfurling herself from Aster, Maia stood, putting her hand out to him. His head tilted with curiosity, but he didn't ask questions as she said her goodnights, the two of them continuing up the stairs in silence. A warmth as intense as the fire still burned between them, growing even stronger as she opened her bedroom door.

Lifting her thick strands of hair from her shoulders, she moved to the vanity, pulling them up with a tie. "Can you help with this dress?" she asked, reaching for the trail of buttons down the back.

Aster bit back a smile, the playfulness in his gaze stealing her breath even through the mirror. Closing the door softly, he placed his jacket across a chair.

"I believe this is the first time you've ever asked me for help," he teased, slowly working the buttons.

"I was saving it for something that wouldn't kill you."

His fingers continued down her back. "I suppose I should appreciate that."

The fabric loosened around her shoulders, and she allowed the dress to cascade to the floor. She held her breath as his eyes trailed over each of her scars and still-healing bruises. Pinching the palms of her hands, she fought the urge to cover them, desperate to hide how frail she had become. As if sensing her tension, he attempted to ease it with a soft kiss on her shoulder.

"There seems to be no end to the ways you take my breath away," he said, palms trailing down her arms and moving to her waist.

She slowly let out her breath, blooming under his touch. "Please, stay with me tonight."

He closed his eyes, and there was a hint of sadness in the pinch of his brow. Maia couldn't help but wonder if they were sharing the same realization—that this might be their last chance to be alone together.

He composed himself, turning her to him and gently lifting her chin. "I'll give you all my nights and days if you'll let me."

Her heart ached while feeling overwhelmingly whole again.

"Then I want to give you every shattered piece of myself I have left," she whispered, leaning into his touch.

His guarded smile confirmed that despite everything they had been through together, there was still that worry in the back of his mind that she didn't care for him as much as he cared for her. Tonight, there would be no more doubts.

Sliding her hand around his neck, she pulled him to her. Every inch of her hummed almost painfully as she pressed her lips softly to his.

His warmth surrounded her, easing the ache of want. Their lips were now desperate for each other, and he pressed his hands to her hips, lifting her legs around his waist.

"Tell me what you want, Maia." His words slipped through ragged breaths. "Whatever it is, it's yours."

Maia licked her swollen lips, lost in his beautiful whiskey gaze, the desire they had for each other now throbbing between them. "All of you."

Whatever shred of composure he had left unraveled, and he crushed his lips to hers. She felt powerful knowing she could make a man as calm and poised as Aster come undone. They moved toward the bed, making up for every kiss they had denied themselves. Every touch they pulled away from too soon.

Gripping his shirt, she pulled it over his head as he laid her gently on the bed. He leaned back, working to remove his boots as she watched him. She wanted to memorize every freckle on his bronze skin, all the different shades of brown in his eyes.

He caught her watching, his gaze darkening as his hand slowly traced her sharp curves. His touch was intoxicating. She closed her eyes, savoring the way her skin tingled as his lips trailed kisses up her stomach to her neck.

"You have no idea the hold you've had over me since the first day I saw you," he confessed against her heated skin.

"You and your beautiful words," she teased. Her hand twisted in his hair while the other trailed down his stomach, working the buttons of his pants. "They're almost as dangerous as the places I've imagined the lips that whisper them."

A low rumble rose from his chest in response, and his grip tightened on her, kisses growing more heated. Her fingers flicked open the last button, and she nudged his pants loose.

They stilled, completely exposed before each other. The flames in his eyes softened to a warm glow. No longer the quick spark of lust, but now the steady glow of devotion.

He placed a soft kiss on her lips. She wanted to savor it, but her body ached, desperate for more as she pressed her bare hips to him. Slowly he filled her in a way that made each of her shattered pieces feel whole. Even in this moment, his gentleness was balanced by the sharp pinch of her nails into his back.

They moved as one, his touch exploring her body, leaving a burning trail of goosebumps while her tongue slid across his. He took his time, learning all of her with each touch, each whisper, each nip of his teeth. She felt herself blooming, climbing, desperate for release.

Taking his hand, she moved it between them. A moan escaped her as his thumb found where she ached for him, slowly tracing circles. She stood on the edge as his teeth grazed her ear.

"Let go, Maia," he whispered breathlessly. "I'm right here."

His words flowed through her, promising her that she would always be safe in his arms. Her grip loosened on him as his lips trailed kisses along her jaw, pace quickening until they both crashed down as one.

He somehow felt light and heavy in her arms, forehead pressed to her shoulder. She ran her hand through his hair, the other trailing down his side, leaving goosebumps on his skin. He smiled, playfully peppering kisses up her neck.

A giggle escaped her and he pulled away, his hooded eyes lost in hers. "You could bring me to my knees with that laugh."

"Good to know," she said, a sly grin crossing her lips.

He laughed, rolling onto his back. Silence had never felt so comforting as it hovered over them like a soft blanket. She glanced at him out of the corner of her eyes, watching the rise and fall of his chest. He lay with his eyes closed, the most beautiful smile on his face.

It was painful how much she wanted to hold on to this moment. To remember every detail of it, of him, and the way he thawed her heart. To forget what morning brought.

"I can feel you watching me," he said, his smile growing as he ran his hand through his hair.

She turned, draping herself over him and resting her head on his chest. His hand found the back of her arm, stroking it with his thumb.

"I wish I would have known you before you arrived in Portico. Before all of this." The heat of the moment had calmed to his usual warmth, and he pulled her close.

She relaxed deeper into him, willing the thundering beat of his heart to slow as her eyes fluttered shut. "You wouldn't have noticed me then."

He shook his head, kissing her temple. "I would notice you anywhere."

It didn't matter if it was true or not, he always found the right words to make her smile. "Then I guess you could have lived a boring life in Williamsburg with me."

His arm tightened around her, lips hovering next to her ear. "Is that what you want? To live a boring life with me?"

His question surprised her. It was filled with the same curiosity he had when their eyes first met. She looked up at him, certain that if she said yes right then, he would have walked away from everything. "A new leader can't live a boring life."

"Titles are meant to be temporary. Eventually, the best thing to do is hand it off and disappear, hopefully somewhere quiet and peaceful." He lifted her hand from his chest, running his thumb over her palm. "Hopefully with you."

She loved the way his eyes seemed lost, tracing the lines of her hand, as if trying to memorize them. "Then I hope one day we can disappear together."

Closing his hand around hers, he pressed it between them like a promise. In this moment, his love filled every broken shred of her with a light that seemed to explode from deep within. She rested her head against his chest, indulging in the dangerously hopeful dream of a future together.

33

SHADOWS

We underestimated their loyalty, and that alone sealed our fate.

W. Wells – 2163.08.26

Hundreds silently waited in the early morning hours for the signal to go to war. The winter fog lay heavy along Canal Row, obscuring them in a flurry of snow. A veil. Just as planned. Off in the distance, Portico guards stood huddled along the frozen water, like a blur of bleeding tombstones.

"How many you think there are?" Sky whispered to Micah, both lying flat on the ground peering through their scopes.

Winter tapped him on the leg. "Five. Tala always sends groups of five."

Sky nodded, adjusting his position. "Work the shots in."

Micah's shoulders tensed, and he let out a slow, steady breath. "Give the word."

Nervously chipping at the black paint on Tala's dagger, Maia glanced at Winter. There were no more speeches to be said. They had reached the point where every word felt too heavy with meaning while equally meaningless.

Encouragement passed around campfires of victory.

Goodbyes replaced with promises to those waiting a few miles back at camp.

The lies needed to fall into marching formation, knowing they didn't have the numbers to win.

Maia's thumb grazed the etching at the hilt of the blade and froze. The black paint had flaked from the smooth surface, revealing an arrow with a line through it. The symbol of Sagittarius. Her father's.

Tala must have taken it as a trophy.

"Take the shot," Winter said.

And just like that, they were at war.

With seven shots, the guards fell, and the world remained eerily quiet for the significance of the moment. Micah and Sky were on their feet, leading a group across the bridge.

"We'll wait for your signal," Winter said as Senna moved to join them. "Make it noticeable."

"Don't worry, you'll see it." Senna lifted her hood, disappearing into the crowd.

Garcia gave Maia a rough pat on the back. "This isn't your father's legacy anymore. This is *your* victory, Sagitta."

Her heart swelled at the respect in his gaze, and she straightened her back. "It's *our* victory."

Face now hardened with determination, he fell into the back of the line, crossing the canal.

"Come on, we need to get in position," Winter said, motioning at the soldiers who remained.

Aster put his hand out to Maia, helping her up, while Rafe loaded his gun, falling in step with Winter. The next part of the plan was all on them. They just needed to find a way into Portico unnoticed. Aster hesitated, tightening his grip around Maia's, eyes filled with words he seemed unable to speak. It was the same look he had last night, even after all the hours they spent tangled together. A desperation for just one more moment.

"It's going to be okay," she said, reaching up and cradling his face in her hand. His brows pinched together, and he closed his eyes, grabbing her arm and pressing a kiss against the inside of her wrist. "If anyone can convince the people within Portico's walls to join us, it's you."

Aster sighed, eyes meeting hers. "Maia, I—"

"Let's fucking go!" Rafe shouted, interrupting him.

A wave of emotions seemed to flood him that she couldn't quite place.

"As long as I'm still standing," Maia said with a reassuring nod.

Aster understood, steeling himself as she pulled away to join the others.

They worked towards the graffiti-covered shell of a building, the same place Rowan had met her what felt like a lifetime ago. Maia's eyes wandered to the watchful gaze of the owl mural. Full circle. Back to where everything started, and she had to believe if he was still here, her father would be proud to be fighting beside her.

Their footsteps echoed off the exposed steel beams above, the moonlight filtering through the thick crawling vines. A glint of light ran along the floor, catching Maia's eye. A wire.

"Wait!"

The explosion threw them on their backs, concrete and steel collapsing around them. A cloud of debris made it impossible to see as Maia choked on the thick air. Trying hard to focus despite the ringing in her ears, she crawled across the rubble.

"Aster!" Her voice sounded muted, as if she were lost somewhere at the bottom of the ocean.

Ignoring the cuts from the jagged wedges of concrete, she desperately threw them from her path. Rafe dropped beside her, his motions as panicked as her pounding heart. She fought the fear radiating from him. Looked past the tears welling in his eyes. None of it would help clear the rubble any faster.

A groan rose from the destruction, and Rafe sobbed in relief. Winter was now beside them, helping him move the final slab of concrete. Maia's heart plummeted so painfully it made her gasp. Blood pooled around a piece of shrapnel lodged in Aster's side. She pressed her hand around it to slow the bleed.

Rafe met her gaze, unable—or unwilling—to ask the questions hidden in his terrified eyes.

"He needs to get to Hannah. *Now.*"

She didn't need to say anything else for him to understand. Aster cried out in pain, face terrifyingly pale as Rafe and Winter lifted him to his feet.

"You three go. Make sure he gets to the healer's tent in one piece," Winter ordered. The soldiers jumped into action. "And don't let anyone fuckin' see him."

Maia closed her eyes, pinching her nails against her palm, taming the emotions threatening to take hold. Her heart split in two, knowing she couldn't follow. She needed to push past the pain and keep to the plan.

With a slow breath, her eyes fluttered open to find them gone—hidden in the fading haze of debris. Across the canal, the bright flashes of gunshots confirmed there was no turning back.

Winter put out her hand, but Maia remained still, dread washing over her like a crashing wave. Aster was the plan. The fight on the other side of the canal was a distraction. The distraction needed for them to sneak into Portico unnoticed. Once behind the walls, it was up to Aster to convince those inside to join their fight.

Even though it had been days ago, Maia could still feel the soft heat of the fire as she sat across from him while he finished his speech.

It had been hours since the others had gone to sleep, but his mind wouldn't rest. She remembered the look on his face when he folded the page—the forced calm. He glanced at her, but the distance in his gaze told her his thoughts were elsewhere.

"If this doesn't work, none of us will survive."

The words weren't for her. They were his unfiltered thoughts, and she saw the small cracks in his confidence.

She walked up behind him, wrapping her arms across his shoulders. "Then you'll make it work."

He lifted the back of her hand to his lips and rested his head against hers, leaving them in a chilling silence.

Maia glanced at her empty, blood-stained hands, knowing that in his pocket were all the carefully chosen words he had prepared. The one thing they needed to win.

"Get the fuck up," Winter said, gripping Maia's arm and pulling her to her feet. "We need to—"

Streams of smoke whizzed into the air across the canal, capturing their attention. There was a moment of silence as the smoke lazily arched back down before exploding into bursts of color.

"That's our signal," Winter said, planting her hands on Maia's shoulder. "We have fifteen minutes to get to the rendezvous point before they pull back. No matter what happens, one of us needs to get there. Do you understand?"

They had written the ending they wanted. Scribbled it onto paper like wishes tossed into wells. The burden as heavy as the rocks each wish had been tied to. Maia steeled herself and nodded.

15 minutes.

Leg aching in protest, Maia jogged past the rubble to the secondary bridge. A steady pop of gunfire echoed behind her, and she glanced over her shoulder to see Winter and her soldiers now shooting at scouts.

Quickening her pace, Maia pushed through the pain, skidding to a stop as another wire glistened in the snow. Tala had rigged the bridge to explode. Doing so ensured there was only one way in. If the wire didn't get them, they had removed enough of the planks to make it impossible to cross.

13 minutes.

"We need to go back," Maia said, ducking behind an Old World steel staircase climbing to something no longer in existence. "The bridge is a trap too."

"Fuck!" Winter shouted, pressing her back against the wide beam support.

The three soldiers remaining hid their fear with greedy gulps of air. Winter's gaze passed between them, the same protective look she gave Briar. This didn't need to be their sacrifice too.

"Cover us from up there," she said, pointing up the steps. The guards' relief was palpable. "Once we're across, you need to find another way out."

They nodded, carefully dulling their steps as they climbed the steel stairs.

Her measured gaze found Maia's next. "You need to make it across. Do you understand?"

She did. Regardless of what happened next, she needed to keep going. No hesitation. Maia nodded, and Winter pulled a large hunting knife from its sheath, lifting her finger to her lips. The only way back was slow and steady, using the darkness and fog to their advantage. Removing one of the three daggers from her hips, Maia slipped out from hiding.

They inched through the shadows, each step cautiously placed to avoid giving away their position. It wasn't until they reached the outer wall of the tunnel that Winter stumbled upon a scout. Covering their mouth, she plunged her knife into their back. The body went limp in her arms, and her eyes grew wide as a grenade slipped from their fingers, rolling across the floor with a clatter.

10 minutes.

Jumping towards Maia, they both collapsed to the floor as it detonated. Gunshots rained from behind them, and Winter flipped over, shooting at the approaching scouts. Through the cloud of smoke, Orion emerged, face pure violence and determination. His wild eyes locked on Maia's as he breathed in the surrounding death.

"I was hoping I'd be able to kill you," Winter said, pushing herself to her feet.

Orion's lip twitched with arrogance as he sized her up. "The leader of Portico's pathetic army. I'm not here for you, but victory will be so much sweeter proving to them how weak you really are."

Winter's nostrils flared just below her piercing. With a measured breath, she holstered her gun.

His laugh was so loud it made Maia flinch. "Weak *and* pretentious."

He holstered his weapon, and Winter slowly circled, waiting for him to follow. A flicker of amusement crossed his lips as he obliged. The moment he did, she charged toward him. He braced himself, taking her shoulder straight on, now locked in their own battle.

Another distraction so Maia could get to the bridge in time. She crept along the wall, stumbling over the debris. The gunfire outside of the concrete cavern occupied most of the scouts, but one caught sight of her, quickly meeting her dagger.

Out of the haze, Orion and Winter barreled towards Maia. He slammed Winter into the wall, her skull meeting the concrete with a sickening crack. A groan escaped her, but she quickly shook it off, forcing her knee into his groin and shoving him away.

5 minutes.

Maia continued along the wall as Orion flipped Winter onto the floor, the impact knocking the wind out of her. He pulled his gun, clicking the hammer into place.

"Guess we're done fighting honorably," she choked out, struggling to catch her breath

He took aim. "If you think honor wins wars, you're just as pathetic as I thought you were." The bang was deafening, and her body went limp.

Maia stood frozen, mouth quivering, eyes wide. She wanted to cry and scream and rush to Winter's side, but if she wanted to survive, she needed to run.

Orion's bullets whizzed past her as she sprinted towards the bridge. She nearly reached the opening of the building when Jackson appeared, her gun aimed at Maia.

4 minutes.

Throwing herself behind a concrete pillar along the canal, Maia sank into the fog, trying to catch her breath while her entire body shook. She glanced over the edge, bodies littering the snow-covered ice. It was too far to fall, especially with her injury.

Her gaze traveled across the canal where Micah and Sky stood back-to-back, shooting at more scouts closing in. Micah took a hit, dropping to the ground as Sky ducked next to him while one of Rafe's collectors covered.

Maia's heart stopped as her eyes scanned Canal Row. Tala's scouts and Orion's rebels were shooting at the guards and collectors still filtering in from Portico. They had remained loyal even if they didn't follow.

Closing her eyes, she took a slow breath. When she opened them again, they met the yellow eyes of the owl. Her father's. And this time, they watched her with conviction.

There was still a chance.

3 minutes.

Orion's footsteps thundered, and his hand came down on her shoulder. Gripping her blade, she thrust it through his forearm. A roar of pain escaped him. In a fit of rage, he ripped the dagger from his arm, tossing it aside and grabbing her by the throat. Panic took hold as she clawed at his arm. He slowly lifted her against the pillar, her feet frantically kicking the air. He didn't need her alive this time.

"I was wrong for thinking you would be any better than your useless parents."

"No," she choked. "You were wrong for thinking you could control me."

Maia's grip weakened as the darkness lurked into her vision. Explosions rattled the pillar behind her, but they weren't enough to keep her from fading. Shouts surrounded them, and she was certain she was hallucinating as Rafe appeared behind Orion.

2 minutes.

Orion's eyes grew wide as Rafe pressed his gun into the back of his head.

"Drop her, or I shoot," Rafe demanded.

Orion's grip loosened around Maia's throat, and she collapsed to the floor. Before she could even suck in a breath, a shot rang above her, and Orion crumpled to the floor.

"Hope it was worth it, asshole," Rafe said, putting two more bullets in his chest.

1 minute.

"No!" Jackson screamed, rushing to Orion. She lifted his head, cradling him in her lap as she rocked back and forth, a tortured cry escaping her. Her bloodshot eyes were teeming with betrayal as they met Maia's. "It didn't need to come to this! *All of this* is your fault, you fucking monster!"

She knew she was a coward for doing it, but Maia looked away, unable to meet the anguish of Jackson's gaze. She had now lost everyone. Right or wrong, even Jackson deserved a chance to mourn. Another grief-stricken sob escaped her as Maia walked away.

Rafe and the soldiers followed her across the bridge, where Garcia was waiting.

"Where's everyone else?" he asked, pulling her down behind a stack of crates.

Her jaw clenched, and she dropped her gaze. "Orion is dead." Her voice was as rough as gravel, and she painfully cleared her throat. Garcia's eyes burned into the side of her face, and she knew where his thoughts were. She wasn't the hero. "Rafe killed him."

Garcia deflated. "Sky and Senna pushed forward thanks to the guards and collectors. Tala wasn't prepared for them to side with us. She ran back to Portico almost immediately."

"Then we should get moving," Rafe said, loading a new clip into his gun.

They jogged through the dwindling battle along the canal towards Portico.

The chime of the bell tower traveled ominously across the deserted gathering grounds, as if announcing their arrival. *The bell tower rings for three reasons: to mark the hour, to warn of attack, or to mourn a fallen leader.* She wondered if it had been the cue for the guards and collectors to choose a side.

The illuminated lanterns between the columns of Council Hall revealed the bloodshed trailing up the bright-white steps. They continued into the rotunda, their steps echoing on the tile floor. Senna motioned for a group to follow, but froze when she spotted Maia. She walked over, throwing her arms around her.

"The chamber doors are locked. They say Tala's behind them. We'll head to the balconies to surround her." She pulled away, eyes finding Maia's. "This has always been your battle. We'll wait for your word."

Maia thumbed the one dagger she had left. The one she saved for Tala. Everything done, all the death and destruction had brought them to this moment. A wolf against a wolf.

"I saw something in your eyes the last time we sat on those steps outside," Senna said, pulling her gun and motioning for the soldiers to start towards the stairs. She looked back at Maia, a dangerous grin creeping across her lips. "I saw you at the center of their destruction. End this."

Maia's back straightened, the fire of Senna's words coursing through every inch of her. Garcia waited for Senna on the steps, whispering something to her as they continued out of sight.

"I ain't gonna be as honorable as them," Rafe said from beside her. "If she attacks, I'm takin' the shot. Aster will never forgive me if I don't."

She glanced at Sky, and his gaze drifted away. He would never promise to be honorable either.

"You'll know if you need to take the shot," she said.

Rafe gave her shoulder a quick squeeze and made his way towards the stairs with Sky's group. The rest that stayed behind waited. She walked past them and pounded on the door.

"It's just me and you!" she shouted, wincing at the sharp pain in her throat.

There was a moment of silence before she heard the slide of a wood brace and the click of a lock. Both doors pulled open to reveal that Tala wasn't alone, but surrounded by her loyal scouts.

With a steady breath, Maia limped forward, lifting her hand for the soldiers to wait when they tried to follow. She continued past Tala's scouts, faces shrouded by hoods as they tracked her. Tala sat in Aquila's chair, twirling a dagger against the podium. The respect in her eyes was no longer hidden.

"I have to say, you're nothing like your father," she said as Maia stopped in the center of the room. "This could all be yours, but instead, you fight for Aster. Why?"

"Because he's nothing like us."

"You mean weak," Tala said, standing from the chair. "He doesn't have what it takes to lead. Even his father knew that. Speaking of, where is our friend? I imagine cowering somewhere instead of fighting for this chair."

"That chair belongs to him. Or did you forget you stole it from him with your forged letter?" Whispers slowly filled the air. "There's a reason Aquila chose him and not you, Tala. Where you and I only understand our blades, he would have done it with his words. That's why he deserves it."

He still had an innocence she wished existed within her, and that felt worthy of protecting.

"Now *that*—" Tala lifted the dagger, pointing it at Maia. Neither of them flinched as the entire room lifted their guns. Tala reveled in the building tension. "Is something your father would have said. A man just as weak as Aster."

"You have nowhere left to run," Maia said, glancing at the glinting gun barrels in the balconies.

"Neither do you, Sagitta. Have you ever wondered what we would be capable of together?"

Maia could almost see the hand of darkness stretch from Portico, shrouding their world in fear. The power of it felt infinite, and Maia hated the temptation it brought. Tala's eyes darkened as she slowly stepped down from the podium.

"We'd never trust each other," Maia said, recognizing Tala's weakness in this game.

Tala stalked forward, holding the dagger behind her back. "I hated you for being another disappointment in our rebellion, but I soon realized the liberation of abandoning allegiance to fight for yourself. That's why you always seemed a step ahead. You weren't trapped by expectations."

Maia took a strategic step forward. "Orion was the disappointment. He was going to take all of this from you if he won."

A genuine smile tugged at Tala's lips. A camaraderie.

"Do you know why I chose the name Scorpius?" A dangerous glint flickered in her eyes. "Legend says it was the scorpion that killed Orion. He was never going to take Portico from me. I promise you that."

Her gaze trailed over her scouts, and Maia took advantage, hand now resting on her hip.

"To be honest, I didn't think he would survive capturing you to begin with. I've watched you transform from a woman scared of the shadows, to one who can manipulate them to her bidding." Tala stepped forward. Close enough to end the game. "I was a bit disappointed when he stumbled through our gates. You should have gone for the—"

Maia ripped the blade from her hip, plunging it into Tala's neck. "Throat?"

Tala's eyes grew wide, her mouth open in a silent scream as her fingers pressed around the blade. She thought she knew Maia, the violence she was now capable of, but she had no idea. The hunter, now the prey.

Maia let go of her blade. "I learned to manipulate more than just the shadows."

Tala collapsed to her knees, and Maia crouched to meet her.

"Lo que el monte nos dio." She gripped the blade, pulling it free. "El monte lo recogió."

Wiping the blood on her pants, Maia stood, sheathing her father's blade. She turned to find the scouts now lowering their hoods as she passed. Their eyes held the same respect she had seen in Tala's, and they followed like a black stain behind her.

34

LIBERATION

In the end, we were all still worthy of redemption.

W. Wells – 2163.08.26

An inescapable heaviness existed after battle. It reached out, touching the earth and spreading like wild vines. Crawling across the blood-splattered snow, still burdened with the dead, and along the collapsed buildings where the innocent had taken shelter, hiding from a war they never wanted. It wrapped around the legs of those still standing, taking root somewhere deep within them. Victory was bittersweet. As it should be.

Maia's boots crunched up the gravel walkway to the Councilor's Manor.

"Evening, Sagitta," one of the guards said, pulling open the heavy doors.

Within the manor, everything remained as it had prior to Aquila's passing. The stiff chairs of the parlor. The mahogany desk in the library where Maia spent her nights hidden away with her new burdens. The bed upstairs where Aster lay heavily sedated, allowing his wound to heal.

She continued past the rose-filled vase in the middle of the foyer and removed her boots. Quietly climbing the stairs, she ambled down the narrow hall, reaching for the handle to Aster's room. She stopped at the sound of Rafe's voice inside.

"You should have seen the ceremony we did for Winter last night. She would have been so fuckin' pissed that everyone made such a big deal about it. The sheer amount of lager would have made up for it though. We buried her with an oak. Maia said it symbolized courage and character or some shit. Guess Winter gets to live her second life as she did her first."

Maia cracked open the door, and Rafe dropped his boots from the bed with surprise. Her heart sank as she realized Aster still remained unconscious.

"Mr. Foster tried a new salve today." Rafe said, standing and removing his jacket from the chair. "He thinks it will work faster. Started cutting down on the sedative too."

Since their victory, Rafe seemed burdened with carrying the poise and diplomacy Aster normally provided. It looked almost painful for him.

"It might work faster if you stopped putting your dirty shoes all over the bed," she said, crossing her arms.

He rolled his eyes, fighting back a yawn. "He doesn't need the sedative with all the boring fuckin' books you read him each night." She bit back a smile, and he squeezed her shoulder on the way out. "Try to get some sleep tonight."

"You too."

Maia dropped her boots beside the door, turning the chair to face Aster. Taking the book from the nightstand, she opened it to where she left off the night before. With his hand in hers, she read until her eyes grew heavy.

A sudden twitch pulled her from a nightmare, and she held her breath, hoping it wasn't her imagination again.

"Aster?" she whispered. His hand attempted to close around hers, and she nearly fell from the chair. "I'm right here. It's okay."

His eyes struggled to open, but his hand was now tight around hers. "I know." His voice was hoarse from days of disuse. "I heard you."

Tears slid down her cheeks, and she pressed his hand to her lips. "I missed you so much."

"I'm sorry."

"What are you apologizing for?"

His pained gaze found hers, wiping the tears from her cheeks. She leaned into his touch—the want so strong it hurt. "Because I had so many opportunities to tell you how much you meant to me," he swallowed, thumb grazing her cheek. "How much I love you, but I never said it. The words just felt hollow and small compared to how I feel when I see you. But it wasn't until I was being dragged away that I realized I spent too much time searching for the words I may never have a chance to say."

That was the difference between them. Injured on the battlefield, his regrets were the words he never told her, while hers were the words in his pocket that would end the war. He would always be the bleeding heart, and she would forever be the bloody blade.

"We already found the words." She stood, softly pressing her lips to his, grateful for the balance he created in her. "As long as I'm still standing."

His brows knit for a second before his face transformed into pure adoration. "As long as I'm still standing," he whispered, his passion igniting each word.

With a sigh, she pulled away. "I should get Mr. Foster while you're awake."

"Not yet."

His hand found hers, and she allowed him to guide her back to his side. They seemed to melt into each other as she rested her head against his chest. It didn't take long before they drifted into a tranquil sleep, floating between who they had been before the war, and who they would have to be after.

⟵———⟶

It took weeks of grueling rehabilitation before Aster was strong enough to leave the manor. When he surfaced, it was the first day Maia felt the sun since the war ended. He took her hand, strolling through the courtyard, stopping to talk with each group they passed.

Maia hadn't realized how suffocating everything had felt before he woke. She breathed in the fresh air her lungs had been craving, melting at the hint of bergamot and cloves now laced in it. Sky was right. The light was so much brighter than before.

War had transformed Aster too. He abandoned his elegant diplomat jacket for more casual civilian clothes. Even with his beard and slightly tousled hair, it was still easy to distinguish the twins with the air of confidence he radiated. It was as if he was finally free to be himself, no longer trapped in his father's expectations. He caught her staring and bit back a smile, attempting to concentrate on the conversation.

"Hey, big man's looking good!" Micah yelled from across the courtyard.

Sky shook his head, grinning at the lift in Aster's brow. Aster apologized to the group for having to cut the conversation short as they approached.

"Glad to have you back," Micah said, putting out his hand. Aster shook it with a conceding smile. "You missed one explosive fight."

"So did you," Sky said, shoving Micah away.

"Don't fuckin' start with me," Micah argued. "I was shot because of you."

"I said I had your *back*. You were in charge of everything in front of you."

Maia couldn't help but laugh, which apparently was a bet the two had.

Sky tossed Micah a coin, his eyes finding Maia's. "Can we talk?"

Micah linked his arm in Aster's, and the two strolled together in the opposite direction.

"You're heading north, aren't you?" she asked as Sky reached for his pendant. His hand hesitated. "Yeah."

"I get it now," she said, chewing on the raw spot on her lip. The sharp edges of his face softened, and he waited for her to continue. "I hope you get your fresh start. Disappear somewhere no one will judge you for the things you did to survive."

Sky slid his necklace from under his shirt. "Mistake not, forgive not," he said, placing it in her hands and closing her fingers around it. She was surprised how light it felt, the cool lacquer soothing against her rough skin. "I was wrong for what I said to you, Maia. I'll never turn you away if you need me. You know where to find me if that day ever comes."

She pulled him into a hug, her chin resting on his boney shoulder. "Be safe, Sky."

"You too," he whispered, his arms thawing around her. He pulled away, his storm-gray eyes dropping quickly from hers as he turned.

Aster walked up beside her as Sky and Micah grabbed their bags. With one last glance over his shoulder, Sky gave her a soft smile and quick nod. A goodbye. For now.

Mr. Foster avoided Sky as they passed each other on the grounds.

"Is the boy leaving?" he asked, his grip tight on the handle of his healing bag. Maia nodded, and his shoulders collapsed with relief. "I will never speak poorly of another, but I did not like him. At all."

"You aren't the first to say that." Maia's lip twitched with amusement, and she turned with Aster back towards the manor. "I'm guessing it's time for my shift at the infirmary?"

Mr. Foster fell in step beside them. "You still have some time. I did, however, want to return something of yours."

Maia tensed as they moved into the shadow of Council Hall.

Mr. Foster opened his bag, removing the three journals. "Apologies for not returning these sooner, but it didn't seem right to add these to your burdens."

The soft leather of the journals felt like an anchor now resting in her hands. She thought she would have adapted to their punishing weight by now. "Thank you for keeping them safe," she said, pulling them to her chest and wrapping her arms around them. "I'm sorry you were caught in the middle of this."

He shook his head as the guards opened the manor gates for them. "My dear, please don't apologize. You've been through so much, and I'm grateful you trusted me with this."

They continued up the manor steps, past the foyer, and into the parlor where the warmth of the fire greeted them. Aster walked to the glass doors overlooking the garden, his hands clasped behind his back.

Maia ran her finger across the embossed name on the bottom corner of the journal. *A. Wells.* She could almost feel Rowan beside her as she walked up to the fireplace. The journals were never meant to be his legacy, but she would ensure he was remembered.

With a deep breath, she threw the journals into the flames, the grip around her chest loosening as she watched the leather blacken and the pages curl. There would be consequences for her actions, there always were, but for now, all she felt was the quiet calm of liberation.

Mr. Foster walked up beside her. "You said it would be up to me to decide the role you've played in this. I can safely say, my dear, you've *always* been the person we can only hope to be one day. Brave, selfless, and true."

Maia met his kind gaze. "Thank you for seeing that in me when no one else did."

"Let this be the beginning of your healing." He squeezed her hand, his eyes hopeful. "Enjoy the rest of your day, Mr. Calderone. We'll continue therapy tomorrow."

"Thank you, sir. I'll walk you out," Aster said, escorting Mr. Foster back to the door.

Maia took a seat on the couch, removing her shoes and curling her feet under her.

"He's right, you know," Aster said, lowering himself beside her.

"You always agree with him," she teased.

Aster smiled, pulling her to his side, thumb grazing her arm. "I know what Tala said to you... about me being weak."

"She was wrong."

"No," he said with a terrifying certainty.

Maia pushed away, looking him in the eyes. "They need your confidence right now, Aster. To see the beauty in this world and the hope you bring to it."

"And I'll give that to them." He sighed, eyes on the flames. "But it won't be enough. We took the Forest Region by force, Maia. It's going to take time to rebuild, and in that time, the other regions will find out. They'll see us for what we are right now..." His eyes found hers. "Weak. And when they do, they'll come for us. Our people need to believe we'll do what it takes to fight back."

"We *will*," she said. There was no other answer.

He smiled softly. "Exactly, and they'll believe it if it comes from you."

Maia tensed, seeing the shadow of darkness stretching out from her again, trailing side by side with his light, and she suddenly understood. The power was always in their balance. The darkness and the light they would need to survive.

"Let them come," she said, easing back into the couch beside him and turning to the flames. "They'll regret seeing us as weak."

"They only see me as weak," he said, leaning into her. "You, Maia, they know are unstoppable."

She crushed her lips to his, the fire igniting between them. A fire so strong and ravenous, it begged to burn their world down.

«———»

Snow flurries lazily drifted down around Maia as she sat on the steps of the guard barracks, watching them slowly erase the earth. A clean slate, and that alone brought comfort to the day ahead.

"Mornin' boss," Briar said, pushing open the patinaed bronze door of the towering brown brick building. "Hannah's on her way down."

The barracks had housed over six hundred guards before the war, but they had yet to count the now-empty rooms. Maia glanced over Briar's head to the intricate black and gold, art déco design above the door.

Iron work snakes slithered up the sides while the center listed partial names of more forgotten men. She wondered who they once were to be immortalized so beautifully, while others became nothing more than vacant beds.

Briar put out his hand to help her up. "So, how does it feel to be co-leader of the Forest Region?"

"Like I might be in over my head."

He grinned. "So, the usual."

Hannah pushed through the door, her cheeks instantly flushing from the cold. She beamed at Maia, a box tucked under her arm with a light-blue ribbon wrapped around it.

"Sorry, the dress wasn't cooperating with the box," she said, her curls bouncing as she descended the steps.

"Thanks again for getting something together so quickly. I know you've been busy in the infirmary wrapping things up," Maia said, reaching for the box.

Despite Hannah's effervescence, the dark circles of fatigue still sat heavy under her eyes.

The first few days after the war, Hannah refused to leave Mr. Foster's side. They worked tirelessly with the other healers and researchers to take care of everyone brought in. Whatever allegiance the injured had before, it no longer mattered. No one was turned away.

But as the days slowly passed, so did the patients beyond their help, and Hannah seemed to realize there was little left she could do. Today she provided Mr. Foster with her last shift sign off, heading back to Williamsburg to live the life Maia had promised her. The one they all deserved.

Hannah pulled the box away with a mischievous smile. "Not yet."

They continued up the road past the training grounds, where Garcia was shouting orders to the guards. He glanced down at his watch, and seeing the time, dismissed them for the day. The group of scouts Maia had sent out to eavesdrop for potential threats in the Coastal Region had just returned.

"The briefing is on your desk, Sagitta," a scout said as they passed. "You'll want to look at it."

Dread tightened her stomach, but she nodded, thanking them for their work. The appreciation on the scouts' faces made it clear that gratitude wasn't something they were accustomed to.

"It already feels different here," Briar said, shielding his eyes from the blinding white of the Council Hall building.

He was right. Inside the gates, they were slowly rebuilding as one. Not just replacing the structures along Canal Row destroyed in battle, but the sparked flame of hope that seemed to temper the winter cold, welcoming the softness of spring. It was what they needed right now, not the fear that kept Maia and Aster up at night.

The bell tower rang out as they started up the steps.

At the top, Hannah held out the box. "I thought it would be more impactful opening it here."

She glanced at the gold placard now hung at the entrance of the building with the inscription:

It was never about having hope.

THE LEGACIES OF TRAITORS

To change the world, you have to give hope.
Andrew Wells

"His legacy brought us here. Now it's time to create your own," Hannah said.

Pulling the blue ribbon loose, Maia carefully lifted the lid. Inside the box was a deep-red, sateen dress, the same color as the roses outside the hedge maze. She removed it, the red flowing against the white steps.

"Aster told me the roses reminded him of you," Hannah said, unable to hide how enamored she was by this.

Maia thought back to Aster's speech during the Ascension Ceremony. *Even the harshest of winters are incapable of muting their resilience.* Her heart swelled. Were those words always for her?

"Thank you," she said, throwing her arms around Hannah.

"It's the least I could do, especially since I'm stealing Briar from you."

She pulled away, her eyes snapping to Briar's.

His wide hand rubbed at the back of his neck. "She asked if I'd go back with her," he said, cheeks instantly flushing. "How could I say no?"

Maia thought her heart might explode. "She can be pretty persuasive when she wants to."

He laughed, the gold flecks gleaming in his soft-green eyes. "Can't imagine how your mom managed the two of you under one roof." There was a second of hesitation before he continued. "We're good?"

"You're the only person I trust to keep her safe."

Briar's hand gripped her shoulder, pulling her into a hug. "Always."

Squeezing him around the waist, she smiled into his jacket, trying hard to tame her emotions as she saw Hannah's future again. A wind chime singing in the breeze as Hannah sat on the back porch, sewing a worn patch on a small pair of pants. Out in the yard, she now saw Briar chasing their children as they laughed, innocent and carefree.

He pulled away, and Hannah tucked herself under his arm. "Please don't be a stranger, Maia. You know there will always be a room waiting for you at home."

"I promise." Maia was grateful that this time it wouldn't be a lie.

"You've outdone yourself again, Hannah," Senna said, ascending the stairs. Her eyes were on the dress in Maia's hand, even as she stood in a stunning rose-gold gown with a heavy, fur shawl. The soft pink, peony-shaped button on the shawl made it clear it was one of Hannah's creations too.

"Thank you," Hannah said, lifting her chin with pride.

"Safe travels back to Williamsburg." Senna took the dress from Maia's arms, pulling her into the rotunda. "Time to get you ready."

It only took a few minutes for Senna to transform Maia with some makeup and a thick, dreaded fishtail braid. They walked into the Council Chambers to find Aster and Rafe waiting.

Maia flushed as Aster's gaze traveled over her, his face an amorous glow. She walked up to him, smoothing the lapels of his tailored navy-blue suit. The top buttons had remained undone, a striking combination of the poise and more carefree side of him.

"Don't tell Hannah, but this dress won't survive the night," he whispered to her.

"Are we going to talk about the fact that Jackson's body *and* the coin from the heist have yet to be found?" Senna asked, pulling them back to the room.

Garcia rushed through the doors, adjusting his black tie and the cuffs of his shirt. "I already told you, I'm not sending the guards out until we finish cleaning up here. Plus, Maia already said we need to focus on distributing the red lung inoculation."

His dark purple suit stole the attention of the room, and he slowed to a swagger, tucking his hands into his pockets.

"None of that matters if Jackson's still out there," Senna argued, turning back to Aster. "We all know she wants Maia dead."

Rafe sat leaned back beside her, his polished shoes up on the table. He didn't look any different from before with his suit vest and newsboy cap. "To be fair, a lot of people want Maia dead."

Maia crossed her arms to keep from flipping him off. "Don't act like you aren't second on her list."

"Good thing I don't have to worry as long as you're still around," Rafe said, grabbing his jacket from the table.

"It's time for our speech." Aster slid his arm around Maia's hips. "We can come back to this conversation tomorrow."

Garcia removed a black leather finger guard from his pocket and slid it over his severed pinky. "I already said what I had to."

"Yes, but not everyone else has," Aster said calmly.

They passed through the rotunda, pushing open the heavy, wooden doors, revealing the crowd gathered in the courtyard. Groups of people in commoner clothes and uniforms, laughing and sharing stories from their day, all grew quiet the moment Aster stepped forward.

"As one, we have defeated our enemy. And as one, we will mourn those we have lost. Tonight, however, we celebrate the countless saved by our actions."

Garcia's gaze found Maia's, and he gave her a reassuring nod. None of this was ever about Maia, though, or Orion, or even the rebellion. It was always what it stood for.

That everyone deserved the opportunity to choose a side, right or wrong. They deserved a chance to be and do better, regardless of their circumstances. They deserved a voice.

Maia rubbed Sky's amulet between her fingers as she stepped forward. The slow curl of lips, dark gazes, and nods of approval fed the fire within her, and she wondered if they were waiting for this moment.

"You fought to make your voices heard—for a chance to become the change you want to see in our world. Don't you *dare* let anyone take that away from you."

The same passion that had brought them to this moment had returned to their faces. Maia found Hannah and Briar watching from the back, pride in their eyes and bags on their backs as they started towards Portico's gates.

It broke her to see them go, but it wasn't fair for her to ask them to stay. She promised them a life they deserved, and she would make sure to keep that promise.

"Tonight, we celebrate another end," Aster continued. "So tomorrow we can rise again!"

The crowd erupted with cheers, and Aster's hand found hers, strong and sure. She had never felt so powerful, the dangerous darkness blooming in her chest, tempered by the hope she saw in everyone's eyes.

She was grateful for the scars that would remain. Reminders of all she sacrificed to become the person they needed to survive the threats now looming beyond their gates. They would celebrate the battle won, but for Maia, it was time to prepare for the war yet to come.

THANK YOU

If you're reading this, you either flipped to the back first like a true rebel, or you just finished *The Legacies of Traitors!* I hope you enjoyed Maia's story of rebellion, betrayal, and finding the strength to create your own legacy. If so, please take a moment to post a review on your preferred platform and tell a friend. Reviews and ratings help us authors find our audience and spread the word on our books.

⟸⟹

Thank you for your support!

Links for Reviews

Goodreads	**Amazon**	**Barnes & Noble**

Acknowledgements

I started writing Legacies eight years ago, so as you can imagine, there are a lot of people to thank for helping me make this book a reality.

First, to my parents, who believed in me and supported my dreams from the moment I put pen to paper. Thank you for being my first fans, and never shying away from the tough critiques. Without that, I wouldn't be the writer I am today.

To my husband for always being the calm in the storms I create. I can't imagine anyone else in this world I would want to share my dreams with.

To my critique partners: Ann Darlington for being my very first beta reader and writing friend. I still remember the exact moment you finished Legacies for the first time. Thank you for believing in me and my story from the beginning, for encouraging me through the lows, and for celebrating with me through the highs. Your friendship truly means the world to me. Nefer Doane, I'm not joking when I say that our calls together give me life. Your excitement and optimism are infectious and inspiring, and I am so grateful for your friendship. Laura Foley, Kate Duarte, and Bria Fournier, for making me fall in love with my story all over again and taking my writing to the next level.

To everyone who has supported me and Legacies: Nisha Tuli for giving me the courage to take the next step with Legacies. I can't thank you enough for all your advice and support to help make my dreams come true. To all my beta readers, Ryan, Kayla, Roni, Rebecca, Chris, and Cortney, for your time and feedback to help make this story into what it is today. To all the amazing rebels in the Legacies cover reveal, street, and ARC teams who have helped spread the word on Legacies. Thank you for making this such a memorable experience. I'm so grateful to all of you for your endless support and excitement for Legacies.

To my cover artist for all their time and patience, all the while creating the cover of my dreams.

To my editor Courtney Hanan for polishing Legacies into an absolute diamond. I couldn't have asked for a better editor. Thanks for all the laughs, for sharing inside jokes, and for making me so excited to get Legacies out to the world. Can't wait to work together again.

Finally, to all of you. Thank you for taking the time to read and joining me on my writing journey. I truly appreciate each and every one of you.

About the Author

C.M. "Christine" Leyva is an adult/new adult speculative fiction author and registered nurse who enjoys writing character-driven fiction about messy, anti-heroes. Her passion for science and medicine is often seen in her stories while exploring the *what-if's* around them. You can find her short fiction in anthologies with Outland Entertainment and Inked in Gray Press, and she is excited to share her debut novel, *The Legacies of Traitors*.

When she's not working on her next manuscript or short story, you can find her attempting home improvement projects, losing herself in a good book, or enjoying a nice glass of wine while working on a puzzle.

For writing updates on book 2 in the Forsaken Legacies Series, exclusive sneak peeks, and exciting news, subscribe to C.M. Leyva's author newsletter at https://www.cmleyvaauthor.com

www.ingramcontent.com/pod-product-compliance
Lightning Source LLC
Chambersburg PA
CBHW031830310726
48972CB00005B/1225